DEATH IN BACTON WOOD

ROSS GREENWOOD

Boldwood

First published in Great Britain in 2024 by Boldwood Books Ltd.

Cover Design by Head Design

Cover Photography: Shutterstock and iStock

A CIP catalogue record for this book is available from the British Library.

Paperback ISBN 978-1-80549-681-6

Large Print ISBN 978-1-80549-682-3

Hardback ISBN 978-1-80549-680-9

Ebook ISBN 978-1-80549-683-0

Kindle ISBN 978-1-80549-684-7

Audio CD ISBN 978-1-80549-675-5

MP3 CD ISBN 978-1-80549-676-2

Digital audio download ISBN 978-1-80549-677-9

Boldwood Books Ltd
23 Bowerdean Street
London SW6 3TN
www.boldwoodbooks.com

For Oscar Taylor
A special boy
See you at the Devonshire

To live is to suffer

To survive is to find some meaning in the suffering

— GORDON W ALLPORT

Make no mistake. It's not revenge he's after.

It's a reckoning.

— DOC HOLLIDAY

NORFOLK MAJOR INVESTIGATION TEAM STRUCTURE

Detective Superintendent
Zara Grave

Detective Chief Inspector
Vince Kettle

Detective Inspector
Vacant

Detective Sergeants
Ashley Knight – Bhavini Kotecha

Detective Constables
Hector Fade – Barry Hooper – Salvador Freitas – Emma Stones – Jan Pederson – Morgan Golding – Zelda Cartwright

Family Liaison Officer
Scott Gorton

Twinned Detective Team Sergeant
Ally Williamson

Forensic Pathologist
Michelle Ma Yun

1

PRESENT DAY

Hamish woke exhausted. He peeled open his eyes, but he still couldn't see anything. It wasn't dark; it was pitch black. He began to pant. His heart raced. Where was he, and how had he got there?

For a moment, Hamish thought he was paralysed, but it was just a deep chill in his bones. He wriggled his toes and fingers, and they moved as instructed. His shoes nipped as they had last night when he'd slipped on the brand-new pair. A worm of recall squirmed its way into his confused mind. He'd gone out for drinks with Max to show their faces. It must have been a mad night. His body ached all over.

It felt as if he'd woken lying in state, with his forearms crossed over his chest. His jeans were damp but that, too, had become a regular occurrence of late.

Hamish attempted a sit-up. His forehead banged something hard, causing him to slump back. It was then that he noticed how still the air was. He lifted his hands and touched a solid object above him. His fingers scrabbled over the smooth surface.

His other senses clicked into gear. He held his breath and heard nothing. Not a thing.

Hamish had a vivid sense of being outside but not outside. Strange smells registered as he inhaled deeply through his nose. Only one nostril was clear. The other was congested with blood or snot. The aroma was earthy, loamy even, but stale. He could have believed he was in a forest if there were any kind of breeze. His chest tightened. He pulled in a shallow breath of sharp air, knowing on an instinctive level that soon there wouldn't be enough of it.

Panic galloped through Hamish.

The horror of his situation was dawning as adrenaline hurtled through his veins. It was too dark. He was too frozen. There was no oxygen. He hyperventilated, but the part of him that had kept him alive when life had gone wrong in the past kicked in. He willed himself to control his breathing, or the inevitable loss of control would swamp him.

After half a minute of slow breaths, his brain fired up. He quelled his fears as he tentatively raised his right fist. It rose over a foot before it hit the flat surface. He lowered his hand, then gently punched up. His reward was a thud.

His left hand, which trembled uncontrollably, joined the other, and both traced the expanse above him. It was clearly wood with symmetrical grooves in it. Smooth, varnished, maybe. He placed his palms on it and pushed. Nothing. His muscles felt newborn weak. He tried again, and there was the slightest shift, but no more.

A wave of claustrophobia washed over him. Bile surged up from his stomach. He forced the burning liquid down his throat with the last remnants of saliva in his arid mouth. He'd had a similar experience as a child. Stuck in a wardrobe during a hide-and-seek game with the other foster kids. His mind started to fold in on itself again as he remembered the pure terror upon believing he would suffocate in that tight space. Back then, he'd screamed for ages, wasting time. Wasting air. Everyone else had been in the garden where they were supposed to be playing.

Yet, he'd calmed himself and eventually booted himself free, so perhaps there was a way out of this.

His hands stretched wider and discovered a piece of metal sticking out of the wood. It had to be a door handle. He was hit by a sudden rush of dizziness. Was he somehow standing after a gas explosion? No. Gravity didn't work like that.

As his fingers crept past the handle, they reached cold, loose lumps. He squeezed one, and it quickly crumbled. The soil fell down, tickling his side where his shirt had risen up to expose frigid flesh.

Mother Nature surrounded him. He imagined it as an omniscient thing, judging him. Hamish knew he would be found lacking.

A scream rose, unbidden, unstoppable, from the darkest depths of his consciousness, which until recently he never even knew existed. His howl echoed around the enclosed space. Then something skittered across his face.

2

DS Ashley Knight's alarm clock came to life. She attempted to roll over to turn it off, but a heavy presence lay on her right arm. She managed to silence the ringing with her left hand, then turned to the beast beside her. DC Barry Hooper. Sometimes referred to himself as Hoops. God. How the hell had she got tangled up in this situation?

When Ashley had first started in the police nearly twenty-years ago, she'd heard the blokes during training joke about chewing their arms off first thing in the morning to avoid waking the person whose house they'd gone back to while wearing beer goggles after the nightclub closed. She'd laughed at the time.

Barry made a piggy snort in his sleep. Ashley blew out a long breath.

While she waited for her limb to be returned to her, she thought about that day's plans. The team had been busy with a spate of armed robberies stretching from Wells to Holme-next-the-Sea, but they'd recently caught the surprisingly young thieves from Wisbech, red-handed.

It was a sad case. The trio were just teenagers and clearly not up to planning a series of thefts on such a scale. None of them were talking, though, which meant they would receive serious jail time. Lads like them just didn't think. Going tooled up for an aggravated burglary might seem funny and cool in the heat of the moment, but it had an offence range of one to thirteen years. The boys would become men while surrounded by career criminals.

Ashley decided she'd drive to Norfolk Constabulary Operations and Communications Centre at Wymondham, referred to as OCC, where she worked in the Major Investigation Team. It was a peaceful place on a Sunday if there wasn't a serious incident occurring. She could steam through her paperwork with no distractions. She also planned to do some last-minute preparation for the Inspector Assessment Day the following week. Ashley wanted to pick DCI Kettle's brains, and she'd heard he was popping in for a few hours.

She felt eyes on her.

'Morning, Barry.'

He groaned.

'My head hurts.'

'Yes, from the whisky you brought round. Nothing good comes of pouring your own measures. You should know that.'

'We had fun, though, didn't we?'

Ashley gave him a tight smile, but something deep inside her treacherously fired up. Barry cleared his throat.

'Okay, Ash, what are we doing?'

She raised her eyebrows.

'I was thinking the same thing,' she said. 'What are we doing? It's as if I've got a dirty secret and I'm too embarrassed to tell anyone. When do we go public? Or do we carry on casually trying to look like friends who enjoy being together until our sanity returns, then pretend it never happened?'

'I meant, what are we doing today? We could try to get a table at The Red Lion, have Sunday lunch, then watch the footie in The Welly. Finish the day off with a tasty burger from their smokehouse.'

Ashley almost levered him out of the bed by struggling to retrieve her trapped arm, but Barry was too solid.

'Don't you want to at least talk about it?' she asked. 'It's getting on for four months.'

'Talking is overrated. Communicating by touch is more important.'

'I'm forty-three, Barry, not eighteen. Now get off my arm, or I'll chew it off and slap some sense into you with the wet end.'

Barry released her arm by rolling on top of her. She found her hands stretching around his muscled back. He was a bit hairy, but she'd never minded that. Barry wriggled himself into position. She ran her tongue over her furry teeth.

'I'm not a ride at the fairground to be clambered onto,' she said.

'Love is a roller coaster.'

Ashley gave him a disdainful look. She tried to push him off, but half-heartedly.

'My breath smells.'

Barry smiled at her.

'I don't mind it dirty.'

3

Hamish didn't know how long he'd screamed and thrashed in his muddy grave, but he was gasping and hoarse by the time the desperation crippling his tired mind finally faded and he gathered himself. His feet and hands ached where they'd pummelled the door and dirt to no avail.

The space he was in was deeper than he'd first thought, which was perhaps the reason he was still alive. It was a simple affair. A hole in the mud with a door placed over it. He had no idea how deep it was or how much earth or maybe stones were piled above him. The door hadn't moved when he'd kicked it.

Hamish centred himself. He often took the mickey out of his best friend, Max, for his hippy crap, but some of it must have sunk in. Calmness was needed. Cool thinking. The burst of adrenaline when he'd lost all control appeared to have purged the shock from his body, but his memory was cloudy.

He recalled being at Max's apartment. Max had insisted on them going for a night on the town to be seen out as friends who were enjoying their lives in Norwich. It was the last thing Hamish had fancied doing, but he'd soon got in the mood for a mad one. He supposed that was part of his problem.

A series of faces flashed through his mind: women, men, police, laughing bouncers. They'd been at The Coliseum, the city's top nightclub and bar. Yet, where did they go after? How the fuck had he ended up alone underground?

Hamish remembered his mobile phone. He reached into his pocket and almost sobbed when he discovered it was there. It was turned off, which was something he rarely did. He pressed the on button and waited for what seemed like forever for it to power up.

'Please,' he whispered, as the Apple icon appeared.

There was at least some juice, as it sprang to life. After thirty seconds, he checked the most important features. There was no signal. The battery. Five per cent. He turned the phone around so he could use the light from the screen to see his sunken jail. The white door above reminded him of the ones inside his own flat.

Sweat and probably alcohol seeped out of his pores again as he realised someone must want him dead. The phone died and plunged him back into nothingness. He didn't have too long to contemplate what that meant because he heard a sound. A scrape or a fluttering. There was something in there with him. He felt the slightest touch on his cheek.

With fingers like claws, Hamish tore at his face again. The scream was childish and high. Tears poured from his eyes. He punched the wood above him harder, but only hurt his hand.

All he had on were a T-shirt, jeans and a sports jacket. Strangely, he envisioned an image of Max shouting encouragement to him as they worked out at the gym. He twisted onto his front and managed to get his knees under his chest. He took three long deep breaths, in and out, then took the weight of the door across his shoulders. With a groan, he summoned all his remaining strength and strained.

It held, then gave slightly near the handle. Hamish shuffled over and tried again. The door shifted upwards a touch on that side, almost as if it were opening. As he persevered, it lifted more easily. With a mighty roar, he strained upward and got a foot down flat. He gathered himself for a final effort, snarled, and burst upwards through the soil and into freezing air to stand shoulder high in a crumbling hole.

Hamish peered around in the dim light to discover himself in a gloomy hollow. His shoulders relaxed with no longer being underground.

A breeze, like a whisper through the treetops, kissed the sweat at his temples and on his forehead. It cleared his head more, but he still couldn't think straight. With the faint glow in the sky, he guessed it was dawn. If they'd left the club when it closed at two, where had he been for four hours?

Hamish checked his other pockets for his debit card and money, but the now useless phone was all he had on him. He clambered from the grave. Looking down, he saw he wore only one shoe. Digging through the soil with his tender hands did not appeal. He just wanted to get out of wherever the hell he was.

Hamish gasped with exhaustion. His arms ached and his groin was on fire. It felt as if he'd survived a plane crash, not a sick prank. Max would never be party to anything like this, even though his brothers might. He pictured Max's kind face. Where the hell was he?

Another cooling gust swept through his sweaty hair, but he wobbled when he spun around to take in the tall sentinels surrounding him. It was noisy compared to where he'd been. The leaves chattered in the breeze like soft applause. A bird tweeted. A solitary voice to herald the new day. Others joined in, as though a slumbering orchestra awakened.

A snapshot of someone gesticulating at him appeared in his

mind, but then vanished. He couldn't pull the image back. Get safe, he thought. Just get home.

The trees reaching into the sky leaned in on him. There seemed to be no path. Hamish forced himself forward and was confronted by thick bushes. A patch of ferns looked easier going, but the fronds eagerly grabbed at his legs as he limped through them. He tripped and fell, which caused unusual sharp pain on the tops of his arms. More injuries on his body registered in his brain with each passing second, as though he'd fallen into the muddy pit from a great height.

Hamish wandered in circles until he lost sight of where he had been buried. As his eyes got used to the gloom, the forest came to life. It sounded as if large animals were scrambling around in the treetops when he passed underneath them, but they were just pigeons who cooed in complaint and flapped away, having been disturbed from their nightly rest. A dog barked in the far distance. A creature cried out nearer by.

Another image burst into Hamish's memory. A snarling, black-faced demon, centimetres from his face. Twigs cracked nearby, jolting him into the present. His vision blurred, and his head spun. He heard a groan. Was it the wind, or the moan of a hunter as it circled its prey?

Should he walk towards what might be a dog walker to ask for help, or would that be to embrace certain death? He didn't recognise the wood, but his watering eyes meant everything seemed slightly out of focus. Didn't they all look the same?

Scudding clouds drifted past a silvery moon to his left. He decided it would be his guide, because the noises would be behind him. Eventually, he'd reach a road or a house. He stumbled across tree roots and muddy puddles, but his heart pumped stronger with each step.

The hound barked again. Louder, closer. He twisted in the

general direction and saw two white glowing eyes watching in the gathering light. They raced towards him. He was too drained to move and could only raise his hands to weakly fend it off. But it was only a muntjac deer, which veered away and disappeared behind a shrub.

Hamish panted with relief.

He hobbled after the deer and, after a minute of stumbling, he found himself on a path. He moved as fast as his sore feet would allow. Oddly, it was the foot which still had a shoe that caused him most bother. A building came into view in the distance as the trees spaced out.

Gasping, he made his way along a well-used track. Out of the forest, it was much lighter. He even managed a chuckle at how he must appear, mud-covered, as he staggered from the shadows.

The structure was a large shed. The garden behind had swings, but the house was in darkness. A car accelerated not far away. He lurched past the dwelling and saw a road ahead. A vehicle drove by but another was coming. Instead of the damp, musty, sour stench of his own fear, he got a whiff of exhaust fumes. It had never been so welcome.

Hamish was spent. His shoeless foot gave way, and he tumbled off the path onto the tarmac. Pain lanced through his knees, while headlights glared. As brakes screeched and tyres slid, Hamish crawled towards the kerb while praying whatever was hurtling towards him would stop in time. Both he and the driver were too slow, and the vehicle careered into him with a solid thud.

4

Ashley stepped out of her house with a frown after what felt like a solid workout. Was her relationship with Barry going anywhere? He was only mid-thirties and not particularly mature. Make that not at all mature. He understood children weren't likely to be part of her future, and said he wasn't bothered. That was all very well in the heady early days, but would it last? Did she want it to?

Ashley had to admit it was nice to be having great sex for the first time in a long time. She also enjoyed leaving him in her bed. It was like saving some chocolate in the fridge for later.

'Hey, lady. You look happy enough to go on a train ride.'

Ashley looked up at her neighbour's bedroom window. The young boy, whose room it was, peered down at her.

'What makes you say that, Oliver?'

'I want to visit my gran in hospital. My mum has a case file to read and says she doesn't have the time. I told her I'd catch the train, then a bus, but she reckons I'm too young.'

'Seeing as you're eleven, then I'd agree.'

'Will you take me, then? Please!'

Ashley considered it for only a moment. Three generations

lived next door. The grandmother, Dana, was on a palliative care ward. Her cancer had finally broken free and spread all over. Ashley had offered to help Oliver's mother because his father wasn't on the scene, and Cherry was wearing many hats, but Ashley struggled to fit much else in when she was at work from early until late.

'So, you really want to visit her?' she asked. 'Will you tidy your room from now on? Help your mum with her chores? Mow the lawn? Buckle down at school?'

'Definitely.'

'Clean and polish my car?'

'Don't push it, lady.'

Ashley laughed.

'Fetch your mum, and we'll agree timings.'

Cherry had been working in London to make her way as a lawyer, but, with Dana's illness, the moment to stay local had come. Cherry wore a big grin when she came to the door.

'You're a lifesaver!'

'It's no problem,' said Ashley with a wink. 'Oliver's promised to be the best boy ever if he gets to go. I'm heading into work to catch up on some paperwork, anyway, and it's not too far away. So, I'll drive him there, then collect him three hours later, if that works?'

'It's okay to drop him at the entrance. I'd trust him to find his way now. He's been a few times. I just don't like the thought of him on his own at busy bus and train stations. If you can pick him up from the ward, though, so he isn't waiting outside, I'd appreciate it. I'll fetch some parking money.'

'No, that's fine. I'd love to see Dana. I'll spend some time with her, too.'

'Tell her I'll be there tomorrow evening. You don't know what a favour this is. I can't get a moment's peace with him in the house.'

'Hey, I'm standing next to you!' shouted Oliver.

They set off in Ashley's old and knackered but reliable Vectra. Oliver didn't shut up for the entire journey. Ashley drove more or less past the Norfolk and Norwich University Hospital on the way to work, so it was hardly an inconvenience. Ashley knew she wouldn't be able to relax if she deposited him at the drop-off point, so she parked and left Oliver ringing the ward buzzer. She then bought two lattes to go from The Pod, a pleasant café next to the east block of the hospital.

By the time Ashley reached the office, she had a sense it would be a good day, which was only reinforced when she spied the DCI in his office. She left one coffee on a free desk, took the other with her and knocked on his open door.

'Morning, sir.'

He noticed the coffee in her hand.

'Ashley. I didn't know you were coming in. Don't suppose that's for me.'

'I was looking forward to it, but okay. You can have it.'

'Very kind.'

'I was also wondering if you had five minutes to discuss the assessment day.'

Kettle was nobody's fool. He rose from his seat and looked out of his office window, spotting Ashley's identical coffee cup at the mostly deserted desks.

'Sneaky,' he said with admiration. 'But not sneaky enough. Is the opportunity to grill me all you've come in for?'

'An hour or so of paperwork, then interview prep. I might nip into town for new work clothes, but I'll probably shop online. The abuse of my threadbare suits has eventually driven me into action.'

'Okay, I need a favour from you after, so it's a deal. Personally, I believe you're more than ready for promotion, so fire away.'

Ashley probed a little about the questions to expect and the types of answer the board would want to hear, but after ten minutes, she realised the assessment day wasn't what was worrying her. She decided to come out with it, hoping Kettle wouldn't tell anyone.

'I'm a little concerned I'm going to get the role,' she said with a smile.

Kettle laughed. 'It will certainly be different. You'll spend more hours in the office. You'll stare at spreadsheets until your eyes hurt, like I'm doing today. You'll feel an extra burden. Not only are the public depending on you, but the whole team becomes your responsibility. I wouldn't expect you to come in on a Thursday looking as if you woke that morning on the floor of The White Horse, either.'

'Ah, you noticed the aftermath of my occasional de-stressing sessions.'

'I could smell them.'

'Last week was an over-exuberant port and Stilton night with my neighbour.'

'I'm only pulling your leg, but I don't expect my DIs to arrive at management meetings smelling like Pepé Le Pew. An inspector sets the standard. The Barry thing will need resolving too. It probably does anyway.'

Ashley's face flared hot.

'Ah. Are any secrets safe here?' she said.

'Not from me.' Kettle smiled. 'Let's see how you perform at the assessment centre. I also need to have a word about Hector. He's been doing some work with me over the last few weeks to give him an insight into higher management roles. I've been impressed. His brain works differently from others. I love a counterweight to conventional thinking, but I sensed a tiny lack of engagement, as if his mind was elsewhere. We mustn't lose people of Hector's calibre.'

Hector Fade was a popular twenty-four-year-old on the Fast

Track programme who'd joined them in April. He was coming up to the end of his two-year spell and had choices to make about where he wanted to work. Ashley knew one of those options was a well-paid job in the private sector. She'd also noticed a slight distancing in his behaviour.

'We've had some shocking incidents to deal with. Maybe it's him adjusting,' she said, trying to give Kettle a reassuring smile.

'I'll leave that with you. Now, let me tell you the cost of my advice.'

'Go on,' said Ashley, now grinning.

'I took a strange call from Control before you arrived. An ambulance attended an RTC on a road near Bacton Wood. It seems a man ran into the path of a van.'

'Suicide. Carelessness. Or drunk. Possibly all three. Probably not a major crime.'

'No, but the paramedic was concerned enough to report it to Control. Uniform met the ambulance at the hospital. The injured party is in an extremely distressed state, covered in bruises and marks, but also mud and moss. Uniform rang it in for us to investigate further, so Emma will be at the hospital in about an hour. I'd like you to have a look, too.'

Ashley's face was now serious.

'What are you saying? That he was running for his life?'

'For want of a better phrase, he'd been buried alive.'

5

Ashley finished most of her paperwork in forty-five minutes so at eleven o'clock, she drove to Norfolk and Norwich University Hospital and met Emma outside A & E.

'Morning, Ems. You're looking rather smart and fabulous.'

'I feel it. I'll tell you more about that later, but this RTC is a weird one.'

'The boss said he'd been buried alive?'

'It sounds like it. The ambulance guys were suspicious, so they mentioned it to the nurses, who've bagged his clothing. They're the threads a young man wears to hit the town nowadays, but it's quality stuff. Decent watch, too. Expensive phone. Leather shoes, although he only had one of them. All covered in mud, as though he's been in a landslide.'

'Which I assume he hasn't?'

'No.'

'Anything off the phone?'

'No, it's an iPhone, but the battery was dead.'

'Shall we go in?'

'It's chaos in there. They're short-staffed as usual, but on top of our guy there's been a four-car pile-up, a fall from height, and multiple cardiac incidents. I asked about the possibility of a side room, but the doctor was called away.'

'Shame.'

'The driver of the van is here as well, also in a distressed state because she was worried she'd killed him. Uniform took a statement. She was delivering a birthday cake nearby, and he staggered into the road right in front of her.'

'But he's not seriously injured?'

'That's the other odd thing. They've checked him over and he's got plenty of bumps, marks and scrapes on him. Damaged nails and sore fingers. There are bruises too, although the emergency doctor said the ones on his legs and arms look a few days old.'

'Sport injuries?'

'Maybe, but there are also some minor burns on his body, and a few careful knife cuts on his thighs.'

'Careful?'

'Yes.'

'As if they were self-inflicted?'

'It is a spot people choose, but the slices are nearer to the groin than usual.'

Ashley didn't like the sound of that.

'Can we talk to him?' she asked.

'Dr Bandera said she'll allow an interview at midday. The victim has agreed to having his wounds photographed, and they've taken blood and urine to run toxicology reports. He's finally given some personal details. His name is Hamish MacDonald. They're dressing his wounds, which all seem minor. The van driver hit the brakes hard and slowed enough to knock him over, but little else. The doc's more concerned with his mental state.'

'PTSD?'

'Drug psychosis was her guess. The doc said how long we get

will be dictated by Hamish's responses because he's started to show hyper-awareness and the beginnings of aggression when pressed for details. His answers have also veered into incoherency. All they're sure of is he lives alone in Norwich at a flat on Lefroy Road. He's twenty-two, date of birth given, and has no next of kin.'

'He hasn't mentioned why he was in the woods?'

'He was out with a friend, Max, but they must have got separated. Said he woke up in a grave. His memory is incomplete, and that's what's upsetting him most.'

Ashley glanced at her watch. They had less than an hour until twelve.

'This could be nothing. Possibly some kind of joke.'

'I know. Or it could be worrying.'

'Let's grab a coffee at The Pod, talk it through, and get the ball rolling.'

'I'll do a background check in case Hamish was recently in Broadmoor or its equivalent.'

'Okay. The question is, do we search Witton Wood before it's trampled to death?'

'How big is it? Wait, I thought it was Bacton Wood?'

'It's kind of both. Locals are more likely to call it Witton, but it's near the village of Bacton, so let's use that before everyone gets confused.'

'Is it big?'

Ashley did a quick search on her phone. 'Two hundred and eighty acres.'

Emma looked upward for a moment.

'A football pitch is a bit over one and a half acres, so that's getting on for two hundred of them. Not quite a needle in a haystack, but it would need a tonne of resources to cover it.'

Ashley rang Kettle and updated him. There was silence as he processed the facts.

'Any previous?'

Ashley repeated the question to Emma, who'd just finished her own call. She nodded.

'Typical troubled juvenile record with minor drug offences.'

'Any hospital orders?'

'No.'

Ashley relayed the information to Kettle.

'I'm not ordering a search on a forest that size without more intel. We have few abductions here, and we'll look like fools if it's unmet mental health needs or drugs. I'll call DS Williamson to see who's available. Did you say you were talking to the victim at twelve?'

'Yes.'

'Ring me after your chat. I've checked for recent missing people in the region, drunken incidents, fights from last night, and it's been remarkably quiet.'

There wasn't much more they could do without speaking to Hamish, so after Ashley finished the call she took the opportunity to catch up with Emma.

'What's got you upbeat, then?' she asked. 'New boyfriend? Friend with benefits?'

Emma Stones was married with three kids to a bloke who'd barely lifted a finger around the house and generally left the child-rearing to her. Emma, who was a tall, curvy and imposing woman, had finally chucked him out a few months ago.

'No, it's the reverse. Hubster has moved back in.'

Ashley managed to hide her complete shock.

'That's a surprise.'

'Yes. He kind of caught me at a low ebb when he asked if he could. The children returned from his grubby apartment and wondered why Daddy would choose to live that way instead of with them. I explained for the umpteenth time we'd been having arguments, but that doesn't compute. They're always rowing with their mates, but they don't then ignore them for three months.'

'Comments from your kids like that can't be easy to hear.'

'No, they aren't, and my youngest whispered a question to me after their father dropped them off.'

'Uh-oh!'

'Yep. He said couldn't I give it another try, just for them?'

'Bless.'

'Broke my heart, but Kevin has been such a dick.'

'He should be the one begging.'

'Exactly. So I wasn't going to reach out, but then he came over.'

'Flowers and chocolates?'

'No, that wouldn't have worked. He arrived when the kids were at school and asked me to sit in his car for ten minutes and let him talk uninterrupted.'

'I'd have needed chocolates.'

Emma smiled.

'I had my police career and focused on the children with my free time, and he had his job. He felt excluded from what I did. To him, he was doing okay by paying for the majority of the mortgage, running the cars and doing property repairs. Although we often got a professional in after to fix his work. The reason he hadn't already been in touch to plead was because he wanted to think about why he'd failed to engage with the family when he had the chance. Did he really want married life?'

'Isn't it a bit late for those questions?'

'True, but his dad worked a lot and was standoffish, so he hadn't had a great father role model. He wants to make amends. He's asked me to help him understand what that role is.'

'And you relented?'

'Yes. If I'm honest, I analysed the bills, and running two houses would mean a lot of sacrifices for the children. I threw him out because I was angry. Maybe I didn't give him enough warning. Anyway, after I lobbed him out, he was warier around me but also more respectful. He brought a bottle of wine when he finally came to talk about everything one evening after the kids were in bed. We chatted, had a glass, and somehow ended up having sex. Very odd. It was lovely, though. Kind of like doing it with a stranger.'

Ashley laughed, but she was a little worried for her friend. Still, it was hard to replace a father, and there'd been no cheating or violence. She did forcibly throw him out the front door, but not from him, anyway. Perhaps a kick up the arse was all he needed.

'Come on, let's head in,' she said.

When they reached A & E, they could see the department was having one of those shifts. There was a long queue at Reception and standing room only in the waiting area. Ashley waved her warrant card and asked if someone could assist them. Half a minute later, a nurse appeared and guided them along a corridor, through a couple of sets of doors, then stopped outside a closed door.

'His shouting was upsetting the other patients, so we bumped him up the queue for their sakes. We've taken him to the toilet. He was fine, but he's still anxious.'

'About anything in particular?'

'Yes, he asked what day it was. I told him it was Sunday. He said it can't be.'

'Why not?'

'Because he went out on Friday night.'

6

The nurse pushed open the door and ushered Ashley and Emma inside. Hamish MacDonald was not far off being curled into the foetal position. His posture and haunted expression were those of an elderly man riddled with disease, even though Hamish had unlined skin and thick dark hair.

'Hi, Hamish. My name's DS Ashley Knight and this is my colleague, DC Emma Stones. How are you feeling?'

To his credit, Hamish pulled himself into a sitting position. He smiled, but it showed both rows of teeth, which Ashley knew meant it was probably fake.

'We're here to ask a few questions, Hamish, then we'll let you rest.'

'I don't want to think about it.' He swallowed deeply. 'I can't.'

Ashley pulled over a chair and sat next to the bed.

'I'm sorry this happened to you. It must have been a terrible experience.'

'I just want to forget.'

'I can understand that, but we need to know what went on. You wouldn't want anybody else to be in danger, would you?'

'No,' he uttered quietly.

Ashley had the impression Hamish was a vulnerable lad with little worldly experience. He was close to retreating into his shell. She gently tapped his arm and nodded at him.

'Please, what do you think happened?'

'I've no idea. I went out with my friend on Friday night. We got drunk and went to a club. I remember vaguely having a good time in there and leaving, but then nothing.'

'Was the next thing you recall waking up in Bacton Wood?'

Hamish grimaced.

'If that's where I was, but I woke in a muddy hole under a door.'

Ashley asked him to give her more detail, which he did. She paused for a moment afterwards to absorb what he'd said.

'Do you believe someone buried you?'

'Yes, I had to dig myself out. How would I bury myself?'

Ashley considered how to word the next question. Emma beat her to it.

'Doesn't it seem unlikely you were buried for thirty hours?'

Hamish rubbed his temples, then his eyes. Ashley noticed a few of his nails were split and others had mud under them.

'I know! It's like a dream where fragments have come back to me. There was a room at a house. I recall alcohol being given to me. No, forced on me. Maybe a party, but that doesn't seem right. I was scared there.'

'Did anyone hurt you?' asked Emma.

'I'm not sure. I have pain everywhere. All of my body aches, not just the side the van hit.'

'Why would someone want to attack you?'

Hamish shook his head. A tear trickled down his cheek.

'They wouldn't.'

'Did you drink too much, or get offered drugs?'

Inside, Ashley smiled at Emma's question. That was another phrase she'd been searching for. Hamish was in no fit state for deceit.

'I can't remember. Perhaps a line or two, just to keep me awake.'

'It sounds like you weren't awake.'

Hamish drifted into a monotone as he continued to talk to them. Emma took detailed notes, but Hamish seemed to live a quiet life as a distribution centre worker for a kitchen and bathroom company, packing boxes for a living. Now he was calmer and communicative, Ashley moved the conversation on to who he was out with.

'You said you were out with Max. Max who? Where can we find him?'

There was little colour left in Hamish's face, but what was there swiftly drained away. His face tensed. Chin forced forward.

'No idea,' he whispered.

'Was he at the party with you?'

'What party?'

'The house after the nightclub?'

Hamish's face creased into an almighty frown as he strained to search through his broken memory. Ashley observed the nurse slip from the room.

'I think so. There was shouting and laughing, maybe. My head was spinning.'

'And Max wasn't in the woods with you?'

Hamish scrunched his eyes up. When he opened them, they were wild. His voice was a bellow.

'God, please! What happened?'

'It's okay, Hamish. Calm down. You're safe here.'

'Trapped!' he screamed. 'They buried me!'

Hamish rolled off the bed, hit the floor, and backed into the corner of the room, banging his head against the wall. He blinked rapidly. His right hand trembled next to the bandage on his left arm, as though he recalled how he'd been hurt. His shoulders shuddered.

The door opened behind Ashley and a southern Asian woman in scrubs entered. Her name tag identified her as Dr Bandera. Hamish stared with fear at first, then relief, as a smiling bald man with big brown eyes followed her in, who immediately reminded Ashley of a short Aldo Zilli, the TV chef. The man had a charm and presence about him. He strode over to Hamish, crouched down, and pulled him into a hug. Hamish bowed his head and rested it on the older man's shoulder.

'Come on, Hamish. Back on the bed,' he said.

'I was under a door,' whispered Hamish.

Hamish allowed himself to be guided to the bed and the man cupped his face.

'It's okay, rest now.'

'I'm sorry. I told them what they asked, but what do they want?'

The new arrival frowned at him. 'Who? The police?'

'No,' Hamish replied. He gritted his teeth again, then spoke through them. 'I don't know. I just don't know.'

Both Hamish's hands began to shake. 'Please leave me alone.'

The doctor cleared her throat. She looked at Ashley and shook her head.

'Okay, let's get everyone out,' said Bandera. 'That should be the last conversation anybody has with Hamish today.'

7

Ashley stopped as she was leaving the room and turned in the doorway.

'We need to talk to him again,' she said. 'Those injuries will need to be properly photographed by CSI. What time in the morning is good for everyone?'

Dr Bandera wasn't much older than the man in the bed and appeared just as exhausted. She walked over and held the door. After a deep breath, she looked Ashley in the eyes.

'Ten. Hopefully, we'll have him rested, fed and washed, but the tests are pretty straightforward, so we at least should have the results back around then. No doubt I'll be here.'

'You took tests? What kind?' asked the short bald man, who was hovering at Ashley's shoulder.

'To see if there was anything strange in his system. If there is, fluids, sleep, and observation are the best way for him to recover. He's highly agitated and could be a danger to himself or others.'

'Strange? What does that mean? Hamish is going to be fine, though, isn't he?'

'He's safe now.'

'Okay. Thank you.'

Something occurred to Ashley. 'Is he seriously dehydrated?'

'Not as much as I'd have expected.'

After a brief nod, Bandera let the door close.

Ashley turned to the man who'd been questioning the medic so forcefully.

'Are you his dad?'

'Like a father, but not his father. My name is Rocco,' he said with a small bow. 'He is super close with my boy, Max. They grew up together, mostly at my house.'

'We've struggled to find a next of kin. Who should we get in touch with?'

'I'm not sure. His parents died when he was little. No siblings. I think he moved recently, but I could call someone who knows where he lives.'

'It's okay, we can find that out,' said Ashley. 'Aren't you concerned?'

'About what?'

'He was out with your son, Max, wasn't he?'

'I presume so. They're thick as thieves, but I received a message from my boy this morning. Max occasionally comes over on a Sunday if he's not too hungover, so I texted him to see if he was coming and he replied he'd be over tomorrow night instead. These youngsters party a lot, so crazy things happen. Especially to Hamish.'

'Do they take drugs?'

'Don't they all? When I was young, the pubs shut at eleven, and clubs at two. Then everyone headed home. This lot don't seem to know when to stop, now there isn't anyone to shout last orders at them. They're at it for days. It's a bizarre new world.'

'Can we have your full name, please?' asked Emma.

'Just call me Rocco. Have you heard of Rocco's Fine Homes in

Norwich?'

Emma and Ashley shook their heads. Then Emma clicked her fingers.

'Do you sell granite worktops?'

'We do.'

'I saw an ad in the *EDP* last week. The price made my eyes water.'

'That's right. We advertise in the *Eastern Daily Press*. Quality costs, or it wouldn't be quality. I'll give you my card. Look. Hamish trusts me, and he works for my company. There won't be anyone else to support him, so I will be here in the morning at ten as well. I'll bring Max and we can discover precisely what has happened. Actually, I'll ring Max now.'

Ashley sensed something was out of kilter. Not being a parent, she wasn't sure exactly how worried she would be if her grown son was involved in a similar situation. Maybe Max had been the one to bury Hamish. Although Hamish's spirit appeared broken by his recent experience in the wood, she suspected he was telling the truth, so he would have probably said if he could recall Max hurting him or if they'd argued.

Rocco seemed to swear in what sounded like Italian as he listened to a recorded message. There was a hint of accent in his voice, but it was faint. He cut the call and gave his phone a dirty glare.

'Max never answers his phone. Says it stresses him out. Can you believe that? Anyway, I gotta go. It's not a problem. I'll find him today, and we'll see you tomorrow.'

He began to walk away.

'Your business card, please,' said Emma.

'Sorry,' he said, passing Emma one out of his wallet.

Ashley handed him hers. He smiled, but as he left, his lips were pursed, and those big brown eyes were narrowed.

8

Ashley and Emma battled their way outside so they could talk. There were ambulances queued up and cars dropping people off.

'What do you reckon?' asked Ashley.

'It's all a bit unlikely sounding. If Hamish was out of his mind on drink and drugs after partying for days, it's more than possible he wandered into a forest, got lost, then passed out. Drugged-up folk thrash around. He might have felt like he was buried.'

'What about the door? It could be serious.'

'Perhaps it was a hallucination, but I agree, if it is a crime, it's a concerning one.'

'What did you think of Rocco?'

'You mean not worrying about his own child?'

'Yeah.'

'As a mother, I'd have been frantic, but I suppose he received a text from him. My kids regularly don't answer their phones to me, either. So, that bit rang true.'

'There were other comments which didn't seem quite right to me though. I can't put my finger on it. What does super close mean? Great friends, or lovers? I reckon Rocco has been dragged to the hospital or elsewhere before because of Max and Hamish. He wasn't at all fazed until Max failed to answer his phone.'

'No, but none of that's necessarily criminal. We've hardly seen Hamish at his best, but he doesn't seem the type to live the kind of life that would put him in danger of being held to ransom or abducted. Crimes like these are often to do with money, and I know the area he lives in. It can be rough around there.'

Ashley looked at her watch.

'I'm running out of time. It's my day off, and I've got a lady to visit here, so I'm finished.'

'The question is,' said Emma, 'should MIT investigate or wait until we speak to Hamish again tomorrow?'

'If there's a crime scene in the woods, it might be compromised by then.'

'Yeah, but closing off a wood that size and keeping it secure would be enough of a job without actually searching it. It's possible someone else sent Rocco the text from Max's phone, but if anyone's going to track Max down, it will be his father, so we can leave that to him.'

'I'll ring Kettle. He can decide. That's why he gets his own office. Can you check the weather forecast for tonight and tomorrow while I call him? He might ask CID or Uniform to head down there if we don't have the manpower.'

Kettle answered swiftly, and she updated him about Hamish and the arrival of Rocco. He'd clearly been considering all angles because he soon made a decision.

'Ally Williamson's managed to get most of his team in. I've spoken to an inspector from PolSA, and he can have a full team down there first thing in the morning. He'll send two officers today to help Ally look into this. Luckily, it's been an afternoon without drama. Uniform units will close the wood off for the rest of the day and ask everyone in there to leave. It's not too heavily used, and most people park at one end. Maybe our guys will see something obvious.'

PolSA stood for Police Search Advisor. They were a team specially trained to search efficiently and effectively while preserving evidence.

Emma tapped Ashley on the shoulder and mimed opening an umbrella.

'The weather forecast isn't the best,' said Ashley to Kettle. 'So, if you've got enough bodies, they could begin where Hamish burst into the road, and move in. There might be a big hole, and he mentioned a door. Perhaps the Grim Reaper will still be there, leaning on his spade.'

'I'm sure Ally's underwear would love that, but let's hope so.'

She chuckled at Kettle's reply.

'Early start for everyone tomorrow, either way,' said Ashley.

'Yes. Regardless of what we find in the wood, you be at the N & N at ten and talk to Hamish as agreed.'

'Okay.'

Most locals referred to the hospital as the Norfolk and Norwich, or simply, the N & N.

'Take Hector with you. He's only got a few weeks now until he needs to decide what his plans are. Fingers crossed, this Rocco and Max are at the hospital when you arrive, and it'll all be down to misadventure.'

'Will do.'

'What was Max's surname?'

Ashley paused. 'We have his dad's business card. Hang on.'

Emma had been listening and a pink bloom came to her cheeks. She showed Ashley the gold embossed thick black card. It had a phone number and just one word written in flamboyant writing. Rocco's.

'Emma's coming back to the office. She'll give it to you then. He runs an established business in town, Rocco's Fine Homes.'

'Okay, I've heard of it. I'll talk to her when she arrives.'

Ashley finished the call with a smile.

'What did he say?' asked Emma.

'They're going to seal up the area as best they can. Ally will take a look this afternoon in case there's anything obvious, but it'll be gloomy down there soon. Right, I'd better get off.'

'Okay, Ash. I'll catch you tomorrow.' Emma scowled. 'Something just dawned on me.'

'What?'

'Hamish had no next of kin, a dead phone and no ID.'

'So?'

'How did Rocco know he was in hospital?'

9

Ashley and Emma concluded that was a question for the next morning. They said goodbye and Ashley ventured back into the hospital to take the lift to the ward where Oliver's gran, Dana, was. Ashley had put little make-up on as she'd not expected close scrutiny and she looked frazzled in the lift mirror. There was redness around her nose and cheeks, which usually meant she was drinking too much. Barry regularly enjoyed a skinful, so he wasn't helping her move closer to sobriety. Or maybe the blotches on her face were down to his stubble.

Dana had a room with three beds but she was the only occupant. She was awake when Ashley arrived. Oliver was asleep on the bed next to her. He didn't look so leggy cuddled in like that and Ashley tiptoed over. Dana took her hand and looked into her eyes. Ashley detected pain in the older woman's expression.

'It's lovely to see you, Ashley.'

'You, too, Dana,' she whispered.

'It's okay. He's out for the count.'

'How are you?'

'Ready.'

'I'm sorry to hear that.'

'Don't be. I have my faith, and I've been fortunate with love and family.'

Ashley felt tears welling up. 'Will you be able to go home again?'

'I chose a hospice for the end, but I've picked up an infection.'

'Do you want anything?'

Dana gave Ashley a tired smile. 'Thank you for bringing Oliver to visit me. He's my only regret.'

Ashley managed to ask why without crying.

'When I first got this diagnosis, I prayed I would last until Oliver was at senior school, so his mum could pursue her career. God answered that prayer, but I won't see Oliver grow into a man, meet his children, celebrate his successes. I suppose we don't get everything we want.'

'That's not a regret. It's just life.'

Dana stroked the boy's head. 'Oliver often got into my bed with me for naps when he was young.'

'You've raised a wonderful boy.'

'He never stopped talking after you dropped him off.'

'I can believe that.'

'Then he ate a load of my sweets and biscuits, washed it down with a Coke from the vending machine, and asked for a cuddle. He dropped right off. This might be his last hug. They tell me I only have a week or so left, at least of lucidity.'

Dana winced and looked over at the morphine drip.

'I need that more and more. It's my time. Can you explain to Cherry not to bring him when she comes tomorrow? I want him to remember me like this. How we were today. I want to say goodbye properly to her, too. Just the two of us.'

'Of course.'

For another half-hour, Ashley sat beside Dana, holding her

hand while she cuddled her grandson. Dana's breathing settled, but she cracked an eye open fifteen minutes later.

'I heard you have a new boyfriend,' she said.

'Bloody hell. Who told you that?'

'I actually heard you!'

Ashley's face blossomed. 'Oh.'

'Are you finally going to settle down? It's about time. Pretty girl like you.'

Ashley shrugged. 'I'm not sure. There are pluses and minuses to this one.'

'Trust me, from a woman who knows. If you're not head over heels at the start, you can do better. Minor problems now become stinkers later on. Like not clearing up spilled milk.'

Dana's Caribbean accent only ever became strong when she was giving life advice and it always made Ashley smile.

'What if I can't do better?'

'Believe in yourself, Ashley. I do. Don't waste time with the wrong person, or you won't be available when the right one comes along.'

Ashley nodded. It was something she already knew. Oliver woke up and clambered off the bed before telling Ashley about his latest football game. When Ashley rose and looked at Dana, she'd fallen asleep. Ashley understood that they'd already said their farewells.

'Are you ready, Oliver?' asked Ashley.

'Wait.'

Oliver took a toy car out of his pocket and rested it on Dana's bedside table.

'Yes, can we go to McDonald's?'

'We'll see. Give your Gran a farewell kiss.'

Oliver marched bravely towards the bed, then reached over and kissed Dana on the forehead. Ashley wasn't aware of the conversations he'd had with his mother about Dana's sickness, but he seemed to know this was goodbye.

'Love you, Gran,' he said, raising his voice.

His grandmother gave no sign she'd heard him.

They left the hospital in silence, but Oliver was chatting nineteen to the dozen again by the time they pulled out of the car park. It was close to four thirty when they reached Cromer after a fast-food excursion on the Norwich ring road. Oliver ran into his house to tell his mum about his day.

Ashley took a minute outside before she headed in to speak with Cherry. Death was familiar to Ashley. Even though she felt choked up by experiences like the one with Dana, they were always lessons to live in the moment. To enjoy your life. She saw the flickering of the TV in her front room and suspected Barry was farting in her dressing gown and watching *Aliens* again. Tonight, she could cope with that if it meant not coming home to an empty house.

As she locked the car door, her phone rang. It was Emma.

'Good news doesn't come on a Sunday at five,' said Ashley after accepting the call.

'Just an update,' replied Emma. 'PolSA and Uniform closed the wood off and got most people back in their cars, but they were running out of daylight. There was no point in tramping about in the dark or organising high-intensity LED lamps and the batteries to power them if we weren't sure we had a missing person. A guy who'd been walking his Beagle all the way around the perimeter was the last member of the public to leave. He said his dog barked at a patch of disturbed earth. When he checked the spot, there was an internal door on its side.'

'Under a door,' said Ashley, repeating what Hamish had said.

'Yes. Hamish's sleeping spot. PolSA made sure there wasn't a body in it before they cordoned it off. They did find a shoe in the hole, which sounds like it matches Hamish's.'

'Okay, is the plan tomorrow the same?'

'Yes. Hector will meet you at Bacton Wood, Mill Road entrance, at eight.'

'Did Kettle consider a helicopter with FLIR in case this Max is still in the wood?'

FLIR stood for Forward-Looking Infrared.

'He decided he couldn't authorise the cost, seeing as the father, Rocco, told us Max has been in touch. We rang Rocco's business number, but it went to voicemail, which just confirmed Kettle's resolve not to bear the expense.'

'His thoughts being if Rocco was worried, he'd have answered his phone or been in touch.'

'Exactly.'

'I don't like this. We should have the helicopter on standby tomorrow, just in case.'

'I'll pass it on.'

'I take it the door and hole looked suspicious.'

'Yes. The lead searcher said it was hard to describe it as anything other than a shallow grave.'

10

Ashley woke at six to an empty bed. Barry had gone home when he couldn't tempt Ashley with a glass of wine, but she'd wanted a clear head in the morning. She half missed his heavy presence, but she also appreciated not having him try to get in the shower with her, and making the kitchen seem as though a gang of teenagers had come over for breakfast. It was a twenty-five-minute drive to Bacton Wood if she went via North Walsham, but, even though it took a bit longer, it was much nicer along the coast, so that was the route she took.

Ashley cruised past the small villages of Overstrand and Sidestrand, then through Trimingham and Mundesley. Autumn was a wonderful time of year in Norfolk. The crowds had gone, especially on that part of the coast, and the pace of life for many residents changed.

One adjustment Ashley had been hoping to make in her life was to be more aware of the moment, and that included the seasons. Norfolk was an incredibly green place in the spring and summer. Trees and bushes surrounded the roads and, as autumn faded, the countryside seemed to shimmer as the leaves shifted through a patchwork of warm and vibrant bronzes, golds and reds.

A flash of lightning far out on the horizon quelled her wonderment, as did being forced to edge inland along the road through Bacton Gas Terminal, an imposing complex of six terminals that supplied a third of the UK's gas needs. Armed police on a walking patrol stared at her car as she drove by. She waved, but they didn't.

Ashley reached Bacton village and was cruising past Castaways and Red House holiday parks just before eight when her phone rang. Twenty-year-old basic Vauxhalls didn't have hands-free, so she had to pick up her phone. The number was unrecognised, but she pulled over anyway.

'Detective Sergeant Ashley Knight speaking.'

'Sergeant. It's Rocco Vialli. We met yesterday at the hospital.'

'Morning, Mr Vialli. How can I help?'

'It's about Max. I rang him many times yesterday, but no luck, so I visited his flat in the town centre and got no answer. His car is there. I called his brother, who knows his friends, and nothing. It's as though he's vanished.'

'Which is understandably a concern after what happened to Hamish.'

'Exactly. I assume you'll be in Bacton Wood this morning, looking into what occurred to Hamish. Should I come down?'

'No, please don't. There'll be no access to the area for civilians and any distractions might disrupt the search. You'll be more help if you continue to hunt for him at your end.'

'So, I will be at the N & N at ten as agreed.'

'Okay, I'll see you there and update you on our progress.'

'That's not soon enough when it's my youngest son in danger. I need an update before that.'

'You told me yesterday you were in contact with him. That information stayed our hand. At the moment, he's just out of contact, unless you have a reason for us to be more concerned? Did he only text you the once yesterday?'

'Yes, but what if a person took his phone and then messaged me?'

'Did the message contain the type of language or abbreviations he would normally use?'

'Yes, but a thief could easily check his previous messages to know that.'

Ashley smiled. Rocco was sharp.

'I'm almost at the location we're interested in now, so give me an hour and I'll call you back.'

'Good. I will also continue the search myself.'

Ashley's mind was whirring as she ended the call. Rocco's information would now send the investigation into overdrive. Max being out of contact for so long, combined with what happened to Hamish, meant they could be dealing with anything from a missing person to multiple kidnappings. They didn't have time to mess around, either. Hamish's escape from a muddy tomb was yesterday. Could someone else still be in one twenty-four hours later? Would they be alive?

She rang Kettle.

'Morning, sir. I'm almost on site. I just spoke to Rocco. He said there's been no show or contact with Hamish's drinking buddy from Friday night, Max. The father is finally anxious. Do we have any choice but to request a flyover?'

'I agree. I'll arrange and liaise with PolSA.'

'Is PolSA definitely using the Mill Road entrance to manage the search as that was where Hamish left the wood?'

'Yes, it's also the closest entry to the north-west section where they located the door and pit. Hector has confirmed he arrived ten minutes ago.'

Ashley finished the call and continued her journey. Five

minutes later, she parked up behind a long row of cars. She got out and looked up at the sky. The grey clouds, which were bunched up like nervous sheep earlier, had lowered and darkened. They seethed as though urging each other on for a fight ahead. Even the wind, which had seemed indifferent when she'd first woken up, had perked up with intent. If the weather deteriorated much further, the helicopter might not fly.

Ashley had pulled on a pair of grey trousers and black shoes, and layered her top half with a T-shirt, thin jumper and a fleece. She opened the boot and sat on the back of her car to take off her footwear, then pulled on her wellies. An old but well-made waterproof jacket would keep most of the elements at bay. She strode down the line of cars and showed her warrant card to an officer where they'd cordoned off the path, which led, by a house, into the woods.

A small crowd of men and women, some in uniform, others in plain clothes, gathered further up at the edge of the wood. She walked down to them, past a garden containing play equipment, and introduced herself. The tall, suited man in charge was Inspector Treharne. Mid-fifties, he'd joined the police in his forties, but he had an eye for this kind of work and promotions had been fast. She'd worked with him once, years ago, when two children had run away. He'd found them alive in the marshes.

'Morning, Ashley. Kettle said to expect you. I hear the ante has been upped.'

'Yes, I assume the bird is on the way.'

'ETA nine a.m. You can come with us to look at what appears to be the hole. It may help with your questioning later. It's not far through the trees. As forests go, it isn't a particularly big one, but it will still take time. Especially if there's nothing more to find.'

'Is it a forest, then? What's the difference?'

'The distinction goes back to medieval times. It's down to

canopy cover and whether the area is big enough to preserve large game, but the terms are pretty interchangeable nowadays.'

'How long for the entire wood to be checked?'

'It depends on how many searchers we have. A couple of days for a cursory check. Getting on for a week for the whole thing to be searched thoroughly. A month scientifically with scanners.'

'Lead the way,' she said.

Treharne let the team head off in front of him. DC Hector Fade was waiting at the back of the group and he smiled at her.

'Did you get here early to make me look bad?' she asked.

'Of course.'

'How are you?' she said as they walked further in.

'Reasonably decent,' he said, dismissing that line of inquiry. 'I've had an update from Emma. What do you think of the fact Max is still missing?'

'It's concerning. Yesterday, Kettle and I were hoping it wouldn't come to searching an entire wood. The potential scale of the crime is a worry, too, because it takes plenty of organisation and expense as well as numerous people to grab two grown men and bury them in a public place.'

'Was Hamish a reliable witness?'

Ashley considered her conversation with him. 'No, he wasn't. I'm not sure if that was guilt, or the fact he'd just been through a horrific experience, or both. Maybe he got dirty burying his best mate.'

'Perhaps Max buried Hamish as a drunken joke, then forgot where. Now he's panicking and run away.'

'That's some gag, and more than a little careless.'

'Young men do silly things, especially under the influence.'

'They do.'

'Although, not all young men,' replied Hector with a smile.

It took only a minute for them to reach the wood proper. A

hundred and fifty football pitches hadn't sounded too big when Emma had mentioned it the previous day, but the trees stretched off endlessly into the distance. The land wasn't as flat as she recalled, having walked in the wood with a friend and her dog a few years back, but there was a clear path to follow.

It seemed a peaceful, sheltered place first thing though, despite the gathering storm overhead. A mist still hung high in the air between the taller trees. The light was soft and cast their surrounds in a warm glow. They'd reached a line of Wellingtonia. Their gnarled bark, with deep furrows and ridges, gave an impression of great age, even though Ashley suspected they were a relatively recent addition. Even so, the evergreen coniferous trees towered above them, giving Ashley a feeling of insignificance.

The wind didn't appear to have as much strength among the trees, which were also known as Giant Sequoias. Ashley recalled her friend telling her they were the largest living species of tree. It was serene under their canopy. A woodpecker half-heartedly drummed somewhere above them.

'Do you know this place well?' asked Hector.

'Yeah, I've been here quite a few times over the years. Mostly the parts everyone walks, although we sometimes cycled here as kids and messed around off the beaten track. It's a sustainable forest with a lot of it only being planted in the middle of the last century.'

'It's definitely atmospheric.'

'I thought you'd like it. I've heard it's haunted too.'

'Really?'

'Yes. They hanged a murderer, William Suffolk, at Norwich Castle around 1800, then brought him here to be gibbeted.'

'Charming. Having now spent time with dead bodies, I can't imagine the aroma from him would pull in the ramblers and picnickers.'

'There was no Netflix, so folk were happy to tolerate that sort of thing for a tasty sausage roll on a comfy blanket.'

Hector chuckled. 'Is it the Scotch eggs doing the haunting?'

'They say you can still sometimes smell the stench, over two hundred years later. Back then, people had to close their windows and shutters because of it.'

'How long was he left there?'

'Years, as an example to others.'

'Bloody hell.'

'His vengeful ghost is said to haunt that spot.'

'Case closed, then. Perhaps Hamish was supposed to be his replacement.'

The path took them on a slight incline. Treharne stopped at the top of it and looked back at Ashley. He pointed down into a small hollow where a grave-shaped hole had collapsed in the peat and moss. A large white door was stuck sideways, as if it were an open entrance to the underworld.

Ashley shivered as she considered the amount of planning that had gone into putting Hamish under it. If Max was also a victim in all this, her hopes for him were fading fast.

11

Ashley stepped gingerly up to where Treharne stood. The path was slippery, and she could feel moisture in the air. Rain would be with them soon. Ashley looked around at the foliage. The trees were a brilliant array of browns, golds and oranges. It was a breathtaking sight with most of the leaves still attached to the branches.

She shook her head at Treharne.

'Infrared won't penetrate this cover.'

'No, it won't, but we'll still be able to rule out vast areas. We have to make assumptions to give us the best chance of finding Max alive.'

Ashley nodded at him to continue.

'If he's here, it's likely they buried them relatively near to each other. Hamish's grave was dug in soft earth. It's much easier to dig. There are fewer tree roots and no packed mud. Maybe Max arose from the dead as well and is long gone.'

'You'll need dogs if the IR cameras can't see in here.'

Treharne smiled, which made Ashley feel foolish saying it. He clearly knew his job.

'Kettle arranged them yesterday,' he said. 'They were on standby if they got the call first thing. They should be here by nine as well. We'll use them to hunt in the areas the helicopter can't check for heat sources. Once the helicopter has run out of fuel, say two hours, and if the hounds come up short, we'll all head in and look for disturbed earth. That will be the clearest sign of another burial. Time isn't our ally in this kind of search.'

Ashley and Hector glanced down at the scene below. At first she thought the Beagle from the previous day must have investigated inside the hole to see if anyone, or anything, was in it, but the soil at the sides was in uniform piles. The grave was easy to spot.

'And the shoe was in there?' said Ashley.

'Yes. There will be photographs on the file shortly,' said Treharne.

'The mud that was removed hasn't been disguised at all, or were those mounds from you guys digging?' asked Hector.

'No, they were present when we arrived. Whoever dug here wasn't bothered about keeping that fact hidden. If Hamish was buried in there, I suspect he was unconscious, possibly drugged. The door may have been used to carry him down here. He goes in, door on top, then earth piled on to hold it down.'

'Yet he survived without a breathing hole,' replied Hector.

'Perhaps the door was placed considerably above him, meaning there would have been plenty of air, or he might not have been in there for long before he sobered or woke up. The strength of desperation of a panicking man would be sufficient to enable him to push up the door, even with the loose earth on it. You need to decide whether he was put in there to die, or if he was put in there to escape.'

'Why would he be buried to escape?' asked Ashley.

'Perhaps it was a warning, like with William Suffolk,' said Hector, who had come to stand next to her.

Ashley thought about that for a moment.

'Yes, but were they warning him, or someone close to him?' she asked.

'That's your job to figure out, but that would be a high-risk play. What if he hadn't woken up?' asked Treharne.

'I read somewhere you can survive in a coffin for around five or six hours until you asphyxiate,' said Ashley.

'Yes, that sounds about right. Plenty long enough to scratch the bottom of the lid with your nails, but I'd say the space above his head was larger than a coffin, so there would be more oxygen, and it wasn't sealed, so air would filter through the loose mud. Maybe he would have lasted two or three times that. As I said, perhaps he came to after being in the ground for only half an hour.'

The sound of approaching rotor blades caused them all to stare upwards.

'Time to get our heat sources out of the area,' said Treharne. 'I'll arrange for them to do this section to begin with, then the handlers can return with the dogs alone so as not to confuse the scent. Once they've done this patch, we'll all come back in.'

Ashley knew they would struggle to protect the scene, especially with a storm threatening, but the first role of the police was to preserve life. They trudged back to the entrance on Mill Road, where the fresh autumnal smell was lost amongst idling engines. Time was running out. Every minute could be the difference between living and dying. The stakes didn't get any higher.

DI Treharne returned to his van and grabbed the phone from inside it to speak to the helicopter crew. Ashley caught sight of the machine overhead. She could see the forward-looking infrared camera mounted underneath it.

Two vans had parked up on the road opposite. Both from the

Dog Support Unit. Ashley smiled as two Springer spaniels were let out of the back of one, their tails wagging frantically. She had seen Chip and Pin in action in the past. They were eager animals who would work all day, never getting bored, their noses glued to trail scents.

A chocolate Labrador sedately dropped down from the other van. He peered at the humans, then his tail wagged ferociously, too, betraying his outer calm.

Ashley had worked with Columbo before as well.

He was the cadaver dog.

12

A sleek Tesla with blacked-out windows drove past Ashley and the line of police as they waited for the hovering helicopter to complete its task in the area that one officer had jokingly referred to as Hamish's hole.

Judging by Hector's distant stare, his mind had gone into overdrive.

'Maybe they'll find three or four people buried in there,' he said. 'Or perhaps it's a weird pagan cult where they get drunk, cavort amongst the trees, then make sacrifices.'

'You're right. They could have been burying men in these woods for decades, and Hamish was the first to escape.'

'I suppose it's possible Hamish and Max made a bizarre suicide pact and Hamish changed his mind.'

Ashley was frowning at the thought of that when a bald man in a sharp business suit left the Tesla, carrying a plastic bag. He marched straight up to Ashley.

'Detective Sergeant,' he said.

'Rocco, I asked you to stay away,' said Ashley calmly, even though she was irritated. He was going through a tough time.

'I brought a towel from Max's house. A pair of underpants from the wash basket, and his pillowcase.'

Ashley blinked at him.

'For the hounds.'

'Oh, well done. That's intelligent thinking.'

Ashley called the dog handlers over and left them talking to Rocco. She strolled over to Treharne and explained who the latest arrival was and what he'd brought.

'Sharp,' said Treharne. 'Especially under stress.'

'Yes, I thought he was on the ball at the hospital. I'm annoyed it didn't come to my mind.'

Treharne smiled. 'Same.'

'Okay,' said Ashley. 'We need to leave in a few minutes to speak with the victim, Hamish, at the N & N. They told me he'd be ready for a conversation at ten a.m. Rocco was supposed to be meeting us there, but I expect he won't want to leave here now.'

'That's understandable.'

'There are guys from Ally Williamson's team here to help and communicate back to OCC. I've got your number. I'll call the moment I have any news.'

'Same here. It was great to see you again, Ashley.'

Ashley nodded, knowing the search couldn't be in better hands. If Max, or anyone else for that matter, was out there, Treharne would find them.

Ten minutes later, Ashley heard the helicopter bank away, then watched as the two dog handlers entered the woods. Pin and Chip scampered ahead, then glanced back for their orders. The other handler coaxed Columbo from the humans, who'd been smothering him in love. Columbo took his time down the path at first with his nose in the air. Then he surged forward.

Rocco stood watching, hand over his mouth. The smart suit he wore fitted him well, but the cool, suave, dominating character of the previous day was gone. All that remained was an anxious father.

Ashley walked towards her vehicle.

'Let's go in yours, Hector. I'll grab my things from mine. I've a feeling we'll be back later.'

Ashley deliberately stayed quiet as they began the journey to Norwich hospital, but Hector didn't take the bait and the silence continued.

'Everything all right?' she asked.

'Yes, why wouldn't it be?'

'You seem a touch detached. Your shoes aren't as shiny as usual, and I haven't choked to death on your expensive scents, or your righteous opinions.'

Even that lure failed to change his expression.

'I forgot to put any aftershave on. I've got a lot on my mind.'

'Penny for them.'

'No, it's stuff I need to work through myself.'

'Gingerpuss still resisting your advances?'

'You shouldn't call her that.'

'Barry says she likes it.'

'Surely you don't take his word on such things.'

'I take it she said no, then?'

'Yes, she turned me down cold. Isn't that simply perfect? When I was content to be celibate, I had women literally chasing me around the university grounds. Now I meet a girl I like, and she'd rather spend the weekend at home with her parents.'

Ashley chuckled. Gabriella was the admin manager at OCC, but she didn't date anyone, never mind work colleagues.

'Go out with someone else. Have fun with Michelle. She'd be happy to chase you around.'

Michelle Ma Yun was the pathologist the team often worked

with. She'd taken a liking to Hector, even with over a decade age gap, but he'd rebuffed her advances.

'She'll be in the mortuary,' said Ashley. 'I don't mind if you pop over. Be romantic. Offer to carry the patient's brains for her.'

Hector chuckled but shook his head.

'I know, I'm crazy. Michelle's lovely, but Gabriella has fired me up in a way I find hard to believe. Her lack of interest is like catnip to me.'

Ashley laughed. 'It's human nature to want what you can't have. Sometimes you have to settle for second best.'

'Is that why you're with Barry?'

'Oh, so quick. Can't Barry and I just be friends?'

Hector scoffed theatrically.

'It's nice to see there's a little life lingering amongst your all-encompassing misery.' Ashley scowled at him. 'What's that supposed to mean, anyway?'

'Is he the man of your dreams? Does he take away your appetite? Do you get butterflies before your dates?'

'Well, I regularly tell Barry he's a nightmare. He's also prone to releasing smells which turn my stomach, and I am apprehensive before we go out, but probably not for the right reasons.'

'Make a joke of it if you like, but you're wasting your time with him. Isn't that the advice you'd give?'

'I hardly have a queue of enthusiastic suitors, and I was lonely.'

'Wars have been fought over such noble motives.'

'Very funny. We don't always get the handsome prince or beautiful princess.'

'I know, but you need more than Barry's willing to give. We can all see it.'

'All of you? Been gossiping, have you? You got the hump when folk were chatting about you behind your back.'

'This is different. That was tittle-tattle. We have your best interests at heart. Besides, there is someone perfect for you, but you're too scared to do anything about it.'

'Bastard,' whispered Ashley under her breath, even though Hector was on the money.

She'd almost had a thing with the divorced Scott Gorton, affectionally known as Flash, but she hadn't been ready. That was years ago, and they'd never found their way back to each other.

She looked over at Hector's grinning face and sneered at him.

'Well, I hope you leave Norfolk, and a flock of sickly seagulls follow you to London and poop on you every time you step from the house.'

'Oh, mature.'

13

When Hector and Ashley arrived at the hospital, they parked up and headed to A & E. It was much calmer, but by no means quiet. Ashley saw Dr Bandera gazing at a vending machine.

'Morning, Doctor,' said Ashley, when she was next to her.

'Oh, sorry. I forgot what I was doing.'

'Hopefully that doesn't happen too often when you're operating.'

Dr Bandera stared blankly at her, clearly beyond jokes. Ashley wondered if she'd even been home.

'Is Hamish MacDonald up to an interview?' she asked.

'Yes, I saw him at eight this morning. He slept well and ate a little cereal. He'll be okay for a short chat, although he's subdued. We did a thorough examination and there were a few strange findings.'

'Such as?'

'Let's talk to Hamish first. He may need directing towards mental health services before he's released. All this might be a cry for help.'

'What do you suspect's wrong with him?'

'It could be many things. Let's hope he opens up.'

As they followed Bandera through the corridors, Hector's long legs made him appear to amble, next to Ashley's shorter stride. He looked down at her.

'Asking people what's wrong with them isn't a great question.'

'No?' she replied.

'No. A trauma-informed response doesn't focus on what's wrong with someone, but rather what they have experienced.'

Ashley rolled her eyes.

'I'd need to study that statement under exam conditions to comment. What do you think of a trauma-informed response, Doc?'

Bandera stopped with her hand on the door of the same room where Hamish had been last time. Her face was gaunt.

'I'm so tired, I'm worried if I sneeze, my eyeballs will fall out.'

She opened the door but didn't enter.

'Oh,' she said.

'What is it?' asked Ashley.

'He's gone.'

Ashley walked past her and stared down at the unmade bed. The bathroom door was ajar, so she pushed it wider. There was nobody inside.

'Did they move him to another department?' she asked.

'No. He wasn't going to leave here until he'd spoken to you. His words, not mine.'

Ashley rubbed her temples while she raced through the implications of Hamish not being there. A nurse walked past in the corridor.

'Nurse!' Ashley shouted, nipping out of the room after her. 'Do you know when Hamish MacDonald was last in here?'

'I spoke to him about thirty minutes ago.'

'Was anyone with him?'

'No, but he seemed agitated.'

'About his missing friend, Max, or our impending visit?'

The woman shrugged. 'Sorry, I didn't ask.'

'Okay, thank you.'

Ashley looked along the corridor ceiling. There were multiple cameras. Bandera beckoned her back into the room.

'I'm going home soon, so I'll tell you this now, or you'll be forever chasing your tails. Hamish had more bruises on his body than he would have received from a low-impact car accident. The cuts on his legs were only a day or two old. They are unlikely to be self-harm, or he'd have started a while ago and be covered in small scars. His hands were damaged. I've seen similar from punching walls. There were two cigarette burns on his body. One on his arm, and one on his scrotum.'

'Possibly self-inflicted?' said Hector.

'I wouldn't say so. Genital self-mutilation is a rare form of self-harm. It does occasionally occur in male patients, but usually only those with severe depression or schizophrenia. Then it's often a single attempt at amputating either the penis or scrotum.'

Hector's lips retreated from his teeth. Bandera nodded.

'Yes. That area is very sensitive, too. If you recall when Hamish was a gibbering wreck yesterday, he said, "I told them what they asked, but what do they want?"'

'I remember,' said Ashley. 'Rocco queried who, but he didn't answer.'

'It could be that he's been a victim of torture, but I'm sure you detectives will work it out.'

Ashley smiled at her.

'We need to find out if he left by himself. I think we can assume he left without stopping to discharge himself.'

'I would say so. If an elephant in pyjamas jogged out of the exit, everyone would just applaud as they'd be pleased there was one less body to deal with.'

Ashley was about to thank Bandera for her help when she remembered the tests.

'Have you had his results back?' she asked.

Bandera looked as if she was about to cry. She managed a nod.

'I'd ask a nurse, but they're as busy as I am. I'll take you to my office. So much for escaping.'

'We appreciate it,' said Hector. 'You're doing a marvellous job.'

'You know how often I hear that? Every day. It helps, but I can actually feel my tank emptying out. I'm spluttering on vapour.'

'Why don't you go home when your shift is done?' he asked. 'Screw the bosses. It's not your fault if they have to close any departments.'

'I was going to do that today, but the other doctor on shift stayed last week for me, so I wouldn't be on my own. It's also extremely hard to wander out knowing someone might die because of it.'

Bandera's office wasn't far. She slumped into her seat behind the desk, nudged her mouse, then typed in her password.

'Did Hamish say anything about wanting to leave?' asked Ashley.

'No, but people up and vanish all the time. It's often part of the process to want to get away from hospital, especially after a tough diagnosis.' Bandera leaned into the screen. 'Ah, interesting. Obviously, we check for drugs in the patients' systems, in case we prescribe medicine that might react with what's already present.'

'Cocaine and alcohol?' guessed Ashley.

'Yes, both. Valium as well. His anxiety levels were off the scale not long after admission, which is common after cocaine, but he has much higher readings of gamma hydroxybutyrate.'

Ashley nodded. 'GHB,' she said slowly. 'The plot thickens.'

'He'd have been crazed with this lot in his system. The combination of those drugs would easily explain any memory loss. I'll show you the picture of the cigarette burn on his arm.'

The image showed a vivid red circle below a tattoo, which was of a wreath and the letters SPQR.

'It's not as bad as I thought,' said Ashley.

'No, it might have been an accident. He was clearly off his face, so he could have been smoking in bed and rolled on a cigarette. Burn pains are incredibly intense, which means the one on his genitals is less easy to explain away. Even the pain on his arm would cause him to shout out. Okay. This has been a great pleasure. I apologise for any flippant comments I may have made, but I really am going home.'

Ashley and Hector said goodbye, then headed for the security office. Ashley had been in there before and knew the man on duty, who soon found the footage, which was crystal clear. Hector and Ashley watched as Hamish was ushered through the hospital by two people in much the same way prisoners were escorted to and from it. All that was missing were the handcuffs.

The staff member rewound the recording so they could observe the other men arrive at A & E. They came in separately, five seconds apart, both wearing medical masks. The bigger of the two, who was also sporting sunglasses, disappeared before returning with Hamish, while the other stayed in the waiting room. Both guys wore baseball caps, pulled down low. Identifying them would be extremely difficult.

Ashley had the footage rewound four times. They left in a straight line. The shorter man kept a hand resting on Hamish's elbow.

It seemed unlikely Hamish was leaving of his own free will.

14

Ashley rang Emma back at OCC and told her about Hamish's disappearing act.

'Shit,' was her reply.

'Precisely. Hector and I will head into the office. Can you ring Control for me and get the ball rolling? We really need to talk to Hamish. Even more so if he's been grabbed against his will. The CCTV shows little of his companions' faces, and they walk off the site, so we don't have a number plate to chase up either.'

'Kettle's already said there'll be a meeting the moment you return. Ally made an instant connection when he heard the name Rocco mentioned. If you're on your way, it'll be covered at the meeting.'

'Okay, we'll be twenty minutes or so.'

Ashley finished the call and walked outside with Hector, who was quiet.

'What's got you thinking?'

'That tattoo.'

'SPRQ or whatever it was.'

'SPQR. It stands for Senātus Populusque Rōmānus.'

'Let me guess, you did Latin at school.'

'Didn't you?'

'Nope. The teachers were too busy showing us how to tie our shoelaces and explaining why licking batteries is a bad idea.'

'Charming. It means The Senate and People of Rome. The tattoo intrigued me.'

'Why?'

'Hamish MacDonald doesn't sound very Italian.'

'I suppose not, but youngsters cover themselves in all kinds of unusual words and images nowadays. Think of the English folk who put Chinese writing on themselves.'

'That's true. GHB is the date-rape drug, isn't it?'

'Right. Did you come across it when you were in uniform?'

'Not really, but I read up about it. It's also taken deliberately, to get a high similar to ecstasy.'

'That's also correct. It's easy to overdo it, though, especially if mixed with alcohol.'

'At which point the user ends up unable to move or unconscious, or even sinking into a coma.'

'Yes, and in liquid form GHB is colourless and slightly salty in taste. So, if someone slips the powder into a strong spirit without anyone spotting them, then the drinker wouldn't notice, either.'

'It's not hard to join up the dots. Hamish gets his drink spiked in the nightclub. He's already taken cocaine and alcohol, so probably assumes his woozy head is related to that. Then he leaves and goes outside, where he feels worse and is an easy target.'

'Those dots lead us to Max being with him at that time. Close friends look out for each other. Perhaps they left together.'

'Let's hope the helicopter finds a heat source in Bacton Wood.'

'Did you know GHB is only detectable in urine for around twelve hours?'

Hector absorbed that fact for a moment and she let him work out what it meant. His eyes narrowed.

'Which means he was probably drugged on Friday night but then again, probably on Saturday night.'

'Yes,' replied Ashley. 'Once in the nightclub, but then where?'

They headed straight to the meeting room when they arrived. DS Ally Williamson's full team was soon present, as was Ashley's, along with representation from a variety of other departments. Ashley brought everyone up to speed, then Kettle took over.

'This is clearly a fast-moving situation. We have to assume, unless we hear otherwise, that Hamish was abducted after a night out. He was taken somewhere where he was drugged, tortured and questioned. On Sunday morning, his captors buried him alive. We don't believe they meant to kill him, so it was a warning. Concerning what, we have no idea. This morning, he vanished from the hospital, possibly under duress. We need him located. Max also needs to be found. We've discovered nothing helpful in the wood so far. It appears out of character for Max not to be in contact with his family for so long, so that's concerning.' Kettle glanced around the room. 'Ally has another layer to add to the case, which gives us the most likely direction to follow.'

Ally Williamson was the detective sergeant for the team that often worked with Ashley's. They tended to specialise in drug cases throughout the region. The county was home to nearly a million inhabitants, but they were spread out over two thousand square miles. Lots of space in the Norfolk countryside meant it had more than its fair share of cannabis farms and places to hide. Ally was a well-liked member of MIT, who accepted the jokes about his mullet hairdo with good grace.

'As you know, we've been struggling with two organisations operating out of Norfolk and Suffolk. One is a group that appears to have a shifting cast of mostly Eastern Europeans.

They call themselves the Vampires. The other mob has a connection to Italy. We suspect the older brothers of running the operation, but we've never been able to pin anything to them. They manage a nightclub in Norwich and are known as the Romans.'

Ashley's ears perked up as she recalled Hamish's tattoo.

'The Coliseum,' she said.

'Correct. It's a popular place and a brilliant cover for an illicit business. It's not certain they are involved, but the brothers' names have come up a few times. Once by a dealer who was going to give evidence against them. I don't know if you recall the case, but, as often happens, he changed his mind. Whoever spoke to him frightened the life out of him. He then disappeared. Word gets around, and that kind of thing sucks the enthusiasm right out of any other potential informants.'

That got a few laughs in the room.

'Hamish had a Roman tattoo on his arm,' said Hector.

'Interesting. I'll come to that. The brothers who run the club are called Tommaso and Lorenzo Vialli. They have a younger brother, who we're pretty certain is an innocent party. Massimiliano.'

'Our missing guy, Max,' said Hector.

'Yes. The nightclub is part of a small conglomerate owned by their father, Carlo Vialli, but he's affectionately known to everyone as Rocco. We're unsure of how much overarching control he has. Using undercover officers, we've caught people in the club with small amounts of drugs, but there's a members-only section, which we only had access to once, and nothing was found.'

'I've seen that section,' said Hector to Ashley's surprise. 'A friend from college came from Norwich and dated Tommaso for a while. I went with her and two other friends to the club. She thought we'd all be able to get in the private part, but only she was allowed in. The bouncer has to use a card on a scanner to open the door.'

'Yes, that delay might have cost us when we arrived to spin the place.'

'My friend declined to go in, but I'll give her a ring to see if she can tell me anything. The relationship didn't last.'

'Please, do,' said Ally. 'We believe the members' area is for their rich mates and acquaintances. There's always at least one bouncer, and we're confident the women who work in there are escorts. Our knowledge of them is vague. We're not sure if they're working there under sufferance to clear the debt from being trafficked here, or are doing so willingly. One girl reckoned she was forced to be a hostess to pay for her route over, but she was here illegally from Sierra Leone, had been shoplifting and no longer worked there. She also disappeared.'

'I assume we've interviewed the older brothers,' said Ashley.

'Yes, no comment. Top-notch lawyers, but they said very little either. We could look at the club's business records, tax returns, but the girls are self-employed. It's up to them to pay their taxes. Obviously, not all of them do.'

'But you don't think Max is involved in anything illicit?' asked Barry.

'No. He works for Rocco's Fine Homes, which is Rocco's main business. It's a high-end bathroom and kitchen distributor. Mostly sells to trade. Seems legit.'

'We could do with looking at the CCTV from the nightclub if they were in there,' said Ashley.

'That might be a problem. To put it mildly, Lorenzo has the hump with us. He accused me of harassing him and his customers. If you remember after that Friday night raid, he threatened to sue. The chance of him providing the footage without a warrant is slim.'

'Could the older brothers be straight up?' asked Sal.

'There's too much smoke for there not to be a little fire. It might just be acquiring narcotics or money for their punters, but that's unlikely.'

'Surely Lorenzo and Tommaso would want Max found,' said Hector. 'Therefore, they'd give us what we need.'

'Maybe. I doubt a magistrate would sign off on any CCTV request because we aren't in contact with Max or Hamish. It's hard to say exactly what's happened at this point. It's possible this Hamish took the drugs himself.'

'Max could be on a real downer at a friend's house,' said Ashley. 'We don't really have cause to look into his affairs at the moment. Maybe he lost his phone.'

'As far as I'm led to believe, Max doesn't take drugs and has little contact with his brothers.'

'He must have had some if he visited their club.'

'Now you see our problem. Our intel is third hand. It's weak. We suspect some of it is from angry ex-employees.'

'And this other group. The Vampires. Are they enemies of the Romans?'

'That's unclear as well. There may have been collaboration between the two parties in the past, but there have also been arguments. The Vampires' businesses operate right at the bottom of society. Heroin, brothels, domestic servitude. Exploitation of all types. There are a lot of fake passports, but the gang hail from all over. Moldova to Montenegro. There's a Mr or Mrs Big somewhere in Europe, but we don't believe they risk visiting here. It's a clever operation, but on an extremely basic, ruthless level.'

The door opened at the back of the room. Ashley peered over her shoulder and saw an admin team member whispering into Gabriella's ear. Gabriella's face fell. She appeared to double-check something, then walked to the front.

'We've had news from Bacton Wood. One of the dogs picked up a scent. He's led them to an area of recently disturbed earth. They're fetching the digging equipment now, but they'll likely stick to spades considering the shallow nature of Hamish's burial.'

Ashley rose from her seat.

'Did they say which dog it was?'

'Yes. It was Columbo.'

15

Ashley looked back at Kettle, who nodded at her.

'DS Knight will head to the scene with DC Hector Fade. The rest of you grab a coffee and have a break. What appears in that hole will dictate where we focus next but I think we can assume it's not going to be positive. For those who don't know, cadaver dogs are similar to pregnancy tests. They rarely make mistakes. They can either smell a dead person or they can't. Ally, stay in the incident room. You run things here, with Ashley dealing out there. I have a meeting with the Chief. Barry, get hold of the pathologist and see if she could attend the wood if called. Time of death might be pivotal. Everyone else back in half an hour, please.'

Ashley and Hector returned to the same car Hector had booked out earlier and they quickly got on their way. The traffic was pretty light with rush hour finished, but a heavy rain was falling. Despite that, they were soon at Mill Road where Hector parked behind Rocco's Tesla. Hector gave it a long stare as he put his coat and walking boots on.

'Yes,' said Ashley. 'Rocco is about to have a terrible morning.'

'How do we deal with him if he gets close to the scene?'

'We'll need Rocco for swift identification. It depends on how he reacts. He might go crazy at the death of his youngest child. If we can keep him away, we'll take a photo of the body and ask for confirmation that way, which will be tough on him, but your concerns are spot on. If he sees his son in the hole, it's likely he'd jump into the grave and compromise any evidence.'

When they reached the entrance to the wood, Ashley sensed the energy in those waiting, despite many of them being drenched.

As she approached the outer cordon, she saw two scene guards, one whom she knew.

'Morning, Ashley. Inspector Treharne said for you and your partner to go in. There's an area to observe from. This officer will escort you.'

'Where's Rocco?' she asked.

'The short bald Italian-looking guy?'

'Yes.'

'He was pacing up and down over there twenty minutes ago. Kept asking questions and trying to get past me when he realised we'd made a discovery.'

'So now he's not here, after seeing the search team enter with spades?'

The PC shrugged. 'Sorry, boss. I've no idea where he went. I was told not to leave my post.'

Ashley considered the size of the area. She turned back to the officer.

'Ring the PolSA team. Tell them Rocco is probably heading to their location. We'll keep an eye out for him en route and apprehend him if possible.'

'Will do, Sarge.'

They followed the officer who was escorting them into the wood. The forestry workers were planting new trees ahead of them, and just before these they turned left. There was a slope up to a hillock a few metres high where Treharne was standing and he beckoned her over.

'You received the message about the dad?' she asked.

'Yes, a father won't respond well to what's likely in there. We've got a team of four working in pairs by hand. The two who aren't digging are looking out for Rocco. There's also the PC recording the scene, who can assist if necessary. If you don't mind heading in, that should be enough bodies if Rocco appears. I know it's not ideal.'

Ashley, Hector, Treharne and their escort carefully walked over. It was surprisingly noisy, with birds tweeting and the rain pattering on the foliage overhead. The wind lifted and swayed the branches in an almost funereal dance, but the air was fresh and crisp, which no doubt would be at odds with what was about to be uncovered.

They'd reached a small glade between bunched-up trees when a shovel made a thud. There were a few more bumps of metal on wood, then a series of scrapings. Ashley, Hector and the other officers formed a cordon five metres from the hole.

'What is it?' Treharne shouted to the diggers.

'It's a white door. Internal. Same as before.'

'Why has it taken so long to reach it?' asked Ashley.

'We didn't want the hole collapsing as we dug, not knowing the door was definitely there to support the earth. There were also big stones and branches in the soil, and the door was deeper.'

Ashley grimaced. Unlike Hamish and his grave, nobody was climbing out of this one without help. After another minute of digging around the door so it could be lifted, the man closest stepped back and put his hand over his nose. Then the others did the same. Few things smelt as awful as a days-old corpse.

Ashley edged forward and looked down at the door. It was identical to the one found in the other hole. One digger, a thick-set woman called Annabel, who wore a large black anorak, pulled down her hood. She dug a step into the side of the trench, where she placed a foot for support. Then she trod into the pit with the other boot, placing it beside the door handle.

Water poured off Annabel's chin. Her brown hair hung limply; wet strands that had escaped her ponytail clung to her face. She didn't appear to notice. Nose twitching, she clenched her teeth, then reached down and pulled on the door handle. It moved a little. Another officer stepped forward, but she waved him away.

Annabel paused, concentrated, and steeled herself. The wood grew quiet, save for the rhythmic drum of water dripping out of the trees and thudding on the shiny white surface next to her. It pattered on the leaves above them, and tapped on their waterproofs. The rain fell gently, like teardrops.

Annabel grunted, then heaved upwards. The door opened with the soil acting as a hinge. Ashley took a step closer. The man inside was naked.

Annabel pushed the door to a right angle, then retreated so everyone could see the victim. His ankles and wrists were bound with cable ties. Eyes open, mouth fixed in a snarl, fingers as claws. All of which indicated asphyxia.

Ashley noticed the face was covered in blood and bruises, but it was the feet and hands caked in mud that grabbed her attention. She tried not to think of the reasons why they'd got that way.

The woman who'd pulled open the door swore. One of the others closed her eyes and turned away. Another coughed. On the dirt-smeared upper arm of the body was the same SPQR tattoo they'd seen on Hamish.

Hector joined Ashley. He stared down impassively.

'I'll call it in,' he said.

'Treharne will do that. This is his show.'

Hector was putting his phone back in his pocket when a

primeval scream pierced the air. It echoed around them. The officers scanned the treeline. The rain had thickened again and teemed down like beaded curtains. A bald man in a sodden suit charged out of the undergrowth towards them.

His face was a mask of anguish. He tripped and fell, howling as he crawled to his feet. Rocco staggered forwards. Grief leached the strength from his stride, so he was stumbling when he reached those who were in his way.

Rocco stopped in front of the closest officer. A huge sob wracked his shoulders. He collapsed onto his knees.

Ashley watched Rocco summon control from deep inside. He pushed himself up, raised his chin.

'Show me,' he gasped. 'I have to see.'

The PC looked over at Ashley, who glanced across at Treharne. He shook his head. Rocco bellowed out and surged forwards, barging the officer out of the way. His expensive-looking brogues sank into the loose wet soil at the edge of the pit as he trod towards his worst nightmare. He tumbled and dropped onto the ground, leaving his face suspended over the hole.

Rocco gazed downwards for three long seconds, then he wept. His head swivelled towards Ashley as he pushed himself up. He made the sign of the cross, a mad expression on his face. His words were gasps.

'It's not Max.'

16

Ashley's jaw dropped. 'It's not?'

Rocco sniffed to clear his nose. 'No. Thank God.'

'I thought with the tattoo it was him.'

Rocco wiped the rain from his face, then spat on the floor. He stood with fervour blazing in his eyes. He appeared to be mumbling to himself.

'I shall be strong, despite what may come. First, I will discover who was responsible.'

Ashley frowned. She stared at the deceased, whose face had been washed clean by the rain.

'Do you recognise this man?'

Rocco blew out a long breath. Then he dragged the forest air deep into his lungs, and released it slowly again.

'No, this guy has light hair, and he's taller than Max. He's got to be connected to the lads, though, because of the tattoo. I don't get involved with their employees or go to the club, but the boys tell me a few of the male staff at the nightclub like to get them. Tommaso and Lorenzo have many tattoos. Huge ones of the

Roman eagle on their backs. Max had a smaller one done to show loyalty and commitment to the family, but he wanted a peaceful, simple life. Sure, he liked The Coliseum to dance, have fun, but his idea of an enjoyable time is expensive coffee, galleries and live music.'

Rocco's swift recovery from his shock was impressive.

'We need to vacate the area,' said Ashley. 'Leave the experts to process the scene.'

Rocco stared up and let the steady raindrops hit his face. He barked a laugh, then gestured to the muddy ground, which had small rivers running through it. The deceased was being submerged in his watery grave.

Ashley and Hector escorted Rocco to the entrance. When they reached it, a smartly dressed, grey-haired man rushed over wearing a long raincoat, which he took off and gave to Rocco. They conversed in rapid Italian. Ashley had an idea.

'Rocco. Wouldn't Lorenzo or Tommaso know who it was back there?'

'Tommaso flew to Italy on Saturday. I've just described the victim to my driver to see if he knew who it was. There are many cousins and friends from home who work for us. Can I take a photo?'

'No,' said Ashley.

'Okay, let me ring Lorenzo. He's taking the club's deliveries, with Tommaso not being about.'

Ashley left him to it as Inspector Treharne came down the path towards them. They stepped away for privacy.

'This leaves you with a big job,' she said. 'How long will it take?'

'Three more days, at least. The forecast is for dry weather tomorrow. We're better off sealing the wood, doing what we can with the area around the two graves, getting the body out and back for a PM, then returning in the morning. The dogs struggle with this type of weather. The spaniels in particular won't stop unless we drag them out of there, but this cold and damp won't do them any good. We have to look after our best asset.'

Treharne turned to stare at the wood and grimaced. 'It's hard to believe there's anyone still out there alive.' He turned back to Ashley. 'We'll set up properly in the morning and bring in exhibit vans and more officers.'

'I take it you aren't hopeful of getting much from the scene after this kind of rain?'

'No, it will have flushed everything away. Footprints, fag butts, maybe discarded clothing, but it also washes things in that were elsewhere. We could get lucky and find something in the hole itself, but that's unlikely. It already resembles the Somme in there. The post-mortem might be more helpful.'

'Okay, we're going to head back. I don't envy you an afternoon in the rain. Splendid work today, though.'

'Too kind,' said Treharne.

'Give me a ring if you stumble upon his wallet.'

Treharne was stifling a chuckle as the stress dissipated, when they both heard a raised voice. It was Rocco pacing up and down while shouting into the phone.

'*Incredibile!*' he muttered after finishing the call.

'Come back to the station and help with our inquiries,' said Ashley. 'Finding Max is our priority.'

'I want to do a bit of investigating of my own. How many tall Italians with blond hair can we have working for us? Lorenzo says it's Paolo, but he'll ring his number to check.'

'Okay, let's take a statement from you now.'

'I must go.'

'Rocco. It's important we see footage of the CCTV from your nightclub on Friday night. We know Max and Hamish were there, so who did they leave with, and when?'

Rocco held her gaze, then he sneezed.

'Sorry, I will talk to Lorenzo and bring it to you.'

Ashley pondered strong-arming him, but at this point his willing help would be invaluable.

'We need it as quickly as possible,' she said. 'I can come to the club and collect it.'

'Okay, I'll speak to him and arrange a time.'

'You'll be allocated a family liaison officer to help you through what I'm sure is a challenging experience.'

Rocco took a deep breath. 'I'm used to solving my own problems.'

'You want your boy back. We have all the resources. Access to the UK's camera network, mobile records, mast information. We're both after the same thing.'

Rocco briefly looked as if he doubted that. Then his mobile rang. He listened for thirty seconds, his eyes widening. He spoke rapidly to whoever had called him, again in Italian. Ashley watched Rocco wither in front of her. He finished the call; the hand carrying the phone hung limp at his side.

'What, Rocco? What's happened?' asked Ashley.

Rocco rubbed his forehead.

'The name of the man in the ditch is likely Paolo. A second-cousin of the boys. Paolo failed to show for work at the club on Saturday night, but he isn't the most dependable, so it wasn't a complete surprise. He didn't answer his phone. Lorenzo said he's still not picking up. Gianluca confirmed nobody has seen him since Friday evening.'

'Who is Gianluca?'

'You don't understand. Paolo is the closest friend of my son Tommaso.'

'So?'

'Paolo was driving Tommaso to the airport on Saturday morning.'

17

Ashley understood the significance straight away.

'Was Paolo dropping Tommaso off at the airport,' she said, 'or going on the trip with him?'

'Both had tickets to fly.'

'Which means if Paolo failed to make it to the airport, then it's likely Tommaso didn't make it either.'

Rocco appeared to be eating sand. He clenched his hands together.

'Right. Lorenzo is trying to ring Tommaso now, but it isn't always easy to contact him over there. I have to go. Please stay in touch. I will ask Lorenzo for the CCTV and have it brought to your station on a memory stick. Email me about anything else you need.'

Rocco handed her a plain white business card showing his full name, email, and even his home address.

Ashley noticed the mobile number differed from the one he had given her before.

'I'll arrange for the family liaison officer to visit your house first thing at nine in the morning.'

'Will you be with them?'

'That's not the usual process.'

Rocco pointed a finger at her. 'Tell them to come with you, or not at all.'

'Rocco, we need to speak to Paolo's next of kin. The more we can learn about him, the faster we'll have an idea of what's occurred.'

Rocco's face was crumpling again. He didn't respond and turned to leave.

'Rocco. Did he tell you Paolo's surname and address?'

Rocco looked very Italian with enormous eyes full of feeling.

'Paolo Moretti. A cousin from Italy. I'll find out. Please. My children. I must go.'

With that, Rocco stormed away. Ashley decided to return to the office with Hector in his car to discuss the case. Hector took his time driving back, giving them both an opportunity to process the previous hour. Ashley made small talk to give Hector a chance to comment, but he kept quiet.

'Imagine what Rocco's going through,' he finally said as they approached OCC. 'How could anyone function?'

'We're all different. Some sink into shock, others deal with it by getting busy.'

'Busy trying to do our job?'

Ashley smiled. 'Yes, that's the problem. If you go after the children of a man like Rocco and get caught by him, you can't expect the justice the legal system provides. We send people to prison. Rocco would send them straight to hell.'

'This could rapidly escalate.'

'I agree. I'll explain it to Kettle. We'll have another meeting tonight, but we need to crack on with inputting everything we have onto the computer first, and I want our team brainstorming as soon as we get back. It's now a murder inquiry, plus three missing people. Two brothers and Hamish.'

'Who knows how many have disappeared? Columbo could have his work cut out down there.'

That was what was concerning Ashley. Chances were, Tommaso and Max were somewhere in that wood, rotting deep in the sodden soil.

Kettle's phone gave her an engaged tone so she left a message, then rang Emma, who picked up. Ashley explained she wanted the team ready for a meeting the moment she got back. If Emma could locate DS Ally Williamson, then request his presence. He should at least attend their later discussion. Gabriella should also be at both.

Ashley made two coffees when they arrived at OCC, while Hector herded everyone available into one of the meeting rooms that was equipped with a whiteboard. Kettle appeared at the door as Ashley was about to begin. He beckoned her outside.

'Sorry to interrupt, but I wanted a quick word so we didn't cross plans. We'll see what tasks HOLMES kicks out tomorrow for us to follow up, but I want Hector to work with Ally. This is his last chance to be on one of these drug cases before he decides where he's heading next.'

'Are you hoping he'll love it enough to stay?'

'Something like that. I passed the details up to the National Crime Agency after the discovery of Paolo. They said to keep them notified of our progress.'

'Okay, although I'm heading to Rocco Vialli's tomorrow with the FLO. I was hoping to take Hector. His parents probably shop at the same places as the Viallis.'

'I've allocated Scott Gorton as liaison, so I'm sure you and he will cope fine. Pay attention to Rocco's furniture, paintings and style. Perhaps mention what you find to Hector. It might tell us a little about the man.'

Ashley considered the involvement of the NCA. 'So, that's your guess. Drugs.'

'Yes. This kind of planning requires money. Drug dealing also brings out the worst in people. Class A and violence are common bedfellows.'

'Ain't that the truth.'

'Make sure everyone stays sharp. This could be brutal.'

Kettle left and Ashley returned to the meeting room and closed the door. She sank into a seat and looked for who was missing.

'Ally not about?' she asked, noticing he was the only one not present.

'No, he said he'll be at the later session,' said Emma.

'Okay, Hector will get you all up to speed.'

Gabriella took notes while Hector spoke, then Ashley rose and moved to the whiteboard.

'Okay. Let's start with the obvious. Who are the most likely suspects?'

'It's got to be organised crime,' said Barry. 'Ally told us the Vampires and the Romans have the odd barney. We know how dishonest drug dealers are. It could be a takeover. The Vampires might be the bigger operation. Ally reckons they bring in loads of different people to bolster their crew when needed.'

'Which means you think they've taken out two of the brothers to weaken the Romans?'

'Yep.'

'There's a flaw in that theory, if someone would like to point it out to Barry.'

'Tommaso is by all accounts the violent one, but it's Lorenzo who is the figurehead of the nightclub,' said Sal. 'He's the head of the snake.'

'Unless it's Rocco,' said Emma.

'Yes, we'll come to that,' said Ashley. 'Let's say for the moment Rocco is either unaware or doesn't care that his sons are up to no good. Assume they are importing or distributing cocaine. It's a real cash spinner, so others would try to target the business, or be after that money.'

'Abduction for ransom,' said Jan. 'Rocco is loaded. I'm sure he'd pay a million for the safe release of two of his family. Perhaps more.'

'Rocco's proved himself very astute,' said Hector. 'He'd know you don't pay blackmailers.'

'Isn't it governments which refuse to pay blackmailers?' asked Bhavini.

Ashley smiled as Bhavini stroked her visible bump while she spoke. 'What are you saying?'

'Maybe Rocco is a cocaine distributor. He'd probably deliver the money and then use violence to get it back.'

'True,' said Ashley.

'A turf shootout is a scary proposition,' said Sal.

'It would be crazy for the Vampires to do it so publicly,' said Barry. 'They don't want us to focus on their activities. They know we're interested in them. I reckon it's more likely a revenge attack, and it's possible Lorenzo wasn't targeted because it was to do with the others.'

'Perhaps the reason Lorenzo hasn't been hit yet was because they want him to suffer the loss of his brothers,' said Ashley.

'Ooh, yes, I like that idea,' said Bhavini. 'Then possibly come for Lorenzo later, after he's suffered days of rage, helplessness and sorrow.'

'Not bad, but surely Lorenzo is on high alert now,' said Sal.

'Rocco, too. The chances of grabbing Lorenzo in the same way they took the other four will be nigh on impossible.'

'Agreed,' said Emma. 'Lorenzo and Rocco will change their routines. Double up on security. Avoid regular haunts and keep low profiles.'

'It'll be interesting to meet this Lorenzo,' said Ashley. 'See what type of guy he is. He could be a stereotypical fiery Italian, or more calm and focused.'

'It could be an argument between brothers,' said Hector. 'Remember Cain and Abel?'

'Right,' said Ashley. 'Let's also not forget, they could be innocent.'

'No way,' said Emma. 'Let's not forget criminals don't tend to rely on us in their hour of need.'

While they were all chuckling, a squall hit the window. Ashley looked outside and pursed her lips as she thought of the search team in the woods.

'Let's crack on before tonight's meeting with the other teams. Emma, liaise with the forensic pathologist, Michelle. She was asked to see the grave with the corpse in situ. See if she can be of any help with the time of death. Judging by the condition, I suspect she'll struggle to be accurate.'

'The other angle is if we consider what's occurred to Hamish and Paolo,' said Jan. 'After all, they're the ones we've found. Both have had horrible experiences being buried alive. One survived, although no doubt traumatised, the other is dead. It's the stuff of nightmares for every person who's ever dreamed, but it does mean we could find the others unscathed.'

Ashley nodded.

'Let's hope we get the other two back alive. It's hard to believe they will have had an experience as awful as Paolo's. He's had the worst death possible.'

Ashley thought of his muddy, damaged hands and feet. He must have wildly attempted to claw himself out, not knowing there was a tonne of dirt above him. She shook her head to dislodge the images.

'I'm not sure that's true,' said Hector. 'Humans have spent millennia dreaming up horrific ways of inflicting pain on their enemies.'

'You can be our torture correspondent,' said Barry.

'Agreed. I could demonstrate on you.'

Ashley cut off Barry's reply.

'Okay, Sal. Background on Paolo, please. Contact the Italian police if he doesn't appear on our records and ask what they have. No doubt they'll need paperwork. We'll need to notify his family over there. One or more of them might want to come over to understand what happened, and we can get official identification, even though Lorenzo should be able to provide it if Paolo's an employee.'

Ashley considered what else needed doing. She turned to Bhavini.

'Bee. Look into Hamish's past and present. In fact, do the social media checks for all involved.'

'Will do.'

'Jan. Ring the nightclub. I'm aware it's Monday afternoon, but someone might pick up. Let's see who answers. Pay them a visit otherwise, but not alone. Take Barry. After, visit the flats we know Hamish and Max live at. It shouldn't be too hard to find where Tommaso lives. Paolo the same.

'Ems. Have a look into the businesses that Rocco runs. Another angle is that he's stiffed his suppliers, and the people he owes don't believe in using the courts to get their money back.'

'Yes, Sarge.'

'I'll have a lengthy list of questions for Rocco and Lorenzo, which I'll email to Rocco. If he doesn't respond sharply, I'll call him. Hector and I will visit his house if there's further delay. Rocco and Lorenzo should be able to easily assist you with a lot of the tasks I've posed, but I have the nasty feeling they'll investigate by themselves before they release everything. He seems the type.'

'Let's assume they're going to drag their heels,' said Barry.

'Agreed. Barry, you start looking into which CCTV we need, both public and from the nightclub. Despite what Rocco said, I believe Lorenzo's going to be difficult about us seeing it.'

'Could we get a warrant for it?' asked Gabriella.

'We considered that earlier, but I hope to keep relations cordial until it becomes impossible. Lorenzo must understand we're best placed to find his brothers. We want his help with interviewing workers, getting a feel for the club, who attends, that sort of thing. If he tells his staff not to talk, we'll struggle to make any progress with that angle.'

'If they're into criminal activities, they'll order everyone to stay quiet, anyway,' said Barry.

'Then at least we'll suspect everyone's silence is down to Lorenzo,' said Ashley.

Her phone rang. She raised a hand to stop the others talking.

'It's Michelle.'

Ashley took the call and listened.

'Okay, brilliant,' she said, then placed her phone back on the table.

'She's at the scene. The team erected a tent, but the hole is in a kind of dip, so the water's pouring in from the surrounding area and has completely submerged the body. Even covering the pit was no good, so they're moving Paolo to the mortuary. Michelle said she'll do the PM straight away with it being so urgent.'

'No more finds?' asked Hector.

'No, the dog units are also leaving. They've had a look around as a team for more disturbed earth, but everything's soaked. We can forget about hearing anything new from there today. Treharne showed Michelle the photos of the pit before it filled. They believe Paolo was buried in a much deeper, narrower space. Michelle suspects he wouldn't have lasted more than a few hours.'

'Nasty way to go,' said Sal.

Ashley's phone beeped to say she'd received a text. The number was unknown, but Rocco had put his name at the start of the message.

This is Rocco. I can confirm. Tommaso never arrived in Italy.

18

A MONTH AGO

Emil ran at the back of the group with the pilot, pretending to find it tough to keep up, but he was conserving his strength. He could have helped carry the boat, but it paid to be underestimated, and he wanted to be close to the man who would be steering.

There was a sense of nervous excitement in the air as there had been in the camp all day. Men had spent their last few coins on shaves and haircuts. It was the way of things. The average time to reach this point, the one of final departure,. was four years from leaving home. Many long, hard, traumatising journeys would hopefully soon be at an end.

The whispered voices of the others ahead were too loud, but palms had been greased. The authorities would arrive a minute too late.

There were gasps of shock, and grins slipped from faces as they stepped into the sea. When the chilly water reached Emil's thighs, it was as though a vice had seized him. He was only in the shallows, but already he felt trapped.

Luckily, Emil was short and slim, and he managed to slip into the last space next to the outboard motor. The pilot, a smiley black man from Tanzania, called Mwamba, was supposed to have saved him the spot, but he looked at Emil as though he'd never seen him before in his life.

Emil had been in live or die situations numerous times fighting for the army. He'd watched as events went wrong. Loyalty or bonhomie soon vanished. Weak friendships were forgotten.

Heroes were rare.

The sea was a millpond. Even at the shore, the waves were gentle ripples. A shout in what Emil suspected was French echoed from the gloom of the beach.

'Come back. Come here,' someone shouted in accented English.

As Emil stared towards the town lights in the distance, a demand in his own language hissed from one of the men on the boat.

'Start the fucking motor.'

Mwamba placed the end of a torch in his mouth and pointed the weak light at the Yamaha engine. He squeezed the primer bulb and turned the ignition on. Emil pictured a horrible image of Mwamba pulling on a cord to no avail, but he twisted a key and the motor purred into life. Emil had used outboards before and relaxed when Mwamba understood to check the cooling water was coming out in a stream. Finally, Mwamba smiled at him.

They'd all paid above the going rate to be in this dinghy. Large boat, they said, expensive motor, few people, perfect night. A premium journey. They were right about the Yamaha, which looked brand new, and the dinghy was big, but money had exchanged hands late on as well. Extra places had been found. Some men might have sneaked among them as the group approached the sea. It was possible some of those onboard were armed. There was no time left to do anything about it now, but the boat sat low in the inky water.

Emil had arrived in the camp only two weeks earlier, but he already knew a few of the others around him. People loved to hear a story, and each tent was the sleeping place of a migrant with a shocking one. Mwamba scanned the hopeful passengers with his torch. They were on their way.

Most Emil didn't know, but then he recognised a big man who'd served time in the same prison as him decades ago. Zoltan. He'd been a desperate, impulsive soldier who'd committed many crimes. Emil wondered if he'd been sent to help as well.

Sammy from Senegal was sitting next to Zoltan and gave Emil a thumbs up. Sammy had flown to Turkey, then entered Greece, where he spent two years in the camp at Samos. Afterwards, he made his way through Bosnia, Croatia, Slovenia and Italy before finally reaching Dunkirk. Sammy was twenty but looked a tired forty.

Mwamba, the pilot, flew to Germany with his brother from Africa and found a bus to France. His brother's leg was crushed between the cab and the trailer as they tried to sneak onto a lorry leaving Calais. Mwamba told Emil via Google Translate he would make his home in England, ready for when his brother recovered. Mwamba was one of the few who didn't have a basic grasp of English from TV.

Three up from him sat a Kurd, Kavek. He'd meandered through Armenia, Turkey, Greece, Bulgaria, Albania, Serbia and all over. He spoke many languages and joked he was Interrailing through Europe. By foot.

Sammy and Kavek had been the ones to organise Emil's seat on the craft. They seemed decent guys. They agreed the torturous trek from Greece to Bulgaria was the worst. It took five or six days and if the authorities caught you, they returned you to the start, sometimes after a beating. Kavek attempted it four times before he made it.

In total, Kavek had been walking for five years. He had only just turned eighteen.

The others appeared as though they hailed from all over. Many would be fleeing persecution and violence. It would take years to get over their experiences. Others were young, strong, twitchy Albanian men, fleeing boredom and poor wages. A couple of them wore thin coats and no life jacket.

There were two women. The first might have been attractive, but she had a nasty bruise on the right side of her face, and the eye on the left was half closed. She wore no make-up on her blemish-free skin. Emil suspected that, for her, the dream had died long ago.

Opposite was the other woman on the boat. Her son, who looked about ten, shivered on her lap. Emil sweated under his layers. He knew not to be fooled by these calm conditions. It would still be bitter out at sea. They would be in the busiest shipping lane in the world and it had extreme tidal currents. Anything could happen. Emil even sported a trapper hat, much of it fur. They'd chuckled at him in the camp, but Emil came from the mountains. He understood how quickly a cold wind could kill. Nobody would be laughing later.

Sammy had told him to tie carrier bags around his ankles for when they got in the boat, or his feet would be wet and uncomfortable. Such good advice. They could be in the water for days. Most of the Albanians were wearing trainers.

Emil gave Sammy a thumbs up in reply and hoped they would all be lucky. They would need to pray for Godspeed and kind currents because, having watched the forecast on Kavek's phone, Emil understood this was merely a brief window in the recent turbulent weather. The thick grey clouds would darken. A storm was brewing.

As they moved further out, the view was total darkness. With the boat's occupants now silent, the only sound was the steady hum of the outboard motor. Mwamba let the throttle out. Emil whispered a prayer. He wasn't the only one.

And they edged further into the void.

19

PRESENT DAY

At a quarter to six, Kettle grabbed Ashley's team and took them into an office. Ashley tried to keep any frustration from showing on her face, knowing if she was feeling it, then her guys would be too, but it had been an infuriating afternoon.

'Sum up, please,' said Kettle.

'I emailed Rocco the questions we wanted answering, but he didn't reply. He answered neither of his phones, even though they rang. I left a message on both. Meanwhile, everyone else has also struggled. The number for The Coliseum went to answerphone, and nobody appeared when we attended and rang the front doorbell.'

'But you're seeing Rocco tomorrow morning.'

'Yes, but we need answers now, so I drove to his house with Hector.'

'I take it he wasn't there either.'

'I'm not sure. He's got a lovely five-bed detached property in Bacton. I expected something much bigger, but the architecture is beautiful. There's a locked gate beside a lowish wall, which Hector clambered over to the porch, but no one answered his knocks despite lights being on inside. His Tesla wasn't there. The gate to the rear has spikes on it. Sal discovered through council records that Lorenzo lives alone next door, but his place was dark with no cars on his drive.'

'What about the other properties we're interested in?'

'There was no sign of Max or Tommaso, who live in the same apartment block, and Hamish hasn't gone back to his flat either.'

'Were they also nice areas?'

'The brothers' neighbourhood was quality,' said Barry, 'but Hamish's area was rough as arseholes. None of their neighbours knew anything.'

Kettle tapped his index finger on the table.

'What about our deceased, Paolo?'

'Jan?' asked Ashley.

'He isn't on any databases anywhere,' he replied. 'If he was driving in the UK, it was on an Italian licence. I've filled in the forms for Border Force to check whether he arrived legally, but they'll take a while. Requests are in with the Italian police to contact his family. The only positive is that none of the three missing men, Max, Tommaso and Hamish, or Paolo for that matter, are on Europol.'

'The other permissions and warrants are being prepared or are in progress, but it's all time we might not have,' said Ashley.

'CCTV?'

'The council footage of the streets near to the nightclub on Friday evening has arrived and is being analysed by Bhavini and two guys from Admin now. Obviously she'll let us know anything pertinent as soon as.'

Kettle shook his head. 'Ally's team have been checking to see if there are any complaints from suppliers or the public. He's also reached out to various contacts to see if the Viallis have upset anyone, but it's like a wall of silence.'

'I know my Mafia films,' said Barry. 'It's *omertà*.'

'I checked Rocco's driving licence and discovered he was born in the north, Milan, so I suppose that fits,' said Emma, 'but his children's place of birth was Norwich.'

'What does *omertà* mean?' asked Jan.

'The obligation never to apply for justice to the legal authorities and never help in any way in the detection of crimes committed against oneself or others,' replied Barry. 'The right to avenge wrongs is kept for the victims and their families.'

Any smiles on the team's faces slipped away, then Hector tutted loudly.

'That's all very well, but the Romans are the victims in all this. There aren't other Italians out to get them.'

'Not that we've seen,' said Kettle. 'Any joy with the movement of their vehicles?'

'Tommaso has a red Audi convertible registered to his home address,' replied Emma. 'Morgan from Ally's team is currently checking the road cameras for its movement history. Obviously, we're restricted on checking all the other vehicles, bank accounts and mobile numbers. As we all know, nobody is obligated to notify anyone else of their movements. Either Hamish, Max or Tommaso could disappear for as long as they liked without letting a single person know. In a way, it's lucky Paolo has been murdered or our hands would be more tied.'

'Rocco's lack of response was the most annoying aspect of the afternoon,' said Ashley. 'He could have given us everything we needed. With the timings from the nightclub CCTV, our searches could have been more targeted, which would have speeded up the process. His disappearing act also brings doubt on everything he's told us.'

'Yes,' said Kettle, thoughtfully. 'Cover it at the main meeting. Let's head there now.'

Ashley was the last to arrive. She marched to the front of the big meeting room and sat between Ally and Kettle, as representatives from all the different departments filtered in. When everyone had arrived, Kettle rose from his seat and cleared his throat.

'Thank you for coming to what is now a murder inquiry. Considering the condition of the body that was found, the disappearance of the man who escaped a similar fate, and the missing brothers, it has become more serious on many levels. Despite all this, we have nothing solid to go on. Much to our horror, we're forced to be detectives.'

A ripple of humour spread across the room.

'Ashley's and Ally's teams are leading the investigation. Ashley as deputy SIO. They're going to update you with their team's progress so far, and the next steps. Then we meet tomorrow morning at ten thirty.'

'Okay,' said Ashley. 'You've now heard who the father is. Carlo "Rocco" Vialli.'

Everyone present nodded.

'Hamish works with Max at Rocco's home improvement company, and Paolo worked for the brothers, Lorenzo and Tommaso, who manage The Coliseum for Rocco.'

Ashley gave them a few seconds to absorb the information.

'To be brief, nobody is talking. We've given Rocco enough time to reply to my questions like he said he would. It appears Rocco's word may not be good.'

'What's the background on his businesses?' asked Det Supt Zara Grave, who stood to the side of Ashley and Kettle.

'Emma's looked into everything from company records to gossip on the Internet. Apart from minor drug finds from various nightclub raids, there's little except for a bitter ex-employee accusing them of running high-end prostitutes with the women working under duress. His other companies are clean. If Rocco is a criminal, then he's a mastermind.'

'What about previous for any of the Viallis?'

'Rocco has a few speeding offences. Max has a no insurance conviction from when he was twenty. Tommaso has minor violence as a teenager, that being common assault, and an ABH from his early twenties. Nothing for years. No prison time. Hamish has a caution for a tiny amount of marijuana and a conditional discharge for an equally small weight of cocaine. Both as a youth. Lorenzo's record is clean.'

'Almost upstanding citizens,' said Zara with a nod. 'Rocco is influential in local politics. He does charity work, has a lot of friends in high places, and holds plenty of influence with those who matter. I understand he's on friendly terms with the *EDP*. Would you agree with treating him as upstanding unless we hear otherwise?'

'I would, ma'am,' said Ashley, 'but Rocco hasn't provided the information we requested. I think it's big red key time for Max, Hamish and Tommaso's properties. Then I want—'

There were good-natured groans as a large beep echoed out of Ashley's suit jacket, causing her to stop mid flow. She checked her phone. It was a message from Rocco.

Apologies. It took time to get what you asked for. I have emailed everything you wanted. I'm terribly busy here, but I'll see you at my house in the morning at nine. More details on the email.

Ashley repeated the text to the room, which caused a rumble of chatter. She opened her emails, then read the contents out. It was all there. Telephone numbers, addresses, car details, and Paolo's family contact in Rome. He said Paolo had been staying with Tommaso in his apartment, but was often back and forth on business trips to Europe, so he didn't have his own place.

Rocco had informed her Lorenzo would meet them at the nightclub at three on Tuesday afternoon. He would have the CCTV footage ready from Friday night from inside the club and outside. Max and Hamish exited at two a.m. on their own. Tommaso and Paolo were present and also went home together. Lorenzo would call in the bouncer who worked the private members' area that evening, as well as the barmaid seen chatting to Max, in case Ashley wanted to talk to them.

Rocco would be able to hand over the keys to all three flats by the next morning.

Zara gave Ashley a smile.

'I don't think we need to batter any doors down just yet.'

20

Ashley was about to argue when Kettle spoke up.

'I agree,' he said. 'If Rocco comes through tomorrow with what we asked for, he'll have been helpful. There's enough to be cracking on with. Everyone spend this evening doing what they can in the office. Let's continue to check CCTV, phone masts, and ANPR, but make sure the PNC is up to date, so HOLMES can do its thing. The search teams will reconvene in the morning at Bacton Wood, and it should be a dry day.'

PNC stood for Police National Computer. It was a computer system used by the police and other UK law enforcement organisations to retrieve real-time information of national and local significance.

'Wait,' said Ashley. 'Why would he have the key to Hamish's flat?'

'You mentioned he was close to the boy.'

'Yes, but he didn't volunteer himself as next of kin. I'm worried he'll visit the properties.'

'Text him to say keep out. If he's already been inside, it's too late now, and at least we'll know they aren't there.' Kettle turned back to the room. 'Before we finish, Ally is going to update you all on the drugs angle.'

Ally stood.

'You should have all now heard of the Vampires and the Romans and understand we suspect them of being responsible for most of the city's class A supply. We've struggled to prosecute anything other than low-level street dealers. We did catch a Romanian holding a kilogram of heroin near Felixstowe port last year, who received eighteen years. He never even confirmed his name.'

Ally paused to check his notes.

'We suspect some dealing goes on through the nightclub, but the drugs are delivered elsewhere. Lorenzo is incredibly sharp. From the scraps of intel we have, they could be moving substantial weights of coke to large dealers in Norwich, who are splitting it to mid- and lower-level crews. Finally, teenagers and children are delivering the product, sometimes on push bikes, to customers' houses.'

'I assume we've arrested people who've bought the end product. What did they say?' asked Sal.

'The usual. Friend of a friend. We find burner phones on the youngsters. Those delivering the goods know virtually nothing, but they understand not to talk. We caught a lad with ten wraps. He was fourteen. We took him out of the area and didn't think he was used again, but the manager of the children's home he was taken to discovered nearly a grand in cash in his room a few weeks later. The kid said it was his savings.'

'Has there been any chatter from the Vampires?' asked Kettle.

'No, I've had my feelers out all day. We have a couple of contacts who say they're as clueless as we are. It's hard to believe they would make a move like this when our guess is that even though their business is bigger, it's different. One informant hinted they are concerned another crew is moving into the area, taking out the Romans first, before they tackle the Vampires. Obviously, we have to take that with a pinch of salt.'

'The Romans use their nightclub as a hub,' said Kettle. 'Explain to the room about the Vampires' café.'

Most of MIT were familiar with the café, but there were trainee detectives, admin members, and others who might not be.

'The Vampires frequent a business in the Larkman area of Norwich. Does exceptionally good Moldovan coffee. It's called Café Soare. Translated from Romanian as The Sun Café. We think deals are done concerning drug distribution but, again, people don't talk to us. There's no product on site. We even had surveillance authorised for a week last year, but there was nothing except idle boasts from teenagers.'

'I reckon they got a tip-off,' said Barry.

'It certainly felt like it,' replied Ally. 'Let's leave the Vampires out of it for the moment. Ashley has the chance to go into Rocco's house tomorrow morning, which is something we've never been able to do. I'm interested to hear how he lives. Does he have servants, or a cleaner? His wife died of a stroke years ago, so is he single? Does a girlfriend live there? Council records state he's on his own, but is that correct?'

'You're closest to these people, Ally,' said Kettle. 'What's your gut feeling about Rocco's involvement?'

'I don't believe he'd be directly involved. He's rich enough not to risk losing everything. Lorenzo, maybe. Max, no. Tommaso is the most likely due to his quick temper. Perhaps this is an argument he started. The family friend, Hamish, might be their weak link. Our people say he's a heavy user of cocaine. I thought he'd just had a mad one when I first heard his story about being buried alive.'

Kettle nodded at him, then addressed the room.

'Anyone else got anything to add?'

'Wasn't there someone found in a forest over in Suffolk a year ago?' asked Morgan from Ally's team.

'No, it was Norfolk,' replied Kettle. 'Two women immigrants without papers or passport. They'd slept in Harrison's Wood on the other side of Norwich. It was a wintry night and one of them died. I'm not sure what happened to them. CID was dealing. You can be a good man and add that to your list of chores.'

Morgan gave a good-natured groan.

'There you have it,' said Kettle. 'Tomorrow could bring us anything. This has been an organised affair. Abducting people and getting away unnoticed is difficult. It's likely they took the men to a house for questioning. Finding that place is imperative. Perhaps Hamish and the others were tortured there. Anyone involved in this operation will probably end up with a life sentence, so they won't be participating on a whim. Somebody, somewhere out there, knows something. Get onto all of your sources.'

He let his words sink in, then continued.

'Our best angle is the transportation. Hamish and Paolo did not reach that wood on foot. They were taken there under duress. How? Max and Tommaso also didn't dematerialise, either. I have a press conference this evening and there'll be a helpline. At the very least, the public might help us find Tommaso's Audi. Have an earlyish night because I'm not sure when you'll next get one.'

Kettle wasn't alone in his thoughts. Ashley suspected that everyone there believed more people would die.

21

Ashley started to send people home at nine and by ten only she, Morgan and Barry remained. Morgan had found Tommaso's car on CCTV leaving the area of the club at four a.m. on the Friday, and picked it up moving past a camera near his apartment. It hadn't shown up anywhere else since then, so it was likely still in the vicinity. He'd left a message with Control that if any response vehicles were having a slow night, they should cruise around that area. It was an affluent place, but there still wouldn't be many red Audis.

The three of them walked to the car park together.

Morgan was a slim, charming black guy from Norwich. He waved goodbye to them and climbed into his shiny green Ford Mustang.

'That dude has worse clothes sense than you,' said Barry.

Ashley playfully elbowed him. 'He's not interested in anything apart from his motor. And don't be so cheeky. I'm slowly upgrading my wardrobe. I've been to Next twice.'

Barry looked down at her scuffed footwear and shook his head as they watched Morgan roar away in his sporty beast.

'Wow,' said Ashley. 'That looks and sounds cool.'

Barry nodded appreciatively. They got in his car, a stylish Seat Ibiza that she knew he'd got on a lease, and he drove Ashley to her vehicle outside Bacton Wood.

'Are Mustangs expensive?' she asked before she got out.

'Mint condition ones like his are. They also need a lot of fine-tuning, so maintenance costs are high, and they eat fuel. He has a wife and two kids as well. I'm amazed she hasn't forced him to sell it and buy a seven-seater Zafira.'

'Sexy.'

'Talking of which, I can come to yours if you like,' he said with a wink.

'I'm knackered. How about a hot chocolate in front of the TV and a cuddle?'

'I suppose I should get an early night. I'll see you tomorrow.'

'Typical,' said Ashley to herself as Barry accelerated away. It was another indication that he wasn't taking the relationship seriously.

She checked in with the officer at the entrance to the wood, but all was quiet.

Ashley cruised home in a distracted state with her mind running through various scenarios that might occur in the morning. She kept coming back to Rocco. It was great he'd given them all the information requested, and she supposed it was reasonable for it to have taken him a while, but she still didn't like the fact he had ignored her calls.

Maybe he was watching the CCTV himself at the time and checking his sons' homes with Lorenzo to make sure they were spotless. Or was he busy making his own plans?

Then she felt guilty. Rocco was at serious risk of losing two of his children. Ashley's email was probably the least of his concerns, and a man like him would prefer to act himself. He might not care about the consequences of that until he'd had time to consider them.

She wondered about the possibility of Rocco having received a ransom note and not telling her. Was he off to a meeting tonight to deliver the cash? She supposed she'd find out more the next morning. Ashley had to admit she was looking forward to seeing inside his house. Sal said Rocco's Fine Homes business turned over ten million a year. Who knew there was so much money in Italian kitchens?

Ashley took a shower at home, then made herself a hot chocolate. The bed seemed large without Barry, but she wasn't bothered. She supposed that had to be a sign, too. As she drifted off, her last thoughts returned to Rocco.

The burning question was, did she trust him?

22

Ashley's eyes blinked open just before six. She allowed her thoughts to wander for a quarter of an hour, enjoying the space in her bed. The heating had kicked in, so she slipped from the sheets and did a few stretches in the pyjamas she'd been wearing. Her running kit was ready on the chair in front of her dressing table and she watched herself in the mirror as she put it on.

Her body had changed. There was even the merest hint of a six-pack. Sex with Barry had done more for her figure than months of jogging. It was much better fun, too. She'd realised, though, their relationship would harm her in the long run. Barry wouldn't consciously hurt Ashley, but he still would if she let herself get attached.

After a few yoga poses, she stepped outside and strode up the street. It was dark, and the streets were empty. Smiling to herself and breathing easily, she ran through the town centre, past the beautiful church, by Peggottys café, down to the petrol station, then powered up the promenade towards the Runtons.

As dawn came, she was rewarded with an apocalyptic sky. Churning clouds of greys and blacks raced out to sea. To her left, the horizon was lighter, hinting promise for the day ahead. She ran through East Runton, where she smiled at Will's Plaice. Barry reckoned they did the best battered sausage on the planet. At West Runton, she breezed down Water Lane, then waved to the friendly guys opening up Seaview Cafe at the slipway as she passed them.

Ashley's spirit lifted as she darted through the shingle on the beach. She let out a cheer. Norfolk at dawn, down by the shore. The never-ending sky, the emptiness, the peace. For the first time in her life, she completely buzzed with the runner's high. Usually there'd be a sense of relaxation and satisfaction afterwards, but that morning she could have run forever.

Thoughts and memories, the faces of colleagues and friends, current and past, filtered through her mind like a slow reel playing. She sent a message of love up into the sharp salty air to her neighbour in hospital. Dana's race was over. She was the competitor who happily sacrificed her own time to help others carry on.

Ashley met another runner coming the other way. As the sun chased away the beaten clouds, they merely grinned at each other, safe with their secret.

At Cromer pier, Ashley was gasping, and she had a stitch, clearly having set much too stiff a pace. She'd resorted to walking and was listing to the right by the time she lurched up the gangway where the boats were pulled up. Mad Geoffrey, a local fisherman, stopped his truck next to her. He wound down his window.

'You're looking well,' he said. 'For a ninety-year-old.'

'It's the exercise. Keeps me fit and healthy.'

Geoffrey laughed.

'Aren't you late?' she said.

'Engine needs a new part. Got my pension now, so I'm taking it easier. How's life for you? I hear you're dating.'

Ashley shook her head at the efficiency of Cromer's grapevine.

'Yeah, well, I couldn't wait for you forever.'

'Sorry, mate. That Kelly Brook's back on the scene again. She keeps me healthy.'

Ashley chuckled and staggered past. She decided on the way home she'd drive to Bacton early and grab breakfast in one of the cafés.

After a shower and a quick Google search of which eateries were open, she texted the FLO, Scott Gorton, and offered to meet him at Cafe Carmel in Bacton. The coast road was clear, and she made good time. Scott's car wasn't outside, but the place looked bright and welcoming, so she headed inside.

The only customer was an older lady reading a book at a table in the corner, so Ashley took a seat next to the window and admired the funky décor.

She grabbed the menu and saw it was a vegan café. Shame she wasn't meeting Hector.

'How can I help?' said the owner, a friendly faced woman with warm eyes.

'Cow's milk?' asked Ashley hopefully.

'No. Oat, almond, soya or coconut.'

'Black coffee, please. A friend's arriving soon, and we'll eat. Do you mind telling me what Bacton is like?'

'Of course. Are you considering a move?'

'Might be too expensive for me.'

'Prices have gone up, but it's so lovely here. Peaceful, you know. There's a slower rhythm to life, so people look out for each other, stop for a chat, that sort of thing.'

'Rocco Vialli lives here.'

'Yes, he does.'

Ashley detected the slightest tension in the woman's smile.

'I'll get your coffee,' she said and left to fetch her order.

Scott breezed in with a grin. She rose to greet him.

'You're a picture of health,' she said.

'Is that a crime?'

'It is if I seem conked out in comparison.'

'You look well, too.'

The familiar tickle of attraction occurred as it often did when she was with him.

'I'm jogging still. I ran at school, but, back then, it was as though I enjoyed the pain. Like it distracted me from everything else, but I'm kind of getting the pleasure angle of it now. Lost weight. I feel decent.'

'Barry must be doing something right.'

Ashley nodded. 'Anyone not know?' she asked.

'I think everyone was surprised.'

Ashley raised an eyebrow.

'Sorry. I suppose I was a little shocked.'

'With him being a bit of a dickhead?'

Scott laughed. 'Exactly! I just wouldn't have thought he was a suitable fit.'

Ashley snapped a reply without thinking.

'What about your unsuitable girlfriend?'

Scott leaned back in his chair and frowned.

'I haven't been seeing anyone.'

'Barry mentioned he spotted you with a beautiful young woman.'

'Jesus, bloody Barry.'

'Isn't it true?'

'He might have seen me with a stunner, but she's my daughter.'

23

Ashley's mouth went dry.

'Can I take your order?' asked the waitress.

'Builder's tea and oat milk, and the breakfast burger with double fakon,' said Scott. 'Have you ordered yet, Ashley? It's excellent here.'

'I suddenly feel like having five Silk Cut and half a bottle of Drambuie.'

'That's the cornerstone of any nutritious breakfast, but go on. Trust me. Make that two burgers, please.'

Ashley had never imagined putting something called fakon in her mouth, but in her stunned state, she agreed.

'So, you aren't dating?' she asked when the waitress was gone.

'No, but I am finally ready. I've been on my own for a long time since the divorce, but I'm centred now.'

'Centred?' said Ashley, slowly raising an eyebrow.

'Bugger off, Ash. Tell me about Rocco Vialli.'

The food arrived just as she'd brought him up to speed. He ate his burger without commenting, so she did the same. She surprised herself by really enjoying it. Maybe she would bring Hector here.

'Situations with men like him are always trickier,' said Scott. 'But no problem. We have to assume he's innocent of anything at this point. Keep him relaxed. He obviously trusts you, which is important. We can put him in the spotlight when we've found his sons. Locating them has to be our focus. How long has it been now?'

'We suspect they both disappeared on Saturday. Max on the way home from the club, and Tommaso as he headed to the airport.'

Scott grimaced.

'Imagine what Rocco's going through. He must understand they're unlikely to be alive.'

'Yes, and it's probably a criminal connection. I'll raise that with him today, which won't be easy. I want him back at OCC, giving us everything he knows, but I'm not sure if I can persuade him.'

'Record the meeting at his house. Did you bring a tape?'

'Yes. He might not like that, either.'

Ashley's phone rang. It was Emma.

'Hi, Ems.'

'Ash, Uniform found Tommaso's Audi early this morning. It's only a few streets away from his flat. The guy who spotted it works in Traffic. He says it appears the same as joyriders' cars do after they've been blocked in by the police, with scratches and scrapes down the side.'

'Okay, thanks. I've got to go to my nine o'clock with Rocco. I won't mention it to him yet. Get the ball rolling on canvassing the vicinity.'

'Already sorted. Kettle has a team heading over there now. All our guys are in and cracking on. There's CCTV in the area, and it's a wealthy place. I bet there are Ring doorbells everywhere. If he was hemmed in there, we should have the registrations of the vehicle or vehicles responsible pretty soon.'

When Ashley finished the call, Scott had paid. She picked up her handbag.

'My treat,' he said. 'Leave your car. We'll walk.'

She followed him outside and they strolled to Rocco's house, which took just over five minutes. A silly part of Ashley almost had her linking arms with him. They crunched up the gravel road for St Georges Close and stopped outside Rocco's large property. Now Ashley was less rushed, she realised the building was much newer than she'd thought, even though it had been built with the traditional red bricks and flint embedded in the walls. A technique that had been used in the area for centuries.

Ashley's heart sank. The gate was locked again. It was 9.03. Ashley's phone beeped to tell her she had received a text from Rocco.

Hi. Sorry, I won't be at home. I had no food with all the drama. I'm at the Poachers Pocket having breakfast. Two minutes away. Come down.

She showed Scott the message.

'Fair enough,' he said.

'Is it?'

'Haven't we just done the same?'

'Yes, but at eight thirty, so we could keep to our agreement.'

Scott rolled his eyes at her, but she couldn't help considering it a power move, which had the added benefit of stopping her snooping around Rocco's house.

The Poachers Pocket was on the other side of Bacton, so they returned to Scott's vehicle, and he drove them to the pub. Ashley had enjoyed a lovely meal at The Poachers one evening with her previous boyfriend before it all went wrong. The beach was directly behind the pub so you could sit on the benches right next to the sea. She'd been so happy.

Scott parked up next to a familiar Tesla. When they got out, Rocco was visible, sitting outside at the back of the building, despite the sky having turned grey and the air being cool. Rocco saw them approach and spoke to the man who'd given him his coat at the wood. The man immediately left the table with his mug and moved to another further down.

Rocco rose as they neared him.

'Morning,' he said. 'Please, take a seat. Coffee, tea, some breakfast?'

'No, thank you,' said Ashley.

She sat on the bench opposite him and spent a moment admiring the view. Rocco had eaten little, if any, of his breakfast.

'Not hungry?' she asked.

'No. How can I eat, when...?'

Ashley smiled softly at him. 'I understand. This is your family liaison officer, Scott Gorton. He'll be your contact from now on if you have any questions.'

'I can't ring you?'

'Scott will be available, while I'll be running the investigation.'

Ashley stared at Rocco while he shook Scott's hand. He was much diminished, as though a vampire had visited him prior to meeting her each time.

'Any news?' asked Rocco.

'Not yet, but we're hopeful today will bring some. We'll have the resources to analyse CCTV and ANPR. If we can get the registration of any suspicious vehicles, that could help. The dogs can work most of the day with no rain and little breeze. If they're in the wood, we will find them.'

'Let us pray, then, for no news today,' he said.

'Rocco. We need you to make a statement at the station with

everything you know. It will be useful in trying to locate your sons.'

'Take your statement now.'

'Okay. I'll need to record it, if that's all right?'

'No, have your friend write it down.'

'It's not the same.'

'Am I on trial?'

'No.'

'I should think not. Ask your questions. I want to help.'

Ashley nodded at Scott, who took out a notepad. She turned back to Rocco, already feeling suspicious of his attitude, and was doubtful he would give them what they needed. Despite what she and Scott discussed about Rocco's presumed innocence, she decided to unsettle him.

'Do you mind telling me how you knew Hamish was in the hospital?'

'Pardon?'

'Hamish didn't have any battery life in his phone and didn't give the details of anyone to contact. Who told you he was at A & E for you to turn up?'

Rocco's reply was quick, but not fast enough for Ashley.

'A friend of mine. A nurse called him.'

Ashley smiled. 'Do they have names?'

'I know his. I don't know hers.'

'What's his?'

'That's not important.'

'We're an experienced detective team. It's best to give us as much information as possible. What might not seem significant now might be the difference between winning and losing later.'

Rocco imperceptibly shook his head.

'I see,' said Ashley. 'Can we be frank with each other?'

Rocco's eyes searched hers and she detected the spark that

remained within him. Rocco was poised, desperate to strike, but he didn't know where to aim.

'It doesn't always pay to be free with talk,' he said.

'Why do you believe your sons were taken?'

'I have no idea. My heart is breaking. I can't even busy myself with action, because nobody knows a thing.'

'These kinds of crimes, the spiking, abduction, murder and burial of men, they're extremely rare and, when they do occur, they're usually connected to criminal enterprises.'

'And?'

'It makes me suspect the victims are involved in gangs or illegal activity.'

'Gangs? My sons are grown-ups.'

'Organised crime, if you prefer.'

'Come on. Just because we're Italian, doesn't make us Mafia. I'm from Milan, not Naples.'

'Can you give me a better explanation why anyone would do this to your family, then?'

Rocco's jaw bunched as he thought. 'No, I cannot.'

'There are courts for legitimate businesses to fight in. Nobody wins with murder.'

'You believe we're involved with shady enterprises. Is that it?'

'It wouldn't surprise me if that was the reason. Maybe it's your children who are. Perhaps only one of them, and the others were collateral damage.'

'My sons wouldn't be so stupid.'

Ashley chanced her arm.

'You must know the nightclub has been raided in the past. Drugs were found. There's been suspicion around it for years.'

'Yes, I did, but the club is their thing, and drugs are par for the course in those kinds of places. One day I'll die, and my sons will take over my legacy, Rocco's Fine Homes. I wanted them to show me they could run a – what was your phrase? – legitimate business.'

'Have they?'

Rocco chuckled. 'Lorenzo has. He is my hope and dreams. The others are good boys, but they don't possess his brains. His organisation. His presence. I shall talk to him.'

'We need to talk to him.'

'You shall this afternoon at the club.'

'Will you be there?'

'No, I told you. It's their enterprise. I'm not involved.'

'So, if anything untoward was going down, you wouldn't know about it?'

Rocco half smiled, then lifted three white envelopes from the table.

'Here are the keys to the flats. Max, Tommaso, Hamish. They are empty, as you'd expect.'

'You see. This is a problem.'

'How so?'

'I texted you yesterday not to go inside.'

'It was too late.'

'You've compromised their homes by entering them since they vanished. It's unlikely we'll get robust evidence from those flats now, and certainly nothing that would stand up in court. You must leave the investigating to us. We'll find your sons if you give us the time, the information, and the space to do it. You'll want whoever's responsible to be prosecuted. Our case will need to be watertight.'

Rocco was unable to prevent his jaw from clenching. It was clear the people involved wouldn't be attending court if he had anything to do with it. He tried a joke to cover his response.

'What do you suspect? That I'll contact the old country and get a hitman sent over? Come on. I'm a businessman. I just want my children back.'

Rocco got up from the bench.

He shook hands with Scott, then Ashley. For a minute, she thought he would kiss her on both cheeks. Rocco beckoned his man over, and they walked away.

'I can see why you're concerned,' said Scott. 'There's no way he's going to keep his nose out of this.'

'Exactly, and that exacerbates our other problem.'

'Nice word, but what do you mean?'

'Do you remember we were worried there might be a dirty cop in our department during the Paradise Park case?'

'Yes. I thought nothing was ever uncovered.'

'You're right, then it went quiet. I have a feeling our rat is very much back in play.'

24

A MONTH AGO

A frightened cry brought the half-dozing Emil fully awake. He blinked salty moisture from his eyes and glanced over the shoulder of the man sagging next to him. A massive ferry filled Emil's vision. Mwamba was slumped over the engine but his head jerked up at the others' shouts. The motor roared in response to Mwamba's urgings. He leaned forward as though it would help increase the speed.

The child opposite Emil also woke up. He stared wide-eyed at the leviathan bearing down on them and let out an exhausted wail. His mother screamed and pulled him tight into her embrace.

Emil knew distances looked shorter than they were at sea, so if the engine held, they might be safe. Safe from the ship, that was. Emil noticed a man had disappeared from near the front of their boat, as though claimed by demons from the deep as they dozed through the night.

The child's teeth chattered. It was the only movement on his expressionless face. Even in the twilight of dawn, the lad's lips appeared blue. Emil unwound his large scarf and passed it to him.

The boy remained impassive, but his mother seized it and wrapped it around the lad's neck.

Emil noticed the waves had increased in size and speed. Three inches of water had materialised in the bottom of the dinghy that hadn't been there a few hours ago. Emil's stomach gurgled. His mouth was dry, which seemed strange surrounded by the sea.

When a wave lifted them up, he saw a welcoming sight. Finally, the cliffs of England. Sammy let out a cheer, which some of the others took up. Many didn't respond, as if they had frozen in place.

The ferry steamed by about fifty metres behind them, so close they could hear the Tannoy. Its wake washed another couple of inches of the English Channel into their boat. The recent full moon meant that as the sun rose, the moon remained visible at the same time so it was like waking in a different world. Both yellow globes popped in and out of view as the thickening clouds raced past them. How had his life, all their lives, come to this?

Emil thought of his warm-hearted wife. Ex-wife, really, although they'd never divorced. When he saw her again just before he left, she smiled at him in her special way, which he felt in his core, even after so many years. Her last words had been, 'Deep down, you are a good man.'

Emil removed his trapper's hat and handed it to the boy. He caught jealous eyes from others on board as they watched him pull the hat on. The lad gave Emil a gap-toothed smile.

Emil suspected they were going to end up swimming the final stretch. If that were so, the hat and scarf would be a burden to him, but he felt better for helping. He wished he had offered them sooner. The swim would be the most dangerous time. Many of those on the boat would be capable only of floating. In the panic, people would get pulled under the waves. Eyes would be gouged. Life jackets would be stolen.

Emil caught Mwamba staring down at the water that swished around his feet.

'We're close, Mwamba,' urged Emil. 'Get as near to the beach as possible.'

'No swim,' replied Mwamba, eyes wild. He cursed in his own language and stared at each face in the boat. Emil knew what he was thinking.

'Then float, Mwamba,' shouted Emil. 'That ferry would have seen our craft and rung the authorities to say we're out here. Help will come.'

Emil noticed a pair of white trainers go up in the air at the front of the craft. It appeared an Albanian had lost consciousness. The youth hadn't worn a hat and his coat had been thin. He was also one of the passengers without a life jacket. The men who seemingly knew him turned around to stare as he splashed into the water behind them, but they didn't shout out. When a much bigger wave raised the boat again, Emil peered back and saw the youngster waving in the sea, but he soon vanished from sight.

Emil observed the other males in the dinghy glare at each other. Fists were clenched. Resolve hardened. The risks had become very real. These were desperate times.

They carried on and the water level in the bottom continued to rise. Emil estimated they were about three hundred metres from land. He could see the beach. It was a swimmable distance for him. He unzipped his coat, ready to discard it.

'Everyone off,' shouted Mwamba. 'Sink! Sink!'

Emil looked down and realised Mwamba wasn't being overdramatic. The craft couldn't bear much more water. They had to lighten the load. Nobody moved.

Mwamba pulled a curved knife from inside his jacket.

'Take,' he said to Emil, indicating for him to grab the handle of the outboard.

As Emil took it, Mwamba walked forwards and started to push people off the boat into the sea. When he reached one of the Albanians, a pistol appeared. The flinty eyed man, without saying a word, shot Mwamba in the chest. Mwamba shrieked, twisted and staggered, taking two with him as he plunged overboard.

The shooter pointed at the others.

'Off,' he snarled.

Someone grabbed Emil's hand. It was the woman. Emil stared at her hand. He didn't want to look at her face.

'Can you swim?' she pleaded.

He yanked his head around but avoided the eyes that he knew would bore into his soul.

'Please,' she said.

'Yes, I can.'

'Save my son, Yusuf. I beg of you.'

Emil glanced up at her. His odds of surviving would suffer if he tried to save anyone but himself. The boy didn't even have a life jacket. His mother didn't either. She shoved the kid at him, who cried out. Emil recalled his wife's words.

Okay, mouthed Emil as another gunshot rang out.

It was too late for the boat. Perhaps too late for them all. In the last few minutes, the clouds had amassed creating a formidable grey ceiling above them, which almost seemed in reach. A flash of lightning lit up the beach. Emil spotted people there, but the waves between them and him had grown in size and strength. A big roller steamed straight over the boat and swept nearly all the remaining occupants overboard.

Emil only remained onboard because he was pressed against the outboard, with the boy clinging to his leg. The mother was gone. Her head appeared for a moment beside them, then she slipped under the waves. Emil never knew her name.

With less weight, the still functioning engine edged them

nearer the beach. Emil took off his life jacket and put it on the boy. It was too big, even when tightened to the max, but was better than nothing. Emil was slipping out of his coat when he noticed the man with the gun staring at him. Apart from the boy, they were the only ones left in the partially submerged dinghy. The killer also had no life jacket.

As the next wave hit them, Emil hooked his arm through the front of the lad's life jacket and let the surge roll them off the back of the boat.

Even though he was prepared for it, the shock of the water drove the air from his lungs. The turbulence twirled him around, and he began to sink. He swallowed a mouthful of sea water as he clung to the boy, then kicked upwards. The child appeared not to struggle, perhaps too exhausted to fight for his life. Maybe he'd accepted his fate.

Emil's head broke the surface. He managed to haul in the chilly air, then closed his eyes as another wave swamped them. To his relief, the current pushed them in the direction of the beach. Emil surfaced and performed a sidestroke. He kicked and swam, almost frantically, dragging the dead-weight boy with him. With the tide's help, he fought his way into the surf zone.

Emil trod water while he summoned one final effort. The boy's eyes were fixed on his and Emil tried to smile.

'Can you kick with your feet if we try to ride the waves to the beach?'

The lad found energy for a cough, but little else.

Emil lay back for another few seconds to steady himself, but the waves were coming fast and often. Energy seeped from his legs. He looked behind and saw a vast dumper thundering towards them.

'Breathe,' he shouted at the boy and shoved him up the wave

as it stormed over them. Emil got a hard slap in the face from it for his reward.

A second wave, taller and faster, rippled and bulged. Emil put his arm around the boy's waist, leaned forward, and tried to swim. His body felt heavy and his lungs tight. He had one last effort in him. He would make it Herculean.

Emil thrashed his legs as fast as he could. The boy had twisted to the side, so he faced Emil, but his eyes were vacant. A surge of sea lifted them. Emil roared as he battled and fought for both their lives, and he felt them being rushed to shore. They surfed closer. When one wave left them behind, another picked them up and propelled them onward. Emil kicked and thrust. When the next wave's energy was spent, he wedged his feet into the sand and held them in the same spot.

He rose from what felt like the depths with Yusuf hooked under his arm. The lad weighed a tonne and slipped from his grasp and Emil didn't have the strength to pull the boy from the water, where he lay face down. A shadow appeared behind them. Emil gritted his teeth and seized the collar of Yusuf's life jacket as a giant breaker thundered into his back. It knocked him off his feet and snatched the lad from his grip with ease.

The powerful force rolled Emil over and over until he was deposited gasping on the sand. The sea retreated, leaving him marooned like a landed fish. He lay there, wheezing, then remembered the kid. Emil rose and noticed there were lights blinking further along the shoreline. There were people running towards him. They didn't appear to be in uniform. Two lumps lay on the beach just up from him. Neither moved.

The closest body was that of the Interrailer, Kavek. Milky, unblinking eyes stared upwards at his God, who had finally deserted him. Kavek, the man who trekked all over Europe as a boy, would now walk only in the sands of heaven.

Yusuf lay next to him, eyes closed. Chest not rising.

Emil contemplated doing mouth to mouth, then Yusuf coughed. Emil laughed, then raised his hands to the sky in adulation. Yusuf and he still had business in this world. They lived.

Emil rose from his haunches, fear driving him along the beach, away from the approaching figures, and into the dark. He hadn't possessed a passport for twenty years, but the waterproof package taped to his chest held a phone, money and contact details. It remained intact.

That was important. He had a train to catch.

25

PRESENT DAY

Scott drove Ashley back to her vehicle.

'Are you saying we still have a snake in the grass?' he asked as she got out.

'Yes. It's hard to believe Rocco's friend is acquainted with a nurse, and she just happened to know Hamish was in A & E, and then decided he might want to hear about it.'

'Rocco is well known.'

'Pah!' said Ashley.

'If so, then who's the rat? From which department?'

'That's the horrible thing. It's likely to be one of mine or Ally's. Only our teams, and perhaps Admin and Control, knew what was happening at the start of all this.'

'Gabriella runs the admin group. I'm happy to put some pressure on her.'

'God, you as well?'

'I was only joking.'

For a few long seconds, Scott appeared as if he was going to comment.

'I'll see you later,' he finally said. 'You know, I've always thought Barry was a bit of a rat.'

'Nah,' she replied. 'He's a weasel. It's slightly different.'

They both laughed and they held each other's gaze longer than necessary, as often occurred when they spent time together.

She returned to her vehicle and tried to focus on the case.

When she arrived at OCC, Ally was also arriving and he waited for her to get out of her car.

'How did it go at Rocco's?'

'He wasn't there.'

'No way.'

'He asked me to meet him at a pub up the road.'

'That's a shame. I was interested in hearing what kind of gaff he had.'

'Me, too. It's like someone warned him we were looking forward to casing his joint.'

Ally looked away for a moment. 'Sometimes this job doesn't play fair.'

'Anyone dodgy in your team?' she asked with a grin.

'Most of them,' he replied. 'Have you noticed you and I have the crappiest cars here?'

'I love the fact I don't give a shit about my motor. AS Joan Collins might say, if it dies, it dies. What's your excuse?'

'I got a divorce.'

'Oh, sorry. I hadn't heard.'

'You wouldn't have. I've always kept my police life separate from my home life after she stopped working here. Anyway, I'm okay. Our daughter had long left home. We're cool.'

They walked in together past Morgan's impressive Ford Mustang and Ally chuckled.

'I should arrest Morgan at his desk right now.'

Ashley smiled despite it not being a laughing matter. She didn't think Morgan was the type to take kickbacks, but he could be desperate for any number of reasons. It was bloody dangerous when the enemy knew your next move, but the worst part was you started to doubt your judgement. It was easy to suspect everyone.

26

Ashley hadn't even taken her coat off when she was summoned to Kettle's office. Bhavini already sat in one of two chairs opposite Kettle, who had a surprisingly animated expression.

'Morning, Ashley. I was telling Bhavini about the first few hours after a baby arrives in the world. I remember my wife and I staring down at my son in his crib at the hospital in stunned silence.'

'Must be quite a moment,' said Ashley.

'Did you immediately feel they were now the most important thing, and you'd do anything for them, or did that take a few weeks or months?' asked Bhavini.

Kettle beamed and, not for the first time, Ashley wondered what he was like out of work. The team knew little about his home life. Was that how she would be if she got the promotion? A person the new recruits feared, or a woman who people called an ice queen behind her back? Someone who, when she entered a room, would cause others to go quiet?

'If I'm honest, it took years for me,' said Kettle. 'I'd just made sergeant when I had my son, and I worked every hour to pay the bills, so my wife could be at home. Then when he was about eight, I took him to his first football match. You know, it was so noisy and busy that he hugged himself into me, but he was excited, as well as scared. I remember watching his face as he stared around and I thought, yes, now I get it. You'll understand when it happens to you.'

Kettle smiled warmly at Ashley. Maybe the gossip hadn't reached him about her inability to have children. Or perhaps he was a good actor. Bhavini gave her a quick, wide-eyed look, which made Ashley grin.

'Right,' said Kettle. 'Let's do a little prep before the meeting. I'm prepared for unwelcome news today.'

Ashley nodded.

'Yes, I'm not hopeful we'll find the brothers in one piece. It's hard enough hiding a dead body, never mind one that's alive and kicking. It sounds like this Tommaso would hate not being in control.'

'All we can do is crack on. Investigate by the numbers,' said Bhavini.

'Bee!' said Ashley. 'You've been watching too many American shows. I assume you mean, as is our traditional British way, we plod on with what we've got.'

'I'm not sure the HOLMES team would see it that way, but I have been binge-watching American series. It's like Bump's and my thing together. I watch TV and stroke him.'

'Him?'

'Sorry, it! I haven't asked. That's the least of my concerns.'

'How are your folks getting their heads around it?' asked Ashley.

'Do you know what? They're loving it. My father in particular.'

'What about the shame and family dishonour?'

'Oh, Ash. The details of my affair with Himansu raced through my parents' community faster than the rumours do here, if that's possible. You wouldn't believe my dad, though. I overheard him on the phone to one of his friends. He was saying, yes, it's difficult. These children have such modern lives, but what can he do if he loves me?'

Ashley squeezed Bhavini's arm.

'Good for you.'

'Yes, and that's why you've been summoned, Ashley,' said Kettle. 'Bhavini will be leaving us on Halloween to start her maternity leave.'

Ashley turned to Bhavini.

'Okay, I kind of had the idea you'd work until the last minute.'

'Me, too, but I've got a crazy nesting feeling occurring. Why not be mellow and take time to fit pleasant, memorable experiences in? My mum hopes to take me shopping for furniture for the baby's room, my sister-in-law is planning long lunches, and my dad has offered to buy clothes. I suspect this case isn't going to end well. I can cope with that now, but I don't want to deliver my baby with brutally tortured bodies on my mind.'

'Brutally tortured?'

'That's what Michelle implied after doing Paolo's post-mortem. She's coming in for our meeting. She enjoys having lunch here, so it's no hassle.'

'Weird to think you'll be having a child in a few months.'

'Tell me about it. I'd like to be in a Zen state. It's stressful enough dealing with the idiotic sperm provider.'

Ashley and Kettle laughed.

'Is Himansu giving you grief?' asked Ashley.

'Yep. He keeps pestering me to meet up. Says he wants to talk about the future. His wife must be the only one in the country who hasn't heard what he's been up to.'

'Sadly, that's often the way.'

'Barry and I did some detective work on who let our secrets slip from our drunken afternoon, and it was Himansu!'

'Himansu was spreading the gossip?'

'Yes, Barry got told two different things by two different officers who work out at his gym. Both said it was Himansu who told them. One was a rumour that I pursued and trapped him!'

'Nasty little shit,' said Ashley. 'Hey, perhaps your dad could visit him.' She put on her best karate voice. 'You take my daughter's virginity. I take your life.'

Bhavini cracked up. 'Poor attempt at a Chinese accent, but no, I can't see it.'

'Your family not into honour killings?'

'No. The newspapers love implying they're happening all the time, but, as I told you, there's so much gossip, little stays a secret for long. My mum did say she wants to kick him where the sun doesn't shine.'

'Don't mind me, ladies,' said Kettle. 'Chat away. Take your time. I've got nothing to do. Any thoughts about the meeting?'

'Let's get the men's flats sealed up as potential crime scenes,' replied Ashley. 'We need to start with door-knocking teams all around Bacton Wood. I wouldn't be surprised if those responsible had a base nearby.'

'I hate to rely on blind luck,' said Kettle ruefully.

Ashley and Bhavini didn't comment. They both knew they were investigating this case with one hand tied behind their backs. If the Viallis, through either Rocco or his sons, were involved in serious crime, then everything they'd been told by them was at best likely to be only a version of the truth. The real questions that needed asking wouldn't be answered, such as which of your drug-dealing partners are liable to want you or your family dead?

'I didn't get to meet Rocco at his home,' said Ashley. 'He went down the pub for breakfast. It made me think about our potential department mole during the Paradise Park investigation.'

Kettle drummed his fingers on the table.

'Do you suspect anyone?'

'Everyone. It was bugging me on the way here. What was the outcome of the internal inquiry?'

Ashley wondered if Kettle would answer that. Professional Standards preferred to operate in the shadows.

'It's still being looked into.'

Ashley understood when she was being fobbed off. It was strange how nobody had been spoken to yet, as far as she knew. Someone must have investigated, but she supposed there was rarely any concrete evidence when it first came to worries about bad officers. That was why when they had one, they tended to escape detection for a while.

'I suppose it was hard to investigate when nearly everyone was dead,' said Bhavini. 'Did anyone ever go to the hotel where they played, and the initial contact was made?'

Kettle shrugged. 'I don't know.'

Ashley didn't believe that. Kettle would have been involved. She recalled the poker tournament, which some people in the Paradise case frequented. Maybe a member of her team or Ally's attended those games.

She looked up to find Kettle appraising her. Ashley was going to send someone to that hotel when the next poker game was on.

She also decided she wouldn't tell Kettle about it beforehand.

27

Ashley grabbed Barry before the meeting.

'Hey, Barry, you didn't tell me Himansu was spreading shit about.'

'Oh, yeah, I forgot. Sneaky prick. He gossiped about Hector being a virgin and about us seeing each other. Bhavini and I were wondering if we should let his wife hear anonymously.'

'Yes, that's a tricky one. Maybe she'd rather not know if there's little she can do about it.'

'Do you know whether Himansu had an arranged marriage?'

'Yes, it was. Bee has also realised she probably wasn't Himansu's first affair. It's difficult with him being the father. You want your child to have a dad if there's the chance of him stepping up.'

Barry nodded grimly. It was something he knew too well.

'Perhaps Himansu will grow up when the baby's born,' he said without conviction.

Ashley shrugged. 'She has family and friends who love her. I think she'll be fine either way. Anyway, I've got a little job for you, Hoops!'

'Oh, no. You only call me that when you need a favour or are taking the piss. Seeing as you've put your foot in it about my own father's vanishing trick, I assume it's going to be the former.'

'Correct! Do you remember Elizabeth used to attend a poker game at The Maids Head Hotel in Norwich?'

'Yeah. That's where she met Deniz, which led to the carnage at Paradise Park.'

'Well, I'm wondering who else she could have met there. It's been more than three months since, so what if you popped down one afternoon when they play. If our informant did frequent the games they might have stopped going after the case was settled, but maybe they started up again.'

'I suppose that's possible. Do you want me to join a game?'

'No. Wait around and see who arrives. You've played poker yourself, so if you get the opportunity to chat to someone, do, but don't waste too much time there. It's just an idea.'

'Come on. You'd need to be crackers to return there when the rumours about a dirty cop were spreading through the department like wildfire.'

'As I said, it's only a thought, but I don't know anyone else who's into gambling.'

'That bloke with the noisy car plays a bit of poker.'

'Morgan, the guy on Ally's team?'

'Yes. Although Ally enjoys a gamble himself.'

'He does?'

'Ally likes the horses. I heard that was why his wife chucked him out, but I'm not sure if that's true.'

Ashley sighed as she headed to the meeting room. She now had suspicions of Morgan and Ally. The insidious nature of corrupt policing could wreck a team's morale in short order.

Kettle stood and brought everyone up to speed. One of the computer systems, HOLMES, had produced myriad leads to follow up, which Kettle distributed to various teams. CSI was going over Tommaso's car with a fine-tooth comb, but there were two other pieces of information gathered that might be critical.

Kettle nodded at Morgan.

'If abducted people are being moved without raising suspicion, they're usually in a van, so that's what we've been focusing on. A blue Transit has been spotted on CCTV, driving around the area near Tommaso's. The better security and cameras at the Gas Terminal have paid off again, because the same van was driven past the entrance. It has a number plate for a 1995 vehicle, but the model being driven wasn't manufactured until the millennium. If it moves now near a main road, with the same plate, we'll know. All mobile units nearby are keeping an eye out for it.'

Kettle cleared his throat.

'This type of case tends to progress rapidly, so let's put in the hard yards this week. That said, the Inspector Assessment Day still goes ahead tomorrow. So, Ashley won't be in. I'll be running her team. Now, anything else before we crack on?'

Scott Gorton was at the meeting.

'I've just taken a call from Paolo's father, who speaks excellent English. As you'd expect, he's devastated.'

'Is he coming over to the UK?' asked Kettle.

'No, he wants his lad's body back as quick as possible. I offered him the chance to visit. We know how helpful that can be for acceptance, but he more or less said, what's the point? His son is dead. Nothing can change that.'

'Was he angry?' asked Ashley.

'No, sad. I'd say defeated, for want of a better word.'

Ashley considered his response.

'Maybe Paolo was no model student back in Italy, then later took up crime. Perhaps his dad had prepared himself for this kind of conversation one day.'

Kettle shrugged.

'It's possible his father understood who he worked for. If any of the Viallis are shady, the wider family will have at least heard rumours. I suspect the Italian community has a few secrets.'

'If we can't get him over here for a visit, I'll broach that over the phone. People tend not to badmouth their own families, but a father's lost his boy. At some point, he'll be raging.'

'It's unfortunate to put him through those kinds of questions, but necessary,' said Kettle. 'After all, we're investigating murder. Right, Ashley is attending Lorenzo's nightclub this afternoon to watch the CCTV from that evening and to interview those present. My guess is Max's and Hamish's drinks were spiked in the club. They might have left in a weakened state or gone back with someone they thought was a friend or potential lover, when the opposite was true.'

'I'll report in as soon as I see the footage,' said Ashley.

'If Ashley's team focus on the flats,' said Ally, 'I'll have my guys prepared for follow-up interviews with anyone we deem suitable. Morgan and Zelda looked into those two women that were found a year ago in Harrison's Wood. Zelda.'

The woman from Ally's team took over.

'Immigration struggled to find out where either of the two women were from. They finally traced the one who died back to Montenegro via DNA and missing persons records. The survivor was granted permission to stay. I've flicked through the file notes, which are massive and don't make easy reading. Forced into prostitution when she arrived here. Given a different name like the other girl. She refused to provide her real name to begin with. They had a harrowing experience.'

'So, she wasn't working at The Coliseum?' said Barry.

'Far from it. She wouldn't give many details for a long time, especially about being trafficked, but eventually she admitted that's what happened to her. I'm going to see if she'll meet me. She may be more open now it's been a while. Maybe this is connected. The Vampires are known to have their fingers in all the rotten pies, even if the Romans are keeping the cream, so to speak. They could be working together. It's incredibly frustrating we know so little about either of these gangs, yet we suspect them of everything.'

'Perhaps Tommaso, or his men, hurt one of the Vampires' women,' said Hector. 'My friend who dated him got back to me. She said Tommaso was never violent to her, but he still scared her. They didn't date for long, but she believed his only focus was making the nightclub a success. Perhaps he tried to recruit some of the Vampires' girls for The Coliseum, and they took offence.'

Kettle rose from his seat.

'It's possible this case will expose everything about these two organisations. I'll have the teams door-knocking around Tommaso's apartment first, and asking if anyone remembers a blue van.'

Kettle tapped the table.

'Be extra careful. We don't know the full picture, and that picture could be as serious as it gets. Whoever's dealing to the masses of Norfolk, whether it be cocaine or heroin, is making a lot of money. For the Romans or the Vampires, it's a big prize to fight over. Risks will be taken. Lies will be told. More lives will be expendable.'

Ashley caught Kettle's attention.

'Go on,' he said.

'Lorenzo will have watched the CCTV already from that night.'

'And wiped it?'

'No, I don't think so. That would implicate him, but he knows more than us at this point. We'll need to keep an eye on him because he might have a suspect in mind. At the moment, only Paolo is dead. It's anyone's guess how Lorenzo will act if the next body we find is one of his brothers.'

28

Ashley returned to the office and logged in to a computer while Jan and Barry hovered next to her.

'Do you still need me to come to the club?' asked Jan.

'No, I should go, considering I have the relationship with the father. Can you help the team looking into the vans in the area, and in particular that false number plate?'

'Will do, boss.'

Jan left them to it.

'What time are we leaving for the nightclub?' asked Barry.

'Two thirty.'

Ashley was still thinking about what Barry said earlier about Ally liking a bet on the gee-gees. Ashley hadn't known that, and she'd worked with Ally for nearly a decade.

'Barry. You drive a pricey car. Are the monthly payments much?'

'They're not cheap, but seeing as I live at my gran's, I've got few outgoings.'

'Does anyone else in the department have any suspicious habits?'

'Only me. My secret vice is having nooky with Velma from *Scooby-Doo*.'

'Interesting, seeing as you aren't, because she's a cartoon character.'

'But I am having sex with her identical twin, you, so that's pretty damn close.'

Ashley mimed being sick in her wastepaper bin and shooed him away.

Admin took up the rest of her time before her meeting with Lorenzo. She had just logged out of her computer when Gabriella arrived at her desk.

'Can I have a quick word?' she asked without any hint of a smile.

'Sure.'

Ashley followed her out to one of the stairwells. Gabriella put her hands on her hips. Dressed in tailored brown trousers and a neatly ironed cream shirt, Gabriella carried off class with ease. Ashley suspected Gabriella could make sackcloth alluring. Gabriella took a deep breath.

'I was wondering if you could do me a favour. People repeatedly ask me to go on dates. I'm not on the market at the moment, which they know. I don't want to keep rebuffing keen suitors at work. It's like I've got a target on my back.'

'Ah, has Hector been overzealous?'

'A little. He is cute, but I'm too distracted by my home life.'

'Hector's a great guy. His heart's in the right place, which is more than most. Some don't appear to have one at all.'

'Yes, it's volume that's my problem. I've been getting peppered with offers from him, and Mark from Custody, and Barry.'

Gabriella bit her lip as she waited for Ashley's response. Ashley's expression twisted into a scowl as the last word sank in.

'For want of a better phrase, my Barry?'

'Yes. I'm so sorry to be the bearer of bad tidings, but I heard you were dating each other.'

Two lines tracked down Gabriella's perfectly made-up face and Ashley gave Gabriella a swift hug.

'Thank you, I really appreciate it.'

Gabriella stepped back as if worried about what the crazy sergeant would do next. Ashley let out a short curse.

'I have been seeing Barry, and a large part of me has been wondering why. Well done for having the balls to tell me, because I can now make a decision with no worries or regrets.'

29

Ashley decided not to mention Gabriella's 'news' to Barry straight away. She supposed she might as well have a little fun at his expense, seeing as he was having some at hers. She met him in the car park, and he drove them to Prince of Wales Road where most of the city's nightclubs were situated. Barry parked on a side street in someone's parking space for their flat and got out.

'Will it be okay here?' she asked.

'Yeah, mate of mine works out at one of the industrial parks, so his place is free during the day. Handy for shopping.'

Ashley realised in all the time she'd been seeing Barry, she hadn't bumped into a single close friend of his. He hadn't mentioned any either. Was that because he had none, or because he liked keeping them separate from his relationships?

'Barry. I've been informed of something interesting. You're aware I experienced a few issues with having a baby.'

'Yes.'

'I received my final results from the specialist. The conclusion is I have a one in five chance of getting pregnant naturally.'

Barry frowned.

'I thought it was like no per cent.'

'Apparently not.'

'You've got a twenty per cent chance?'

'That's generally what one in five means.'

He clasped his hands together.

'We haven't been taking precautions.'

'Scary, isn't it? Imagine, we could be heading to parenthood and not even know.'

Ashley glanced at Barry's face to confirm the colour was leaching from it. His tongue had frozen.

'I was thinking,' she said. 'Perhaps we should trial you moving in. We've been getting on well, and you already stay over a lot. Let's see how it goes.'

'I'm not sure we're there yet.'

'How about the new year?'

'Yeah, maybe.'

'Now's the perfect time to tell you I love you.'

Barry came to an abrupt halt outside the entrance to The Coliseum. She watched his squirrel-sized brain process all the nuts she'd thrown at it. Then, finally, the dull bulb inside his head glowed dimly as he understood what was happening.

'You're mean,' he said.

'What?'

'Gingerpuss told you,' he said.

'Told me what?'

'Devious cow. Typical woman who can't keep a secret.'

'Barry. You're unreal. The only bovine in this discussion is you.'

'It was only a joke. I ask her out all the time.'

'What if she'd said okay?'

Barry at least had the grace to look shifty. There was no reply to the doorbell at the nightclub entrance, so he knocked hard on the glass.

'I take it our little thing is over,' he said.

'Oh, yes.'

'Anything I can say to change your mind?'

'Hell, no.'

'Ah, well. I enjoyed it while it lasted.'

'Screw you, Barry.'

Ashley smiled as she waited. It had been fun, distracting, but deep down she was glad it was over. Barry would be fine. He'd just move on to his next victim.

The guy who let them into the club was tall with wide shoulders, with a lived-in face and the physique of a man capable of efficient violence.

'Lorenzo will see you in the private bar. Follow me, please.'

They wandered through the foyer and into the club itself. Ashley's clubbing days in Norwich were long gone. This one hadn't been open back then, or perhaps it had, but under a different name.

Ashley had investigated a lot of crimes in nightclubs during her career in uniform. They tended to have a grim vibe when the lights were turned on, but The Coliseum appeared more a selection of trendy bars around a large dance floor and was in excellent order. The big guy took them to the third floor, scanned a card against a reader, then opened a glass door to what was clearly a luxurious private area.

Ashley paused at the door and scoped the room. The lounge was cleverly laid out. The restricted section had all glass windows etched with the logo of the club, so they would feel part of the nightclub, but those on the outside would struggle to peer in. Their escort took a stool at the bar. A good-looking man, wide brown eyes, a strong jawline and dark hair that just about curled onto his blue shirt collar, sat at the nearest booth to the entrance with a laptop in front of him. He slid out from his seat.

'Thank you for coming. I'm Lorenzo, the manager.'

'DS Ashley Knight, DC Barry Hooper. Thanks for meeting us.'

Ashley shook his hand and wasn't surprised to find Lorenzo exuded confidence and was clearly in control, despite his short stature. He was in the mould of his father, but middle-aged spread hadn't yet begun its attack and his hair was thick and lustrous. Ashley suspected he didn't weigh much more than she did.

'Please sit down,' he said. 'I'll show you the CCTV, which I'm sure you'll agree is interesting.'

Ashley let Lorenzo lead the conversation and took a seat next to him with Barry on his other side.

'Here. This is what we've seen. It appears Hamish and Max were chatting with these two girls about an hour before they left. We know the guys visited the toilet together and left their drinks. Watch. One woman scans around, then deliberately stands in front of the table so her friend is hidden from the cameras. When the boys return, their new friends only stay for a few minutes. Then they leave the club and turn right outside. Maybe you can trace them from there.'

Ashley took a few moments to consider her reply.

'This footage would have been helpful earlier.'

'Who knew?' said Lorenzo, throwing his arms in the air. 'I thought the lads were lying low with hangovers. Hamish is well known for drinking too much.'

'Yet you still have him in your club?'

'Yes, he's like family from being Max's mate at school. That way, I can keep an eye on them both. Look, this is them leaving half an hour later.'

Ashley observed as Max and Hamish staggered towards the exit. Hamish could barely walk, but Max didn't seem to mind too much and laughed as he supported his friend past a camera, almost tripping up himself. The recording quality was top-notch.

'I assume you've watched it all,' she said with a smile.

'Of course. He's my little brother.'

'There's nothing else incriminating?'

'No.'

'Does anybody know who the women are?'

'No. I've been collating as much information as possible for you. I didn't want you to have to keep coming back. We think one of the girls was here a few months ago. Gianluca remembers her trying to blag her way past him.'

Lorenzo beckoned over the man who'd brought them up the stairs. He sauntered over.

'Yes, it was definitely her. She was dressed differently, and her hair had changed, but the cute smile and flirting technique were memorable because of her intensity. Some will do anything to get into the private area. My job is to stop them.'

Ashley wondered if Gianluca took advantage of the keen girls with promises of admission, but Lorenzo already didn't seem a man to cross. That made the fact someone had attacked his family all the more concerning.

'Who might have kidnapped your brothers?' asked Barry. 'Point us in the right direction.'

'That's why you're here. I'm clueless.'

Ashley wondered how many levels there were to that reply. Was he saying if he knew, then he would have resolved it without their help?

'No ransom notes? No strange communications? No threats?' asked Barry.

Lorenzo gesticulated as he spoke. It reminded Ashley of someone, but she couldn't place the memory.

'People don't threaten me. Why would they? I run the best club in town, but if they wanted my crown, they should compete honestly. They should clean their carpets. Sell decent liquor. That'd be a start.'

Ashley detected a hint of an Italian accent in his speech, but he was born in Norwich. She suspected it was put on as part of his suave and sophisticated persona.

'So, you don't think the competition on Prince of Wales Road could be responsible?' asked Ashley.

'No, but I have no idea who might be. It's crazy. We don't understand. I just want my brothers back. Please, find them for us.'

'Okay, let's begin with the girls you suspect of spiking either or both of Max's and Hamish's drinks.'

'Yes.'

'Did they pay by card?'

'No, I checked the cameras. Cash for everything, including entrance. One of them sported large trendy tinted glasses and the other had a funky haircut which covered half her face, so Gianluca asked his security friends in a few of the other bars and clubs if anyone recognised or remembered them. They said no. Norwich isn't that big of a place, so pretty, hip types like them get noticed. Who knows? Maybe they're innocent. Perhaps they'll come back this Friday, and I'll be able to ask them myself.'

Ashley briefly observed Lorenzo, who had a distant cold look on his face. She hoped for the girls' sakes they didn't show this weekend, but it sounded as if they had set out to be unrecognisable.

'Do you know where Hamish is?' she asked.

'No. I heard he walked out of the hospital.'

'You don't have any idea where he could be?'

Lorenzo's gaze briefly rested on her before he shrugged and looked away.

'If you'd been through an experience like Hamish's,' he said, 'I suspect you might disappear as well. At least until your attackers were arrested.'

'I suppose.'

Lorenzo clicked his fingers, and a young girl came into the room from behind the bar. She was heavily made-up and looked uninterested. Lorenzo introduced her as the manager who ran the section where the lads had been buying their drinks that night. After a few minutes of chat, Ashley gave up on her. Barry had been recording everything in his notebook, but she suspected he agreed with her, and they were getting a whitewashed version of events.

A small white envelope sat on the table. Lorenzo pushed it over to them.

'Memory stick with the CCTV on it. Anything else I can help you with, then give me or my father a call.'

'I'm not sure I have your number.'

Lorenzo reached into his pocket and drew out a gold-embossed black business card identical to the one Rocco gave her. This time the name on it was simply Lorenzo.

Lorenzo insisted on escorting Ashley and Barry back to the foyer, where he showed them a picture on the wall, of him, Tommaso and Max leaning against a balcony, all looking cool. Despite what she'd heard about Max not being close to the others, he was beaming at the camera. He and Lorenzo had similar slim figures while Tommaso was noticeably thicker set and taller. Ashley commented on it.

'Yes. Tommaso took after our dear mother.'

Lorenzo made the sign of the cross, which reminded Ashley that his mother had passed and stopped her asking any more questions.

Lorenzo firmly shook both their hands and held eye contact.

'We'll speak soon,' he said.

'Is business good?' asked Barry.

'Very. The average spend per clubber is around fifty pounds. A thousand people come through the door. Even I can cope with that maths.'

When Ashley and Barry stepped outside, she felt disorientated, like leaving the cinema mid-afternoon. They blinked as they strolled along the quiet street. It was hard to imagine this road once ranked as the fourth most dangerous in England for drinking. Covid had done for a lot of the nightlife in Norwich. When they reached their car, Barry said what they were both thinking.

'That's not the first time Lorenzo's spoken to the police about what's happened.'

'No, but apart from his having an insider feeding him information, which is infuriating, his response makes it worse.'

'How come?'

'Lorenzo still appears to be in the dark after seeing the footage or he'd be acting on what he knows. Which probably means Rocco is none the wiser, either.'

'Their minions will be working overtime in the background to discover what's going on.'

'I'm sure they are, but the most likely explanation is another crime outfit. Yet if he wasn't exaggerating back then, he's taking fifty grand a night. That's serious, honest money.'

'The books are probably cooked to hide the avalanche of illicit dough.'

'Maybe, but surely if it were a rival after any business of Lorenzo's, he'd have a clue, but he seems as genuinely confused as we are.'

'Someone's got to be mad or confident to take on the Viallis.'

'I agree, but which is it?'

Barry shook his head. 'Who knows? I will say I found it hard to read Lorenzo.'

Ashley nodded. She could imagine Lorenzo a charming host,

but she could also see him holding a smoking pistol, before handing it to Gianluca to dispose of. The way Lorenzo's body moved with energy made her suspect he would make a great dancer or lover, but it was easy to picture his face twisted with rage and splattered with blood.

She decided it was best to treat Lorenzo as an enigma until she knew otherwise. The rich and powerful didn't come to Norwich for light entertainment. Lorenzo had to be offering them an experience they couldn't get elsewhere.

It wasn't much of a leap to guess that might be illegal, but somebody, somewhere, had decided the Viallis' business needed to be curtailed.

And they were prepared to kill to make that happen.

30

Ashley woke the next morning at five. With no chance of getting back to sleep, she clambered out of bed and stared out of the window at another grey dawn. Raindrops pattered against the glass. Her shoulders tightened. It was an important day. One that would affect her career, and therefore the rest of her life.

Ashley pulled on a pair of leggings and a top but had no intention of going running. She wanted to practise her answers to the questions she was likely to get at the assessment centre. She wasn't sure she'd accept the job if she got it, but it would be better to have the option, and she didn't want to be unprepared. They would interview a focused woman with ambition, then it would be her choice.

Before she left the room, she glanced back and thought of the last few months. There were no regrets. Barry was gone from her bed, but he'd never been in her heart. Perhaps she'd used him as much as he had her. There were no hard feelings.

After twenty minutes of stretches and some yoga, she wandered into the lounge and gazed at herself in the mirror. Cursing, she put her glasses on so she could see better. Bloody Barry. She really did look like Velma, but a maturing one.

Ashley stared at a picture of herself and her father on the mantelpiece when she was only around six. She was on his knee while he peeled an apple with his penknife. Peeling an apple that way had been a habit she'd taken up but recently dropped. It was another crutch, for which she had no further need.

Ashley's thoughts slipped to Scott Gorton. Overnight, her feelings had slotted into place around him. He would also meet a focused Ashley in the near future, who would ask him out on a date, of that she was now sure. Although she ought to let that side of the bed get cold again, if only for decency's sake.

Ashley climbed the stairs and opened her wardrobe. She took out the new navy tailored single-breasted suit jacket, tailored trousers, shoes and blue blouse she'd ordered from the Next catalogue. It had been a rash decision one boozy Sunday with Barry when he'd been giving her grief about her clothes. When the items had arrived, she'd almost not opened them. The price had seemed ridiculously expensive for clothes, but Barry had laughed and asked her what she was saving her money for.

When she'd come downstairs ten minutes later, posing in those two-inch heels, Barry's jaw had clattered to the floor. Then he'd chased her back upstairs and ensured she wouldn't be able to return anything. It had been a heady moment, which had made her believe there was more in the relationship than there was. But she needed more than lust.

At eight, after practising her answers out loud began to make her hoarse, she got in her car, even though she would be early. Her mind drifted to the case. She and Barry had gone back to the office with the club's CCTV and let those present watch it. Detectives from various teams had filtered in from their investigations, but nothing had become clear. The searchers in the wood had also come up empty-handed. After ten minutes of consideration, Ashley pushed the investigation to one side and turned the radio on.

Ashley was singing along to 'The Final Countdown' when she approached the turning for OCC. She cursed, knowing she shouldn't go in, but indicated, and took the road towards it.

When she stepped into the office, Emma whistled at her.

'Power, baby!' she shouted.

Sal, Hector and Barry were also in.

'You look like an inspector,' said Hector with a smile.

'Don't worry, Fast Track,' said Barry. 'I'm sure you'll be dressed the same way one day soon.'

Even Hector smiled at that.

'Why have you come in, Ashley?' asked Sal.

'The interviews are at Suffolk HQ in Martlesham at eleven, so I was passing. I woke up early, and I didn't want to rattle around the house for hours, overthinking things, so I thought I'd get there without stressing and grab a coffee. There was time to pop in here.'

Sal shook his head and laughed. 'Witness's story is highly suspect, my lud.'

'Hilarious. Any overnight developments?' she asked him.

'I was up early, too. I wanted to check the CCTV of those men picking up Hamish from the hospital, see if I might spot them on the footage from the nightclub.'

Ashley punched Sal gently on the arm.

'Sal, you're a genius. One of the people who collected Hamish seemed a big unit, as was the doorman, Gianluca, who met us yesterday. There can't be too many twenty-stone ogres wandering around Norwich. Get the recording up, and we'll see if it's him.'

The door opened behind her and Ally marched in with Zelda and Morgan. Ally picked up on the energy in the room.

'What is it?' he asked.

'We think we have a lead,' said Ashley. 'Zelda, did you and Morgan manage to speak to the woman who was found in Harrison's Wood?'

'Yes,' she replied. 'Her name was Drita Grbić. That's why we're here at the crack of dawn as well. Drita told Immigration, in an interview after they were found, that she and Olga, the lady who died, had come from Montenegro. Drita gave few details at the time because she didn't want to relive it, but she wants to put the record straight.'

'What brought that on?' asked Ashley.

'My guess is the guilt has been getting to her, then we got in touch, which she saw as a sign.'

'What kind of guilt?'

'Survivor's. She'd clearly been through a horrible ordeal, but she knows if people like her don't step forward, then more will go through what she did. Someone from Border Force came with us. They reassured Drita she wouldn't be deported whatever she said, so now was the time for the truth.'

'Let's hear it.'

'Okay. She knew Olga was from Montenegro because they spoke the same language, but they came here separately and didn't know each other. Drita met Olga in one of the brothels they were forced to work in to pay off their journey. That was nearly four years ago.'

'They were in one for three years?' asked Sal incredulously.

'Two for Drita. Longer for Olga. Their passports were taken, no money or phone, force-fed drugs, and generally abused in every way. She didn't go into it, but she's unable to have children now. There was a man at her house, a massive bloke. I assume she chose a certain type of boyfriend after her ordeal. He had to calm her down.'

Ashley thought of Gianluca.

'Was he strong, with a craggy face?'

'Strong, yes. Craggy, no. I'd say he was in his sixties. He's most likely rich. She probably wants a partner who can protect her physically and financially.'

Ashley's fists clenched, even though she'd heard comparable stories many times over. Zelda continued.

'Do you remember a report of gunfire in Catton a year ago, but nothing ever came of it?' asked Morgan.

'Rings a vague bell,' said Ashley.

'Drita explained they were shunted from house to house, but at the last place there was an argument with a punter over payment. Security threw him out, but he returned with a gun. He stood outside and said he was going to kill everyone in there. The madam of the property and the security guy both fled out the back after the enraged punter shot through the front door lock, so Drita and Olga ran, too. They hid for a few days with no idea where to run to or who to ask for help, huddling together in the woods for warmth. Drita woke up one morning, and Olga didn't.'

'Bastards,' muttered Ashley.

She pushed her feelings to one side and checked her watch. There were ten minutes before she needed to leave.

'A harrowing tale, but I'm not sure it's especially relevant to our case.'

'That's what I thought, but I asked her about the nationality of the people traffickers. Initially, they were all Slavic, but the final few legs, which got them into the country, were in a shipping container. Drita saw a sign when they were allowed to use the toilet, which said they were heading towards Rotterdam. The men who arranged that leg were Italian.'

31

Sal had pulled up the footage from A & E at the same moment as Morgan dropped his bombshell. They all stared at the large presence who escorted Hamish out of A & E. The man was the right size, but, under a cap and thick coat, it was difficult to say if it was the bouncer from The Coliseum.

Kettle appeared in the office and received a rapid update. He told Sal to rerun the recording.

Ashley nudged Barry and pointed at the second figure, who held the door for the big man and Hamish to leave the hospital. That person made a call when he got outside. His arms waved theatrically as he spoke.

'Lorenzo,' whispered Ashley.

'Gotcha,' growled Barry.

'Is it definitely him?' asked Emma.

'Roll it again, please,' said Ashley.

She watched it twice more.

'Yes. I've got his mobile number now, so we could check phone masts in the area, which would also put him at the scene, assuming he wasn't using a burner.'

'So, Lorenzo turned up at A & E,' said Emma, 'grabbed Hamish, made him disappear, then told us he knows nothing about it. There is a list of offences within that.'

Kettle came closer. 'What exactly are you saying?'

Ashley was still wide-eyed at Lorenzo's smooth ability to deceive them.

'We're pretty certain Lorenzo and Gianluca collected Hamish from the N & N, and Hamish has now vanished.'

'Okay. It doesn't mean Lorenzo has him. He may have taken him for breakfast, talked to him, then sent him on his way.'

'Surely an innocent person would have mentioned it yesterday. He lied to my face when he said he'd heard Hamish had walked out of his room.'

'That gives us grounds for a warrant to check for Hamish at Lorenzo's house. It's some distance from being chargeable, but he's certainly wasted our time. I suspect he'd insist Hamish told him he needed to leave the hospital, and he helped him. Then he'll say Hamish wanted to vanish and begged Lorenzo not to tell anyone until it was safe to do so.'

'It's a flimsy defence,' said Sal.

'Yes, but will Hamish say otherwise when we find him? Lorenzo would have ordered him to keep quiet. We still don't know what we're dealing with here. I have concerns for Hamish's safety, but surely Lorenzo isn't a danger to him.'

Kettle didn't appear convinced by his own argument.

'Could Lorenzo be responsible for all this?' asked Barry.

'What? Took his own brothers out?' asked Sal.

'I can't get my head around it either,' said Morgan.

Ashley looked at the other officers in the room. Sal, Barry, Hector, Ally, Zelda and Morgan were the only ones present. She glanced at Kettle.

'We don't want word reaching Lorenzo that we're coming,' she said. 'If Hamish is at his house, we can catch him red-handed.'

'Agreed. We'll be the only people who know this search warrant will be going down. Sal, sort the paperwork. Barry, Hector, Zelda, and Morgan, you'll be knocking on the door. Ally, you run the show because Ashley has a busy day ahead of her in Suffolk.'

Ashley involuntarily recoiled with envy at missing out. For a second, she considered missing the assessment centre, but swiftly realised that would be daft.

'Okay,' she said. 'I'd better set off. Happy hunting, guys. Keep me posted. Make sure someone visits Rocco's Fine Homes and questions them about Hamish and Max. Don't let Rocco know you're visiting. Maybe ask employees after they've left the building if nobody inside is helpful.'

Kettle shook his head at her. 'Leave! It's a tiring day, Ashley. And drive home afterwards, or I'll think you believe we can't cope without you.'

Ashley grinned at him.

'Sneaky, sir. I'll talk to you in the morning. I assume you're sending a team down to the Vampire Café.'

'Go!' they all shouted.

Kettle pointed towards the exit, but he was smiling.

Ashley picked up her coat and bag and headed downstairs. Jan was arriving and passed her on the stairs.

'Ashley,' he said. 'Before you leave, we traced the false plates for the van. They came from a breaker's yard that went bust years ago. They were for a Mini. We'll struggle to connect that up now.'

'Cheers, Jan. I'll see you tomorrow.'

'I also heard Tommaso had been sighted in Norwich town centre. A man with a foreign accent rang the helpline, but they were vague and didn't leave a name or contact number.'

'Those responsible have been smart so far. It was probably a distraction tactic,' she replied, then nodded firmly. 'Okay, wish me luck.'

'Good luck.'

She returned to her car, opened the satnav on her phone, and chose Suffolk's HQ as the destination. As she pulled out of the car park, she couldn't help focussing on the fact that if Lorenzo got a tip-off this time, they could narrow down who the informant was.

It would be one of the six other people in that room.

32

Ted Philbin swung his old Volvo estate into the car park on Blue Boar Lane. He raised an eyebrow when a blue Transit van accelerated from one of the other spaces. Ted had thought he'd have the place to himself seeing as there would barely be enough moonlight to see the paths. Saying that, he occasionally came across the odd pair of what he suspected were illicit lovers here from time to time.

He grabbed his flask of coffee, stepped out of his vehicle, and stared around at the silent gloom. Perfect. Dawn was twenty minutes away, but Harrison's Wood was small and familiar. If necessary, he had his torch. As he walked to the back of the car, his ears tuned into the forest, and he relaxed to the quietest of murmurs as the breeze tickled his skin. He calmed again. He strengthened. That was how he coped.

Ted stretched his neck, then opened the boot and Lucy, his Jack Russell, leapt out. She tore around and around, yelping, then hared off into the bushes. Ted shook his head at the lairy thing. Eight years old and she was still hyperactive. The dog had been a puppy when his wife, Kay, first started showing signs of trouble.

Kay loved the hound unconditionally and fussed over it throughout the day, even now, when she rarely showed emotion to anyone else.

His job, driving up and down Britain's main arteries, and a half-hour walk with Lucy at the start of each day, had kept him as sane and solid as the pooch was wild and frantic. Although in the house, around Kay, she remained calm and affectionate.

Kay's older sister did the long hours of care while he worked. Something neither had planned on having to do in their sixties, but together they'd managed. Lately, it seemed there would be no end. Ted shrugged. He'd decided at the beginning that dementia wouldn't beat them. Whatever happened. After all, he wasn't fighting a war, although it sometimes felt that way.

The stench of petrol caught him unawares as he turned a corner on the main path. The scent was so alien to the normal aromas of the damp wood. Lucy returned to him, sniffed the air, then raced off through the ferns.

Perhaps youngsters had got out of that van and tried to light a fire to keep warm. Ted wasn't too worried. Everything was too wet to burn. It intrigued him, though, and the tranquillity he'd been feeling had gone. He followed his dog. Occasionally, a joyrider stole a motorbike and drove it around these paths at dusk, but he'd not seen one for years. The last kid who'd done it had hit a post and nearly died, which was a salutary lesson for anybody else considering it.

As he came upon a clearing in the gloom, leaves fell about him like gentle snow. The carpet beneath cushioned his steps, which made him feel as if he were tiptoeing. But as the trees rustled around him, Ted was the one to have the surprise. The whispers in the branches ceased, as did his heart. His knees threatened to give way.

A young man, mouth taped, was slumped in a rickety

wooden armchair. His wrists were tied between his knees, and his ankles were bound together. Bundles of sticks and paper surrounded him. Planks had been placed across his thighs, over his shoulders and above him as if he were within the timber frame of a tent. A lantern rested on the arms of the chair. It contained a lit candle.

Ted stepped nearer, thinking the victim was unconscious, but the man's eyes blinked open. They swiftly focused on Ted's face and bulged, perhaps through pain, or more likely terror. Ted licked his lips. Was this person pleading with him to come closer or warning him to stay away?

'Are you okay?' asked Ted, who then felt stupid.

All the lad could do was tremble.

Ted traipsed around what could only be described as a pyre. When the wind blew the pungent, heavy air into his face, he gagged at the intrusive smell. Had everything been soaked in fuel? He eyed the flickering flame in the lantern and wondered what the chances of the fumes igniting were, even if the lantern wasn't knocked over by the person struggling.

Ted glanced into the darkness at the edge of his vision and worried whether he was alone. The wind caressed the treetops as though hushing them. Surely, the perpetrators meant this man to die. Maybe his abductors had thought nobody would come for a hike this early, and they would have plenty of time to watch their captive burn. Were they now watching him?

Ted paused in front of the victim and recalled the dark shapes in the cab of the blue van, who must have been responsible for this. A voice in his head told him he should be more concerned by the situation, but the previous eight years had taught him that he could cope with anything. Frustrated ranting, rage, and physical attacks coming out of the blue had become everyday experiences. So, for Ted, surprises held no power. It was as though he had a buffer to shock, which was just as well, or he'd have folded long ago.

Underneath the chair, firelighters were scattered. Ted looked up into the haunted eyes, which had started to roll. Despite the cool air, sweat poured down the youngster's face. Lucy sat next to Ted and howled.

Ted wondered if he should leave the wood, knowing he must if he wanted to get a signal to call for help, but would he return to a pile of ash?

Ted crouched and reached towards the lantern and the lad whimpered.

33

Ashley woke the next morning and breathed a sigh of relief. The assessment day was over. She had decided at the interview to be honest and reveal all her hopes and concerns. Whatever happened now, her participation in the decision had finished, which left her to concentrate on the case at hand.

She grabbed her phone and reread the text she'd received last night from Jan.

We arrived at Lorenzo's property, but no answer. His father, Rocco, came over as we prepared to break in. Rocco had a key and showed us around. Nothing to report. No sign of Hamish. Place looks like a rich man's bachelor pad.

Ashley recalled meeting the polished Lorenzo. He didn't seem the type to do without female company. Perhaps he enjoyed playing the field. Ashley tried to listen to her gut feeling, but she didn't have one. That was unusual and in itself still spoke volumes. It meant the solution would likely come out of left field, and whenever people were unaccounted for, events often came to an abrupt conclusion. That didn't bode well.

The sky was a deep blue and the air crisp when she stepped from the house not long after seven. It was sunglasses and warm jumper weather. Ashley loved this time of year, yet her mood sank the more she thought about the missing men.

Ashley turned the radio on and turned up the volume for 'Dancing Queen', but for once, she didn't sing along.

She took the quicker route through North Walsham but was oblivious to the changing sky as it shifted from purple through to aqua, while an orange glow blossomed to her left over the sea. It wasn't a surprise when her phone rang. She pulled over and answered the call from Emma.

'Morning, Sarge. Control have just informed me they're dealing with a 999 call. A dog walker in Harrison's Wood discovered a man first thing sitting on top of what sounds like a funeral pyre. Uniform and Sal, who was on call, are at the scene. An IC1 was tied up, then a small petrol-soaked bonfire was gathered around him, with a kind of miner's oil lantern to supply the spark. The guy's clothing appears to have been doused as well. I assume the idea was if he struggled, the lamp would fall and ignite the fuel, and up he'd go.'

'Christ. What's the situation? Is the victim safe?'

Emma barked a short laugh.

'Sorry. Perhaps I should have started with him being alive. The gent who found him was worried about booby traps, but in the end, he poured his coffee over the flame. I had a word with the response officer, who said Ted Philbin, a lorry driver in his sixties, then pulled the guy off the seat. He was only loosely secured.'

'I don't suppose he needed to be strapped in. One move and boom.'

'Exactly, but someone went to a lot of effort for him to survive.'

'Yes, excellent point. What time was all this?'

'Six-thirtyish, so it was pretty dark. Perhaps they weren't expecting to be interrupted.'

Ashley nibbled her finger.

'No,' she finally said. 'I don't think so. They killed Paolo efficiently enough. It's not a big forest. Whoever was responsible would hear another vehicle arrive, never mind a dog crashing through the undergrowth as it approached. They could have flung a match in at any point if they wanted it done.'

'That's true, and a lone, older man wouldn't have concerned them. Look at the violence they've inflicted already.'

'Agreed. Hurting him would not bother them at all.'

'It has to be a them. Three people, or at least two strong ones.'

'There would've been plenty of planning, too.'

'Right, so they weren't trying to murder him. It was another scare tactic.'

'Yes, although I doubt they'd have been too upset if he had burned, but maybe it wasn't a warning to the victim, but to someone else. I take it we don't know his name.'

'No, the victim had slipped into a deep state of shock by the time the response vehicle arrived. He was in poor condition. Wearing only a T-shirt and jeans, no shoes or socks, no ID, but he's awake now, and the ambulance guys are talking to him. They'll be leaving for the Norfolk & Norwich shortly.'

'I'll head straight to the hospital and meet them there. Anyone else in except you?'

'Bee's called in to say she'll be late.'

'Is she okay?'

'Yes, just didn't sleep with Bruce moving around.'

'Bruce?'

'After Bruce Lee, for his karate expertise.'

Ashley laughed. She had a wide range of emotions when she thought of Bhavini being a mother. Naturally, she was a little jealous, wistful, maybe, but also proud and pleased. Ashley felt relieved that the overriding feeling was one of happiness for her friend.

'Are you still there?' asked Emma. 'Jan's arrived. Shall I send him down to the N & N?'

'Yes, do that. I heard the search of Lorenzo's house didn't help. Did I miss anything else yesterday?'

'Morgan has been investigating the comments from that woman, Drita Grbić, who was found in the wood with the other lady who escaped the brothel.'

'Oh, God. That was at Harrison's Wood, too. Perhaps it's a link.'

'You're right. I suppose they're a different kind of victim, but it'd be quite a coincidence if it wasn't connected. Morgan said it took a while to locate Olga's family after her death because they had no surname. Turned out Olga wasn't her first name either. It was Jelena. As you know, folk disappear all the time with these human traffickers, especially women.'

'We'd better refer to her as Jelena from now on.'

'Sure. Jelena was finally linked to Montenegro's capital. Morgan said he'll talk to you when you get back, but he's found a number for the local police in Podgorica. They helped repatriate the body and liaised with the family.'

'Is Morgan in yet?'

'No, Ally and he are on a first-aid refresher today. Morgan emailed you the details.'

'Okay. I'll ring you as soon as I find out what's what at the hospital.'

'Wait a minute. Sal called in on another line. He's got the name for the poor bloke in the pyre.'

'Who is it?'

'Hang on.'

Ashley listened to Emma shouting in the background, then she came back on the line.

'Max Vialli.'

34

Ashley drove leisurely towards the hospital so she could focus on the case. The nurses would assess Max when he arrived, so she had time to mull over her next moves. The first consideration was when to tell Max's father they had found one of his two missing sons. She assumed Rocco would then inform Lorenzo. The concern, and the last thing Ashley wanted, was Max disappearing as Hamish had.

Jan was wearing sunglasses and leaning against his vehicle in the car park when Ashley pulled in.

'Morning,' said Ashley.

'Morning.'

'You got here quick. How are you?'

'Good, you?'

'Good.'

Ashley couldn't help smiling at him. Jan wasn't one to waste words.

'I went in,' he said. 'They said to come back in fifteen after they've settled him.'

Ashley didn't think that sounded promising.

'Come on,' she said. 'Let's grab a coffee. I'll give Kettle a quick ring. Treharne has another wood to search.'

Ashley spent ten minutes on the phone with her boss while Jan bought them drinks. They took a seat.

'Big surprise Max is alive,' he said.

'Yes, my thoughts exactly.'

'Did you hear about the van?'

'No.'

'When the gentleman who found Max reached the wood, there was a van leaving.'

'An old blue one?'

'Yes. Uniform are on it, and all the road cameras are primed for it to appear.'

'What do you reckon is going on, Jan?'

'I can't see this Rocco guy being implicated in people trafficking, nor this Lorenzo. Possibly drugs. Goes hand in hand with nightclubs. Perhaps they acquire girls from the Vampires when they've been brought into the country, but you'd have expected more intel from a range of sources. Those involved let things slip over time. Snippets built up.'

'Funny how Lorenzo knew not to be at his house.'

'Yes. That's worrying. Let's hope he doesn't turn up for a while.'

'I think we have grounds for taking him to the station, so maybe that would be a bad thing.'

'What are the odds it's Rocco who arrives here?'

'Short,' replied Ashley glumly.

Ashley and Jan left the café and trudged through the doors into A & E. Sadly, it was a place she knew too well. Jan went to speak to a PC inside while Ashley stood behind an old man who was the only one in the queue at the reception desk. She felt a tap on her elbow. It was Dr Bandera, looking like a different person.

'Business or personal?' asked the doctor.

'Definitely business. You remember the young man who was buried?'

'That kind of experience is hard to forget. I even dreamt about it.'

'Well, the friend he was out with the night he was missing has been discovered in another wood.'

'Buried?'

'No. He was also alive, but at risk of being burned to death.'

'But he wasn't?'

'No. He would have arrived within the hour. Have you just started?'

'I wasn't due to start until midday, but they called. I've been away on a two-day training course. Follow me and I'll take you through. What happened to the guy we cared for last time, Hamish?'

Ashley wanted to be honest with the helpful doctor.

'We don't know.'

Bandera frowned, then shrugged. It wasn't her problem.

'The bed would have come in handy.'

Ashley was unsure if it was an attempt at humour, so she didn't comment.

The hospital felt different. Busy still, but with more efficient control than wartime panic. Bandera chatted to one of the nurses, then directed the officers to a side room.

She paused outside.

'Like Hamish, Max got agitated in A & E, so they brought him here. There didn't seem to be any critical injuries, so they decided it was better to keep him calm. He didn't reply when they queried if anyone had hurt him, but apparently he walked down here okay.'

She pushed the door open to reveal Max lying on a bed in a hospital gown, seemingly asleep.

His face was filthy, but it was more the look of someone who hadn't washed for a week, rather than fresh dirt. A young nurse sat beside Max.

'How is he?' asked Bandera.

'Quiet,' she said, turning to them. 'He's clearly been through a tough ordeal. We'll monitor him for shock.'

Ashley noticed the nurse's skin was in rude health, but she wore the gaze of a forty-year-old. Even so, her look was nothing compared to the haunted visage of the man on the bed, whose eyes had opened. Ashley recalled TV footage of the aftermath of earthquakes, where survivors were pulled from fallen buildings, days after the event. Gaunt and wracked by exhaustion, starvation and dehydration, with expressions that shifted from relief to disbelief, then guilt and despair.

Ashley had a quandary. An experience like this might push Max's mental health over the edge. If it wasn't already there. His brother, Tommaso, was nowhere to be seen though, and there could be others who'd been taken, or more people facing the threat of abduction. Paolo was dead. The culprits were still free. MIT was nowhere close to finding them.

Investigations were always a jigsaw. Sometimes they solved the investigation without all the pieces. In this case, they had no idea of the puzzle size, or even what the picture was. At that moment, Max was by far their best hope.

'Can you talk to us, Max?' asked Jan. 'Tell us what happened?'

Max shook his head.

'We're trying to find your brother. Can you help?'

Max shook his head again. A tear slid down his cheek. He rubbed it off, which left a cleaner patch.

'After what you've been through, we know it's hard,' said Ashley. 'There are specialists who can support you. Would it help to chat with them?'

'No,' he muttered.

'Max can stay in this room,' said the nurse. 'Someone will be with him all the time until he's stable. I asked him if he wanted something to assist with sleeping, but he was clear about not wanting anything.'

Ashley licked her lips. She glanced at Jan, who nodded. They had to ask.

'Max. Please explain what happened.'

'No,' he whispered and closed his eyes.

Ashley wondered if having Rocco there might be beneficial. He would insist on knowing where his son had been for six days, but at least then, Max could lean on him. He would need all the support he could get.

'Has anybody contacted his next of kin?' she asked.

The nurse shrugged. 'I don't think so. Max didn't say anything apart from his name. He refused a shower and only let us touch him to clean his wounds, but he did hand over his clothes. He had nothing to identify him, and no phone.'

'Max,' said Ashley. 'Shall I ring your father to tell him you're here?'

It was like finding someone dead on a battlefield and have them turn to you and open their eyes. Max came alive. His eyebrows raised.

'No. Do not let anyone know I am here,' he shouted.

'You're safe here, Max, but your brother's still missing,' said Jan.

'Tommaso,' replied Max slowly.

'Yes,' said Ashley. 'We believe he vanished on Saturday shortly after he left the house for the airport.'

Max swallowed. His voice was back to a whisper.

'I've seen Tommaso. They took him away.'

35

Jan carefully pulled over a seat and took out his pocket notebook. Ashley moved closer to the bed. Bandera asked the nurse to leave, saying she'd stay.

'When?' asked Ashley.

Max shook his head.

'Can you tell me where?' she asked.

Max sniffed.

Ashley smiled at him. She wondered if it was wise to push him any further at this point. After a minute of silence, she rose from her seat, stood next to him, and rested a hand on his arm. Max looked up at her.

'Okay, I'll try.'

'That's all we ask.'

'I never knew the location,' he said. 'A room. A house.' A brief grim chuckle came out. 'Just a normal home, but I seem to remember no internal doors.' Max blinked, and for the first time his eyes appeared to focus on what he'd been through.

'Max, this could be really important to our investigation,' said

Ashley. 'It's vital we find out what happened so we help anyone else who might be in danger.'

Max's chin wobbled as he spoke.

'They kept us in armchairs, tied up, blindfolds, gags, bright lights, beatings.'

'Us?'

'Hamish and me. I listened to his cries and screams. He would have heard mine. Then I woke up and I couldn't hear him breathing. They'd forced me to swallow pills.' Max wrung his hands. 'You have to believe me!'

'We believe you.'

'Later, when I'd lost all track of time, my blindfold was yanked off. They helped Tommaso into the room.'

'Alive or dead?'

'He was still standing, but he was in tatters. Blood all over him. Only one eye was open. They wanted answers.' He choked a sob back. 'So many questions.'

'Who was asking them?'

'I don't know.'

'Big or small? Male? Female?'

'I struggled to take my eyes off Tommaso. I think there were two. A bigger guy, and a thinner, shorter one.'

'Both male?'

'Hard to say. Could have been a woman. Slim, anyway. They had balaclavas. You know, like paramilitary. Not English.'

'Irish?'

'No.'

'Could you guess their nationalities?'

'No. Only one asked the questions. His English was okay, but there was another who spoke with him. Deep and guttural. Perhaps he was Russian.'

'So, they were both men.'

Max rubbed the side of his head.

'God, it's all hazy.'

'Us knowing the number of people involved is significant. Did you hear three voices?' she asked.

Max cringed at his memories. 'Hearing was all I had for most of the time. And pain.'

'They hurt you again and again?'

'Yes,' he whispered. 'But not like they'd hurt Tommaso. They dragged him away. Oh my God. Hamish!'

Ashley remembered Max didn't know Hamish was safe. Probably safe.

'Max. Hamish was found near Bacton Wood on Sunday morning.'

'Oh, God. No, no, no.'

Tears streamed down Max's face. Not sobs nor weeping, more water pouring from something that was broken beyond repair. As if all hope were gone.

'He's alive. Hamish was here in this hospital. He's okay.'

'He is?'

Max gritted his teeth and lifted himself up onto his elbows. His gown moved and Ashley noticed the identical SPQR tattoo that Hamish had on the same arm.

'Thank you. He's really okay?'

Ashley swallowed.

'Yes, but there's some confusion around his location.'

At Max's frown, she explained.

'Hamish told us how he'd been buried in a wood and climbed out of the hole. He had injuries, but he would have recovered. Then he got up from his bed and left. It seems two people came to collect him. We're not sure who they were.'

'Russians?'

'More likely friends.'

'Who?'

Ashley didn't comment.

Max spat out the answer, but there was also concern on his face. Or possibly fear.

'Lorenzo.'

Ashley's mind tried to follow the implications of Max's guess.

'Why do you think it was Lorenzo who came?' asked Jan.

'They kept asking the same questions, but I don't know anything. That's what I told them. Nothing. I go to work, little else. The nightclub is nothing to do with me. I just want to be left alone with my friend.'

'Tell us, Max. We have to locate Hamish and Tommaso. They're likely to be alive like you.'

Max laughed again. A slow cackle that tailed off.

'I died a thousand times in that room. I accepted it.'

'Can you guess what Lorenzo has got himself involved in?' asked Ashley.

'No.'

'Has he tangled himself up with the wrong people?'

'I can't talk to the police. You understand why.'

'Tell me why.'

Max's head flopped back down on the pillow. Saliva drooled from his mouth. His face scrunched up.

Ashley could see he was closing down. She would get little more out of him, but what was he saying? That Max wasn't involved in anything illegal, but Lorenzo was? And why wouldn't he want his father to know he was here? What was his relationship with Lorenzo like? Troubled, by the sounds of it.

Max also seemed to have scant concern for Tommaso's whereabouts.

'Why go to their club?' she asked.

'They think I'm a liability. It's a way of keeping them off our backs. Hamish and I should have run when we had the chance.'

Ashley noted his last statement but didn't probe.

'You can talk to us,' she said. 'We can protect you.'

Max grunted. 'No more questions.'

Ashley nodded. She was about to leave when Max barked out, 'Wait!'

'What is it?'

'Find Hamish, and I'll give you all I know.'

Max turned to face the wall, but his voice was loud.

'Doctor. Knock me out, and don't tell anyone I'm here. I can't take any more.'

36

Bandera left the room. She returned with the nurse, who was holding a medicine tray.

'We're going to leave now, Max,' said Ashley. 'I'll come back tomorrow, hopefully with good news for you.'

Max didn't reply. His shoulders moved up and down in an unnatural rhythm from his breathing.

Ashley and Jan waited outside until Bandera finished with Max. Bandera appeared concerned.

'He'll be out and then drowsy for the next twenty-four hours,' she said. 'No visitors, as he asked. Will you be putting an officer on his door, after what happened to Hamish?'

Bandera smiled sweetly. Ashley reciprocated.

'Yes, of course. Jan can arrange that now. There's an officer in A & E in the meantime.'

'I'll ask one of our security guys to come while we wait for your cogs to turn.'

'Okay, we'll stay until they arrive. Can you check to see if anyone has turned up looking for him?'

Bandera raised an eyebrow. Ashley laughed.

'Sorry. You probably want to focus on saving lives.'

'It's okay. I'll find out when I ring Security. I need to get an update from Reception and the charge nurse, anyway. Stay here and I'll be back in fifteen minutes.'

Jan called Control after she'd gone while Ashley checked her emails. Morgan had sent her a police contact number in Podgorica. Ashley had a few minutes, so she copied the telephone number and rang it.

The female voice that answered sounded Russian, although Ashley's only experience of the language was Dolph Lundgren in *Rocky IV*.

Ashley spoke slowly with her request, then the woman transferred her without further comment. Another voice with a similar accent picked up, this time male. He simply said, 'Hello.'

'Hi, my name is DS Ashley Knight, from Norfolk Constabulary's Major Investigation Team in England.'

'Good morning. I am Inspector Djokovic. How may I help?'

'I'm ringing regarding a young lady from your country who died over here in a wood about a year ago.'

'Jelena Popovic.'

Ashley's eyebrows rose.

'Yes,' she said.

'Don't be too surprised. Even out here in the wilds of Montenegro, it is not a usual occurrence. Did you know our country is one of the fastest-growing economies in eastern Europe?'

'I didn't. How familiar are you with what happened?'

'Very. The girl was the sister of a rich, influential businessperson and politician in the city. I am acquainted with him and was informed at the time of his desperation and sorrow.'

'I'm investigating a case here, and I was wondering if the incidents might be connected to Jelena's death. Maybe some kind of revenge.'

'You have called a long way to go fishing. There are official rules on such things. Avenues to take.'

Ashley smiled. His English was excellent, and she could detect a smile behind the accent.

'Not fishing, just after a little background. None of the new victims are Montenegrin. I have no suspects.'

'What you're wondering is if she had any family who would hit back. Am I right?'

Djokovic was certainly on the ball.

'I would be curious about that,' she said.

'It must be getting on for six months ago when we found out. A private investigator from our end went to talk to your officers, which Jelena's relatives paid for. We are unfamiliar with your customs and cities, which are vastly different from ours. I understand there were no leads. It seems they applied for positions in London. Administrative roles in large companies with a room included. Secretaries and translators. That kind of plausible thing. They would swiftly get a visa later if they work hard.'

'Jobs that don't exist. Twenty to a house. Visas that never arrive.'

'Yes, and passports are taken at the start. By then, it's too late. They have entered the belly of the beast, and you can imagine how it ends.'

'Why would she risk that if her brother was rich and influential?'

'It was four years ago they left. He was wealthy, but that's not to say his family was, and he wasn't a politician at that time. The trafficked girls are naïve, and they can pay the ultimate price. This would have put a flame in his heart to do something, but it is extremely hard. There is shame and silence from the victims, and those things are black curtains to the investigations.'

'What's the brother's name?'

'Dragan. Dragan Popovic.'

'What about a father or uncles?'

'No, I don't think so.'

'You said they. Did Jelena go with a friend?'

'She went with her sister.'

37

Ashley almost swore in the face of Bandera, who had returned and was standing next to her. Ashley held a finger up to her.

'She had a sister?' she said to Djokovic.

'Yes. A girl of incredible beauty.'

Ashley hadn't read the files, but surely Ally's team would have mentioned a sibling.

'That's the first I've heard of a sister.'

'That is perhaps because her trail went cold in Slovenia. There are rumours that an organisation or person called Typhon is the cause of much misery in Eastern Europe. Or so they suspect. We know nothing of him except his legend. Their low-level workers occasionally fall into our traps, but they comprehend little of the network they are in. We put them in prison. Ours are different from yours. The other inmates have been known to kill them. That way silence is preserved, and the myth grows.'

'And what did Dragan do about this second sister? What was her name?'

'Jasmina. Europol managed to track the traffickers responsible for moving the girls out of Montenegro and we arrested them.

They had been hired to take a collection of young women from our country and others nearby, like Kosovo and Serbia, to Slovenia. They knew nothing more. I expect they committed the usual crimes by such men. Robbing them. Threatening them.'

'Rape and beatings?'

'Actually, not that. This group said they received explicit orders not to damage the goods.'

'Interesting.'

'Yes. As I mentioned, once the passport is gone and the victims are in a different country, their fates are tied to the people traffickers. They have to hope they survive. All they know at that point is they are the lambs to slaughter. If you follow my meaning.'

'Yes, and even if they make it alive to their final destination, what's waiting can be worse than the journey.'

'*Da*, that is the truth.'

Ashley couldn't help thinking of the beautiful women at Lorenzo's club.

'This Jasmina was attractive, you said.'

'Incredibly. To look at her face was almost painful, and as for her eyes. If you had the choice to stare into them, or visit heaven, then paradise would wait. Or so they tell me.'

Ashley laughed along with him. She suspected she'd enjoy staring into Inspector Djokovic's eyes.

'She could have been a model, then?'

'Perhaps, but for a Montenegrin, she was small. The whole family is short.'

'I don't suppose this Typhon is Italian?'

'No. They say he is the product of the wars here. A bastard who crawled from the inferno of those days. Maybe Kosovan, maybe Slovenian, Yugoslav, nobody knows. Definitely eastern-European, although it's funny you should mention that. The gang we caught talked like the canaries in the hope of leniency. They admitted there were two sisters. The leader recognised the photos of both of them. He recalled the moment Jasmina was separated from the rest.'

Ashley grimaced.

'And?' she croaked.

'He said the men who took her were Italian.'

38

Ashley could almost hear gears tumbling and the pieces slotting into position in her head.

'Thank you. You've been extremely helpful. I have a lot of questions, but you're right, I should run this through official channels now there's a possible link. There'll be an authorisation information request completed and sent to you today. Could you make sure it's approved quickly at your end?'

'No problem. Give me your email, and I'll send you my direct contact details.'

'Thank you. Last question. Is the gang leader who trafficked Jelena and Jasmina out of Montenegro still alive?'

'We knew he would be in danger if we put him in jail, so we placed him in a secure house in the countryside. The cities here are civilised, but outside them it is quiet. People lead simple lives. He should have been safe, but both he and his handlers were murdered a month later. I'm afraid we have rats. We left two men protecting him but they were taken out with a knife. Throats cut. The informant bled to death, impaled on a stake in the garden, as though Dracula himself had killed him.'

Ashley's ears pricked up.

'Interesting. Have you heard of a group by the name of the Vampires?'

'No.'

'Pity. Perhaps this Typhon was responsible?'

'It's where my bet would be. Information is often bought for little money, and wages here can be low, which means there are leaks everywhere.'

Ashley knew that only too well but said nothing. Ashley gave him her email address.

'Thanks again, Inspector.'

'Call me Ivan. I will speak to Dragan for you. See if he knows more. I heard he had been thinking about sending another private detective, but if you can't solve it, then what is the chance for someone from our country?'

'This Typhon sounds like he's decided the best way to keep his secrets is to take out anyone who could implicate him. He might include those who did business with him. Italian or otherwise.'

'That may be so. Good luck with your investigation. I'll talk to you soon.'

Ashley's mind was already whirring as she said goodbye. Bandera had wandered away to give her privacy, but she had just returned with Jan and a security officer in uniform.

'Mr Allardyce has been briefed,' said Jan. 'He understands not to let anyone inside without Dr Bandera's permission and that he will be relieved by an officer team shortly. Dr Bandera has found Max a room elsewhere with his name down as unknown.'

'Perfect.'

Two orderlies arrived, spoke to Bandera, then strolled into Max's room to move him. Ashley glanced at Max as they wheeled him out. He was quietly snoring and finally looked at peace.

Allardyce went with the orderlies, which left her and Jan with Bandera.

'Are the hospital staff in any danger?' asked Bandera.

Ashley shook her head.

'I don't believe so, but I'll inform the senior investigating officer for this investigation when I leave here. DCI Kettle will be cautious, so you may find he liaises with your security to strengthen things here.'

'Strengthen things?' asked Bandera with a wry smile.

Ashley chuckled.

'Stern men and women with guns might appear, just in case.'

'Fair enough.'

Ashley didn't want to enter into specifics with the doctor, but there had been an elevation of risk since Hamish was there.

'A man has lost his life connected to this, so everyone should be vigilant.'

'You'd be surprised by how many gunshots and knife wounds I've seen over the last few years. Britain is changing.'

Ashley couldn't argue with that. 'I know.'

'Sometimes the mental scars of the injuries are worse than the physical. It makes me fearful about Hamish's and Max's futures after both having gone through this.'

'Do you mean they'll struggle to get over it?' asked Jan.

'Sorry, I'll explain. I told you I found it hard to erase the Hamish incident from my mind. Well, if these criminals were trying to murder people, then they've been doing a rotten job. There have to be easier ways than going to these lengths, even if they were sending out a warning, but it dawned on me what the reason might be.'

'Go on,' urged Jan.

'Think about it. If you kill, you get your revenge once. But damage someone's soul, and they suffer forever.'

39

Ashley returned to her car and drove behind Jan's on the way to the operations and communications centre. The doctor's words rattled around in her head. Maybe this Typhon killed the subordinates in Europe, but only warned his partners. Or did he want them to suffer first? Perhaps he wasn't anything to do with this at all. It could still be a gang war between the Romans and the Vampires. The latter were eastern-European. It was annoying that Morgan and Ally were on a course, but she could speak to Zelda from their team before the next meeting.

When Ashley reached OCC, she nipped to the canteen for a sandwich, and noticed Zelda sitting on her own.

'I hear you've had a busy morning,' said Zelda.

'You could say that. Got a minute?'

Ashley spent ten minutes bringing her up to speed.

'Damn,' replied Zelda. 'I read most of the file, and I saw there was a sister who was missing elsewhere in Europe. The investigators left it there, assuming she never arrived in England. Are you saying she did?'

'No. I'm just throwing shit at the blanket and hoping some sticks.'

'Charming saying. I need to borrow it.'

'Lorenzo and Tommaso have foreign workers at their bars,' said Ashley. 'It's feasible she still came over.'

'It's possible she was so pretty that they transported her over separately to make sure she arrived in one piece.'

'That seems unlikely. The trafficker they caught mentioned they had strict instructions to bring all the girls to the UK unharmed. It sounds as if they took them to Rotterdam port in Holland and brought them across in containers on lorries. Roll on, roll off.'

'These operations tend to be undertaken by a chain of gangs. Separate groups facilitate the movement through their country to the next border. Although Drita, the one who survived, said her and Olga ended up working in a small brothel. Seems unlikely a man like Lorenzo would be interested in the grubby end of the market.'

'Some men get off on the sleaze aspect of it.'

Zelda pulled a face. 'That's true.'

'Does the file have clear pictures of both girls in it?'

'Yes, I believe so. Passport photos.'

'Print a few copies off and bring them to the meeting, would you? I may have a plan.'

'Uh-oh!'

* * *

Ashley spent the rest of the day catching up on her admin. Just before the teams all gathered at four, she rang the hospital to check up on Max. A protection team was in place. Max was asleep, but his vitals were okay. Bandera had been to Max's room a few minutes before Ashley called. Nobody had looked for Max in A & E, or, as far as she knew, contacted the switchboard. Ashley walked to the meeting knowing her idea might work.

As Kettle started the discussion, Ashley noticed Hector wasn't present. She couldn't remember seeing him in the office. Kettle immediately gave the floor to Ashley, so she stood and updated them. She handed over to Barry to talk through his and Emma's visit to Rocco's warehouse.

'We arrived and went to the reception desk. It was almost as if they were expecting us. We waited ten minutes, then a manager took us on a guided tour. It was a smart operation. All the kitchens and bathrooms units are handmade at a factory outside Milan. The marble comes from Tuscany. Both are imported here and distributed all over the UK.'

'Does it come through Rotterdam by container?'

Barry looked over at Emma.

'No,' she said. 'They drive it here. It travels through the tunnel. They had the odd bit of damage when they used shipping, so it wasn't worth the saving. I'm guessing the profit margins are large.'

'Perhaps this Jasmina was brought to England that way,' said Ashley.

Barry shrugged. 'Possibly. It's a lot of trouble and risk for one woman.'

Barry smiled as a torrent of abuse hit him. Even Kettle had a chuckle at his expense.

'On that note, Barry, we'll move on,' he said. 'It seems doubtful Rocco's involved in this. Zelda, you have two photographs to pass around.'

Zelda distributed the A4 pictures of Jasmina and Jelena, and Barry let out a low whistle. Ashley stared at her copy and was lost for words. Jelena looked a pleasant young lady, but her sister, Jasmina, was something else. There was an ethereal quality to her that pulled you into the page. The photograph appeared professional. It was hard to believe it was a passport picture.

Kettle spent a few seconds staring at it.

'She's striking, but we've had no intel that she's in this country. Nobody's seen her for four years. Ashley, did you uncover why nobody came looking for them back then?'

'Not a clear reason. Zelda?'

'It'll be the usual. The family won't know exactly where they were heading. The women who've been trafficked usually feel ashamed they've been duped and abused. Time ticks by. Trails go cold.'

'This is all interesting, but we desperately need to find Lorenzo or Hamish,' said Kettle.

Nobody replied and Kettle swore under his breath.

'Anyone familiar with a person or organisation called Typhon?'

'I've heard the name before,' said Zelda. 'We have intel from abroad that Typhon exists, but no one we've picked up has ever mentioned it. I'll check on the PNC and with Ally. He should know more.'

'Right,' said Kettle. 'What about Rocco? Was he at his warehouse?'

'No,' said Emma. 'The manager said he'd been there earlier, though.'

'Okay. It's interesting Max turned up, but not Tommaso. And, Jan, you said Max claimed to have seen Tommaso wherever they were?'

'Yes. We suspect their abductors rented a house, and that's where they kept them.'

'We could really do with finding it, but it's worse than a needle in a haystack in that part of the county. There are so many isolated houses and bungalows, cottages, caravans and chalets, plenty of which are only used during the summer. The place they're using could be anywhere within a half-hour's drive.'

Emma cleared her throat.

'One minor point to mention. We hung around outside and chatted to a few of the workers when they were leaving at lunchtime,' she said. 'They were happy employees. The only slight negatives we heard concerned Hamish. A woman implied he wasn't the most dependable. One of the blokes joked he must be shagging the boss's daughter.'

'Sounds as if he's doing the boss's son,' said Barry.

'Yes, I think we all got that, Barry,' said Kettle. 'Let's get the paperwork up to date before we go home tonight. Treharne's team has begun in Harrison's Wood. I have the feeling if we don't uncover something new, Tommaso is going to appear shortly, anyway.'

'Is Lorenzo's nightclub open for business?' asked Ashley.

'No. Their website has an error message,' said Sal. 'There was no answer when I called, but their Insta page and Facebook said it's closed all week due to water damage.'

A few tuts spread through the room. Ashley knew it would have been helpful to visit the venue when it was operating. Revellers usually revisited the same establishment if they'd had a fun time previously. The bar staff would also all have been there. Even if Lorenzo had told them to keep quiet, they could get something from them. If they found an employee who felt poorly treated, they might prove highly informative.

'There'll be no leaking pipes in there,' said Kettle. 'It makes me suspect Lorenzo is holed up with Hamish. Maybe in that nightclub. If we have nothing more by tomorrow, we'll try for a search warrant.'

'Perhaps Lorenzo's been taken by the kidnappers,' said Zelda. 'They might have recaptured Hamish at the same time.'

Kettle looked over at Ashley.

'That doesn't ring true,' she said. 'Rocco understands we're probably his best shot at finding his family. And currently he only has one son whose liberty is intact. He'd be onto me if he couldn't locate Lorenzo. I wouldn't be shocked if Rocco knows where he is. Hence him not answering his mobile to me.'

'I'm about sick of this Rocco using us like his own team of PIs. Ashley, can you track him down?'

'We could use ANPR to narrow down where his car has been. Do we have enough suspicion to ask for his call records?'

'Probably not. Unfortunately, being unhelpful isn't breaking any of our laws.'

'I might be able to do better than that, anyway,' said Ashley. 'He isn't aware Max is safe yet. I'm sure if Rocco knew, he, or someone he's instructed, would head straight to the hospital.'

'But Max told us he didn't want anyone to know he was in the N & N.'

'Yes, but we don't have to reveal his location. I'll text Rocco the news that Max has been discovered alive, but nothing more. He might ring me, but if he doesn't, he'll guess where the most likely place Max would be sent to.'

'A & E, where we'll be waiting?'

'Yes. I expect Rocco to remain evasive, but we'll learn more from how he behaves.'

'That's true.'

'And who's to say Max gets what he wants? This is a police investigation and other lives are at risk, including that of his own brother. He knows more than he's told us.'

'Yes, this is much bigger than him.'

'It might be wise to double Max's guard if we do this, but I don't think he's in danger now.'

Kettle pondered her plan.

'Why not text Rocco and say we've found Max, and he's alive and relatively unscathed? Tell him Max is helping us with our inquiries.'

Ashley grinned.

'That's an even better idea. Rocco will come straight here.'

40

Ashley stayed behind after the discussion closed and sent the text. Kettle didn't leave the room either.

'Assuming he takes the bait, who will you interview Rocco with?' he asked. 'It's a shame Hector's not here. He seems to unsettle the suspects. Sorry, I mean people kind enough to help us with our investigations.'

Ashley gave Kettle's joke a slight nod, but Hector hadn't told her he was away.

'Where is he?' she asked.

'He had a meeting in London, so he left at midday. Should be back tomorrow to spend the day with Ally.'

'Was his meeting today to do with his future?'

'Do I look like his secretary?'

Ashley knew the job Hector had been offered in the private sector was based in Highbury, north London, so suspected that was where he'd gone. She smiled at her boss.

'I think you'd make a great secretary.'

'Cheeky.'

'I'll take Sal in with me. Rocco's into appearances, so he might underestimate him.'

'Good idea. I'll be here until late.'

Kettle looked pained.

'What is it?' she asked.

'Our investigation is moving too slowly.'

Ashley had to agree.

'I know. Hamish was taken to a wood from wherever they're being held, then Paolo, now Max. It's likely Tommaso's going to appear in a forest soon.'

She didn't need to add that the pertinent fact would be whether they found him dead or alive. Kettle stood to leave.

'I'll talk to you later.'

'Before you disappear, Max has taken a sedative today, but I reckon I can get him to break ranks tomorrow. He doesn't seem the type to be involved in anything dodgy, and that's my gut talking. I believe he's in a loving relationship with Hamish. It's more than possible Lorenzo is holding Hamish in a place we'd never find. I assume for his safety, but it might also be to stop him chatting with us. Perhaps it's a property under company ownership, which Max is aware of. If I persuade him love trumps loyalty, we'll have our first real insight into what's happening.'

'Excellent. Remember, there's a killer about, and who knows what the Viallis are capable of? We don't want to wander in between warring factions when we're only armed with sharp tongues.'

Ashley hadn't noticed Barry hanging around just outside the doorway of the room until Kettle stopped in front of him.

'You look shifty,' said Kettle to Barry.

'I prefer to call it focused.'

'Hmm.'

When Kettle had left the room, Ashley beckoned Barry over.

'Sal's interviewing with me, if that's what you're after.'

'No, it's not that.'

'Go on.'

'I was wondering if you fancied hanging out at the weekend, assuming we're not busy at work.'

'You appear to be confused about what splitting up means.'

Barry's expression was blank for a few seconds.

'Just kidding,' he said with an unconvincing smile. 'It's something else. Sal and I were talking about how Rocco was told Hamish was at the hospital the morning he was brought in, yet he doesn't know Max is there.'

'Go on.'

'It made me consider who isn't working today.'

'The nurse who gave out the information?'

'Come on, there is no nurse. Think. Nobody's spilled the beans about Max's location.'

'Yes. That had occurred to me.'

'Ally and Morgan aren't in. They're on a course.'

'I can see a two-plus-two thing coming here. Loads of us have been in and out, including Hector.'

Barry waved a finger. 'I knew he was bent.'

'Get on with it, Barry.'

'Our team is straight. I'm sure of it, but I am suspicious of Morgan, Ally, and Zelda. You got me thinking when you mentioned visiting that hotel to see if our snitch had returned. I'll go to Rocco's distribution centre tomorrow and find out if anyone knows them. They'd have no reason to have been there unless they were up to no good. I can tell by your face you don't like my plan, but it's worth a shot.'

Ashley understood it wouldn't provide absolute proof, but somebody in their organisation was giving out information. It had to stop.

'Aren't you off tomorrow?' she asked.

'Yeah, but I'll come into the office and take some sneaky photos of those three. If nothing's occurring, everyone will be here. I'll act casual. Then I'll leave and head to Rocco's and ask around. If nobody's seen them there, then it's cool. We'll forget about it.'

'Okay. I appreciate the extra effort, but be discreet.'

'It's my middle name.'

'I thought that was pinhead.'

Barry chuckled.

'We could meet up, you know, from time to time. No strings.'

Ashley huffed. 'Let me explain. When people are lonely, they attach themselves to relationships that aren't healthy for them.'

'Are you referring to domestic abuse?'

'I suppose a few end up like that, but no, I'm talking about couples not being a close enough fit to begin with. If partners don't have the same goals, or aren't willing to grow together, then a relationship is doomed.'

'What?'

'Okay, I'm not a fucking poet. What I am saying is they start something that's unlikely to pan out well. It could be years down the line, which means they've wasted all that time. There'll be many missed opportunities in between.'

'I thought we were having fun.'

'We were, but luckily I came to my senses and swiftly realised what an absolute ballbag you are.'

'Charming.'

'Am I right?'

Barry was quiet for a moment.

'I guess settling down isn't high on my agenda.'

Barry looked up at the ceiling and Ashley guessed he wasn't

contemplating the sort of future he wanted. She was confirmed correct when he smiled and pointed a finger at her.

'You're going to ask Flash out.'

'You're going to be a bruised ballbag in a minute.'

Ashley was saved from committing grievous bodily harm when her phone beeped. It was a text from Rocco. His reply was simple.

I'll be there in half an hour.

41

Rocco arrived twenty-five minutes later. Ashley was waiting for him at Reception. She struggled to understand exactly what it must be like to have two missing children in such circumstances, but clearly the toll would be heavy indeed.

Rocco raced in, resembling a man who'd won on a big bet with his last pound.

'Max is alive and well?' he asked, almost violently shaking her hand.

'Yes, he is. Come with me, please, and we'll talk about it.'

Ashley escorted Rocco to a meeting room, as opposed to an official interview room, where Sal was waiting with recorder and a notebook. Sal looked small and inconsequential behind the big desk. He'd undone his tie and there was a brown stain on the front of his shirt.

'My colleague will take notes for me.'

'I don't understand,' said Rocco. 'Where's my boy?'

A vein pulsed at Rocco's temple, but he pulled a chair out and slumped into it. He ran a hand through his hair, which Ashley could have sworn was thinner and greyer than the first time they'd met.

'Thank you for helping with our inquiries, Rocco. Your son Max was found and is safe, but he needs to rest and get his head together. He asked to be left alone for twenty-four hours to gather his thoughts, after enduring such a draining experience.'

'Where was he?'

'He was discovered in Harrison's Wood, north-east of the city.'

Rocco frowned. 'Buried?'

'No, not buried. He was in some danger, but if whoever put him there wanted him dead, then he would be. That gives us hope for Tommaso.'

Rocco grimaced and rubbed his temples.

Sal cleared his throat.

'I'm very sorry about what's happening to your family, but we need to ask you some difficult questions.'

'What?'

'Any advice you can give us today may assist in finding your missing son. Honesty is important to ensure we're looking in the right direction. Please take your time because I can't write very quickly.'

Ashley wasn't sure if Rocco released a small laugh or a cry.

'Cases don't get more serious,' she said. 'A man has died. People were tortured. We don't know who's involved. It could even be to do with you.'

'You think I'd abduct my own sons?'

'No, we don't think that, but it's obvious we're not being told the full story.'

'Cut this shit out. Where's my boy?'

'Max is an adult,' said Ashley. 'If he wishes to be alone, that's his call, don't you think?'

'He doesn't know what he wants,' he growled.

For a few seconds, Ashley saw the Rocco of old. A week of not eating or sleeping would be enough to drive any man to the edge of a breakdown, never mind one who'd also been separated from his sons.

'We can't reunite you with Max just yet, but he is fine. I'm sure you agree we should direct all our focus, all of our remaining energy, on ensuring Tommaso is safe too.'

Rocco barked out a short laugh. 'Talk about honesty. You tricked me into coming here.'

He covered his face. There was some dirt under his fingernails. His hands were blotchy, as was his forehead, which had a sheen of sweat across it, despite the cool air in the room. He seemed to find it difficult to focus on Ashley when he looked up at her.

'Whatever,' he whispered. 'Ask your questions. Reunite my family.'

'Okay.' Ashley turned to Sal. 'Is there anything you wish to ask Rocco at this point?'

Sal coughed, then gave Rocco an innocent smile.

'I've been confused by the case. The person I would most like a chat with is Hamish. Have you any idea where he is?'

'Why would I know?'

'Can you tell us where Lorenzo is, then?'

'He's gone to ground.'

'Even from his father?'

Ashley sensed a tightening in Rocco's jaw and a change in the energy coming from him. He shifted his gaze to Sal.

'Do you have boys?'

'Yes.'

'Do they always listen to you?'

Sal's smile grew. 'No, not all the time.'

Rocco waved a hand in the air, in much the same way Lorenzo did when he spoke.

'Exactly. They believe they know best, but they know nothing.'

'Lorenzo knows where Hamish is,' said Ashley.

'Why do you believe that?'

'We saw him escort Hamish out of the hospital on CCTV.'

Rocco broke eye contact for a second. His eyes were narrower when he returned Ashley's gaze.

'I expect Hamish feels the same as Max and Lorenzo,' he said. 'It seems as if everyone wants to run away. As you say, be safe.'

'I agree, but it doesn't make it any easier to find Tommaso. They might know a tiny morsel, which could lead us to a house, or the next wood, or to something we haven't considered.'

Rocco shook his head as though trying to clear it.

'I understand. I will attempt to reach Lorenzo.'

'Who do you suspect is doing all this?' asked Sal.

Rocco leaned back in his chair, jutted his chin out, and swore.

'I don't have a clue. If I did, I wouldn't be sitting here with you. I'd be doing to them what they've done to me.'

'Vigilante justice only leads to more problems, Rocco,' said Ashley. 'You know that.'

Rocco's anger gave him a burst of energy and clarity.

'Do you mean leave it to you? How are you doing? It's been five days for Tommaso. Why don't you do your job as police? I'll do mine as a father. I have everyone looking for these men. Everyone! I've ordered protection from abroad to come over. If necessary, I'll spend every penny I own to find my children, and if someone hurts them, I'd borrow money to take my revenge.'

Rocco's shoulders heaved as he fought to regain control.

'I believe this is an attack on Lorenzo,' said Sal quietly.

'Phht! Then why is he still alive and Paolo dead? Why were his brothers taken and abused, and not him?'

'I think criminals are threatening Lorenzo. Warning him. They've shown how easy it is to take his family any time they want.

Do with them what they like. If they're in business with Lorenzo, then this is perhaps a bargaining tactic. Sign the deal or else.'

'Don't be ridiculous. Who would work with such people?'

Ashley noticed Rocco's burst of vigour ebb then fade before her. His voice was softer when he spoke.

'I'm so worried.'

'Lorenzo works in the nightclub game,' said Sal. 'He mingles with wealthy and powerful people and makes a lot of money, all in the public eye.'

'So?'

'Maybe someone wants a piece of the pie.'

'Rubbish. The business would just fold.'

'Perhaps there's a drug angle,' said Ashley.

'No. You guys have been hounding him for years over that. There is no significant drug dealing at the club, or you'd have uncovered it. Besides. If Lorenzo was in any kind of serious trouble, he would come to me.'

'Okay,' said Sal. 'What would you have done if he had?'

'Same as I'm doing now. Put out feelers. Called in people to fucking sort whatever it was. I worked too hard all my life to create a family business. No idiots are going to get away with stealing what is mine. How about I ask what you are doing?'

'We need to speak to Lorenzo and Hamish, but they're gone.' Ashley laid down her ace. 'Perhaps Max will talk to us.'

Rocco had been staring at Sal but now he shifted his eyes across to Ashley and smiled.

'I wish he knew something to tell you. He's a simple boy. Works hard but no ambition. He lacks drive, which is also a phrase that applies to the drunken fairy he beds.'

Ashley cocked her head to one side. Rocco glanced away.

'So, Hamish and Max are a couple?' she asked.

'Yes, from school days. Since I took Hamish under my wing.'

Ashley struggled to decipher Rocco's expression. Was it regret?

'What do you think of their relationship?'

'Sorry, I shouldn't use phrases like that. It's okay. Well, sure, I wouldn't have wished for it. I pray for more grandchildren.'

'Being gay is no barrier to that these days.'

'Look. If he's happy, I'm happy. The world changes fast, but it's not always easy for my generation to keep up.'

'How many grandkids do you have?'

'Two.'

For the first time that evening, Rocco's shoulders dropped and his face relaxed. Ashley and Sal kept quiet.

'They are wonderful. So wonderful, you know? They are the future. So innocent. They call me Ro-Ro. I would do anything, anything, to protect them.'

'Are they Lorenzo's or Tommaso's?'

They saw a shard of the steel, which had made Rocco one of the area's richest men. He inhaled deeply, bared his teeth, and leaned back in his seat.

'They are a secret. The finest jewels to be protected.'

'Why would they need protecting?' asked Sal.

Rocco did another wave of his hands.

'All this. Build a legacy, spend years, spill tears. Others always try to take it away. And they will destroy what they cannot thieve.'

Ashley felt a shred of sympathy for him, but she suspected someone in his family had done something so awful that another party felt compelled to commit acts that had been shocking even for experienced officers.

'To be honest, Rocco, I'm surprised anyone would hurt your children. They must know it would cause you great pain, but perhaps, more importantly, make you incredibly angry.'

'Nobody is more shocked than me.'

Rocco's passion for his grandchildren had drained him. His head bowed.

Ashley saw her opportunity.

'Lorenzo employs attractive women at the club. When powerful men see things they want, they won't take no for an answer.'

'I don't understand what you mean.'

'A young woman was found dead in the woods a year or so ago. I wondered whether she may have worked at the nightclub?'

Rocco looked up through heavy eyes.

'No way. The girls are well cared for. They are part of the fabric of the place.'

'You can't tell me they are only there to talk.'

Rocco smirked.

'Of course not, but Lorenzo runs the club. The women are paid handsomely. My understanding is they may sleep with the rich clientele if they want. If they like them and can squeeze cash or jewellery out of it, or if they don't fancy them but wish to earn money, then it's their call. Sure, Lorenzo and Tommaso intend for the guys to enjoy themselves, but those girls are safe. They are under their protection.'

Ashley held Rocco's gaze. A shadow crossed his face. He had a secret.

She suspected it was the key to the entire case.

42

When Mary-Rose Meyler stepped outside her house with her father's ancient winter jacket on, the wind tugged at the big hood. She had few other options, though, as her warmest coats were still at the university halls. In the rush to escape, she'd only brought her laptop and phone, and the clothes she stood in.

Her stomach rolled as she remembered walking in on her boyfriend and her so-called best friend. After a few deep breaths, she pushed the memories aside. He wasn't worth it, even though, at that moment, it hurt.

Mary-Rose stamped down the street and walked towards the beach while trying to keep her head high. She pulled in the sea air and the weight on her heart lifted. All her old schoolfriends lived along this stretch of the Norfolk coast. Hemsby, Bacton, Walcott, Eccles-on-Sea, Ostend, and so many more. All quaint villages, full of character and history, but she had loved living in Happisburgh. It was home.

Mary-Rose glanced seaward. Her eyes narrowed at the dense dark-grey wall out there.

She walked down Beach Road to the car park and trotted along the steep sandy slope without too much concern. She'd hopefully be enjoying tea and toast when that front hit, although the weather could move at breathtaking speed. Almost like time-lapse photography. You could get four seasons in a few minutes. Happisburgh was often in the news for erosion and houses plunging off clifftops, but the land had been losing its war with the sea for thousands of years. The unpredictable climate was just one reason why.

Most tourists headed right towards Cart Gap, but Mary-Rose turned left where enormous stones had been dropped in another attempt to preserve the cliffs. Everything about this stretch of coast made her feel insignificant. The huge grey boulders, the vast skies, the endless sand, starry nights and raging storms, and the power of the sea. Mary-Rose became nothing. Her existence a grain of sand on the beach of time. Humankind dwarfed in comparison. Down there, she could cope with anything, because her problems were trivial. She was just a girl.

The waves roared their agreement and yearned to claim her, as they pounded on the barrier of stones that kept them from their prey. But no! They wouldn't win today. She would survive and fight on. Mary-Rose's pace picked up. She grinned as energy flowed through her. She would love again.

A cacophony of shrieking caught her attention. Gulls circled ahead. They banked in the breeze above, arguing amongst themselves, pecking at each other. An unpleasant smell drifted over. She suspected they were fighting over a dead seal.

Mary-Rose hated finding seals. They made her so sad and so she was tempted not to investigate, but she knew she would. Occasionally, they were injured or exhausted, and the sanctuary would collect them. Her stomach twisted once more, but it was now fear at what she might find.

Mary-Rose was edging through the sand to the shingle, and

the large clumps of earth that the furious elements had torn from the hillside, when she saw a bare foot sticking up in the air. She paused.

People partied by the shore all the time. She told herself they regularly slept it off in the marram grass. But few snoozed down there in October. The wind whistled around her, yet the stench was stronger. Her nose twitched. It didn't smell like a dead seal.

Mary-Rose nibbled her finger. Hairs rose on the back of her neck. The beach was empty except for her and whatever was ahead, but the foot hadn't moved. She surged forward to get it over with, ready to sprint back the way she'd come, but watched her footing. It had better not be a pervert or flasher.

Three metres away, she looked up. The foot was attached to a leg, but at an impossible angle. Mary-Rose steadied herself, then tiptoed forward. She frowned. Was it a dummy? The figure appeared to be male, but it wasn't easy to be sure. She was within two metres when the empty eye socket came into view.

Mary-Rose, the wind, the seabirds, and perhaps the gods themselves, all screamed as one.

43

Ashley was huffing and puffing on the lounge floor, trying and failing to get into a yoga pose from a tutorial she'd found online, when her phone rang. It was Control.

'Good morning, Sergeant Knight. A body has been discovered on Happisburgh Beach.'

Ashley couldn't say she was surprised.

'Has it been identified?'

'No. Male is all we have so far. I have to warn you. It's a gruesome find.'

'Is anyone else en route?'

'Uniform has that part of the beach blocked off. It's down from the car park. DC Hector Fade was on call. He's on his way. DCI Kettle has asked for both you and DS Williamson to attend.'

'Okay, I'm not far away. ETA eight o'clock.'

Ashley said goodbye and raced upstairs. She glanced out of the window at the weather, then pulled a thick jumper on over her work blouse. Ten minutes later, she'd brushed her hair and teeth and dashed out of the door. There was no time for a shower.

Once someone died, there usually wasn't an incredible rush,

but as it could be Tommaso, that would mean informing Rocco. Who knew how he would react? Ashley knew she might be the best person to let him know.

Twenty-five minutes later, she reached the road up to Happisburgh car park. It was already cordoned off. Ashley wound down her window to show the PC her warrant card, then recognised the woman who used to work in Control and had taken a job as a police officer after being inspired by Ashley.

'Hey, Jenny. It's great to see you again, and you look very smart. Are you going to let me in?'

'Hi, Ashley. Nice to see you, too. This is my first day out as part of my training. I hope they don't want me down there. The other trainee with me had to go home.'

Ashley almost stalled the car. That was more worrying than being warned by Control to prepare herself. Seeing the recently deceased was what you signed up for when you became police. Jenny wrote Ashley's name down and moved the barrier.

'Thanks for being such a great source of inspo for me.'

Ashley drove off, smiling and confused. She parked and grabbed her heavy-duty coat from the boot. She couldn't help but chuckle when she spotted Ally's beaten-up old saloon next to Hector's electric car.

It had been a while since she'd been to Happisburgh, pronounced hayz-buh-ruh. She remembered taking the wanker whom she'd been dating, and who had turned out to be happily married, to the lighthouse on their second date. Still operating, it was the only independently run one in the country and was maintained and operated entirely by voluntary contributions. She faintly recalled a wonderful view of the area, which was mentioned in the Domesday book, but she and the dickhead had only had eyes for each other. She should visit again to erase the memories.

The weak sun, which had peeked out of the odd break in the clouds when she'd earlier glanced out of the window, was long gone and an ominous sea mist was rolling in. Ashley knew the tides and the weather were unpredictable, dangerous and destructive on that section of the east coast, and not to be underestimated.

She nodded at a uniformed officer who looked green around the gills as she picked her way down the sand ramp that led to the beach. Right would take her to Cart Gap, which was where they stationed the lifeboat. It had previously been at Happisburgh until the coastal erosion had got too much. Sea Palling was five miles away and walkable if the tide was out.

Ashley turned left though, and approached the inner cordon. A grim-faced officer wrote her name down but didn't comment. Further up, she spotted a group of officers and two plain-clothes men: Ally and Hector. They were all staring at the bottom of the cliff.

Ashley trudged through the shingle. The wind buffeted her like blows from a soft pillow. With that breeze, the mist would be with them soon. Visibility would rapidly fall to metres, making crime-scene management difficult. The sea thundered close to her but was hidden behind some rocks. When Ashley reached the onlookers, she followed their line of sight, then gasped.

She wasn't sure what she was looking at. It could have been a mannequin due to the lack of features between its legs, but the muscular structure of the body indicated it was a large naked man. The skin was a mess and almost completely red. Ashley had attended a scene where someone fell six storeys, but they hadn't looked like this.

'My Lord,' was all she said.

'It's safe to say He was absent when this occurred,' said Ally. 'I've never seen anything remotely similar.'

Ashley stepped forward on the plates that had been laid to

protect the scene. The man lay supine on a massive lump of soil that had dropped away from the cliff. Ashley glanced around. It seemed unlikely he was brought down here. The fall would have shattered most of his bones, but she hoped he wasn't alive at the time. His head lolled back, neck clearly broken, so it appeared as if his remaining eye stared behind him. Ashley had a closer look at the face, but that was ruined, too. She glanced at Hector. His expression was impassive. He no longer looked twenty-four.

'What do we know?' she asked him.

'Not much. A student, home from uni, came for a morning walk, and found him lying here. It's not as if he was concealed, but these wounds wouldn't have come from a fall.'

'Have you checked his arm for a tattoo like Max and Hamish's?' asked Ashley.

'I could just make one out,' said Hector.

'It's as if he's been flayed alive.'

'This would appear more of a scourging than a flaying.'

Ally and Ashley turned to Hector as a light mist floated around them. The air rapidly cooled and dampened as it thickened. Ashley felt droplets of moisture forming on her face. As the weather front rolled in, it felt as if the sky were falling down, leaving them in a surreal environment that muffled the invisible waves as they crashed against the rocks.

'What's the difference?' asked Ashley.

'Flaying is known colloquially as skinning. It's a slow, painful but careful execution. Scourging was another form of torture, which was anything but gentle. Brutal and inhumane, and delivered by a flagrum, it was one of the most feared of all punishments.'

As Hector spoke in a monotone, the fog enveloped them. The victim seemed to shimmer as he was shrouded from view.

'Do you two believe in the principles of pathetic fallacy?' asked Hector.

'I'll answer when I understand the question,' said Ally.

'It's when a writer attributes human emotion to objects, nature or animals. An example being when ominous weather denotes impending doom.'

'Oh, great,' said Ashley.

Ally couldn't help himself. 'What's a flagrum, and how do you know so much about it?'

'I took ancient history as my fourth A-level subject. I found it compelling.'

'You did four A levels?' asked Ally.

'Didn't you?'

Ally shared a grin with Ashley. 'Maybe not quite that many. Carry on, please.'

'The flagrum used in scourging was a whip consisting of three or more leather tails that had plumbatae. Simply put, small metal balls or sheep bones were a feature at the end of each tail.'

'I think I saw something like that on *Ben Hur*,' said Ally.

'The number of lashes depended upon the cruelty of the executioners,' continued Hector. 'The more they administered, the swifter the death. The social standing and their crime usually dictated what happened next. Sometimes they would be left to suffer.'

'Surely someone wouldn't live long with these sorts of injuries,' said Ashley, gesturing in the direction of the body.

'You'd be surprised. The plumbatae dug deep into the flesh, ripping skin, small blood vessels, muscle and nerves. The victim would vomit, experience tremors and seizures, and slip in and out of consciousness. Each excruciating strike elicited shrieks of pain. But it wasn't necessarily deadly.'

'So, they could live for days in agony?' asked Ashley.

'Yes, although if the torturer put some real effort in, the ribs would fracture, making breathing painful. The plumbatae could lacerate the liver and maybe the spleen. Then death would be quicker.'

'So, if this attack wasn't meant to kill and occurred days ago...' said Ashley.

'Then this man has suffered in a way that's almost impossible to comprehend.'

'And then they threw him off a cliff,' said Ally, flatly.

'A merciful release, I should think,' said Hector.

Ashley summed up out loud.

'Perhaps Tommaso was the target in all of this. Four men were taken and questioned. Hamish and Max don't seem to be involved. Paolo sounds as if he was in the thick of it, but maybe it was all to do with revenge against Tommaso for something he did. This all feels incredibly personal. Someone has gone to great lengths to ensure their victim has experienced the most painful death possible. Assuming this is Tommaso, then all those missing are accounted for.'

'Perhaps it's over,' said Hector. 'Maybe Lorenzo wasn't involved in whatever Tommaso was up to his neck in.'

'I think Tommaso and Lorenzo are bound together,' said Ashley, wiping her damp face with her hands. 'Well, we have a job to do. The undertakers should be able to get their collection vehicle down that ramp if they're careful. I assume CSI is on the way, but the beach won't tell them much unless something came down with him.'

Hector shook his head in disgust.

'What type of person could inflict this punishment on another human being?'

'An incredibly warped and violent sicko,' said Ally.

'Or perhaps a very angry one,' said Hector. 'This is off the scale.'

Ashley's mind linked the scene in front of her to the brutal death that Ivan had described of the trafficker and the officers with him. She remembered Hector hadn't been in the previous day.

'Hector, a few things came up at yesterday's meeting. A police officer in Montenegro told me that there was a gang of some kind in Europe who were prone to killing the people who crossed them. A people trafficker who was caught by the authorities didn't keep his mouth shut and was murdered.'

'What sort of gang are they?'

'That's the problem. They don't really know. The name used was Typhon. It's a nickname for a person or a group who are responsible for serious crimes in eastern Europe.'

'Isn't this Typhon thing a Slavic issue a long way from here?' asked Ally.

'Yes, but their victim was impaled, which is barbaric. That word well describes what we're looking at now.'

'Zelda checked into Typhon and rang me last night,' said Ally. 'The National Crime Agency is aware of the name, but they don't seem to have much on it. That's assuming they're not keeping their cards close to their chests.'

'I meant to google the word. Does it stand for something other than wind?'

Ally shrugged. 'No idea.'

'It's Greek,' said Hector. 'Typhon was a monstrous serpentine giant, and up there with the deadliest creatures in Greek mythology. After Zeus defeated the Titans, the mother of all life, Gaia, had one more child, Typhon. He became the father of most of the well-known monsters. Hydra, Ladon, Cerberus, Chimera, the Sphinx and so on.'

'He must have been a proud dad,' said Ally.

'It was said Typhon had enormous strength with many heads, hands, and wings. Squirming coils of snakes stretched from his massive thighs. He was a match even for Zeus himself, who was only victorious by dropping Mount Etna on top of him, imprisoning Typhon inside it.'

'You're a clever one,' said Ally, without malice.

'Seeing as you're such a genius,' said Ashley, 'what does a great source of inspo mean?'

'Something or someone that serves as inspiration or motivation.'

Ashley smiled at Jenny's compliment, but it felt as though the chilly, wet air was seeping into her clothes. She was about to return to her car to update Kettle when a ragged cry came from the direction of the ramp. Something was moving across the shingle towards them with slow, heavy stomps. They all turned and faced the sounds. A uniformed sergeant trudged to meet the ever-louder crunches. He removed his baton.

'Stop there!' a female voice ordered from somewhere within the fog.

A sound screeched into the wind, ricocheting off the hillside. High-pitched, desperate, inhuman. As though wrenched from the bowels of hell.

A dark shape materialised in the misty air and lurched towards them.

44

As the figure neared, they heard the female voice again and Ashley recognised it as Jenny's.

'Please, sir. Stop.'

Then another shape appeared. A male voice rang out.

'That's far enough, sir. This is a crime scene.'

Ashley guessed who it was, just as Rocco pleaded with the scene guard to let him through.

'My son! It's Tommaso. I know it. Please, I have to be with him.'

Ashley considered the state of the victim. No father should see that. She glanced at Hector, who was wearing a new and expensive-looking short bomber jacket with a fur collar. Ally, on the other hand, had a long trench coat on, which appeared like something a dog would lie on in the boot of the car.

'Ally. Would you mind using your overcoat to cover the body? If it's Tommaso, we shouldn't prevent Rocco from being with his son, but we can stop him from seeing most of the mutilation.'

Ally didn't think twice and whipped his coat off. Ashley also understood that a quick identification by Rocco would be handy, but felt it better left unsaid.

'Hector. Escort him over here.'

Rocco would charge over and compromise the scene, but it was clear by the victim's broken back he'd landed on the boulder from height.

Ashley watched Hector walk out of the mist with Rocco. He had his arm around the much shorter man's shoulders. Both men wore expensive slip-on shoes, but that was where the similarity ended. Rocco had a large sheepskin jacket on, but Ashley could detect blue and white striped pyjamas on underneath. Ashley stepped forward to meet him. She shook his hand, holding onto his elbow as she did so. Rocco's eyes were hollowed out.

'Is it him?'

She grimaced. 'We believe so.'

'Where is he?'

'Rocco. You don't have to do this now. We'll have him taken to the hospital shortly. You can spend time with him there.'

Rocco's voice was louder.

'No. A man should be with his boy.'

Ashley took a deep breath.

'Okay. Come with me.'

Keeping hold of his arm, Ashley guided him further through the swirling mist. The others present, hair slick with the moisture from the air, backed away, to give Rocco privacy. Someone needed to stay with him and Ashley nodded she would do.

Rocco slipped and staggered at the shingle's edge, where it met the mud deposits from the cliffs. He rubbed his eyes, then he noticed Ally's blue coat draped over a large lump. Ashley watched as Rocco's gaze moved along the jacket to the claret face and thick hair. Blood appeared to drip from the shoulders, even though it was more likely water.

Rocco reacted as if he'd been physically assaulted. He grabbed his stomach, doubled over, and vomited. All that shot out was thin liquid, further proof of the man's suffering. It spattered like acid on the ground before him.

A whimper came from Rocco's throat as his teeth gritted. He pushed himself onward. Still supporting his arms, Ashley trudged with him. A death march. Rocco's face so grim, even the wind fell back in fear.

He gently removed Ashley's hand from his arm, collapsed to his knees next to the hood of the coat, which partially covered the ruined face. Rocco's shaking fingers hovered above the body. Grabbing the material, he lifted the hood and pulled it away to expose the savaged flesh on the chest of his second born. Ashley was much closer to the face and less shocked than she had been before as she absorbed the catastrophic injuries in detail.

Ally's coat slid from Rocco's hands. He leaned back on his haunches, opened out his arms and yelled long and loud into the fog. It was a sound of pain, but also a release of tension. He twisted to stare up into Ashley's eyes.

'It's not Tommaso.'

45

Rocco made the sign of the cross. Ashley noticed he did it slowly, which reminded her of when Lorenzo had done it the same way. Ashley helped Rocco to his feet.

'As you might understand, we need to respect the deceased and keep the area and any facts private for the moment.'

Rocco whimpered. It was the second time he'd expected to have lost a son. Each emotional blow would take its toll. Rocco would be close to defeat, or perhaps surrender.

'I can't believe what's happening. My head is spinning.'

'Rocco. How did you know to come here?'

Rocco tried to centre himself, but his breathing was erratic, and he wore a mad smile.

'The radio, I think. Lorenzo heard about an incident here and rang me. I came straight down. Hah! In my pyjamas.'

Ashley left it at that, but it was highly unlikely a news channel would have the details, and the police had been using the Airwave communication system for decades, which was digitally encrypted. Nobody could listen in.

Ashley turned her attention to the deceased. He looked a comparable size to Tommaso, but the face was severely damaged, and the hair matted with blood.

'Do you recognise him?' she asked.

Ashley realised immediately that Rocco knew who it was. She could also see he was debating whether to tell her, but he nodded.

'Gianluca. The head of security from the nightclub. We didn't open the place due to all of this, but he was there last night helping restock and get it ready for when this is all over. He was supposed to see Lorenzo when he'd finished but never showed.'

'I thought you weren't involved with the staff at the club.'

Rocco's eyes narrowed.

'It's a crisis. We all muck in.'

Ashley looked at the victim. He had exuded strength when she'd met him. Whoever had done this must have possessed plenty of their own.

'I haven't met Tommaso in the flesh, but I can see a similarity.'

'I saw Gianluca once from behind at Lorenzo's and thought it was Tommaso. Similar build and thick Italian hair, the identical tattoo on his arm. Tommaso also has a much bigger tattoo on his back. It fills it. Lorenzo, too. I told you a few of the others got SPQR done to show loyalty.'

'Loyalty to what? To Rome?'

Rocco closed his mouth and rubbed his face, appearing to realise he'd let something slip.

'You know how young men are. They love to be part of a gang.'

'Didn't you say your sons had grown up now?'

'You know what I mean. Lorenzo and Tommaso are a handsome pair with a successful business. Gianluca, Max, Hamish, they all want a little piece for themselves. Others too, you understand the difference?'

Ashley wasn't sure she did.

Relief was shedding from Rocco in waves, despite the fact someone high up in Lorenzo's circle had recently been thrown from a cliff.

'And where is Lorenzo?' she asked.

'He is in hiding. A hotel we use. I have my best man at his side, brought over from the continent. He will protect him. Nobody else but them and me has a clue where he is. Family only.'

'Tell me where he is so I can speak to him.'

'Are you family?'

Irritation flashed through Ashley's mind.

'Don't you want our help in finding Tommaso?'

Ashley wondered when Rocco was going to understand the significance of Gianluca's fate. The doorman had probably been grabbed somewhere late last night. Tommaso had been missing for much longer. Rocco ignored the question.

'Rocco, are you fixating on the fact that even though Max and Hamish were punished, they were released with no permanent physical injuries?'

'Not hoping, praying for the same with Tommaso.'

A light rain fell as Ashley wondered about loyalty. Paolo and Gianluca had paid the ultimate price for theirs, but Max and Tommaso were more important figures. They were family. Perhaps whoever was responsible had killed the expendables, knowing if they went too far, there'd be no more business done with the Viallis.

Ashley was about to guide Rocco back to the slope and away from the scene when a uniformed constable sprinted out of the mist to their right.

'Ally sent me to fetch you. You're needed further along the beach.'

Ashley walked with him until she could talk out of Rocco's earshot.

'What is it?'

'We've found another body.'

46

Ashley checked the young PC's face and could see from the strain in his eyes that a bad morning had just got worse.

'Is it similar to this?'

'Almost identical.'

'Does the deceased have a large tattoo on his back?'

'Yes. This one is also naked, but he landed chest down. He looks weirdly peaceful, but it's obvious he was abused in the same manner as the first guy before he was pushed over the top.'

'Has the victim been covered as best we can?'

The officer nodded.

'Okay. Stay here and keep everyone else away from this body until CSI arrive.'

Hector trudged over as well.

'Go on ahead, Hector. Let the officers down there know I'm on my way with Rocco.'

Ashley spun around and strode towards Rocco. He looked old and insignificant, perhaps for the first time in his life, as he waited to hear what they all knew must surely come. Ashley nodded at him.

'There's another victim further down the beach. If you'd like to follow me and check if you know who it is, that would be helpful.'

They lumbered through the sand. Ashley had to help Rocco, whose knees threatened to give way. They reached two PCs and Hector, but she couldn't spot a victim.

'He's fallen tight against the cliff face,' said Hector, 'and is concealed by the marram.'

Ashley supported Rocco again. The response officers would have done a recce up here when the first victim was found, but she could understand how the victim might have been missed as she was almost on top of the body before she saw it.

Rocco knew it was his son immediately. 'No-o-o!'

His roar of pain was far deeper, more powerful, and more penetrating, than the wild North Sea behind him. He knelt beside Tommaso's bloody head and took it in his hands.

Ashley picked her way through the coarse grass, which was common to Norfolk's sandy beaches, and stood next to Hector.

'Okay?' she asked.

'Kind of. I'm a bit concerned I'm getting used to seeing sights like this.'

'It can feel like a conveyor belt at times.'

A faint buzz came from Hector. He removed his phone from his pocket and answered it.

'Yes, she's here,' he said and passed it to her. 'CSI. Gerald.'

'Hi, Gerald,' said Ashley. 'How are you?'

'Fabulous. Sorry, I missed the Bacton Wood incidents. I was on a fishing trip. Control sent me to Harrison's Wood this morning to help Treharne, but he's done with his preliminary searches. We heard you've discovered the missing son.'

'We've just found him.'

'Excellent, or is that not good?'

'There are two bodies. Both deceased.'

'Sorry to hear that. I'll head down to you and process the scene. Is it likely to give us anything?'

'No. As a rough summary, I would say both men were tortured elsewhere, driven here and thrown over the edge of the cliffs.'

'I do love looking for a needle in a haystack when there's no needle.'

Ashley smiled, but it wasn't a time for laughter.

'Let's hope one of the people responsible dropped their phone,' said Gerald.

'That's the spirit. I haven't had any messages from Treharne, so I assume there's no news.'

'Correct. Zero to report at this point. His team have been thorough and he's confident there are no other disturbances to the ground like there were for the two burials. It's a lot smaller wood. He doesn't believe anything else is here. Obviously we can't say what the tests will produce. There's been clothing and personal items found.'

'Has Treharne spoken to Kettle?'

'Yes, he's on the phone to him now. It looks as though they're calling it a day. I think the locals are ready to get their dog-walking routes back, judging by their antics.'

'What do you mean?'

'The officers on night patrol both had all their tyres let down, an idiot dug a deep narrow hole in the middle of the path and covered it with ferns, which almost broke one of Treharne's team's legs, and another fool emptied a load of rubbish bins at the main vehicle entrance, which they drove through first thing. The PolSA team will be glad to see the back of the place, and they all need admin time. I'll be over to your beach shortly to check what needs to be done.'

'Okay. Thank everyone from all of us for their efforts in those woods. Can't have been easy under the conditions.'

'I don't think it will have been too bad for them. There are worse places than here to work. It's not too dreadful a morning in the woods.'

'It's misty, cold and breezy down here.'

'Exactly. Give me trees and birdsong any day, even if it is raining.'

Ashley was smiling as she finished the call, but another bout of Rocco sobbing at the sky soon wiped it from her face. She beckoned Ally and Hector further up the beach so they could talk privately. One of the uniformed crew had given Ally a Hi-Vis jacket that was slightly too big and really didn't suit him. It was hard to picture the man as he would have been in similar attire when he started nearly thirty years ago.

'How do you want to play this?' asked Ally.

'I'd like you to stay and help uniform and CSI with the scene. I'm expecting a call from abroad soon, but I'm heading to the N & N to visit Max.'

'Rocco may still have guessed he was there.'

'That's my concern, so it'll be interesting if anyone has tried to reach him in the hospital. I'm hoping Hector will find common ground with Max.'

'And why is that?' asked Hector.

'You both grew up with powerful fathers.'

'Fair enough. I do know plenty about that.'

'Ally, I've only got Sal, Emma and Jan back at HQ. Can you ask Zelda and Morgan to assist them? Bee's baby is draining the energy from her, and Barry's supposed to be off today. There'll be CCTV around here. It's a reasonably affluent area. That blue van was probably how the victims were transported. We're still flying blind without having a solid idea of what's going on here, but my gut tells me Lorenzo is key.'

'Same,' said Hector.

'Which means Max and Rocco might not be involved. I reckon Lorenzo and Tommaso are in deep. Drugs, trafficking, maybe organised crime in all its glory. We'll need to notify the NCA of our suspicion.'

'I can sort that,' said Ally. 'Do you really believe Rocco or Max will tell us the truth now Tommaso has died?'

Ashley considered the ties that bound these types of families.

'Perhaps not the truth, but they might give us something as the weight of losing Tommaso crushes them. At this point, they have nowhere to direct their anger. They appear to be in the dark as much as we are.'

'Not quite as much as us,' said Hector. 'Rocco got here a bit too quickly for my liking.'

'No, I suppose not,' said Ashley with a rueful nod. 'Ally, Scott Gorton's in today. See if he can come straight down here. Leave Rocco with Tommaso until Scott arrives, then let Scott manage him. It's also possible Rocco is a target, so take that into account.'

'Don't worry. I'll make sure he doesn't freeze to death.'

'Ring Kettle. Tell him we need the cliff line walked from here to Sea Palling and then down to Bacton Gas Terminal, to check for any more drop-offs.'

Ally and Ashley shared a look. As always, dark humour would get them through. Hector shook his head but appeared to be coping well.

Ashley was looking forward to the car journey with him. He wouldn't be able to escape from her interrogation. Before they left, Ashley walked over to Rocco, who swayed with the long grass next to his deceased son. His eyes had closed, and his face was white and drawn. He drooped, like a toy that had run out of batteries.

'Rocco. Let's get you back in the warmth.'

Rocco didn't move.

'We'll need to get Tommaso off the beach soon, so the investigators can do their job. The person responsible is still out there. The liaison officer you met at the pub will arrive shortly, and he'll arrange for you and Tommaso to go to the hospital. You have my number. Please use it for anything.'

As Ashley stepped away, Rocco croaked a reply.

'Thank you, Ashley. Thank you.'

She turned back to him. His shoulders shook as he sobbed.

'It doesn't seem real,' he said. 'I must get a message to Lorenzo and warn him to be careful.'

Ashley kept quiet, but she couldn't have agreed more.

47

Ashley and Hector stamped back to the car park through the shingle.

'We'll go in your car,' she said. 'Assuming you have enough juice.'

Hector's vehicle beeped, and they got in.

'You're going to grill me while I drive, aren't you?' he said.

'See. You have learned something from me and my underhand ways.'

Ashley's phone let her know she had a voicemail from a missed call. She listened to it and cursed.

'That was the police in Montenegro,' she said.

'You should have bought a phone on Three to use on the beach, like I did, and learned from my intelligent ways.'

'I don't need one if you're about.'

'Ah, but let's not forget, a week from today, I'll be going. Whether it's to a different department or a different job, I'm leaving either way.'

'Part of me was hoping you'd stay.'

Hector didn't look at her. He started the vehicle and pulled away, driving along the narrow lane back to Beach Road.

'Which part?' he asked.

'The bit that likes you. Enjoys having you around. Respects those intelligent ways.'

'And the part that wants me to leave?'

Tears welled in Ashley's eyes. Hector was turning her into a big softie.

'You're a young man with potential. It'd be a crime to keep you here in Norfolk, at least for this phase of your career. There's an entire world out there for you to tackle. Perhaps you're destined for greatness.'

'You do important work here.'

'I guess. It's hardly global, though, is it?'

'The Americans were interested in the Paradise Park investigation.'

Ashley ignored him as he tried to humour her. She was focussed on one thing.

'Have you decided?' she asked.

'No. I need to let Kettle know my plans soon, though. I wondered if you could arrange a leaving meal for me, assuming the case is solved or has settled to some degree. Kettle said I could head off at that point.'

'Sure. What do you fancy?'

'How about that sundown thingy at The Grove you were telling me about?'

'Norfolk tapas, pizza, seafood and ice cream in the massive tipi.'

'Yeah, sounds brilliant.'

'I'll see if I can book it in. I'm fairly sure they put heaters on if it's cold. Shall I invite all the team? Include Kettle? How about Ally's lot?'

Hector considered it for a moment.

'Just our team and Kettle. Joan and Arthur, too. Michelle, of course. Maybe even Gerald.'

'Even Barry?'

Hector blew out a big breath. 'I suppose so.'

'Gingerpuss?'

'Gabriella? That'd be nice.'

Ashley suspected he would find it more than nice.

'Mission accepted.'

'Don't you need to ring Montenegro?' he asked, blushing.

'No, I'll wait until we get to the hospital. The signal will drop in and out on the country roads. We'll talk instead.'

Hector chuckled.

'I thought detectives were the experts in deception. Using guile to squeeze intelligence and confessions out of the most hardy and suspicious of criminals. You're like Ronald McDonald running through a minefield.'

'That's normally true, but it's not far, so there's little time for craftiness. I'm your boss, so you have to answer.'

'I dived in the sea to save you, so I get a pass.'

'Ooh, look at you, laying down your ace.'

'Sorry, but I'd rather not talk about it now. I've booked golf with Jan this weekend. Last round we played, he barely spoke to me all the way round. It was so relaxing, and it let me organise my thoughts. I'll tell you all next Friday at The Grove.'

'Drama queen.'

'Something occurred to me on the beach, though. You know we were talking about Greek mythology?'

'About Typhon?'

'Yes. My mind naturally linked it to Roman mythology.'

'Naturally.'

Hector nudged her with his elbow.

'Aren't they the same?' she asked.

'Kind of, but there's a lack of anthropomorphism in early Roman myths.'

Ashley groaned. 'Kill me now.'

Hector laughed. 'Basically, the Greek gods are more human, and are talked of in human form. Picture handsome Zeus holding bolts of lightning. Roman myths were less about physical form.'

'Are you going to blame all this on Dolos?'

Hector glanced at her.

'Outstanding. Are you fascinated by mythology too?'

'No, it was in Sal's crossword last week. The God of lies, cunning, deception, and all-round sneakiness. He joked it sounded like the God of criminals. I still don't get your point though.'

'It had me thinking about the Viallis' nickname. Consider the types of punishment that have been meted out.'

'Torture, burial, a bonfire, and free flying lessons.'

'Torture by scourging. Jesus was scourged before his death by Romans, and the other victims weren't just buried and burnt, but buried alive and potentially burned alive.'

'Max and Hamish survived.'

'Yes, but they could've easily died. Now we have today. Both men thrashed to within an inch of their lives, then thrown off cliffs to their deaths. They are all methods used by the Romans when they had their empire.'

'Yes, and it's all sickening. What are you saying?'

'I'm coming to that. This isn't about money or drugs, or at least not directly. I don't reckon the Vampires have anything to do with this. They'd simply want the Romans all dead so they could take over their business.'

'So, it's revenge.'

'Yes, but not just vengeance. I think these crimes are also a message. Communication in its most brutal form. They're shouting, this is what happens when you insult us, attack us, hurt our family, whatever it is. They know they call themselves the Romans, so they're punishing them with their own techniques from the past. Someone, or an organisation, has carefully planned this. Time and money have been invested. If we can find out what Tommaso did that caused him to be tortured in this way, well, we'll be eating tapas and pizza on my last night washed down with champagne.'

Ashley looked out of the window at the beautiful autumn trees. Even just a few miles from the coast, there was no fog.

'Yet,' she said, 'Lorenzo is still alive and he's seemingly in charge.'

'Yes. That was bugging me, too, until I saw Rocco weeping over his middle son. Then I think I understood.'

'Go on.'

'It's not the natural order of things when a child dies before the parent, but consider losing a brother, too.'

'Right, there's frustration for the survivors. Fury. Fear. Helplessness. The stolen years. The knowing you're next. All of that.'

'Precisely.' Hector hit the steering wheel. 'It's been a progression. Hamish, Paolo, Max, Gianluca and now Tommaso.'

'Why kill Paolo and Gianluca, but not Hamish and Max?'

'I don't know.'

A surge of adrenaline pulsed through Ashley's veins.

'Do you remember Morgan telling us it was Italians who arranged the final leg of the trafficked journey?'

'Yes.'

'People holding out from torture is bullshit for the movies. If you grabbed hold of a pair of pliers and headed for a man's genitals, he'd tell you everything he knows.'

Hector gave Ashley a huge, respectful grin.

'Brilliant,' he said. 'Max and Hamish couldn't admit to anything because they weren't involved. They knew nothing. Tommaso, Paolo and Gianluca, on the other hand, probably had something to confess.'

'And then they were treated accordingly.'

'Which brings us to Lorenzo.' Hector took a deep breath. 'Is the worst yet to come?'

Ashley understood his point completely.

Perhaps everything so far had been part of Lorenzo's punishment.

48

Hector pulled into the car park at the hospital and prised his tall frame from the vehicle. Ashley followed him out.

'So, Lorenzo's next?' she asked.

'Yes.'

'You don't reckon they'll come back for Max?'

'No. Look at how efficient they've been.'

'It's almost like they're the ones with an insider, rather than Lorenzo, or Rocco.'

'I've been thinking,' said Hector. 'If Lorenzo is heavily involved, he must understand they'll be coming for him so won't he already be in hiding?'

'We have to assume the kidnappers know where he is. Interviewing techniques don't need to be fine-tuned when you've got a lit cigarette and a flabellum in your arsenal.'

'Flagellum. A flabellum is Latin for a ceremonial fan.'

Ashley shook her head.

'What are we going to do without you? Maybe if we explain to Max that this isn't over, it will loosen his tongue.'

'That's possible. Remember, you said the ultimate target could be Rocco himself. To live is to suffer, to survive is to find some meaning in the suffering. Friedrich Nietzsche is often given the credit for that, but it was Gordon Allport.'

Ashley nodded. Rocco was certainly in torment.

'I'll update Control and call the police in Montenegro while you get Max's room location.'

'Okay.'

Hector marched through the entrance, then headed in the direction of the security office while Ashley remained outside. She considered Max's loyalty to his father and brother. Would he know where the hotel was that Rocco said Lorenzo was in? She hoped so because the police would struggle to protect Lorenzo if they couldn't find him.

Ashley rang Control first and gave them an update and then she sent Ally a text with her concerns. He texted straight back saying he understood and informed her Scott had just arrived at Happisburgh beach with Zelda. Ashley asked Ally if he was on the Three network. Of course, was his reply.

Ashley found the number for Ivan in Montenegro and rang it. Kettle often joked that one of the perks of being a sergeant was free international calls. A man answered in rapid dialect, but she suspected it was the detective she'd spoken to before.

'Hello. May I speak to Ivan?'

'E-van, please. Is that Ashley Knight from England?'

'Yes, Ivan,' she replied, pronouncing his name properly. 'Did you receive our official request for information?'

'We did, but I don't believe it's necessary.'

'Oh, why's that?'

'You tell me the reason for your call first.'

'Okay. I was wondering if you'd had a chance to chat with Dragan, the brother of the girl who died in the woods?'

'Excellent pronunciation, and no. I spoke to the mother of Jasmina and Jelena.'

'What did she have to say?'

'When the girls went missing it devastated the family. Both her girls were gone. Jelena wrote for two years, but never gave a return address. She said she was okay, the country was strange, but she was having fun. Her job was perfect.'

Ashley frowned. It was common for those who ended up in forced prostitution or domestic servitude to be coerced into writing letters home to say they were happy, and everything was fine. Return addresses weren't provided. That way, nobody came looking for them.

'But the stunning sister, Jasmina, never kept in touch with her mum?'

'No. Jelena said in one communication that Jasmina and she got separated in Slovenia, which makes me suspect there's a connection.'

Ashley considered that for a moment, but it didn't compute.

'Sorry. Can you explain?'

'The individual who either permitted or forced Jelena to write those letters to her mother saying life was good allowed her to mention her sister vanished in Slovenia. That's not normal. Usually there are no details like that. So maybe the person who kidnapped Jasmina told Jelena's handler to leave it in the letter.'

'Right. That way her mum would think Jasmina was somewhere in Slovenia and didn't make it to England, when she may well have done.'

Ashley mulled it over in her head. Had Jasmina been separated because of her looks and fast-tracked to Lorenzo's club somehow? Had she eventually become an enthusiastic worker there, and was she still in the UK? Or was she now dead?

Ashley decided to update Ivan on the latest developments and he whistled afterwards.

'That is extreme, but I have heard of similar punishments, some recently. The world is becoming an even more violent place.'

'I'm beginning to wonder if someone is taking retribution on the Viallis. If not for Jelena specifically, then for all the women who have been tricked from their homes.'

'Do you have proof the Viallis are traffickers?'

'No. I was just thinking out loud. You mentioned the guy you arrested said the people who took Jasmina were Italian. That is at least a link, and if you found it, then it's possible Dragan's investigator also uncovered it. Perhaps it brought him all the way to Norfolk and now Dragan is having his revenge for his dead sisters.'

'I suppose that's a reasonable assumption. Dragan has money, but, logistically, it wouldn't be easy from here.'

'You mentioned we only notified you of Jelena's passing within the last six months. I assume her DNA linked her back to Montenegro.'

'Yes, the bodies are regularly discovered decomposed. Even with people like Jasmina, people's faces change a lot in death, and they tend to be malnourished. It's hard. Every year, hundreds of thousands go missing in Europe. Half of them are children.'

'Wow, so many.'

'Lots of families are ripped apart.'

'I don't suppose Dragan is on holiday here with all of his largest and most well-armed friends?'

Ivan laughed loudly.

'No, I think he was on TV last night. Hang on.'

Ivan didn't bother putting her on mute. She listened as he shouted, then someone hollered back, then they bellowed at each other, a third voice joined in, then they all cracked up.

'Yes, it was a live show. Politics. Modern rubbish, according to my boss, but my youngest colleague reckoned they were progressive ideas. Both agreed it was all probably lies.'

'But Dragan is wealthy.'

'Wealthy here, but that's not rich by your standards.'

'Are there any other relatives? Half-brothers? What about her dad?'

'The mother swore when I asked about the girls' father. Explained he was a monster who died a long time ago. She'd spit on his grave if she knew where it was.'

'At least he made an impression.'

Ivan chuckled. 'I love English humour. Sarcasm. Very funny.'

'You said you've heard of similar types of incidents. Would that be in your country?'

'Yes. *Krvna osveta.* Are you familiar with the term?'

'No.'

'It's like a law of vendetta here and means blood feud. It is usually triggered by murder or rape. The most serious crimes. The victim's relatives then fulfil the social obligation of avenging the victim. That would be the only solution to maintain their honour.'

'Which would mean they'd kill the person responsible?'

'Krvna osveta gives them permission to target all the males in the killer's family, and anyone else who gets in their way.'

'Is it still legal over there?'

'Of course not. Do you imagine me coming to work via horse and cart?'

Ashley laughed.

'Perhaps a state-of-the-art cart. You know, the latest model. All chrome.'

Ivan guffawed.

'Wait until I tell the guys. Feuds were common when our society had weak laws, which were occasionally not enforced.

Justice wasn't done, so the relatives did it themselves, but it's not been practised here for nearly two-hundred years.'

'Okay, thanks for your help, Ivan. I appreciate it.'

Ashley noticed Hector step outside the hospital, but she'd thought of one last question.

'Ivan. How does it stop? Surely they'd have to kill everyone in the family, and all of their friends, or it would end up in an insane tit-for-tat.'

'Excellent. You understand why they are illegal. They often finish in a bloodbath.'

49

Hector was relieved to inform Ashley there'd been no disturbances in A & E, at the main entrance, or at Max's room, which he'd been given directions to, on the far side of the hospital. Ashley gave him the latest from her call with Ivan as they went inside to Max's ward. Hector raised an eyebrow but didn't comment.

The officer outside Max's room was enjoying a lengthy yawn as she and Hector approached. Ashley strode right up to him, so she was the first thing he saw when he peeled open his eyes. He jumped to his feet when Ashley showed him her warrant card.

'Sorry, Sarge. I've been here since last night. My partner's just gone to the toilet.'

'You're forgiven. Both of you get yourselves a decent coffee. I'm sure we'll be fine with him for quarter of an hour. Nothing to report?'

'No. He only woke a little while ago. I heard the toilet flush. The nurse said he's drowsy.'

Ashley and Hector stepped into the room and discovered Max lying on his side, but he was awake and staring at them. His hands were bunched under his chin in a manner that reminded Ashley of a baseball pitcher. She glanced around. It was hard to say whether Max's face or the walls were greyer.

Ashley pulled up a chair and sat, bringing herself on eye level with him.

'Hi, Max, do you remember me from this morning? I'm DS Ashley Knight. This is my colleague, DC Hector Fade. You suggested coming back, so we're here to offer support.'

There was another seat in the corner. Hector grabbed it and put it next to Ashley's. He removed his pocket notebook from his coat as Max's eyes followed his movements.

'How are you feeling?' asked Hector.

Max just blinked.

Ashley had spent the final part of the car journey wondering what she should tell Max today. She'd decided his mental health would dictate how they acted. Would the information about Tommaso be better coming from her or Rocco? She suspected Max's relationship with his dad wasn't like the one Rocco had with his older sons.

'We're searching for Hamish,' she said. 'No news is hopefully good news.'

Max's eyes tracked over to her.

'Talk to me, Max, please. We're concerned for Hamish.'

Max moistened his parched and cracked lips.

'I was expecting visitors. Just not you. Seeing as you haven't found Hamish.'

'You expected Lorenzo to come and collect you?'

Max scrunched his eyes up as he nodded. A tear squeezed from each eye. Ashley's heart went out to this young man, but she had a job to do. If they failed to crack the case, it was clearly going to escalate.

'Max. We're concerned about your family's safety. Someone is attacking everything the Viallis hold dear. Gianluca has been killed.'

Max's eyes opened, but there was no emotion there.

'We're worried about you, too. We can help you. Get you somewhere safe.'

'All I want is to be with Hamish.'

'We can't find Lorenzo, either. It's likely Hamish is with him.'

'Lorenzo will be with Tommaso.'

Ashley looked over at Hector, who shrugged.

Ashley scooted her chair closer and rested a hand on Max's clenched fists.

'Lorenzo isn't with Tommaso, Max. I'm so sorry, but Tommaso died with Gianluca.'

Ashley expected Max to shove her hand away, but he didn't. Instead, he opened his hands, let hers in, then squeezed his fingers shut. Max's fingers were ice cold. He closed his eyes again, and tears flowed freely now. Ashley kept quiet for a minute and remained still. It was Max who broke the silence.

'I don't know what to do,' he whispered.

'There are killers out there. Attacking your family. We're concerned Lorenzo is next.'

Ashley paused to give Max time to connect the dots.

'Hamish,' he gasped.

'Yes,' said Ashley. 'I think they're together. We believe you and Hamish aren't involved in any of this, but if Lorenzo is a target, Hamish could end up as collateral damage. Please, talk to us.'

'I can't,' he muttered after a pause.

'Max, you must. Would Hamish want to be with Lorenzo?'

Max shook his head, his expression taut with emotional pain. Ashley had to push him for more.

'Is Hamish even safe from Lorenzo?'

A focus gradually rose on Max's face. He spoke louder.

'I've always been told family comes first.'

'Max. Look where you are. Understand what's happened. You're here alone. Trying to make sense of it by yourself. Hamish and you have been tortured. Questioned. For something which was nothing to do with either of you.'

Max rubbed his temples. His voice dropped back down.

'I heard them.'

'Heard them doing what?'

'Hurt other people.'

Ashley paused at the change of direction.

'Who was hurting them?'

'The people who took me.'

'Where?'

'At the place. They blindfolded me, but I listened to screams.'

'Whose?'

'I can't be certain. Hamish, probably, but I've never heard him scream like that before. They must have slipped me something. I don't take drugs, but everything's so hazy.'

'Give us snippets if it's all you have. Tell us what might have happened.'

Max rolled onto his back and spoke to the ceiling.

'I'm fairly sure they threatened to kill Hamish if I refused to talk, but I didn't know the answers to their questions. I kept telling them that, or at least I think I did. They told me Hamish would be killed. My blindfold was removed a few times. Once, when they took Hamish away for the last time. He was covered in blood. Again, when they brought Tommaso in. And then in the woods, so I could see the chair.'

Max licked his lips once more. His voice quivered.

'I thought I was going to burn,' he said, with his words returning to a whisper.

'We don't think they planned to kill you.'

Max's expression softened.

'My dad changed after my mum died. He and I were a long way from close before that. He shifted from being distant to becoming all about family. If I tell you anything, it'll hurt him. I can't implicate my father. He's innocent. It's Lorenzo who's evil.'

Max rolled over and faced away from them. Ashley stood.

'I bet you're thirsty. Shall I fetch you an ice-cold Coke from the machine?'

After a few seconds, Max nodded his head. Ashley nodded at Hector. As Ashley left, Hector took over.

'You know, Max. We're the same age, and my father has cast a big shadow over my life. He was a powerful man, too. It's difficult to escape, but you must. Or you'll never be free.'

Ashley peered through the window of the door as it closed behind her.

Max had turned around.

50

Ashley found a male nurse outside.

'Hi, can you tell me where the nearest vending machine is and whether Max is allowed a fizzy drink?'

'Sure, one floor up, and yes. The sugar will do him some good.'

She took her phone out as she trotted up the stairs and checked her emails. There was one from Sal.

A van was seen on CCTV going past The Hill House Inn, Happisburgh, about four a.m. this morning. Vehicle spotted further up on council cameras heading in the direction of Bacton. Different registration and colour (dark grey) but otherwise identical to the blue van we've been searching for. Door-knocking teams in action still, returning to houses missed. No more bodies on the beach or clifftop.

Scott had emailed a minute ago.

At the scene now. Rocco having last few minutes with his son, then will return to the car park while they remove the bodies. He says he has calls to make, so I offered to let him do them in my car while we wait for them to finish. I'll ring if anything pertinent comes out of him.

There was a text from Barry.

At Rocco's distribution centre. Shown a few workers the pictures of Ally, Morgan, and Zelda. No joy. Security here now. He seems foreign with poor English. Won't allow me in to ask women on reception. Doesn't seem to care about my warrant card, but I don't want any escalation. Will persist.

Ashley found the vending machine. Two pound fifty for a bottle of Coca-Cola. She bought two, and a can of Mountain Dew for Hector. Barry had called it chilled nocturnal animal's piss when Hector once opened a can in the office. Ashley doubted she'd ever be able to drink it again. She balanced them precariously on each other and padded back to the room.

Ashley decided to give Hector fifteen minutes. She rested the drinks on a windowsill and stared outside while she waited. A car screeched up outside A & E and stopped on double yellows. The driver, a middle-aged guy, shoved his door open and jumped out of his seat. He ran around to the passenger side, yanked the door open, leaned in and reappeared carrying a big lad who appeared to be in his early teens. The man staggered under the weight, then stomped towards the entrance. Even from so far away, Ashley could detect the anguish and desperation on the father's face. She thought of Rocco.

Her mobile rang.

'Ashley Knight.'

'Ivan here. I have a change of information.'

'Okay.'

'When we talked about the Popovics, I told you the girls'

mother informed me that her husband died, years back. It sounds as if that was wishful thinking.'

'You're saying he could be alive?'

'Yes, and maybe that fact is something important. My boss knew him from decades ago. He was well known to the authorities after the wars were over. Many men struggled to deal with what they had done. For some, it was as if the fighting never ended. They took their aggression home to their families. Apparently, the dad realised he was a danger to everyone around him and left to live up in the middle of nowhere, where there are no rules, no police, only wilderness.'

'How long ago was this?'

'Twenty years.'

'And he's not been seen since?'

'Not here, but the chief heard a rumour the father was in the city centre a few months ago. He can't be sure of the date, but, considering what's happened, he said it was vital that I tell you.'

'Okay, but he must be pretty old now, so he's unlikely to be involved.'

'The chief knew him before all the fighting. The man had a bad reputation as a youth, but wars let men like him off the leash. Once their darkness has been released, it can never be returned.'

Ashley wondered if all Montenegrins were as dramatic.

'Okay,' she said. 'Let's assume this father has headed to the UK after living in the hills for two decades. Surely he wouldn't have the resources or contacts to commit this series of offences.'

'No, that's my chief's point. He would not, but Dragan might. Perhaps Dragan is the gunpowder, and his dad is the missile.'

It was a timely metaphor.

'So, the Popovics' two beloved daughters go missing four years ago. One keeps in sporadic but distant contact, which then stops. A year ago, Jelena is discovered dead in a wood with no ID. She's eventually traced to the Popovics, and they're informed of their tragic loss within the last six months. They decide to avenge their honour in blood. After some investigation, they link everything to Lorenzo and his trafficking. Then the aggrieved patriarch, a man damaged from the horrors of the Balkan wars, heads here to wipe out Lorenzo's family.'

'Correct.'

'It seems a lot of effort. Why not simply come over here, then torture and kill Lorenzo?'

'Their anger is terrible. His death is not enough, and you are forgetting the most important thing.'

'Which is?'

'Jasmina is still missing. It is likely she is dead, but the Popovics need answers, or they won't be able to make their peace. The Viallis don't sound the type to talk without persuasion. There is a phrase in your language. To kill two birds with one stone. They will find the truth about Jasmina and have their vengeance at the same time.'

Ashley considered his words. It was the best explanation they had right now. Perhaps it was why Rocco and Lorenzo had no idea what was going on. As she'd suspected it might, this danger came out of left field. They had to locate the hotel where Lorenzo was staying. She hated to consider his fate if he were taken, considering what had been done to Tommaso and Gianluca.

Ashley knew little about torture, but would anyone have kept quiet under such punishment? Certainly, hired hands, like Gianluca and Paolo, would have shouted out at the first glimpse of a snipping tool.

'There is one more thing,' said Ivan. 'A lifer escaped from a prison here with outside help. His whereabouts are also unknown. I'm not sure if he's connected, but one of his known acquaintances was the father.'

'I'm assuming this escapee is as violent as the father.'

'Zoltan Andrijević is much, much worse. He is a man of extreme violence who killed for sport.'

'Brilliant.'

'Sorry, but it is important you hear.'

'What does he look like?'

'Big man. Bald head. His prison picture is ten years old unfortunately, but I'll email it to you.'

'Okay. Thanks for calling. Your information has been extremely helpful. Could you send any information you have to me and whatever photographs you can get your hands on?'

'Of course. I will look into the father for you.'

'Do you have his description?'

Ashley again heard Ivan talk to someone else. There was no laughter.

'Not a great one,' he said. 'Grey hair. Average height. Thin. Craggy face. Terrible eyes.'

'Terrible eyes?'

'Yes, you know. Vacant, haunted, mesmerising, ruthless. You're really putting my vocabulary to the test.'

'Your English is impressive. So, these girls probably inherited their soulful eyes from their father.'

'Yes.'

'What's his name?'

'He is called Emil.'

51

Ashley had a question on the tip of her tongue.

'Wait. You said this guy was a criminal and has lived in the back of beyond. Would he be able to get a passport?'

'I checked. No passport.'

'So how would he get here, then?'

'I thought anyone could wander into your country when they fancied.'

Ashley smiled. 'Sometimes it seems that way.'

'Maybe he got a false passport, or he could have come like his daughters did in a container or bought a seat on a boat across the Channel. While his son is not super rich, he would easily have money for an illegal crossing.'

'Will you talk to Emil's son, Dragan?'

Ivan laughed. 'And ask him if he's paid for his father to go on a homicidal holiday to the UK?'

Ashley grinned as her mobile vibrated. Barry was ringing her.

'Okay, Ivan. I'll be in touch.'

She took the waiting call.

'Yes, Barry.'

'I waited outside Rocco's Fine Homes because that security fella was walking up and down in front of the door, but he answered his phone, then jogged away to a car. He drove swiftly away.'

'And?'

'Well, my path is clear now.'

'Why not ring me afterwards, or do you want me to shout go-go-go?'

'Oh, I wanted to hear how your chat with Max went before I headed in.'

'Hector's working on him.'

'Great.'

'Be vigilant, Barry. I reckon that security bloke is actually a close protection officer that Rocco brought over from abroad.'

'I thought it was weird to have someone like that outside a kitchen place.'

'Barry, people have died!'

'I suppose so. Right, let's see if I can flush this rat out.'

'Wait. Describe the security guy.'

'Typical henchman. Bald, heavy, combo of fat and muscle. Fortyish. The kind of guy who could run through walls without slowing down. But he's gone, so I'm heading in.'

Ashley cut the call and returned to Max's room. She was about to enter when Scott rang her.

'Ashley speaking.'

'Hi. I need to be quick. I'm still in the car park. Rocco has nipped to the toilet block. He made three calls in my car. I was wondering if it would bother him with me listening, but he spoke in Italian.'

'Which you speak fluently?'

'If only life was like that.'

'Do you have any idea who he rang?'

'The first one could have been Lorenzo. Even in a foreign language, the tone was different from the other conversations. The next was more formal. It was the third which was odd. I suspect he can be a bit theatrical, but at the end of the call he repeated with genuine desperation something like *salvalo, per favore, salvalo*.'

'*Salvalo?*'

'Yes. I put it through Google Translate. I think it means, save him, please, save him.'

Ashley felt she was peppering Scott with a machine gun as she rapidly hit him with facts about Rocco upping his security, and what Ivan had told her about the possibility of a vengeful father.

'Okay,' said Scott calmly. 'That certainly sounds plausible. I don't know what I'd do if someone hurt my daughter and the law didn't make them pay. Especially if I knew where they lived and that they were doing it to others. It's also not a surprise that Rocco hired a top bodyguard.'

'Agreed. What are your plans now?'

'Rocco wants to follow the undertaker's van to the hospital. His car's here, but I'll drive him if he lets me. Someone's meeting him there with a change of clothes.'

'Right. Be careful, Scott. There are lunatics around, and they might be after Rocco. If they wanted Lorenzo to suffer, murdering his father would achieve that, just as well as killing his brothers.'

'Will do, Ash.'

Ashley peeked through the window into Max's room and saw him and Hector talking. Max even had half a smile on his face and some colour had returned to his cheeks. The corridor was empty, so Ashley rang Kettle at OCC and updated him.

Kettle was quiet as he digested the information.

'You've got to discover the location of this hotel they're staying in.'

Ashley listened as murmured voices and gentle laughter echoed from Max's room.

'I think we're about to get it,' she said, looking at the door.

Ashley bid goodbye to Kettle, grabbed the cans, and nudged the door open with her elbow.

Max was sitting up. He saw the drinks and took his with a smile.

'Sorry I've been a while, Max. You look a little better, if you don't mind me saying.'

Max ran a hand through his thick hair.

'It's probably gallows humour. Hector's been talking to me about the changes he made in his life. How it's normal to love and want to protect your family, but it's also okay to want to live separately. Ignore them if necessary.'

'Is that what you want?'

'I need out. I've got money saved. If you find Hamish, I'm going to vanish with him to a friend's house. Then we're applying for working holiday visas to Australia. We've looked into it. You'll never hear from us again. Even though it pains me to say it, neither will my father or Lorenzo.'

'Do you have any serious physical injuries?'

'No, my captors explained how they were going to slice off my balls. They ran the blade along my thighs, cutting me, and they repeatedly slapped my face, but it was mostly verbal threats. I told them I hated Tommaso, and that Lorenzo scares me. It was the truth. I said I'd answer any questions I was able to, so I did. I tried to help them.'

Max's mouth formed a grimace of shame.

'Don't worry, Max. You did what you had to do. We'll put you somewhere secure in the meantime.'

'Thank you.'

'Max, you talked to your captors, now talk to me,' urged Ashley, but it was Hector who replied.

'We've been waiting for you to return. Max has a story to tell us. He won't repeat it again because of respect for his dad. If he's taken to court, he will deny ever saying it.'

'Okay,' said Ashley, although the police were bound to report it, and Max could find himself in trouble at court if he refused to repeat what he'd said.

'I've already said we'll put him up in a safe place for a few days, so he can sort his finances and his plans out.'

Ashley looked back at Max and gave him a noncommittal nod.

'We need to know where Lorenzo is.'

Max lifted his chin.

'I'll give you the address of the hotel, but first, I have a terrible tale to tell.'

52

Normally, when my dad took his boys to Italy, we wouldn't stray far from Rome or Milan, but this time, four years ago, he stayed home. The vacation was different from the start, because we flew to Marco Polo airport near Venice.

On the second morning, Tommaso said he had business and would meet us in Udine in a few days, leaving Lorenzo to show me around Venice. Lorenzo was kind of showing off, but I didn't mind. I felt like a prince.

I had mixed feelings about my brothers when I was younger. Tommaso was four years older and tended to be rough with me. He never hit hard, but neither did he show affection.

Lorenzo was two years older than Tommaso, so it was quite a gap to me. He was often kind, but in a controlling way. Growing up, he showed me off as the young handsome one, until I told the family I might be gay.

My father, Rocco, reassured me I'd always be loved, whatever I wanted from life. He still couldn't resist saying it was lucky he had two other sons to continue his legacy. Tommaso saw my revelation as weakness. He barely spoke to me again.

Lorenzo took me for a meal shortly afterwards and asked outright. Was Hamish my boyfriend? I'd already learned to be wary of Lorenzo. There was a possessive and dominating side to him that made me edgy. If Lorenzo wanted something to be a certain way, it was. Almost at any cost. When he got whatever it was he desired, he would enjoy it, but then, he wouldn't let anyone else have it. He'd rather destroy than share. Traits like that aren't normal.

So, I told Lorenzo that Hamish and me were close, but simply good friends now, helping each other through life. I even lied about having feelings for women, too.

Lorenzo stared long and hard that day, before finally smiling. He calmly thanked me for my honesty, which caused my insides to squirm, then explained how it was probably best for the family if I kept my private life private in the future. I immediately realised, at some point, I would need to escape.

Everything settled down afterwards. I kept to the edges of most family occasions, but still went on and enjoyed the luxury Vialli holidays, all paid for by Rocco. My dad made them fun, and my brothers left me alone. Until this one when he didn't come.

After Lorenzo showed me the sights of Venice, he drove us to Udine in an open-top car and booked into Castello di Buttrio, a castle hotel that dominated the vine-covered slopes surrounding it.

We spent a day in Udine with all its incredible architecture. It was eye-opening, and only ruined by me knowing it would have been more perfect with Hamish present. Then Tommaso showed up for breakfast, leading to an instant tension over coffee and croissants.

After we'd eaten, a long, sleek, black Mercedes arrived and took the three of us over the border into Slovenia. I plucked up the courage to ask where we were going, but Tommaso told me to keep quiet. Slovenia proved beautiful, but I struggled to enjoy the view. When I looked out of the rear window, two white vans and another Mercedes followed. When I glanced back many hours later, the same three vehicles remained behind.

It was dusk when our car stopped in the middle of nowhere. We seemed to be in a meadow next to a forest, which stretched far away into the mountains.

'Out,' instructed Lorenzo.

My brothers and I left the car, but the driver didn't. A pistol handle stuck out the back of Tommaso's belt. Lorenzo raised the vehicle's boot, then bent and fiddled with something inside. He came away empty-handed, but left it open. I could hardly breathe.

'What's going on?' I asked.

'We're meeting friends,' replied Lorenzo.

I wondered what kind of friends would need loaded weapons present.

After thirty minutes of my brothers' chain-smoking in silence, lights appeared through the towering trees.

'Come,' said Tommaso to me. 'Say nothing.'

I followed, with Lorenzo next to me. The RV trundled to a stop at the edge of the forest. Two men clambered from each side of the cab. The dense wood made it difficult to see beyond a few feet, but moonlight filtered through the thick canopy and lit up their stern faces. I slowed, but Tommaso and Lorenzo strode towards them and shook hands.

My brothers spoke to one of the new arrivals in rapid Italian. I took a few paces nearer to hear them better. As I'm the youngest, my parents hadn't been as bothered about me learning the language, so I'm rusty and struggled to understand them. It was as if they were speaking in code.

I made out the words *quindici* and *vediamoli*, which I knew meant *fifteen* and *let's see them*. Tommaso opened the side door of the RV and went inside. He shouted *uscire. Get out*.

I couldn't believe my eyes when a young woman appeared at the door and stepped down. More followed. Tommaso being last out.

'Formare una linea,' he growled.

'Senor.' One of the girls shuffled forwards, her gaze down submissively. '*Per favore*.'

Tommaso waited until she was close, then he slapped her face and sent her spinning.

'*Formare una linea!*' ordered Tommaso.

My mouth went dry. Many were teenagers.

The door of the Mercedes that had been following us opened, and an older, bone-thin man with a flat nose walked towards Lorenzo. They exchanged handshakes, then ambled towards the first woman in the line. Flatnose held a small torch. He shone it into her face.

'Mula,' said Lorenzo.

Flatnose pointed at the girl.

'*Ricordalo*,' he shouted. *Remember it*.

He shifted two steps to the left, so he was in front of the next person, and shone the beam on her face.

'*Cavalla*,' said Lorenzo.

They progressed down the row. There were more *mula* than *cavalla*. It was obvious those who were more attractive got tagged as *cavalla*. I felt sicker and sicker as each torch beam lit up a terrified girl. Most of them wilted under the spotlight. A couple glared defiantly ahead.

The light reflected onto the faces of Lorenzo, Tommaso and Flatnose, making them seem old and wizened. Tommaso also appeared demented. When they approached the second to last in the row, the driver of the RV took a step forwards.

'Sorellas,' he said. *Sisters.*

The torch lit up the first of them. She was petite, but with prominent features. Pretty, without being beautiful.

'Cavalla,' said Lorenzo.

The second girl's attractiveness was impossible to miss. Even from my distant position, I noticed the shift in my brother's posture. She was a touch taller than her sister, but still little more than five feet. Her looks were almost elven. I've never seen anyone so striking. Judging by how he puffed himself up, neither had Lorenzo.

I watched with horror as Lorenzo reached over and gently lifted the woman's chin, forcing her to meet his stare. She glared rebelliously back for a second, then looked away.

'Unicorno,' said Lorenzo.

He turned to Flatnose and spoke slow and heavy.

'Andare. Termini normali. Processo usuale. Sai cosa fare se hai problemi.'

I could just about translate.

Go. Normal terms. Usual process. You know what to do if you have problems.

I'm not stupid, and I read the news. It was obvious what I was witnessing, but it wouldn't sink into my brain. My mind had been stunned. I remained glued to the spot while the girls were shepherded to the waiting vans. All except the *unicorno*, who Flatnose escorted to the rear seats of his car.

'Get used to it,' snarled Tommaso as he walked past me so near we bumped shoulders. I stared after him as an owl hooted in the trees overhead, then glided away. My innocence departing with it.

Lorenzo came and stood next to me. He wore the same expression I had seen many times before, when we were growing up. One of want and desire. A face of determination.

'Don't look so shocked,' said Lorenzo. 'That was your introduction to the new family business.'

53

PRESENT DAY

Max's cheeks reddened further as he told his tale, which Ashley suspected was guilt. It was a troubling tale, but it also made sense.

Criminal gangs containing family members were the hardest to infiltrate. Ashley knew if you combined those close units with cross-border movement of either drugs or people, then their behaviour could continue unchecked for years.

'How long has Lorenzo been running the club, Max?' she asked.

'About six years. After my mum died, Dad wanted them to have a focus and learn properly about business. Accounts, cash flow, stock. Lorenzo and Tommaso had been living like playboys until then. Dad had been addicted to work, so he decided to take a step back and push them forward.'

'So, you don't think he's involved in any of this?'

'No. My mum dying was a wake-up call for him. What was all the money for if he spent his life in his office? He planned lots of family meals. You understand? All of us coming over to his lovely house and garden with our partners. Or huge gatherings at posh restaurants. He still had the kitchen business to focus on.'

'Surely, he must have suspected there might have been something untoward going on at the club with all the police raids. It was in the *Eastern Daily Press*, for God's sake.'

'My father has always been blinkered when it comes to Lorenzo. He's the image of him in looks and stature. Tommaso was always his strong, silent son, and look at me. Hah!'

Ashley recalled Rocco saying, 'Hah'. He and Max were probably more similar than he thought. Max's face twisted into a frown. Ashley kept quiet, knowing he was on a roll. Max's voice quietened.

'Lorenzo has poise, class, and brains. Dad can't see the darkness in him. Hamish and I joked that Lorenzo has the Scarface complex, like in the film. You know, where you believe your own hype. The need to be the ruler of your domain. To be the best. Lorenzo knows he is destined to be the king, but his personality is twisted. He thinks the rules don't apply to him. Anyone outside his circle is a commodity to be used. Their lives can be ruined as long as Prince Lorenzo gets what he wants.'

'Whose lives?' asked Hector.

'I can't talk about that. I've gone too far already. Lorenzo would kill me without skipping a beat if he knew I talked to you.'

'Wasn't Al Pacino's demise in *Scarface* hastened by cocaine?' asked Ashley. 'Do Lorenzo and Tommaso have the same problem?'

'I doubt it. The pair of them are mad enough without any of that. They'd have killed half of Norwich by now. Lorenzo would hate the loss of control. They did have problems with drug dealers at the nightclub to start with, and the place was dirty and outdated. Lorenzo considered it a reflection of himself so he built something magnificent. The Coliseum. Tommaso and Gianluca cleared out the scum. It became the best party in town. Guests came from London and all over. The finest women were on tap.'

'Who were trafficked,' stated Hector.

Max cringed.

'I went to the members' area when I was told to, but I usually stayed in the club. You could tell some of the members' girls weren't happy. Their smiles never reached their eyes while they spent evenings dodging pawing fingers, but that wasn't all of them. Some loved it. I occasionally talked to them. Pretended I was bisexual. One evening, I paid a girl to come home with me and we played Scrabble. She was Czech, and she beat me.'

'The fact she got used to it doesn't make trafficking any more acceptable,' said Hector.

'No, she applied for the job. She was stunning. These rich men were putty in her hands. She told me she eased cash from them like squeezing water from a sponge. It was to set her and her child up for life. When she saved enough money, they would leave the UK forever. It's the oldest career in the world, after all. Nobody really bothered the girls, or Gianluca would have thrown them out.'

'Did the Czech woman leave the country?' asked Hector.

'Yes, after three months. Lorenzo was pissed off because she was so popular. She just disappeared and it made me realise what Hamish and I should do.'

'But some girls were trafficked?' asked Ashley.

'Yes, I think so. Lorenzo wanted a revolving door of women. Fresh meat every few months. Diverse types. Exotic foreigners aren't easy to get out here in Norfolk, so they were brought in from abroad. They were paying off their journeys. The usual story. To be fair to Lorenzo, most repaid their debts and left the club after six months. A few chose to stay.'

'I expect they were institutionalised by that point,' said Hector.

Ashley gave him a warning glance. They were here for information, not to give Max a lecture on exploitation.

'So, Max,' she said. 'This must have been so tough on you. Your own brothers immersed in something like this. Did they force you to help with the business?'

'No, of course not. When I got back, I told my dad I couldn't work under Lorenzo.'

'Did your father know the type of operation he was running?'

'He always insisted the club was for Lorenzo to operate as he wished, but he would talk to him if I didn't want to be involved.'

'Did you mention this *mula* and *cavalla* stuff to Rocco?'

Max wiped his eyes as he remembered the conversation.

'No, I couldn't. You see?' Big eyes stared at Hector, then Ashley. 'Lorenzo is the future.'

'Even if he's breaking the law?' asked Hector.

'It's not for me to question his behaviour. My dad wouldn't want to hear it.'

Ashley wasn't quite sure what to make of that, but she wanted to keep him talking. She allowed him a few seconds to compose himself. He wrung his hands.

'What is this *mula* thing?' she asked. '*Mula*, I assume is a mule, so I'm thinking drugs. Those women were used to move heroin or cocaine.'

'Right.'

'What is *cavalla*?'

'*Cavalla* means horse,' said Hector.

'Yes,' said Max, looking away. 'It was their joke. Those poor girls were for riding.'

54

Ashley shielded the look of distaste and irritation that automatically appeared on her face by scratching her nose.

'At the club?' asked Ashley.

'No. They weren't pretty enough for the private members' area. Those girls were given to the Vampires for their business. They were brought over by lorry or in containers, the mules came individually with fake papers or hidden in car boots, or they were forced to take their chances on the boats across the Channel. Either way, they carried packages with them. They often ended up in domestic jobs for little money.'

'What if anyone refused?' asked Hector.

Max shrugged and put his head in his hands.

'Max. How do you know all this if you never worked for Lorenzo?' asked Ashley.

'After the girls were taken away in Slovenia, Lorenzo left in the other Mercedes. Tommaso drove me back to Udine, then just he and I flew home together. He loosely explained how the business operated on the way, thinking I would join them.'

'Ah, so your dad agreed you didn't need to be involved, but he wasn't aware of what Tommaso told you,' said Hector.

'Exactly.'

'I bet your brothers were furious when they found out what your father said, and Tommaso had already revealed the truth about the nightclub to you.'

'It was worse than that. Lorenzo and Tommaso took me to dinner and warned me. They threatened me that I might believe I only work for Rocco's Fine Homes, but I'm involved in everything. I would sink or swim with them. So, I knew escaping was my only option, but we had no money. Hamish and I tried to save, but we needed to hide our relationship. He rented a shitty flat, which still ate up our funds, but we spent all our time with each other. It just never seemed the right moment to vanish until recently.'

'So, that's why when you went to his club, you would pretend to get drunk and chat women up as if everything was fine,' said Hector.

Max nodded.

'Well, we tried, but Lorenzo's no fool. He must have been suspicious. Hamish had a tough upbringing with no parents. At times, he took drugs, but he managed to break the habit more or less. The last three months, when we were almost ready to leave, Hamish suddenly slipped back on them big time. I thought the pressure had got to him, but I was wrong. It was Lorenzo. He'd been supplying them to Hamish for free, and his addiction grew. Hamish became so paranoid and erratic. I didn't think I could get him out of here like that.'

'But you do now?' asked Ashley.

'Yes, we still have to go. Far away. I'll get Hamish off the junk myself miles from here, and then our lives can start.'

Hector had been ready to say something. Ashley gestured for him to speak.

'Unicorno,' he said. 'Unicorn. Those were the ones who ended up as hostesses for Lorenzo?'

'Yes. They were the absolute beauties. Their transport was by private car with quality documents, or even a yacht. It's easy to visit an island like England without going through Customs if you are prepared to pay.'

'I find it hard to believe your father didn't suspect Lorenzo was up to something illegal.'

Max scoffed. 'Ah, you see, Lorenzo was always the golden boy, and then he laid the golden egg, or his girlfriend, Vittoria, did.'

'Ah ha!' said Ashley. 'They gave Rocco what he most desired. A grandchild.'

'Not just one, but two. Both strapping boys. They're two and three now. My father's pride and joy. Even Lorenzo can't compete. Raffaele and little Rocco. Rocchino, we call him. The most handsome, sweet kids you could ever meet. They are hidden from the world. Safe in the hotel.'

Ashley stiffened at the word. They were approaching the vital part of the interview. She glanced into Max's eyes with concern that he might not tell them the truth, but Max had rediscovered his resolve. His jaw clenched and unclenched. Then he smiled.

'Fuck Lorenzo.'

'It's not a hotel, is it?' asked Hector.

'No,' said Max. 'That's a secret word.'

'Where are they, Max?' asked Ashley.

'They're in Overstrand. It's a small place near Cromer.'

Ashley nodded calmly when he gave her the address, as though she'd vaguely heard of it. She knew the location in the village intimately, seeing as it was only a mile from her house.

'Well done, Max. So, Lorenzo lives there with the kids and Vittoria.'

'No. He lives in that big property next to my dad. The Overstrand cottage is for her and the children. It's their prison. I told you. Lorenzo collects things, and that includes people. Even if he doesn't want them any more, nobody else can have them. Vittoria is a lovely person. She is a beautiful tiger, but he keeps her in a cage, locked away from the rest of the world.'

Ashley bobbed her head at him. He had at least inherited Rocco's expressive nature. She had to respect him for having the strength to shatter the family code finally. Max had put himself in a lot of danger, assuming he was telling the truth.

The most important thing was they now knew the location for Lorenzo's children. Most sociopathic Alpha males considered their offspring reflections of their identity, even if they might not love them in the conventional way. Combined with what Rocco had said, Lorenzo was likely to be holed up with them.

Ashley's mind was in its tying-up-loose-ends mode.

'Max. The two sisters who were at the end of the line. One of them was branded *cavalla*. What exactly happened to those girls?'

'I'm not sure. Tommaso explained once that, after the women go to the Vampires, it's none of our business. I assume they'd need to work off their debt like the others.'

'It sounds as if one was a woman called Jelena. She was found in a wood a year ago, having finally escaped from their clutches after three years.'

Max's face froze. He spluttered out a question.

'She was still working for them, after three years?'

'Yes.'

'Where is she now?'

'Jelena was discovered dead.'

His eyes stretched like saucers. Max was finally struck mute.

'I'm sorry,' said Hector. 'It's hard to believe. But we don't know what happened to her sister, Jasmina. You told us she was *unicorno*. Which means she would have come to work for Lorenzo in the club. Did you see her there? I understand it was a long time ago, but you also mentioned she was someone you'd never forget.'

Max shook his head, still dumbstruck. Ashley put a hand on his arm.

'People are looking for her, Max. We must find where she is, or what happened to her. Her devastated family is desperate to know if she's alive.'

Again, Max couldn't look her in the eye.

'You don't understand. Jasmina is now called Vittoria.'

55

Hector recovered faster than Ashley.

'You're saying Lorenzo spotted her in that Slovenian line-up and brought her over to this country, where he impregnated her, twice, and kept her in a house in Overstrand.'

'Yes. She never worked in the club.'

'Is Jasmina there of her own free will?' asked Ashley.

'She wasn't. Only my dad or us boys visit them on Harbord Road, or Lorenzo drives her either to Rocco's when he holds garden parties, or to restaurants for celebratory meals.'

'What do you mean, she wasn't?'

'When she was pregnant with their second son, Raffaele, she collared me in Rocco's garden when my brothers and dad had gone for a business discussion. Jasmina wanted to go home to Montenegro. She begged me to help her.'

'Why didn't she leave, or did she have no money? I bet he took her passport.'

'Both, but she wasn't stupid. She understood she only need visit a police station and explain, except Lorenzo had told her if she left him, he would kill her sister, Jelena, who was in the same situation in a different city.'

'That's awful,' said Hector.

Ashley puffed out a breath at Hector's use of words. Awful didn't even come close.

'She's happy now, though. A few months ago, she told Lorenzo it was time for her to accept her role here as mother to her children and build a life in Overstrand. Lorenzo said she wanted to get married, but no date has been set.'

Ashley suspected Lorenzo liked Vittoria right where he had her. Ashley was thinking about what else Max could tell them when his eyes widened. His hand came to his mouth.

'Oh, no.' He groaned, closing his eyes as his pale features turned grey.

'What?'

'I think... all this talk of Overstrand. It's coming back to me.'

'Try to explain,' urged Ashley.

'The men who took me. I told them everything, including the cottage's address.'

Ashley quickly understood the implications.

'Which means the people responsible know where Jasmina is living.'

Max wasn't listening. He appeared to be thinking back to that moment. He looked up with a pained expression, close to tears.

'The man said he forgave me.'

Ashley assumed whoever was doing this wouldn't have raced around to the property. They had shown patience and planned every step so far, but it was no wonder they hadn't been worried about finding Lorenzo. Max would have revealed Jasmina's location during the first few nights of questioning. They would have guessed Lorenzo would be there at some point.

What was worrying was why Max was alive. Did they think he

wouldn't talk because doing so would drop his brother in it with their father, or was it because the attackers were ready to move? Perhaps they suspected Max dared not tell Lorenzo he'd blabbed the location to them. They'd been right about that.

'I'm going to nip into the corridor and make a few calls. Hector, see if Max wants a bite to eat or a coffee.'

Ashley left the room and rang Kettle. She imagined him nodding grimly after she repeated what Max told them.

'Now we're getting somewhere.'

'Yes, finally. Hector and I will come back to OCC. Max has an evaluation to pass, but then he'll be discharged. We need to get him a long way from here, especially with Rocco heading to the mortuary.'

'What are the dangers if anyone turns up unannounced at Vittoria's house?'

'We should call her Jasmina.'

'Agreed. Those bastards stole their lives and their names.'

'The risks for Jasmina's rescuers are serious. Guns are a real possibility.'

'I meant for us.'

'Sorry, you're wondering what Lorenzo's capable of if the police knock?'

'Yes, that is my concern.'

'My guess would be nothing. Assuming she's there, we should get her out today.'

'Really?'

'If we turn up mob handed, what can he do? Remember, his family are the recent victims in all this. He probably won't suspect we're onto his trafficking until the moment we arrive. Lorenzo will front it out, confident our evidence is weak.'

'Will Max testify?'

'He said not, but he knew about all this and kept it to himself.

I wouldn't be surprised if the CPS charge him with conspiring to commit an offence of human trafficking. We have plenty of leverage. Who knows what might unravel if it all falls apart? Drita may give evidence. Oh, shit! I forgot about the danger to Jasmina.'

Kettle growled his reply. 'Yes. The biggest threat to Lorenzo's freedom will be standing next to him.'

'Would he kill the mother of his children in front of the police?'

'Doubtful, but he may take her hostage.'

'No, it's too messy. Behave like that, and he ends up in prison for a long time for that crime alone, never mind his other sins. He'd be a sitting duck in jail. Whereas we may struggle to get anything to stick on the trafficking. If we'd had better intel, Ally would've collared him ages ago. The odds are he tries to run. If he turns himself in later, I doubt it would lead to custody if we can't prove the rest.'

'Yes, he's likely to have brilliant counsel and watertight phone and bank records. She's our best chance of a prosecution, though.'

Ashley's phone vibrated to indicate she had a call holding. She ignored it.

'Yes, but she's a foreign national who, strictly speaking, entered the country illegally. She'll probably go back to Montenegro and want to put it all behind her. How many victims like her hang around for the trial, even with the option of video links nowadays?'

'If he's as ruthless as we think, he'll threaten to end his own children's lives if she talks, not hers. Nothing will bring her sister home, so like so many victims she'll disappear.'

'We've got the added problem of the sisters' angry father, Emil. If he's here and responsible, he's not working on his own. His son has money and influence, so it could be a reasonable team. We need to head to Overstrand, hopefully find Lorenzo and Jasmina, get them in custody, and go from there.'

'Agreed, but it's too dangerous without at least having Tasers. Hang on.'

Ashley received a text as Kettle put her on hold. It was Barry.

Call me asap.

Kettle came back on the line a minute later while Ashley was patrolling the hospital corridor like an expectant father.

'Ally's leaving Happisburgh beach shortly,' he said. 'I've redirected him to Overstrand. A response vehicle, double teamed, both Taser trained, will leave Sprowston nick within fifteen minutes. If you arrive before them, wait down the street. Only engage if it looks like Lorenzo's disappearing.'

'Okay. There might be kids present, so send Emma down, too. Rocco mentioned he was bringing over protection for his family, so Lorenzo's liable to have at least one security person with him.'

'There's a motorbike from Traffic finishing up at a domestic not far away. I'll request him or her too. This situation isn't ideal, but time is clearly of the essence. I'll set up a command room here.'

'Perfect, I'll ring Ally and confirm where to meet.'

Ashley thought for a moment he was going to tell her to be cautious before he cut the call, but instead he snarled, 'Don't lose him.'

Ashley rang Ally, who picked up immediately. She explained.

'I'll be there before you,' he said. 'How do you want to play it?'

'The property is down Harbord Road. There are two routes in and out, but they all lead to Cromer Road. He won't be expecting us, so if he leaves for any reason, he should turn onto High Street near the convenience store.'

'Okay. Kettle said Sal will send me details of the cars registered to Lorenzo's home address, but I doubt he'll be in one of them. I'll keep my eyes peeled until you and the backup arrive. I assume Kettle's happy for us to block him in or even shunt him if it's safe to do so.'

Ashley smiled.

'Yes, although he'd never admit to it. Let's hope it doesn't come to that. In forty-five minutes, we'll have enough bodies to knock on the door.'

'Okay. Morgan and Zelda checked out the Vampires café again. It's all closed up. Looks dead.'

Ashley told him what Max had given them.

'Well done. That's more than we've ever got out of anyone else. I reckon the Vampires were probably working for Rocco or Lorenzo. They must have heard what's happening and gone to ground.'

'Sounds like Lorenzo was gifted the nightclub to run and went rogue with it.'

'Right. Look, I'll talk to you in Overstrand. I'm going to set off.'

Ashley spent a minute writing in her notebook, then saw the uniformed officer who had been sitting outside Max's hospital room had returned and was waiting at the nurses' desk with his colleague.

She beckoned him over.

'We're leaving. There'll be developments over the next few hours, so check in with Control every fifteen minutes, or if you're in any way suspicious. More officers are coming to support you, then we'll move Max to somewhere safe.'

'Yes, Sarge. No worries.'

Hector left Max's room.

'He wants to sleep for a bit. Get his head around what he's told us. He feels guilty he didn't help Jasmina or Jelena, but he's still scared. I reminded him Tommaso's gone, and he can't hurt him.'

'Well, it's a little late for that. It's good he's been honest now, but the time for the truth was when he first came back from Slovenia.'

'I'm not sure many nineteen-year-olds would have done that. What's the plan?'

'We're going for Lorenzo. Whether we'll have enough evidence or witnesses to charge him isn't clear, but we also have a duty of care to protect him from Emil. I wouldn't be surprised if Emil's team have been scoping the place ever since they found out its location. Jasmina and the children also need removing immediately.'

'Let's hope we aren't too late.'

Ashley had the feeling it would be touch and go.

'I agree. Come on, we'll update Control on the way.'

When they got in the car and began their journey, Ashley rang Barry on speaker phone.

'You took your time,' was his first comment.

'Quiet. There's a cottage where we suspect Lorenzo is hiding up, or at least where his girlfriend and children are.'

'Where?'

'Overstrand. A minute's walk from the paper shop.'

'Do you need a hand? I can be there in three quarters of an hour.'

'Okay. I've got Hector and Ally, and uniform backup with Tasers. Come down, though, but do it discreetly. Get in touch when you're five minutes away. How did you get on?'

'I took the photographs in and spoke to the receptionist. She works part-time and said none of them were familiar, but Rocco has a small gym there for them all to use. She told me the other receptionist was working out in it and showed me down there. The second woman was no actor. One picture caused an immediate response. She was worried about upsetting Rocco because she loves her job. I soon cut that shit out. Turns out our informant has been here numerous times.'

'Spit it out. Who's the rat, Barry?'

'DS Ally Williamson.'

56

Ashley's instant reaction was to stick up for Ally. She felt herself puffing up.

'No way, he's sound.'

'Ashley!' Barry barked down the phone.

'I've worked with him for nearly a decade.'

'I've known him longer. Think about it, Ash. We've all suspected something hasn't been right for a while. Even if we weren't asking ourselves if we had a snake in the grass, we've been concerned about the poor clear-up rate with the drugs in the area.'

'You know how difficult it is to get inside tightly run crime families.'

'The last six months, it's been obvious information is leaking out. Look at the case in Paradise Park. They knew some things before I did.'

Ashley opened her mouth to reply, but she was already deflating. Ally had almost been an enigma in the department. Wacky hair, cheap suits, loved a joke. His knowledge and ability to keep his finger on the pulse of such a vast area was hard to fathom for the new detectives. He was someone to look up to.

Ashley recalled Ally telling her about his divorce. Had he seemed a person beaten down by life? Not quite at vagrant levels, but he was unshaven and unkempt. Had the dude who was once bohemian slipped to a man in need of salvation, and resorted to desperation?

Her pause gave Barry the opportunity to press his advantage.

'You must have heard the rumours about gambling.'

'Only from you, and wasn't that on horses?'

'If he's an addict, he'll be betting on everything from Shergar turning up again, to aliens running the Tory party. We have nothing on these Vampires and Romans, apart from what we've found out during this investigation, yet they're probably familiar with the menu in our canteen.'

'Okay, but having been at Rocco's business doesn't confirm he's corrupt. There might be a sound explanation. He could have been double-checking all manner of things.'

'Yeah, of course. That's what I thought. I guess we could check the crime recording database, and everything should go in the murder book.'

'Exactly. I bet it's on both.'

'Well, I got Sal to investigate before I rang you.'

'Shit.'

'Yeah. I'm having it out with Ally today. You've seen what happens when cops go bad, Ashley. I'll see you soon.'

'Wait!' The line was dead. 'Fuck.'

'It appears Ally has been unethical,' said Hector.

'Your vocabulary does him an injustice. If he is bent, his behaviour makes all our lives more dangerous. Barry's on the money. Corruption is a cancer. If it's not hit early and aggressively, it spreads and is much more difficult to cure. Ally's also a DS, to complicate matters. Youngsters like Morgan and Zelda are vulnerable to getting influenced by him.'

'Then it's not only Ally's career at risk.'

'Exactly. The thing is, we don't have unarguable proof yet. The police officer in Montenegro suggested that when the beast of war was let out, there's no putting it back. It's the same with dishonesty. If this gets out, it won't matter if Ally is guilty or not. His career will be over. Fuck!'

'What?'

'It's probably over already.'

'Why?'

'Barry knows. Sal knows. We know.'

'Ah, I see. So, the virus will spread regardless. At least you'll be able to tell if I've improved at judging people's behaviour in a few minutes.'

'What do you mean?'

'Ally's meeting us at Overstrand. We're on our way to confront Lorenzo, and Barry suspects Ally's been feeding him and Rocco intel. Ally and Lorenzo may try to act distant, even though they are likely well acquainted. The best actors in the world with months of practice might struggle to pull that off.'

'That's true. Ally won't be looking forward to it, but at least he's had a chance to prepare. Lorenzo won't have a clue we're coming.'

'Not unless Ally rings him on the way.'

Ashley's mind was firing off connections.

'But that might give us proof if Ally calls him.'

'Surely Ally would have a burner phone.'

'Maybe, but he'll be panicking. We can confiscate Lorenzo's mobile. It should be possible to use phone masts to isolate where his calls came from. Ally is on his way from Happisburgh, which means he'd have rung while he was on the coast road.'

'Good point.'

'But an angry Barry appearing won't be helpful.'

'I agree. Now is not the time for an altercation.'

'What Ally needs is a chat with Kettle on video back at OCC, not a scuffle on the high street of a quiet village. That's assuming Kettle doesn't simply suspend Ally and notify Professional Standards or the Independent Office for Police Conduct.'

With that in mind, she called Barry back, but it rang out.

She imagined him, teeth gritted, chin over the steering wheel. A committed driver leading the field at Le Mans.

Ashley tutted loudly with the confirmation. 'So, Ally has definitely been visiting the warehouse for no obvious reason.'

'Yes?'

'That's not Lorenzo's domain at all, only Rocco's.'

Hector smiled as he swung wide to overtake a mobility scooter, which also had a focussed occupant who drove as though he were in the world's most famous automobile race.

'The plot thickens,' he replied. 'Perhaps when Rocco said, "Like a father, but not his father", when asked about Hamish, he meant he was the Godfather.'

Ashley didn't even chuckle. She considered ringing Kettle, but suspected he might say abort. If they had a dirty officer, Ashley wanted to know. The dice were rolling and would stop in ten minutes. She was inclined to let them land.

Her phone rang. She stared at the screen for a few seconds when she saw who it was.

'Yes, Ally,' she said after hitting accept.

'I got a puncture, but I've used one of those rapid repair kits, so I'm back on my way. ETA fifteen minutes.'

'Okay, no worries. We should be there by then.'

Ashley cut the call and closed her eyes to think.

57

Lorenzo finished the conversation with his informant and placed his mobile on the arm of the garden bench. The sea fret from earlier had gone, but he still zipped up his Armani quilted jacket and wished he had gloves. Jasmina had brought the children out to play on the grass in hats and gloves. She was laughing at Raffaele as he thundered around. The little boy raised his hand to get his attention.

'Dadda,' the kid shouted.

Lorenzo stared at his son, then at the person he considered his property. She looked wonderful. Even though the cottage was registered under the name Vittoria, he never called her that. She was Jasmina, his beautiful flower. Always.

He clapped his hands at Raffaele with a joy he didn't feel inside, and rarely had done at any point in his life. Love was something he struggled with, while possession could be easily understood. Jasmina laughed as Rocchino kicked the ball into an imaginary goal and cheered. She'd changed over the last couple of months. It showed in her face, in the way she talked, even the way she made love. She was giving herself to him, as opposed to

Lorenzo taking what he wanted. He wasn't entirely sure he preferred it.

Lorenzo recalled his father's phone call telling him what had happened on the beach. His mind brought up the framed photograph of the three brothers together in the nightclub. He suspected love wasn't what he felt for Tommaso, who had been an unlikeable, violent creature. Lorenzo's affection towards him was more that of liking and respecting a particularly efficient guard dog. His loyalty would be missed.

How dared someone do that to him? Lorenzo choked back his anger. There would be a time for making those responsible pay. He would make sure of it. At least now, after hearing the message from his inside man, Lorenzo knew why his organisation had been decimated.

It was that meeting in the forests of Slovenia four years ago that had led to this disaster. He stood and forced a smile on his face for Jasmina.

'I have some business to attend to.'

'Oh. The boys have enjoyed having you here these last few days. It's lovely for them to spend so much time with you.' She met his gaze. 'It's been good for all of us.'

Jasmina walked towards him wearing one of her stunning smiles and rested her hand on his arm. He barely felt it through his thick coat. Even so, he wanted it gone.

'It has been great. I'll be back soon. A few days, then all this recent drama will be over.'

Jasmina looked nonplussed. He supposed she didn't know anything had changed, apart from it not being usual for him to be with her for so long. He hadn't mentioned Tommaso's demise, or the fact Max had gone missing. Max was the only person she seemed to relax with, although Lorenzo understood why that wasn't surprising.

'I could cook a meal for us,' said Jasmina. 'We can have *Ispod Saca* and make it an occasion. I have the meat in the freezer. You loved the previous one.'

Lorenzo struggled to maintain his composure. He'd eaten the meal thinking back then about another young lady who had rebuffed his charms, and he'd barely tasted what Jasmina had explained was the Montenegrin equivalent of an English Sunday roast.

'Stop tempting me when I have to go,' he said. 'It's not easy to leave, but I must. Look after my kids.'

Lorenzo strode inside with a frown, which she couldn't see. He'd meant to say our kids. In the lounge at the front sat the man Rocco had brought over from abroad to protect Lorenzo. His name was Quinto, and he was cleaning his Beretta 92 for the fifth or sixth time.

Lorenzo had stopped looking over his shoulder when Quinto took up his post. Quinto had been hawk-eyed at first, but the guy seemed distracted now. Lorenzo could tell when a man's mind wasn't on the job. He felt like slapping him, but Gianluca, Paolo and Tommaso were gone. Quinto was all he had. He just had to hope his protector hadn't been paid to become his attacker.

'Time to leave,' said Lorenzo in Italian.

'Why? It's safe here, or have you heard otherwise?'

'We've discovered the likely cause of our recent bother might be Jasmina's family from back home.'

'And they are aware you're here?'

'Only Tommaso, Max, Rocco and I knew about this place, but it is no longer a secret. They will be coming for her. It has to be their end game.'

'Would Tommaso have talked before he died?'

'No, I don't think so, but if they really hurt him, who knows? Max, on the other hand, is still alive, so he probably did.'

Lorenzo knew Max had talked. His informant had told him, but he didn't want to admit his brother's weakness to a stranger.

'Okay, let's go,' said Quinto. 'It's better to be safe than sorry. There's another place that Rocco told me about. We'll wait there. No problem.'

Lorenzo tutted. He hated sitting around doing nothing, and he'd smoked his last cigar.

'Stop at the store for a minute. I need a few things.'

They strode from the house and got in the maroon Nissan Pathfinder. Lorenzo had to admit it was an excellent choice of car. Strong and powerful, but not too ostentatious. Quinto started the engine and pulled away. He turned left at High Street and cruised past the shop to check out the immediate area.

There was a middle-aged couple strolling hand in hand further up the road. They were the only people he could see, so he spun the car around and parked at a spot directly outside the store. A grey-haired man stepped gingerly out of the doorway with his newspaper tucked under his arm. Leaves twirled in the air from the towering trees that lined the pavement. The old-timer grimaced, then limped down the street in the direction of The White Horse.

Lorenzo stepped out of the SUV and walked around the bonnet to the pavement. He waited outside while an elderly woman left the store carrying a cake as though it might explode.

Quinto wound down the window and grinned.

'Be careful in there, Lorenzo.'

Lorenzo glanced at the woman in front of him with annoyance. She contemplated the kerb as though it were a cliff edge, then doddered further up where it had been dropped.

'If your time's up,' he said to Quinto with half a smile, 'what can you do?'

Lorenzo walked into the cool interior, grabbed *Men's Health* from a magazine stand, then chose some fruit. There were no other customers. He dawdled near the chocolate and cold drinks, before selecting a Diet Coke and a Crunchie. At the till, he remembered his so-called bodyguard waiting outside, so he went back and got the same again. Maybe it would wake the guy up.

'What cigars do you have?' he asked the assistant at the counter.

The server raised a finger as she counted the receipts in front of her. She shook her head and started again. Lorenzo's blood boiled. Why was she taking so long? Lorenzo knew he was being paranoid, about her and Quinto. No one rushed in Overstrand.

A car door opened and slammed outside. Lorenzo looked behind him at the entrance. Seconds ticked by, but nobody appeared.

58

Quinto observed as Lorenzo strolled into the convenience store. It was one of those establishments that hung all its wares outside the shop so you couldn't see inside, but he struggled to imagine an assailant lurking in Overstrand. Just being in the village was like taking a mild sedative. Quinto took a deep breath of the autumn air and tried to focus.

He'd become a bodyguard twenty years ago after his ejection from the Italian army over an unauthorised shooting. That had been a shame. Soldiering suited him. Quinto understood too well, from that experience and many since, that it was often the places where you least expected trouble that caused you bother. After all, a few weeks ago, the previous person he'd been protecting had perished in the toilet of an exclusive restaurant on the Amalfi coast.

The owner of the security company had bellowed at Quinto and told him to take this last-minute job in England. Quinto had said he didn't want to, but fuck-ups left you with few options, and his boss had owed someone a favour. Quinto had rapidly understood that if he wanted to work in the Italian protection industry ever again, he would need to fulfil the contract. It would take a fortnight at most.

There were two issues in play. The first was Quinto had been living on his past reputation. He had a rep as a man prepared to put himself in danger for his clients, but that person was gone. Once, he even took a bullet in an insane firefight in Tripoli. Quinto shivered. Never again. It bloody hurt. Still, it was hard to picture anything like that in Norfolk.

It was an incredible place. Dawn and dusk left you speechless, and it was so green and relaxing. He just wanted to sit under some shade with a cold drink and watch the world go by, not pander to ungrateful rich nut-jobs, who he suspected, on the grand scale of things, were better off dead. There lay the second issue. Quinto didn't care any more, and he'd been forming a plan.

He almost had the money for a quiet café back home in Sardinia. Among his own people. Not a business as such, but a lifestyle. Great menu, top wines, find a girl, settle down, get fat together. He could hardly wait. There was nothing compared to an Italian woman. A voluptuous, tanned brunette, knowing glint in her eye, bringing him a delicious soup of mussels, clams and octopus cooked in vermentino wine with olive oil, garlic, onion, parsley and chilli peppers, sprang to his mind. Quinto had been daydreaming in the restaurant about such a lady when a hired gun had shot the Amalfi asset in the head while he was taking a piss.

That brought Quinto's mind back to the task at hand. What the hell was taking Lorenzo so long? He should check. As he looked down to find the control for closing his window, a fist jabbed into the vehicle. The assailant buried the three-inch blade gripped inside it to the hilt in Quinto's neck.

While Quinto's life oozed from him, his door was opened. The knifeman located the button Quinto had been searching for, closed the window, then quietly closed the car door.

The final thing Quinto saw via the car's wing mirror was the grey-haired guy, who'd limped down the street with his paper earlier, stare intently at the entrance to the shop. After a few seconds, he retreated purposefully to an old-fashioned phone box on the corner. He hauled open the door and stepped out of sight.

Quinto reached up and gasped as he pulled the knife out. Blood gushed from the wound like a fountain. He smeared his dripping hand down the driver's side window, then pictured his café and the woman, both of which he'd never know.

Then Quinto drew his last breath.

59

Emil stared through the windows of the phone box, which he'd been using to watch the people passing by, and spotted the bloody smudge on the Pathfinder's window. Lorenzo had to notice it the moment he returned outside.

The people Emil was working with rushed past on the other side of the road as they headed to their van. Emil knew the shop had no customers because he'd been counting the shoppers in and out. He guessed at a minute for Lorenzo to go in, pay, and leave. Where the hell was he?

It didn't matter. The street was empty so Lorenzo was his now. If Lorenzo attempted to escape in the car, the driver slumped over the wheel wouldn't be swiftly moved. Emil just had to stop Lorenzo from getting around the passenger side and locking the doors.

Emil withdrew the hunting knife Zoltan had given him in case of trouble. It was a vicious thing. Lorenzo would soon be pressed against the van with the blade against his windpipe, knowing judgement was on the agenda.

Emil's mind wandered for a second to his dead daughter,

Jelena. His favourite growing up. Jasmina had the looks, but Jelena had been sunshine in a bottle. Balm for Emil's tortured soul. When he'd been with her, there had been reason and purpose to his world, and his rage could sleep. It was everyone else who got him angry. None more so than this motherfucker, who had driven that innocent young girl into prostitution. A man responsible for her death.

Emil's skin tingled as his fury sprang to life and he gagged at the thought of how his child had suffered. He pushed the heavy, metal telephone box door open as if it were made of balsa wood. Energy crackled through his body in the same way it had when he'd burst into the homes of his enemies during the wars and slaughtered everyone present.

Emil gritted his teeth and tried to ignore the roaring in his ears. Lorenzo deserved to die in the street like a dog, cut from ear to ear and sternum to groin, even though that wasn't the plan. Emil grinned a rictus smile as he imagined using his own hands to pull the man's innards out.

Lorenzo stepped from the doorway of the shop and was tucking his wallet back inside his jacket's inner pocket when he glanced up. Emil had timed it to perfection. He rushed at Lorenzo, raising the knife towards his throat.

Emil snarled, then roared. Saliva sprayed from his mouth. His brain felt as if it were trying to break free from his skull. Boiling blood coursed through his veins. Emil let the moment take him, welcomed it, as he had so many times before.

He would gut this pig on the pavement, and the whole world would see!

60

Lorenzo was on high alert as he came out of the shop. The first thing that caught his attention was the bloody handprint on the inside of the Pathfinder's driver's side window. Out of the corner of his vision, he saw a person gripping a large knife bearing down on him. Their eyes met. Time slowed.

Lorenzo immediately recognised the similarity of the man to the mother of his children. The big eyes, the perfectly proportioned features, but his brain also registered the lined skin and grey hair as he took one long step back. It must be her father. He had a face that had seen many winters, and eyes that had seen it all.

Lorenzo's heartbeat carried on at the same rate, and his body didn't tense. He knew panic didn't help and he'd never felt it anyway. The assailant closed in. His expression one of madness, on a man who would welcome death.

Lorenzo's hand was already in his jacket. He let go of the wallet and seized the handle of the pistol in the holster next to his chest. He flicked off the safety as he pulled the gun out. With the man only half a metre away, Lorenzo crouched, which dragged the elbow of the hand holding the weapon down to his hip but left the gun pointing up.

With a smile forming, and at point-blank range, Lorenzo blasted a hole in the man's stomach. He dropped at Lorenzo's feet with a thud.

The air rang with the explosion. Lorenzo knew he had seconds to get away. He stepped from the prone figure and opened the door to the Pathfinder, reaching in to unclip Quinto's seat belt. Lorenzo grabbed his shoulder and hauled him out of the vehicle.

Lorenzo was quick, both on the draw and with his attempt at escape, but the person who approached from behind did so silently. They held a weapon that had many names: blackjack, sap, cosh. A heavy leather pouch filled with lead. It came down in a blur on Lorenzo's crown.

Lorenzo's eyes rolled into the back of his head, but he didn't have time to hit the pavement. He was caught and dragged into the middle of the street where a grey van screeched to a halt beside him, and his captor threw him inside.

They drove Lorenzo swiftly to Cromer Road, then through Sidestrand. The driver indicated right to go down Top Road. They'd take their prisoner through quiet roads to an empty bungalow, which was located near Bacton Wood.

61

Hector and Ashley were on Cromer Road approaching Sidestrand when she received a call from Control.

'Afternoon, Sergeant Knight. Gunshot has been heard on Overstrand High Street. That's a weapon fired in Overstrand. State your location.'

'A mile away.'

'I would advise not to go in until other units have arrived.'

Ashley glanced over at Hector, who nodded.

'I'm nearly there. Two minutes. There might be children at risk. We'll turn right down Carr Lane and follow High Street back to the end of Mundesley Road without stopping and do a recce. Proceeding with caution. Would you like us to stay on the line?'

'Yes, please, we'll monitor at this end and direct resources as needed.'

Hector turned right, then left. They passed The Sea Marge Hotel and soon approached The White Horse. The street was rarely busy, but it was as though the plague were in town. Ashley put Control on speaker.

'There aren't any pedestrians in sight. A maroon Pathfinder

parked outside the store, facing north, has its offside door open. There's a body on the ground next to the vehicle. It looks like a lot of blood, and this person isn't moving.'

They drove past a large puddle of dark red liquid on the pavement, with a streak leading to a traditional phone box.

Ashley couldn't drive past. She placed her hand on Hector's arm. 'Stop here.'

He nodded again and pulled over. Long seconds ticked by.

'Control, I think we've missed whatever happened here. It appears the offenders have left the scene already.'

Ashley peered along the street, then back the way they had come. A car approached from the opposite direction. It cruised past. An old couple were inside, laughing at a private joke.

Hector pointed forwards. The door of the store had opened and a lady with frizzy grey hair poked her head out. Her eyes narrowed, but she stepped outside. She held a green first-aid kit. Ashley smiled at her bravery.

'Control. People are starting to appear. We're going to leave the car to check injuries. Will advise if the situation changes. Ambulance and uniform both needed.'

'Confirmed. Marked car ETA two minutes.'

Ashley stuck her phone in a pocket and jumped out of the vehicle.

'Get our first-aid kit, Hector.'

Ashley jogged along the white lines in the middle of High Street. A smiling woman driving a Porsche Boxster appeared at the junction with Cliff Road. Ashley held her hand up to indicate for her to stop, then directed her past Hector's car and away from the scene.

Hector ran along the pavement towards the woman from the shop.

'Back inside, madam,' he ordered. 'Ring 999, please, and explain what you've seen. Lock your door.'

He knelt down next to the body as the lady backed away.

Ashley shouted over the road to a man who'd left his house.

'Please stay in your property, sir.'

'I heard a gun fire. A man was bundled into a van.'

'That's why we need you to remain inside. This is a crime scene. Wait. Can you describe the person who was taken?'

'Short, kind of Italian-looking, handsome, head full of black hair.'

'Thank you, sir. I'll have someone knock on your door shortly.'

Ashley turned around and looked at the trail of blood that stretched away from outside the shop. The stain got thinner, then stopped at the phone box. Ashley walked over and peered through the top of the murky glass. It seemed empty. She crouched and saw a dense object in there. A trickle of dark liquid had seeped from under the door and was soaking into the concrete.

Control would have sent the ambulance, but it might take twenty minutes to arrive if there wasn't one in Cromer. Ashley looked back at Hector, who'd risen from the other victim. He shook his head.

Ashley eased the phone-box door open. It was heavy and the rusty hinges creaked, which forced her to grab the side with both hands. She sneaked a look inside. A person was slumped in a seated position, their chin hovering near their knees. A lethal-looking knife lay on the floor. Ashley rested her foot on it, then scraped it out behind her.

'Emil?' she said.

The grey head lifted, and a tired old man looked into her eyes.

'*Da*.'

She crouched.

'Let's get you out of there.'

He raised his hand in the same manner she'd used to stop the car a moment ago, but his face creased with pain.

'*Ne.*'

Ashley remained crouching.

'We need to treat your wounds. You're bleeding.'

'Too late,' he said slowly, in heavily accented English.

'Are you a doctor?' she asked.

Emil tried to smile, but he winced and cried out.

'*Ne.* I am ready. *Krvna osveta* is finished. I killed those men.'

Ashley knew Emil was out of time.

'Did Lorenzo shoot you?'

'*Da.* He will pay. Then. It is over. Please!'

Emil twisted towards Ashley as blood drooled out of his mouth. He began to tip out of the phone box but Ashley held him in place, fearing the worst. Emil's face greyed before her. He bared his teeth, yellow and tobacco stained.

'Please,' he wheezed at her, with breath from a crypt.

Emil's hand reached out and she grabbed it and gently squeezed. His skin was slimy with fresh blood.

'What do you want?' she asked.

'Jasmina. She. Is. Here.'

Emil's teeth chattered as each word took its toll.

'In. This. Village.'

His head bowed. Ashley thought he had passed until he strained and lifted it once more.

'Help her home.'

Two breaths burst from Emil, the final one tailing off.

'Promise. Save her,' came out of him as gasps.

'I will,' said Ashley quietly, but he had gone.

Emil died over fifteen hundred miles from home, but just a little over twenty miles from where his youngest daughter had perished in a cold wood, and not two hundred metres from where his eldest child had spent the last four years in captivity. But his journey was over.

As Ashley prised Emil's slippery fingers from hers, she felt hostage to the promise she'd uttered as he'd passed away.

A car pulled up behind her and its door opened. She glanced over her shoulder and watched Ally get out. This was no time for confrontation.

'Either you or Hector speak to the guy in that house,' she shouted at him, pointing to the property of the man who'd seen the kidnap take place.

Ally stared around in disbelief at the scene, but Ashley's mind was on Jasmina. She heard multiple sirens in the distance. The address they'd been given by Max was round the corner. Ashley let the door close on Emil, then she sprinted towards it.

62

Ashley knew Harbord Road well from an aggravated burglary she'd attended many years ago, not long after she'd returned to her hometown. She ran hard and found the number she wanted. At first glance it was a big, detached house, but up closer she could see it had once been much smaller but was now extended. It looked picturesque, with a pretty porch at the front. She opened the low metal gate, walked up the path to a solid-looking front door with no glass, and pressed the bell.

She waited with her heart in her mouth for thirty seconds, then poked the button again.

Ally had returned to his car to follow. He pulled up on the road behind her and got out.

'Hector has the scene,' he said. 'Response vehicles are arriving. Ambulance ten minutes, but they might as well turn around.'

'Let's see what we find here first,' said Ashley, not bringing herself to look at him.

Ashley gave the bell one last try, then looked for a way of breaking in. There was a gate to the right of the property, which she walked over and shook. The shiny padlock on it was solid and appeared new. She shouted through to the garden.

'Jasmina! Vittoria!'

Ashley paused, trying to hear if anyone was at the back, but that seemed unlikely. The sea breeze would make it cold this close to the beach. She attempted to peer through the windows on the downstairs floor, but thick curtains had been pulled across. She debated whether to shout police through the letterbox, quickly deciding she should. When she tried to push the flap open, it had been fixed in place.

A sharp shriek of tyres grabbed her attention. Barry's car sped down the street and screeched to a halt. He climbed out and marched towards Ally, who had been at the gate looking at the upstairs windows for life. Ally took a step back as Barry's hand came up. He jabbed a finger in Ally's face.

'You're busted. I know it's you.'

'What are you on about?'

'You're the mole.'

'Don't talk crap.'

'Admit it. Now!'

Ally looked over at Ashley, who held his gaze. Ally glowered back at Barry.

'Fuck off, Barry. I don't answer to you.'

Barry lost whatever cool he had remaining. Ashley thought he was going to punch Ally but instead he shoved him backwards. The effect was much the same, as Ally stumbled and landed on his arse. Barry stood over him, fist waving in the air like Muhammad Ali over Sonny Liston.

'Maybe it's time you did. Why have you been visiting Rocco at his distribution centre?'

Ally wearily hauled himself to his feet and backed away.

'It's background work.'

'Then why isn't it on the database?'

'We wanted to keep it quiet.'

'We? Do you mean you and Rocco?'

'You idiot. Kettle and me. It's not just you who thinks we have a dirty cop.'

Barry's eyes narrowed.

'Enough, you two,' shouted Ashley.

She was about to add more when she sensed they were being watched. At first, Ashley thought it was a child behind the iron gate. Ashley stepped over to what she could now see was a beautiful but diminutive woman with huge sorrowful eyes, who stared through the bars like a prisoner on death row.

'Hi,' said Ashley, stepping towards her. 'I'm Detective Sergeant Ashley Knight. Norfolk Police. We're here to help.'

Ashley held up her warrant card. The woman remained stone-faced until a tight smile cracked her face.

'Looks as though you were about to start fighting.'

'We've had a trying day, but everything's fine now,' said Ashley, giving her a comforting nod. 'Are you Jasmina?'

'Yes. How did you know?'

'It's a long story. Without being dramatic, we can save you, assuming that's what you want.'

Jasmina's hands trembled on the gate bars. Her eyes filled with tears.

'Oh, God. Please help us.'

'Can you let me in?'

'I don't have the key to the lock. Only he has it, but I can open the front door.'

'Okay, we'll wait there.'

Ashley walked to the door, then turned to the two men behind her, who were both watching from the end of the path.

'Cut it out. We deal with this first. Jasmina and her children are in danger. Once they're safe, we'll talk about what Barry said.'

Barry and Ally nodded, but neither looked at the other.

A lock clicked behind Ashley, and Jasmina appeared in the doorway. She was tiny, like a doll, and, like Barbie, she wore the finest clothes and make-up.

'There's a camera,' she said, pointing up. 'They are everywhere. Microphones too. I can't tell you anything or go anywhere, or he'll be so mad.'

Camera was the first word where Ashley detected a strong foreign accent, with Jasmina emphasising all three syllables.

'You mean Lorenzo?' asked Ashley.

'Yes. He told me he had some business for a while, but he lies to catch me out.'

'We believe Lorenzo has been kidnapped.'

Jasmina's face showed no emotion.

'Who by?'

'We're not sure at this point.'

'What for?'

'Something to do with his lifestyle, work, his past. Could be a few things.'

'I can't say I'm surprised. Come in, but you must be quick.'

Ashley looked up at the camera. A red light flashed on it.

'Are the boys here?'

'You know about them?'

'Yes, Rocco and Raffaele.'

'They are watching TV.'

'Can you fetch them and collect a few of their toys? A day bag, perhaps. I'd like to get you out of here and to the station, where you'll be safe.'

Jasmina shook her head.

'My children are my priority. I have to stay. We'll never be safe from Lorenzo, and neither will my sister.'

Jasmina's resolve wavered, but she crossed her arms.

Ashley considered telling her about her sister to shock her into action, but she worried it might be too damaging. Jasmina picked up on her struggle.

'What is it?'

'Jasmina, I want you to trust me. I'll explain everything at the station. We're going to help you get home to your family in Montenegro. I can have your personal items collected from here another time. Lorenzo, assuming he survives whatever's happened to him, will no longer control your life. Or your children's.'

Jasmina considered her words for a second. Her mouth formed a jagged line, then she fled back into the house, reappearing twenty seconds later with both children in her arms and an expression of total determination.

'Don't you want to take anything else?' asked Ashley.

Jasmina looked her in the eye.

'We have all that we need.'

63

Ashley shepherded Jasmina out of the doorway. Both young boys stared dolefully over their mother's shoulder at Ashley as Jasmina serenely cruised down the path, head held high. Emma had arrived and was waiting at the gate.

'Good timing, Emma,' said Ashley. 'This is Jasmina, Rocco, and Raffaele.'

Emma gave Jasmina a reassuring smile.

'Ally,' said Ashley, 'you and Emma escort these guys back to OCC. Set them up in the visitors' room. The usual drill. Barry, Hector and I will start searching here, then I'll return and talk to Jasmina. See if Scott Gorton is around, but I'll probably use Emma for the discussion.'

Barry opened his mouth.

'Quiet,' snapped Ashley. 'Get inside and check nobody else is in there.'

'There's a basement room,' said Jasmina. 'I don't know the code. It's where I was first held.'

Ashley couldn't stop herself from frowning.

'Is there someone in there now?'

'I think so. I've heard the television.'

'Have they shouted or screamed?'

'No. Just watched TV, but I dared not cry out either.'

Emma helped Jasmina into the middle seat of Ally's Ford pool car and tugged the belt across her. The children were too small for their own seats, but both had clamped themselves to Jasmina's arms, anyway. Emma got in the passenger side. Ally opened the driver's door and looked back at Ashley before he stepped inside.

'Drive carefully,' said Ashley. 'I'll be back in an hour or so.'

'Will do.'

'Tell me it isn't true, Ally.'

Ally held her gaze for a moment.

'It's not true.'

He dropped his eyes, got in the vehicle, shut the door, started the engine, and pulled away. Ashley shoved her feelings to one side because she was unsure whether to believe him. Her heart wanted to, but detectives trusted their instincts and hers were muddled.

Ashley rang Control and updated them, then she called Hector on High Street.

'Sarge,' he replied. 'Uniform have the scene controlled. Road is closed. Units are arriving in droves now, so I'll take a full statement from the man who observed some of what happened. I had a quick word with him to assess any further risk. He was outside the front door of his house and heard a car backfire.'

'He didn't see who shot Emil?'

'No, but he saw them bundle what I'm ninety-nine per cent certain was Lorenzo into the van.'

'Then they burned rubber and left.'

'That's the weird thing. He thought it seemed organised. He wondered whether a production company was shooting a film for a second, but when he spotted Emil dragging himself away leaving a trail of blood, he panicked. The guy was embarrassed to say he ran inside and peeked through the curtains. He was the first person to ring 999.'

'Did the shopkeeper see anything?'

'No, she confirmed she'd seen Lorenzo frequently, but he never made small talk. She didn't know his name, but the description fits. When she heard the explosion shortly after he bought a pack of cigars, she assumed it was a firework, but after a few minutes, she got curious and looked outside. She has agreed to shut the shop while the road's closed. I can take a statement from her after I speak to the other witness.'

Ashley pictured the street.

'Grab the nearest sergeant and ask nicely if they'll arrange some door knockers for you.'

'Frank Levine's here, so I'm sure he'll give us a hand.'

Ashley smiled as she recalled the grizzled officer who'd helped them with the recent case in Hunstanton.

'There are only about twenty houses with a view of the shop. Ask him to visit that side of the road first, then do the other side. Perhaps somebody noticed the van waiting if nothing else.'

'Do you reckon Emil's team was staking Lorenzo's place out?'

'Yes. It's difficult to purchase a gun in this country. You need connections and plenty of money, so I suspect they wouldn't have fancied storming the house without firearms, knowing Lorenzo probably had one. The easiest thing would be to pick Lorenzo up when he left the property. That's when he'd be most vulnerable. They knew Lorenzo would leave eventually, so they watched and waited.'

'That's clever. They took Max and Hamish when they weren't expecting it but waited for Lorenzo until they had tortured Jasmina's location out of the others.'

'I believe they wanted to inflict the maximum emotional toll on Lorenzo as well.'

'Wouldn't their van have struggled to chase after a Pathfinder?'

'Valid point. Blocking it in as opposed to ramming it would have been a better option, which could have been the plan before he got out at the shop.'

Hector was on the ball.

'Which means they likely had two vehicles here.'

'Yes. These are expensive houses. I'm betting at least a few have Ring doorbells or similar. If the residents are retired, they might have noticed a vehicle outside their property for an unusual length of time, especially if it had people in it.'

'I'll get on it.'

'The important thing is we find the people who took Lorenzo. It looks like Emil's team killed the driver of the Nissan, probably while Lorenzo was in the shop. Rocco said he brought his best man over to protect his family. His best wasn't good enough. I expect Lorenzo shot Emil after coming outside, even though Emil probably thought he had the element of surprise.'

'That was a nasty-looking knife found at the scene.'

'There you go. Apart from the obvious weapon offences, Lorenzo could claim he shot Emil in self-defence, so our focus needs to be on saving his life. To do that, we need to locate him.'

Hector breathed hard down the phone.

'They have what they came for,' he said. 'I hold little hope for Lorenzo unless we can track down that van. I suppose the concern now is whether it's over, or if Rocco is the final target.'

'Emil said it was over with Lorenzo, but the person who might give us better information about that is Jasmina. Barry and I are going to check inside the property, then I'll go back to OCC to discuss everything with her. You stay here until you hear otherwise. Interview Jasmina's neighbours after you've finished on High Street.'

'All in hand,' said Hector, and cut the call.

Ashley marched past Barry up the garden path.

'Don't you think there was a better place for a discussion with Ally?'

'I was angry, and he's bent. I know it.'

'What if he isn't? And now he has time to prepare his story.'

'If Kettle doesn't back him up about not putting his visits to Rocco on the system, then he's toast.'

'I suspect with you telling everyone, his career is over regardless. Which would be unfortunate if he's innocent.'

Barry's face fell as he realised what he'd done.

'Leave it for now. You do upstairs, I'll do down.'

They stopped at the entrance and put disposable gloves and shoe coverings on. Barry made a pretend gun with his fingers and moved in. Ashley muttered, 'Child,' then followed.

The house was pretty from outside, but inside it was stunning. Ashley knew nothing about top-of-the-line furniture and furnishings, but guessed everything was the finest money could buy. There was a wood-burning stove in the lounge, and an Aga in the fitted kitchen, which had a lovely marble work surface, no doubt from Rocco's Fine Homes, but little in the way of personal touches.

There were a few oil paintings and professionally done photographs, but there were none of the random silly pictures that happy mothers loved putting up of their families. The ones slightly out of focus, or with people half in shot. No daft smiles or closed eyes. Photographs that held so much more because they weren't just images, they were also memories.

'What's it like upstairs?' shouted Ashley.

'Hotel,' replied Barry.

Ashley did a circuit and discovered nothing untoward. The

fridge was fully stocked with Marks & Spencer's produce. Ashley would bet on it being delivered by Ocado, so Jasmina didn't need to leave home to shop. Ashley finally found two crayon drawings on the side of a cabinet. There was also a photo of a proud Rocco and the kids in a frame on the windowsill.

There was only one door that could lead to a basement. It was the same style of wood, possibly mahogany, as the others, but when she opened it, she was greeted by another door, which was metal. There was a number pad above the handle.

Ashley rapped on the solid surface. The noise was dull, which suggested it was well fitted and probably soundproofed. Ashley shouted at it, anyway.

'Police. We're coming in. Let us know you're there.'

Barry appeared next to her and gave the door a solid boot.

'I doubt the enforcer will work on a door like this.'

'No.'

Ashley rang Kettle, explained what she needed and hoped it wouldn't take long. They would need the paperwork for entry, but lives were at risk. Kettle would have the authority to order it done.

They used a locksmith service called LockRite for this part of Norfolk. Luckily, he was based in Cromer, so, assuming he wasn't on another job, he could be there in five minutes. They weren't robbing a bank vault, so it would be quick. She'd found few things were hard to open with the right tools if you didn't mind wrecking the door and making a lot of noise.

If anyone was down there, it was hardly surprising they kept schtum. They'd likely be petrified and would have been warned about being quiet.

'I'm pleased we can't get in. Who knows what's waiting down there?' asked Barry.

'Are you worried there's a monster down there?'

'It might be a shoot first, ask questions later type of monster.'

'Come on, Barry. This hasn't been your finest hour. I should think that, considering they've been locked in some kind of dungeon, it's more than likely they'll be pleased to see us.'

'I suppose.'

They did a further sweep, checking in cupboards and drawers, but nothing seemed out of place. Ashley's phone rang.

'Hi, Control. That was quick.'

'The locksmith is in Trimingham installing an alarm, so he'll come straight down. Uniform on High Street will be aware.'

'Ask Sal Freitas at OCC to meet with the tenant, Jasmina, who should arrive shortly. She'll give permission for us to open the basement door, but preservation of life is plausible otherwise. Someone could be in trouble down there.'

Ashley knew she was just dotting the Is. They had enough. She and Barry checked the garden and garage while they waited but nothing grabbed their attention in either.

Ashley shook the hand of the locksmith when he arrived. He was a friendly middle-aged chap she'd worked with many times when she was in uniform. They were always in need of someone to make properties secure after robberies and burglaries. After ten minutes of deafening drilling, he hooked a tool into the door and yanked it open.

'Do you want me to stay?' he asked.

'No, this will be a crime scene for a while yet.'

When he'd left, Ashley pulled the door wide.

'Police! Everything's okay. I'm coming down.'

She tiptoed down the steps to a narrow hall with two doors. One was ajar and led to a toilet. The other was shut. She pushed it wide to reveal an open living area with a large TV on the wall.

In front of it, with a pale, blotchy and sweaty face, was Hamish.

64

Ashley stepped inside the room and glanced around. Apart from a vinegary smell, nothing seemed untoward. Ashley spotted an air vent on the wall, but she supposed that would be normal for any basement conversion.

'Hi, Hamish. Everything okay?'

'You mean except from being in here?'

Hamish looked shifty. His eyes drifted past her to the kitchen area, where she noticed a roll of foil next to a white rock. She turned back to him, and he avoided her gaze.

'We're not here to judge you, Hamish. Just to make sure you're safe.'

'I have to remain here.'

'Do you want to stay?'

Hamish shook his head. 'He told me not to leave.'

'Lorenzo's gone.'

Hamish got up from his seat. His clothes were crumpled, and his T-shirt had stains on the front. He was barefoot.

'He'll be back,' he said, but a light had come on in his eyes. 'Gone where?'

'We suspect the same place your kidnappers took you.'

Hamish shrugged.

'They let me go.'

'You and Max were the lucky ones.'

Hamish's whole face lit up. He rushed towards her.

'He's okay?'

'Yes, he's looking forward to seeing you.'

'Is it possible for me to see him now?'

'Yes. We'll take you to HQ. I'll ask someone to fetch Max. He's probably still at the hospital. We have a few questions, but you can both help answer them.'

'Where's Tommaso?'

'I'm afraid he's dead.'

'Good.'

Hamish slipped by her and ran up the stairs. Ashley took a quick look around and shook her head. How many others had been in this prison cell?

Ashley caught up with Barry as he guided a blinking Hamish out into the daylight.

She rang Control.

'DC Hooper and DS Knight will be returning to OCC with a Hamish MacDonald. The same who was in the N & N last weekend.'

'DS Knight, that's confirmed.'

'Hamish has no immediate medical concerns, but request for health assessment upon arrival. ETA sixty minutes.'

Outside, Ashley stared at the cottage. What sort of monster was Lorenzo?

Barry drove to the top of Harbord Road and stopped at the cordon. Ashley got out and explained to the officer where they were going and that someone would need to guard the Harbord Road property. He lifted the tape and let them through. Ashley tried to chat to Hamish, but he didn't engage and stared out of the window.

Back at OCC, she would arrange for him to do a recorded interview, but she suspected Hamish knew little more than what he'd told them before. Lorenzo probably took him from the hospital, then stuck him in his cell. That way, Hamish spoke to nobody. Perhaps he was also a form of security to keep Max quiet.

As they approached the turning for the N & N, Barry looked over at her.

'We might as well take Hamish to the hospital. They can assess him. If him and Max have anything to say, we'll hear it straight away.'

'Makes sense.'

Barry indicated, and they left the parkway. Fifteen minutes later, they were witness to an emotional reunion between Hamish and Max.

Hamish explained to Max what had happened to him, which made Max furious, until he heard the news about Lorenzo's abduction. The gravity of that rapidly sank in.

'They'll torture and kill him,' he said.

Ashley nodded. 'Are you certain there's nothing either of you can tell us which will help us find him?'

'I wouldn't say if I knew,' snarled Hamish. 'Let him receive his punishment.'

Max had his head in his hands. He glanced up.

'My poor father. He's going to lose his heir and the spare in the space of a few days.'

'Can you both take a moment to recall when you were questioned? Are you sure it was just Lorenzo and Tommaso they were asking about? Or was it Rocco as well?'

'My memories are rubbish, but I remember thinking about Lorenzo. I don't think Rocco figured,' said Hamish.

'They grilled me about both to start with,' said Max, 'but my dad wouldn't be involved in this kind of madness. I should have told him what Lorenzo and Tommaso were up to, but how could I? He favoured them. He always did.'

Max was beginning to irritate Ashley. If he hated it all so much, then he could have left a long time ago. She'd put money on the flat he lived in being paid for by the family, and no doubt he had a cushy position at Rocco's Fine Homes. Just because he had declined participation in the trafficking, it didn't make him innocent. Morally, he'd fallen well short by keeping quiet. Legally he was also in trouble.

Still, he didn't need that placing on him yet. The Crown Prosecution Service would probably consider his involvement when the dust settled. Even if they didn't charge him, Ashley would ensure he understood there was blood on his hands.

65

Hamish had nothing much to say about being kept in Lorenzo's basement. He had been escorted from the hospital and put down there for his safekeeping. The expression on Lorenzo's face had prevented him from objecting. He hadn't been mistreated and Lorenzo had brought him drugs and food. The time had drifted away.

Ashley and Barry left the couple to their reunion after Max gave them the address of a cheap hotel where they would head later that evening when Max was discharged. It would keep them off the grid until Lorenzo was released or his fate was known. Max had no intention of speaking to Rocco. He was done with the Viallis' family businesses, but he and Hamish wouldn't be doing any interviews without a solicitor. That slightly concerned Ashley, but she wanted to get back to OCC.

When she reached the office, Ashley prepared with Emma for their discussion with Jasmina Popovic. Ashley knew what she had been through. The local authority's crisis team were on their way. There were also specialist officers for this kind of thing if needed, but Ashley had detected a steel core in Jasmina. She believed the woman would cooperate enthusiastically now she was free of Lorenzo's clutches, but Jasmina was also going to hear the devastating truth about her father and sister.

Ashley was pleased when Scott appeared a few minutes before they began, so she brought him up to speed.

'Right. Let's see how Jasmina is, then ask how she'd like to proceed. Maybe she won't talk right now, or perhaps she won't want you there, Scott, but we'll let her guide us. Annoyingly, we've no idea who was helping Emil. If we're not careful, everyone will be dead or gone.'

Kettle strode into the office.

'Sorry to impose,' he said, without looking concerned if he was. 'I want to convene a quick meeting, so all departments are up to speed with events this morning. Ashley, you'll be at the front with me.'

Ten minutes later, forty people had gathered in the conference room. Kettle clapped his hands together.

'The Det Supt has authorised unlimited overtime to anyone for the next twenty-four hours. Hotel Nine Nine will also be flying all over the target area.'

Ashley nodded her head. Hotel Nine Nine was the call sign for NPAS, the National Police Air Service. A helicopter would be an incredible asset in the pursuit of vehicles.

'We must find that van, if we're to have any chance of getting to Lorenzo before his punishment starts,' she said. 'It's possible the motivation to torture him won't be as strong if Emil was the driving force behind this, but if, as we suspect, the girls' brother funded everything back in Montenegro, we need to assume Lorenzo's capture will proceed to its conclusion. Unless we can stop it.'

'It's liable to be another statement death,' said Sal.

'Yes, although without Emil, they're a man down,' said Kettle.

'Whatever they have planned won't be as easy, but I wouldn't be surprised if Lorenzo's already praying for a quick end.'

'Emil's death doesn't give us much except confirmation all of this is related to the trafficking of his daughters,' said Ashley. 'The question is, who was helping Emil? It's got to be at least two people so, with Emil gone, they may be down to just two. I expect once Lorenzo has been dealt with, they'll run.'

'I agree. Border Force are assisting us, but they haven't been able to provide a great deal of help. There are only around a thousand Montenegrins officially in this country, and they're generally law-abiding. Border Force has no record of Emil arriving, so he came illegally. The individuals helping him probably arrived the same way. If we don't catch them and they decide it's time to leave, the hope of a successful resolution falls dramatically.'

'Exactly,' said Ashley. 'As a country, we're struggling to stop folk getting in, so you can imagine how porous our borders are for those who want to go the other way.'

'We're going to flood the area from Cromer to Sea Palling and inland with officers in the hope we get lucky. We'll have an ARV on standby for twenty-four hours. I'm afraid that's all at this point, unless Jasmina gives us any direction from what she knows of the Vialli family's movements. There must be something we've missed, or perhaps a link that isn't obvious. Keep thinking, people. I understand Hector has now interviewed a witness who saw the van and the person in it.'

Kettle nodded to the back of the room, where Gabriella was waiting.

'Yes. He rang in a few minutes ago. A retired schoolteacher, who likes to keep an eye on the street because she lives not far from the school, spotted a grey van parked up near her house. She assumed it was a tradesman's vehicle, but noticed the driver didn't seem to do any work. It was parked up from dawn this morning. It may have been there before.'

Gabriella quickly checked her notes. 'The driver fits the description of Emil. Slim, grey hair, lined face. However, she said there was another man who came to the window and spoke to the driver. Much taller, much broader. A little younger. He swapped seats with Emil at one point. The teacher was inside, but she's hard of hearing, so she wouldn't have heard any shooting.'

'Was this big guy the person who grabbed Lorenzo in the street?'

Gabriella turned her million-watt smile on Ashley.

'Yes, but he had a helper. The man who heard the shot and came out said he saw a grey van arrive in the middle of the street. A huge bloke jumped out of the passenger side, opened the side door, then dragged a man, most likely Lorenzo, out from behind a maroon Nissan Pathfinder. He picked Lorenzo up like a parent would a child and raced around the vehicle and threw him inside. That was the witness's phrase. The large guy also got in the van via the side door. Interestingly, his accomplice was a woman.'

'You'd need to be very strong to lift a man that easily,' said Emma.

'Yes, although we estimate Lorenzo's weight to be around ten stones, so we're not talking Hafþór Björnsson levels of strength here.'

Kettle frowned. Ashley whispered in his ear.

'He was the Mountain in *Game of Thrones.*'

That didn't seem to help, but he nodded anyway.

'Hector gave me a summary of his working hypothesis,' said Gabriella. 'I'll read it out.'

Gabriella turned a sheet of paper over.

'Hector believes Emil was given the address of Jasmina's home by Max under questioning. Emil's crew dealt with Max and

Hamish, then Paolo and Tommaso, and finally Gianluca, before waiting outside the Overstrand place for Lorenzo to arrive or leave. We suspect Lorenzo was there already but kept a low profile until today when he left with his minder. Lorenzo stopped at the shop, giving Emil's team the opportunity to grab him. We can assume they wanted to take him alive because they could have killed him when he left the store.'

'They probably haven't got guns themselves, so it was always going to be risky,' said Ashley.

'That's true,' said Kettle.

'Lorenzo's death wouldn't have been enough,' said Ashley. 'He needed to suffer like the others.'

Gabriella glanced at her notebook again.

'While Lorenzo was in the shop, the minder, who was likely the guy Rocco brought over to protect his son, was fatally stabbed in the neck. When Lorenzo came out, Emil probably tried to collar him, not suspecting Lorenzo was armed. Even so, Lorenzo must have been quick because he managed to get his firearm out and shoot Emil in the stomach.'

A thought occurred to Ashley.

'It's possible Emil sacrificed himself as a distraction to give one of his team the chance to sneak up and knock Lorenzo out. It sounds as if Lorenzo was unconscious when he was put in the van.'

'Yes, he didn't appear to struggle,' said Gabriella. 'After Lorenzo was grabbed, they drove off in the direction of Sidestrand, possibly to their base where they've been holding their victims, which we suspect is somewhere near Bacton Wood. After checking the map, it's likely they took Top Road, or they would have passed various members of our team.'

'I assume we have no further sightings of the vehicle?' asked Kettle.

'Not yet. But we're hopeful. Morgan has more on that.'

Morgan spoke with enthusiasm.

'When the door-knocking teams talked to various residents in the surrounding areas over the last week, numerous had Ring doorbells or similar, which looked out on the main road through the villages. They kept a record. Zelda is on her way to those properties now. We may be able to trace the van's route back to its base using what they give us and with ANPR.'

Ashley nodded. If the van triggered a camera at Trimingham, but then not one further up at Mundesley, they could narrow down their search.

'Hector also thinks we might get some joy from a doorbell cam in Overstrand,' said Gabriella. 'That part of Overstrand doesn't receive too much passing traffic at this time of year. It's out of season, so most of the residents would stick to Mundesley Road. He believes there were two vehicles used by the gang. The van and another. That second vehicle will have driven past the shop, maybe more than once. He estimates there will only be two hundred or so vehicle registrations to check.'

A chuckle spread through the room, but it was excellent work. The problem was it would take hours. As always, time was not their ally.

Ashley was only half listening. Her voice was little more than a whisper, but it stunned the room.

'I've just realised who was part of Emil's team.'

66

Ashley cleared her throat as she stood. The room quietened.

'I've been struggling to imagine who would get involved in something like this. It's murder for a start. We know from our recent experiences at Paradise Park what people are capable of doing for money, but this is different. Who can tell me why?'

Emma spoke up.

'It's vicious to the point of sadism. Max and Hamish survived, but the experience will scar them for the rest of their lives. Tommaso and Gianluca were brutalised before their deaths. Paolo suffered badly as well.'

Ashley glanced around and noticed Ally wasn't present.

'Yes,' she said. 'Their bodies were difficult to look at. What kind of stomach would you need to inflict those wounds? Who could do that to another human being?'

'It must be personal unless it was a complete psychopath,' said Jan.

'Spot on. This was personal for Emil, but others were involved. It must have meant something more than money for them as well. So, who else wanted revenge on the Viallis? Who among their victims is likely to be so filled with rage, they would be party to the horrific torture we've been shown? And focus on that. They want the world watching.'

'When the details of Tommaso and Gianluca's deaths get out, it will be on every TV station on the planet,' said Jan.

'Fuck,' said Morgan, who then put his hand to his mouth.

Ashley nodded at him to continue. He closed his eyes.

'It's Drita.'

'Why?'

'It has to be Drita. Lorenzo gave her to the Vampires, and she spent two years being moved around the country from brothel to brothel, being forced to take heroin, while being raped and abused.'

'You spoke to her at home. Describe the man who was there.'

'He was huge. Tall and broad.'

Murmurs spread through the room.

'Yes. We don't know his story, but perhaps he's in love with Drita, and this is obviously important to her. If what happened to her had been inflicted on me, maybe I'd get involved. I'd have grabbed the spade and buried them myself. In a way, she's giving them a dose of their own medicine. The guys who died lived a fate worse than death first, like she did.'

'I'm sorry,' said Morgan, who had a sheen of sweat on his forehead. 'Drita's involvement should have occurred to me, but do you know what it also probably means?'

Ashley shook her head.

'I bet she was one of the two women in the club the night Hamish got drugged.'

Ashley managed to stop herself swearing. Barry didn't. Ashley took a deep breath.

'Don't worry about it now, Morgan,' said Ashley. 'We can check

Lorenzo's CCTV, but they were disguised. You and Zelda head straight to her address with uniform backup.'

'We have the ARV on call,' said Kettle. 'I'll arrange for them to be there as well.'

'Excellent,' said Ashley. 'The people involved will be desperate to escape now, so they could be capable of anything. The significant planning, and the cruelty, are off the scale. If they finish up in front of a judge, it's life sentences all around, so be aware of that.'

Ashley paused while she considered Drita's involvement. She remembered Hector's comment about the probability of Emil's team having another vehicle in Overstrand.

'Drita escaped over a year ago. I suspect she has a car, and I wouldn't be surprised if that was used to stake out Jasmina and the children's house in Overstrand. If they're knocking people out, then it might have been used to transport bodies in the boot. Sal, get on it, and let Morgan know what you discover while he's en route.'

'Will do,' said Sal.

'I'm going to talk with Jasmina now. Email me anything that might be pertinent, and I'll check as soon as I'm finished with her. You might find the car is still on High Street because they both left in the van. If we narrow down the likely direction of that vehicle, we can tighten the noose. The van will be parked somewhere in the Bacton area. The fact we haven't found it means we're probably looking for a property with a garage or a shed. Perhaps it's under a tarpaulin. They took a live hostage. One Drita despises. Lorenzo's clock, assuming it hasn't already stopped, is ticking.'

'I'll return to the hospital and ask Hamish and Max to focus on their captivity,' said Barry. 'Women's voices. Maybe the sounds of farm machinery, that sort of thing. I'll get persuasive if they pull that *I want a solicitor* bollocks.'

'Good. Emma, call the mortuary and see if Michelle has anything from the bodies. Hector pointed out these are all methods of execution from ancient times. They've been dramatic, but in doing so, with moving around, they've put themselves at risk of being discovered. Emil might not have cared too much about getting caught. They were his daughters. Even so, it's likely the others are planning their escape. They'll be holed up by now, but I agree with Hector. They'll want to make a theatrical sign-off with Lorenzo.'

Ashley left that comment hanging in the air.

'Let's get to it,' she said.

Grim faces dispersed from the room.

'Sergeant, a moment of your time,' asked Kettle as she was leaving.

The way he said it made her glance back with concern.

'What is it?'

Kettle waited for everyone to depart. Ashley had guessed the topic by the time they were alone.

'Ally Williamson,' she said.

'Yes.'

'Where is he?'

'He's now on leave.'

'I assume you mean suspended?'

Kettle took a deep breath.

'I was aware he was going to see Rocco.'

'You were?'

'Yes, although I'm not entirely sure he's been honest about what else he's been up to, but there are complications. I'd appreciate it not being discussed, although I recognise the cat is out of the bag. Barry told Sal, who mentioned it to Emma and Jan. Everybody at OCC will have heard by tomorrow. Nobody will trust Ally now, whether he's responsible or not.'

'I know,' she said, 'but the evidence points to him doing something untoward.'

'It seems so.'

'It's hard to believe he's guilty.'

Kettle gave her a sad smile.

'We're all guilty of making mistakes.'

67

Ashley didn't have time to digest his cryptic comment. Half an hour later, she, Emma, and Scott entered the room where Jasmina was waiting with the children.

'Hi,' said Ashley. 'How are you all?'

'Coping. What's going on?'

'We'd like to discuss what happened to you, so we know what we're dealing with.'

Jasmina stood and glanced at Scott.

'You've met Emma. This is Scott Gorton. He's one of our family liaison officers, if you don't mind him sitting in.'

Jasmina's lips pursed.

'I do not care about that. My only concern is my family's safety. If Lorenzo turns up and finds me gone, there'll be hell to pay. Who will protect me? Where can I go?'

'Scott can help. The local authority have safe refuges to place you in, until we see what happens with Lorenzo. We'll take notes, if that's okay.'

'Can we talk here? I want to be able to keep my eye on the kids.

Perhaps Emma will play with them here. They found her funny during the journey.'

'Of course,' said Emma. 'You have a chat with Ashley and Scott, and I'll keep them occupied.'

Ashley and Scott set up at a table in the far corner. He took his notebook out and Jasmina sat in front of them. Ashley struggled to say exactly what made her so attractive. It was as if everything was perfectly proportioned. Her teeth were beautiful, but maybe a shade too white to be natural. Jasmina caught the focus of her gaze, smiled, then tapped one of her front teeth with a manicured fingernail.

'Even the prisoners have veneers in Lorenzo's jail.'

'Perhaps you could start from the beginning,' said Ashley.

Jasmina puffed out her cheeks.

'It seems so long ago. First, even though my heart already knows, is my sister, Jelena, alive?'

'I'm so sorry.'

Jasmina twisted around and looked at Rocchino and Raffaele, who were giggling at Emma's face-pulling. She returned her gaze to Ashley. Jasmina's expression remained unchanged.

'Jelena would have loved them.'

'I'm sorry, Jasmina. Were you close as children?'

Jasmina's features softened.

'I suppose the usual. Love and hate growing up. She used to steal my perfume all the time and then deny it, even though I could smell it on her. I often shouted at her, but when she was older she told me why she did it.'

Jasmina looked into Ashley's eyes. Ashley swallowed.

'Because she wanted to be just like you.'

'Yes.' Jasmina's fists clenched. 'Poor Jelena.'

'Are you okay to continue, or would you prefer some time?'

'I'm fine. Don't think me hard. I have grieved for her many

times, and I shall again. It's necessary that I am strong now, for them.'

'Okay. Tell us what happened after you applied for jobs in the UK.'

Jasmina leaned back in her chair as if to say, how did you know? Then she shrugged.

'Jelena was desperate to leave Montenegro and spotted an advert. She loved Insta and TikTok, followed influencers, all of that. She imagined being here, perfecting our English, sending money home, seeing all the sights. Her enthusiasm swept me up, even though I wasn't hopeful, but I believed I could always return if it didn't work out.'

Jasmina stared hard at Scott, then Ashley, as if expecting them to comment that she had been a fool. Both knew better.

'They picked everyone up with a grand bus, very new, then our passports were taken at the first border. They were never returned. We were taken off the bus soon after for a toilet break, and they shoved us into a big, old motorhome. We travelled for days and days on little roads. Nobody told us anything. The blinds were pulled. We had no clue where we were. One girl complained about the toilet, so they stopped in a forest for us to relieve ourselves. We never laid eyes on her again. The drivers seemed troubled afterwards.'

'I'm sorry to hear that.'

'Her name was Mira Bajić. I hope she ran away. I'll tell her family of her bravery if she did not. Lorenzo separated me from the others in what I later learned was Slovenia. I was so stunned that I left without saying goodbye to Jelena. I didn't realise it would be the last time I saw her.'

A tear welled in Jasmina's eye, then trickled down her cheek. She scrubbed it away with the back of her hand.

'I was driven in a car then, through Italy and into France.

Lorenzo was charming and showed me the sights as we passed through small towns and hamlets. We stopped at a chalet in a quiet village, but I had my own room. I kept asking about my sister. He said she will be in England when we arrive. When I asked why we were being treated in that way, he got this look in his eyes. It would be an expression I came to understand very well, and one I understood to fear.'

Scott was busy making notes, so Ashley continued.

'Did you come straight to Overstrand?'

'Yes, we caught a ferry. Lorenzo took care of paperwork, so I never left the car. I arrived, and he lured me into the basement, telling me it was for my own safety. I was scared he would murder me, even though he continued to be kind. It drove me crazy, like he was doing me a favour. He'd call me the most beautiful woman he'd ever seen, and we'd be happy together. After a few days, he marched down the stairs and wanted more than to talk. I said no. Not until I see Jelena. That was a mistake.'

Jasmina's eyes narrowed as she remembered.

'The next few weeks were tough. It must have been then when I fell pregnant. I'm ashamed that I had to, now, what is your phrase? Go with the flow? I couldn't take any more pain. No more nightly beatings if I resisted. At six weeks, I could tell, but he was so rough with me. I didn't know whether to mention it because I might become unwanted, but by then, death had lost its sting.'

Jasmina's face twisted into a tight smile. She focused on the table.

'As you must imagine, I've watched a lot of TV in four years. I've picked up many odd phrases. Anyway, I told him about the baby. It became even weirder afterwards. He changed. I can only assume he wanted children and thought I would give him handsome ones. I suppose he got that right.'

'Did he let you out of the basement?'

'No, he kept me there until I was nearly to term, then he let me into the house. Rocco was delivered in a private hospital. I don't know where the time has gone since. He began sleeping with me again, but normally, as though we were husband and wife. I had a baby to protect, so what could I do?'

Jasmina looked up. She wanted a reply.

'You did what you had to.'

'Yes, but I will never forget the shame. He stole my youth from me. My happiness.' Jasmina clenched her fists. She gasped and closed her eyes. 'My innocence.'

Ashley sat in silence, allowing Jasmina the time to compose herself. When she was ready, Jasmina flexed her hands and slowed her breathing.

'I asked after Jelena on so many occasions that it began to make him angry. He told me she was in a similar situation, but I would see her soon. Always soon. Lorenzo said we could take our kids to the park together, but there were no children for Jelena, were there?'

Ashley slowly shook her head.

'And that is it. As the years passed, he allowed me more freedom. I could go to the shop, take the kids to nursery, be his partner at meals. Just living a terrible lie. I dreamt of killing him, but my boys were too precious to risk, and also there was Jelena. I couldn't chance it, even though I knew she was probably dead.'

'You survived.'

'But she did not. I want to get out of your country and go home to mine. Will you help me?'

'Of course. Our focus is your safety. We just have a few loose ends to tie up. Can you tell me about Lorenzo's father, Rocco? Do you see him much?'

Jasmina relaxed slightly.

'He visited not long before I had Rocchino. Lorenzo told big

Rocco we had been dating but split up because I was returning to Montenegro, but then I discovered my pregnancy and came back. He said if I didn't go along with these lies, he would kill my sister. That was the first occasion he threatened her life. Later he mentioned it often until he understood saying he would hurt our children had more effect.'

'That's so evil,' said Ashley.

'It has all been evil. Rocco was generous to us with his time and money. He treated us as family. The kids love him. He comes around often, buys many gifts, and even took my older boy to McDonald's in Cromer. Rocco tells him about the places they will go. Football matches. Films they'll watch, that sort of thing.'

'And Tommaso?'

'Tommaso scares me. I avoid that evil man if possible, but I have little to do with him. Lorenzo, on the other hand, is demonic. That is the only word that fits. I hope he is burning in hell.'

68

Ashley decided to probe more about Rocco.

'Rocco clearly loves his children. Does he suspect anything?'

'No, I don't think so. Over the years, I've become a brilliant actor. I planned to leave when Raffaele was a little older. I was so scared Lorenzo would make me have another baby, but he rarely wants to sleep with me now. When I got an infection down there, I went to the surgery, and told the doctor I wanted a coil. The doctor saw my bruises but didn't comment. He fitted it and said Lorenzo would never know.'

'Did you see much of Max or Hamish?'

'I met Hamish but we only spoke briefly. He appeared withdrawn, but Max was also kind. I asked him to help me, but I believe he was as trapped as I was. I considered asking Rocco, but Lorenzo is the apple of his eye, so I kept quiet. Now, I have answered your questions. Please tell me how you found us. How do you know about my sister? Who has taken Lorenzo? I don't understand. I want to hear everything.'

Ashley took a deep breath.

'This is what we think has happened. It won't be easy for you.'

'Not hearing doesn't make it any less true. Give me the news. I don't want to be spared.'

'Your sister escaped from forced prostitution a year ago with a woman called Drita. Jelena died from hypothermia while hiding in a wood, but Drita survived. If she knew your sister's real name, she didn't reveal it. Perhaps Jelena told her not to say because of the shame of what happened to them. Maybe she didn't want your mother to know, so the authorities struggled to locate your family to inform them. A special department linked her DNA to Montenegro, where you both had been reported missing. Your mother recognised the photo.'

Jasmina's face finally crumpled, and she let out a sob.

'Mamma! My poor Mamma,' she wailed. 'Jelena!'

Ashley reached over the table and took her hands. Jasmina swiftly pulled herself together, let go of Ashley's hands, and gestured for her to continue.

'It sounds as if your brother, Dragan, investigated the crimes to find out more, but it was your dad who came to this country.'

'My father?'

'Yes. We suspect to fetch you. He used some non-conventional methods.'

Jasmina's eyes narrowed.

'My father is not a nice person. He was rarely around when we were young, and later disappeared. My mum had to raise us on her own, but it was better that way. Many men were damaged beyond repair by our wars. Emil Popovic was one.'

Ashley considered glossing over what had happened, but she needed this woman onside, and she had been honest with them.

'We think it was your father who took Hamish and Max after a night out last Friday, then questioned them using torture. Hamish was buried alive but escaped. Max was put on a funeral pyre but also survived. Two of Lorenzo's staff were not so lucky and were killed. Tommaso is also dead.'

Jasmina nodded firmly but didn't comment. Ashley noted a small glint of satisfaction flash across her face.

'Was Lorenzo at your home this morning?'

'He has been at the cottage for days. It felt like he was hiding. He's not stayed so long before. It was oddly okay. I have been upbeat with Lorenzo recently, even trying to make love to him, to hope he dropped his guard for when I fled. But I have no money and no passport, so I kept putting it off. There's no Internet in the house, only TV. I saw on daytime programmes there are places which can help, but it is such a risk with young children. Lorenzo is rich and ruthless.' She flicked a glance at Ashley. 'I do not know if your police are corrupt, but I decided to try because Jelena would have wanted me to after all this time, even if she was in danger.'

'This morning when Lorenzo left your place, Emil and two others, who we believe are Drita and her boyfriend, tried to abduct him. Lorenzo's driver was stabbed, but he shot your father. I'm sad to say he has died.'

Jasmina flinched.

'But they still took Lorenzo?'

'Yes. We're currently searching for him.'

'How did Tommaso die?'

Ashley deliberated on her reply.

'Terribly.'

Jasmina smiled. It was the first one that touched her eyes.

'Don't search too hard for Lorenzo on my behalf.'

Scott coughed next to Ashley.

'That's not how it works,' she said. 'Do you have any idea where Lorenzo might have been taken?'

'No, of course not. Why would I? I've barely left the village, and then never alone.'

'Did anyone come to visit you? Any messages reach you?'

Jasmina shook her head.

'Did Lorenzo tell you anything? Perhaps let something slip in the bedroom?'

'Lorenzo was cruel. He called me his *cavalla* and said I was only good for riding. Later, he told me I was nothing but a mare.'

69

There was a knock at the door. The victim support team from the council had arrived. Ashley stepped outside and gave them an update, then introduced them to Jasmina and the children. Ashley took Emma and Scott away to a meeting room.

'I heard most of the conversation,' said Emma. 'It made me feel like torturing Lorenzo myself.'

'It's hard to believe all that's been going on, right under our noses,' said Scott.

'Not hard, sickening,' said Ashley, 'but we know it happens.'

'Jasmina was right,' said Emma. 'Part of me doesn't care if we don't find him in time. The joys of being police, eh?'

'I want him found so we have the bastard behind bars and can give that poor woman some closure.'

'I'll go for another chat in a bit, maybe just her and me,' said Emma. 'She might open up a bit more with general talk about what her plans are for the future.'

'Great idea.'

Gabriella must have noticed them return to the office. She walked over.

'Can I have a quick word?'

'Of course.'

'Morgan and Zelda have been to Drita's house. There's nobody home. Curtains drawn upstairs and downstairs. Uniform are knocking on her neighbours' doors, and we're looking into her background. Entry warrant is with the magistrates. Sal checked with DVLA, and she owns a Mazda. He's linked it already to the footage Hector provided. Her car was parked next to St Martin's church in Overstrand. Sal also found what is likely Drita and the big guy walking up the High Street hand in hand. They're wearing hats, and she has a scarf, but there weren't many people around, and his size gives him away in a village with lots of pensioners. We've obtained a mobile number for her, but it's off.'

'Did they pinpoint the van's movements using the other cameras?' asked Ashley.

'Kind of. It went through the outskirts of Mundesley, so they drove back along the coast roads. The vehicle didn't reach as far as Walcott. Unfortunately, that still gives us a large area, especially if we consider everything inland to North Walsham. Any available units are on their way. Kettle's doing a live interview on the BBC, to ask for the public's help in locating the van.'

Ashley saw Hector arrive in the office and called him in. He smiled at Gabriella without blushing. Perhaps he'd given up on her.

'Any news?' asked Ashley.

'Yes, but of the bad variety.'

'Go on.'

'Rocco arrived at Overstrand. He'd received a text from Lorenzo's phone.'

'When?'

'About half an hour after he was abducted.'

'Which I assume Lorenzo didn't send.'

'No, it wasn't even a threat. It was a statement of events.'

Hector rummaged in his pocket and brought out his phone.

'I got Rocco to forward the message to me. It's easier if I read it out.'

The tension rose in the room. Hector's expression was grim.

'It appears you were innocent, but your older sons were not. The blood feud is now settled. They called themselves the Romans. It is fitting they died like Roman scum.'

'That doesn't sound promising for Lorenzo,' said Emma. 'Texts were sent from Max's phone after he was abducted, so they have form for it.'

'It sounds as if Lorenzo's already dead,' said Scott.

Hector waited until he had their attention back.

'As I mentioned before, the methods so far inflicted on the Viallis were all taken from antiquity. Rome was a patriarchal and hierarchical society. Roman men held all the power. Fathers in particular. Usually, only low-level citizens were sentenced to die by burning, being buried or being thrown from cliffs, but the Romans tortured, not only to emphasise the low status of the convict, but to dishonour and humiliate the higher born. The killers are telling the world that the Viallis are the lowest of the low.'

'You're saying Lorenzo will meet a similar and equally unpleasant end,' said Emma.

'Yes. Use your imagination. My guess is they will have saved the worst 'til last.'

70

Ashley rang Michelle after the meeting to see when she was doing the post-mortems on Gianluca and Tommaso.

'I'm starting them soon. Do you have a preference on which order I do them in? Looking at the bodies, they've been through the same ordeal.'

'I'll come down for a chat and get it first-hand. It'll be Hector and me. No drooling.'

'Ah, no worries. I reckon I might have a date soon with another guy, so I may be able to control myself.'

'I'll look forward to hearing about it.'

'I hope I have something to tell you.'

'Is Paolo's PM finished?'

'Yes, I'm about to hit send on that, but I'll update you when you arrive. It's been a long time since I did anything this gruesome.'

'I assume you've heard a man called Emil Popovic will be with you by day's end, and a John Doe from the same shooting and stabbing this morning.'

'I did. It never rains but it pours.'

'See you soon.'

Ashley hadn't considered the extra impact of this case on Michelle. She was used to seeing dead bodies, but Ashley suspected even Michelle would struggle with so many gruesome deaths, especially as she had to imagine what each victim had been through, and, more importantly, whether they were still alive during the ordeal. Post-mortems took around three hours. That was more than enough time for those images to burrow into Michelle's brain permanently.

Ashley had all the time in the world for Michelle. She was a lovely person. Like Ashley, she worked hard and was lonely. Ashley hoped her date went well and made a mental note to double-check she was still coming to Hector's leaving do.

Ashley and Hector caught up with an hour's paperwork, then got in Hector's car and drove to the hospital. There'd been no sightings of the grey van. A tension had hung heavy in the office as everyone waited for Lorenzo to be found. It was a bit of a relief to get out of there.

Hector was quiet until they reached the mortuary. Just before they walked in, he asked about Ally.

'I can't believe he's a wrong 'un. It's really shocked me.'

'Things like that do. We all think we're superb judges of character, so it's a surprise when that's proven so wrong. It's an important lesson for you, and a pointed reminder for us oldies who've been through it before.'

'Which is?'

'You never truly know anyone. People's lives can be affected in a thousand ways, and they might respond in a thousand more. You can't see inside their heads.'

'I suppose that's why we have a defence of temporary insanity.'

'Exactly. We're all walking a tightrope. It's only a matter of time before someone else slips off.'

Hector smiled.

'I'm going to miss your advice. I just feel so stunned.'

'Hang around long enough, and you'll come to expect it. These things are good for your career. They're a fabulous lesson in human behaviour. Possibly not great for eight hours of shut-eye but don't take it personally. I bet everyone at OCC is wondering how they didn't see it. That's probably why he went under the radar, assuming, of course, he is dirty.'

'Do you think he is?'

'I still want to say no. I know that man, and I would have trusted him with my life. Barry would have done, too. It's why he was so angry.'

'I felt similar, but there's no getting past the fact information is leaking out of our department.'

'Precisely, and if it isn't Ally, then it's someone else, which is even more worrying.'

A receptionist buzzed them into the mortuary, and they were soon in scrubs and staring over Tommaso. Michelle was ready to start.

'I won't need to get physical while you're here. Observations should be enough for you. Start the recording, please, Sally.'

Michelle waited until Sally, her anatomical pathology technician, had everything prepared. Michelle confirmed Tommaso's details, then began.

'Subject is prone. Back shows a large tattoo. Letters SPQR have been tattooed below a large eagle. The flesh around the tattoo has been heavily scoured, as has the skin all over the body, even the soles of the feet. There has been heavy blood loss, most likely ante-mortem. Suspect would have been in considerable pain. Correction, make that agony.'

'Enough loss of blood to kill him?' asked Hector.

'No,' said Michelle, grimly. 'Close, but unlikely. Sally, assist me in turning over Mr Vialli.'

Even Ashley balked at the damage that had been done to Tommaso. His chest looked as if a lawnmower had run over it.

'The sternum, shoulder blades and the front of the ribs are broken, suggesting he landed face down after falling from the cliff. I expect to find many of the internal organs torn from position, due to the force of the impact. The skull has a depressed frontal fracture, which would likely be fatal. Both sets of tibia and fibula have snapped. The chance of the victim surviving such a fall was zero.'

Ashley gestured to the corpse on the trolley next to her.

'I assume conclusions are similar for Gianluca.'

'He landed on his back, but yes, his was a fatal drop too. I noticed many of his fingers had been broken, whereas Tommaso's fingernails were missing.'

'Same tattoo as Tommaso?' asked Hector.

'Similar, but smaller and on the upper arm. No eagle,' replied Michelle.

Ashley nodded at Hector. 'The same as Max and Hamish.'

'Maybe Tommaso's is bigger because he is one of the main men,' said Hector. 'I expect his brother, Lorenzo, has the larger design.'

'Rocco told me the older brothers had larger tattoos.'

'We occasionally get gang markings. It would make sense if Tommaso was a leader and Gianluca a follower, but that's conjecture. Perhaps Tommaso and Lorenzo simply liked bigger tattoos.'

Another mortuary assistant entered the room.

'Emil Popovic and John Doe have arrived and have been processed. I'll put Emil in the other room.'

'Come with me, Ashley,' said Michelle.

They made small talk while they walked to the room.

'So, about your potential date,' she said to Michelle. 'Spill the beans.'

'No, I don't want to jinx it. He hasn't asked me out properly yet. We're jockeying for position.'

Ashley couldn't help thinking of Lorenzo's *cavalla* tag, so she was pleased to be distracted when Emil was brought in, and she could focus on the job at hand.

'Do you need quick information on both of the new arrivals?' asked Michelle.

'I saw both wounds at the scene,' said Hector. 'Emil was hit at close range. I noted the powder burns on his shirt.'

Michelle unzipped Emil's body bag and checked his chest.

'Very close. His skin is also burnt.'

'I thought people could survive wounds to the abdomen if help was fast to arrive.'

Michelle smiled at Hector, then had a swift look over the body. She lifted Emil's right shoulder.

'It looks as though he was shot by someone crouching. The bullet entered his stomach, but the weapon was pointed upwards. The exit wound would indicate the right lung has been destroyed as the projectile came out behind his shoulder blade. He'd have bled out quickly. Perhaps a minute or two. It's extremely tricky to stabilise those injuries unless you're a combat medic.'

'Any tattoos?'

Michelle pointed at Emil's arms and then his stomach.

'A few smudged and old ones. Maybe prison tats. He's had a hard life, judging by his skin. Numerous serious traumas. Looks like another bullet wound. Was he a soldier?'

Ashley nodded.

'And the man with no name?'

Michelle called for the other corpse to be brought in. She made a cursory check when it arrived.

'Nothing, although he also has more than his fair share of

scars. If the other tattoos are gang-related, this person wasn't affiliated to whatever their collective was called.'

'The Romans,' said Hector.

'Makes sense. I need to move these bodies to the room with the fridges. I'll continue with Tommaso.'

'That's great,' said Ashley. 'We appreciate you staying late.'

'No problem.'

They returned to Tommaso's body.

'Would you like the lowdown on the buried victim, Paolo?' asked Michelle.

'Yes,' said Hector.

'He was bound and placed in the hole. There was significant mud under the remaining toenails and fingernails, suggesting he tried to dig himself out by any means possible. His pose in death is typical of asphyxiation, but he'd also been maltreated beforehand. Cigarette burns, and, by the looks of it, some kind of electric shock treatment. Possibly a Taser, but the skin has been singed, so more likely a wire from the mains.'

'I have the feeling we're in for a long one tonight, so ring me if anything comes up,' said Ashley.

'Are you expecting more bodies?'

'Tommaso's brother, Lorenzo, was picked up by the same crew who inflicted the damage on Tommaso and Gianluca.'

Michelle looked down at Tommaso's ruined body.

'I'm not religious, but may his god have mercy on his soul.'

71

Ashley cadged a lift from one of the admin team back to her car in Happisburgh at seven. She drove home parched and hungry. The officers searching for the van had found no sight of it, so it was a case of waiting for a phone call while she took some down time. Her mobile rang the second she shut her front door. She groaned, then remembered it could be important. It was Scott Gorton.

'Hi, Scott.'

'Hi, Ash. I thought I'd let you know about my follow-up chat with Jasmina.'

'No worries. I'm just pleased it's not Control dragging me back before I've eaten.'

'Still work, unfortunately.'

For a moment, Ashley considered seeing if Scott fancied going to Hector's leaving meal the following Friday, but Hector had said who he wanted there, and Scott hadn't been on the list, so she didn't ask.

'No problem. How's Jasmina?'

'I have to say, I like her. She's showing a lot of strength, but the signs of PTSD are present, and she's trying to push this whole saga from her mind.'

'I take it she's hoping to leave Norfolk straight away. We could do with questioning her after we find Lorenzo. Dead or alive.'

'Jasmina's planning to stay for a few weeks. The kids are confused, so she wants to get them back at nursery, then tell them they have a holiday coming up. The children have friends there and are happy, so she hopes that settles them.'

'If Lorenzo dies?'

'Yes. If he survives, then she's on the next plane out of here.'

'Did you speak to Rocco?'

'Yes. He was in an awful state, but even more credit to Jasmina because she calmed him down.'

'Surely she's not still happy talking to him?'

'Yep. She heard Rocco shouting when we brought him in. He clearly dotes on those grandchildren. Imagine, though, how his life has imploded. To lose a son in the way Tommaso died. It doesn't look encouraging for Lorenzo, and Max still hasn't been in touch with him.'

'Even though Max doesn't want to talk to him, surely a message would be normal, even if it was only to say he's fine. It makes me suspect that Rocco, like Max, isn't as ignorant of all this as they've made out. I assume everyone's kept clear of the possibility of Rocco perverting the course of justice by receiving tip-offs from Ally.'

'Yes, I checked with Kettle beforehand. He said it's best left for the moment. They need to talk to Ally under caution. Find out exactly what's gone on. He's been told to report to the Met police next week for interview and is suspended in the meantime.'

'Makes sense to keep any internal meetings out of the area. I wonder if there'll be a fudge up. Consider the two involved. Ally's done nearly thirty years, is close to retirement, and he's recently gone through a divorce. Rocco's favourite sons will probably both have been brutally murdered after we failed to locate them.'

'True. They won't be in a rush to see that in media reports, and right now all they have is Ally not recording his visits to Rocco's business.'

'I bet there will be more if they dig.'

'Maybe, but it's not a problem for today, so I'll let you go. There is one last thing I don't like.'

'That doesn't sound good.'

'The message that was sent to Rocco's phone pinged off a mast in North Walsham.'

'Shit, so perhaps the kidnappers weren't going near Bacton Wood. For all we know, they might have killed Lorenzo and left Norfolk. Or at least taken him with them.'

'Yes, that's possible.'

'Bollocks.'

'My words exactly. I'll see you tomorrow.'

Ashley said goodbye to Scott and put the hob on to cook a nice piece of steak. It had been hanging around a while but was only a day out of date. The edges of it were tinged a little brown, but it smelled okay.

She read her emails and found The Grove had confirmed her booking. Drinks at six, food at seven. All the people she'd invited had agreed to come, although Kettle had emailed to say he could only do the first hour.

He said he'd see her on Friday during the day anyway because that was when he was announcing the results of the Inspector Assessment Day.

72

Ashley didn't get the quality night of sleep she hoped for because her brain wouldn't be quiet. Her phone rang at five in the morning. She struggled to understand the implications of what Control were saying to begin with.

'You're ringing me about a domestic?' she asked.

'No, a reported domestic. Screaming was heard in a bungalow.'

'When was this?'

'The report came through an hour ago, but the noise occurred at about eight yesterday evening.'

'I assume someone's been out to the property.'

'Yes. The caller was a passing dog walker. He wasn't sure whether it was a cry of pain or pleasure. He couldn't sleep, so his wife told him to call us. Better to be safe than sorry.'

'Good for her.'

'He said it was a woman's voice, but it was more likely she was the aggressor, not a victim.'

'Right, and what did the residents say when we attended?'

'No one answered the door, but they spoke to the closest house about two-hundred metres away. They said the place was empty after the tenant moved into a nursing home four months ago and recently died. They'd noticed a van coming and going, but it looked like a carpenter doing some work, so they weren't worried.'

'Location?'

'On the edge of Edingthorpe.'

Ashley leapt out of bed. That wasn't far from Bacton.

'I'm on my way. What's the situation on the ground?'

'Uniform are outside. There's still no answer. They decided to check with you or the SIO to see what you want to do.'

That sounded like buck-passing to Ashley, but who knew what they'd find inside? It could well be dangerous.

'Where's the ARV?'

'Twenty minutes away.'

'Is the helicopter around?'

'Refuelling, but it can be there in half an hour.'

Ashley put the phone on speaker and slipped into a pair of loose jeans. The helicopters had only around two hours of airtime. It was a big area with a lot of criss-crossing roads. The chopper might come in handy later. She had a thought of the route she'd take.

'Keep it grounded for the moment but have them on standby. Ensure the bungalow has a tight cordon. Call the ARV. I'll be thirty minutes, anyway. Then we go in.'

'Understood. Notify us when you're nearly at the scene.'

Ashley didn't bother brushing her teeth. She pulled on a pair of boots and a coat and was out of the door. They had enough manpower to cope without her waking anyone else up, so she drove straight there with her mind whirring.

Ashley suspected the screaming wasn't from the victim. It would be Drita, as she took her revenge.

73

Ashley arrived at Edingthorpe twenty-five minutes later and turned onto Rectory Road. It was narrow, with just about enough room for two cars to pass, and without streetlights. She slowed down as something swift scampered across the tarmac in front of her. Flashing lights glowed in the distance as though aliens had landed.

The ARV was parked up, and the two occupants had removed their Heckler & Koch MP5s from the rear of their vehicle. Ashley introduced herself. Uniform at the scene already had them up to speed.

The ARV crew set off with an officer holding the big red key and another with a loudhailer, while Ashley updated Control. If anyone was in the dwelling, they'd be well aware the police had arrived. Ashley couldn't say if that made the situation more or less dangerous.

The team disappeared down the drive, which was surrounded by mature trees. The large bungalow at the bottom remained mostly out of sight. Four marked response estate cars and two vans were present, but everyone had left their vehicles in case they were needed to head in. No one said a word, with all of their ears tuned in for any reply to the loudhailer's request to come out, but also for the possibility of shooting.

They listened as a second warning rang out and then the sound of splintering wood followed. More shouts filtered through the early morning air, then 'clear' was bellowed as each room was checked. Five minutes felt like an eternity until one of the officers reappeared.

'Nobody's home, but this is the right location.'

Ashley wondered if the moonlight was making him look pale, or if the sights he'd just seen in the bungalow were responsible.

'Is the scene secure?'

He nodded.

'Follow me,' she said.

She gave orders for the rest of the waiting officers to stay where they were and trod carefully down the drive. The driveway was a muddy track, which would leave footprints. A mist hung suspended a foot above the ground, giving the place an ethereal feel. It was deathly quiet, with the wind too weak to even rustle the leaves on the trees. She looked over at the empty fields. There was nothing like searching for murderers in the middle of the countryside in the milky twilight.

First, she had to look inside the bungalow and Ashley steeled herself for what lay ahead.

When they reached the end of the drive, one of the ARV crewmen was crouched and looking at the ground. Using his torch, he pointed to markings on the drive. It was pitch black surrounding the building, so the lines he traced were clear.

'These are recent because it rained around midnight,' he said. 'I'd guess there were at least two vehicles here, and, judging by the width of the tyre marks, one of them was probably a van.'

Ashley glanced over to the left at a large garage where the

tracks led. No prizes for guessing where they hid the vehicles when not in use. It was strange to think the helicopter would have flown overhead and looked down on this building, but there were thousands of places similar in Norfolk.

'What's in the garage?'

'A set of blank number plates and some tins of vehicle paint. There's a trestle and a big toolbox. Someone's been sawing pretty big pieces of wood. The evidence in the bungalow is different.'

Ashley nodded at the man, who shook his head.

The front door was ajar with a PC standing beside it. He'd placed the big red key on the ground and had his hand to his nose. He passed her his torch.

Ashley recognised the scent of blood before she'd even edged in the doorway. There was an undercurrent of decay and faeces to the aroma as well. Ashley had been to an abattoir once, and it had smelled similar.

She put on a pair of gloves and stepped inside. The stench was far stronger and she breathed slowly through her mouth. The kitchen was the first room she entered. She considered putting the light on, but a light switch was one of the best places to find fingerprints, so she ran the torch beam around the room in a circle instead. Bottles of water, sandwich wrappers, discarded cereal boxes, opened tins and coffee jars littered the worktops.

There were no internal doors, even though the hinges remained. The mystery of where Hamish and Paolo's coffin lids had come from was solved.

She walked into the next room. Restraints hung from each of the four corners of a table, which was covered in a dark dried liquid and what she guessed were pieces of skin. More operating table, than dining table.

She crouched and stared at a dark puddle on the floor. The centre still appeared wet. It must be blood, and it had been spilled recently, maybe within two or three hours. Ashley took her phone out of her pocket.

'Hi, Control. DS Ashley Knight. Instruct Hotel Nine Nine to go up and head to my location. Suspects liable to have been in the area in the last few hours.'

On the seats, which had been pushed up against the walls, sat piles of clothing. A weapon rested on one chair. A flail. It was home-made – a piece of wood with leather thongs fastened to it. On those thongs she could see nails affixed along the length. She glanced at the parquet floor. It was mostly free of debris, but what looked like teeth lay strewn among the odd bits of rubbish. Fingernails, too.

As Ashley circled the table, she almost trod on a short, thick tree branch. It was stained dark red. The leather of the wooden flail was the same colour.

The next room had a white door that was identical to the ones placed over Max and Hamish in the wood. She pushed it wide and entered a lounge that stank of death. The couch had a blanket laid over it, but, even with a remote control on the arm, the space was not being used for its intended purpose.

Both armchairs were heavily soiled. A coil rope lay around both of them. Plastic cable ties were scattered on the floor. On a nest of tables sat a knife, a hammer, and a pair of pliers. All of them had reddish brown stains. Beside them was an electric cable and two dishcloths twisted in the manner of blindfolds, or maybe gags. She moistened her lips and moved on.

Ashley moved through another identical door and headed further along a corridor. It was a long bungalow. The next room was a bedroom containing a large double bed. Both sides appeared slept in. The other rooms held single beds without bedding, with the final door leading to a family bathroom. She returned to the first bedroom and found an en suite. Scummy brown water sat in the shower tray, which made her suspect it had been recently used, perhaps to wash blood away.

Ashley headed back along the corridor and took a left at another door, where she entered a hall. On the left was a bathroom. Ahead was the doorless kitchen. She strode through and rushed outside. Five metres from the bungalow, she leaned backwards and forced the fetid fumes from her lungs, then she gratefully sucked in the clean country air.

'There's a loft space,' said one of the ARV officers. 'We looked, but we didn't go inside. Seems unused.'

'Our perpetrators have left,' she replied. 'But they haven't been gone long.'

She heard the crackle of a radio from down the lane.

'Cordon this off, guys. I'll update Control. CSI will have a field day in there.'

A female officer ran down the drive.

'We set up cameras along a few of the roads in the surrounding area because there were so many interlinking routes. They're watching them back at OCC. A vehicle has just gone through one near Bacton Wood.'

'What kind of vehicle?'

'It was a grey van.'

74

Zoltan pulled out of the field where he'd been waiting under a tree for the first hint of daylight. He'd driven there after watching a screaming Drita whip Lorenzo to the gates of damnation. He'd had to stop her in the end or Lorenzo would already be dead, and that wasn't part of Dragan's plan.

Zoltan had felt nothing watching Drita's blows rain down on Lorenzo. He didn't particularly care if Lorenzo deserved it or not, but for them to go to all this trouble, Zoltan assumed he did.

From the moment Zoltan had met Drita, he'd known she'd been damaged beyond repair. He knew the look. He wore it himself.

She flinched every time he accidentally brushed past her. Zoltan knew victims like her. People who would never be the same. It was common when ruthless invading armies entered civilian areas. The officers encouraged it. Zoltan couldn't forget playing his part in all that, too. He sometimes wondered if that person had really been him.

To be fair to her, Drita was responsible for improving their plan. Dragan's detective had found her address and asked if she wanted to be involved. She'd offered her house as a base and acquired the van for them. In Overstrand, she had been cool, and it had been her idea to send the text messages to Rocco. First from Max's mobile after drugging him, then from Lorenzo's. She'd earlier told Zoltan to drive towards North Walsham to further confuse the police. Lorenzo had given her the code for his phone after Drita had said he would have one chance to provide it, or she would immediately cut his index finger off and open it that way.

Drita had lost control only when it had come to punishing Lorenzo and that was understandable. The experience the brothers had inflicted on her had ruined her life. It was only right they should lose theirs. The night Drita had seen Tommaso in the club and dropped a pill in Hamish's drink, she'd said she wanted to stab the Italian to death there and then. Tommaso and Paolo had been present when she was trafficked. It was Tommaso who had labelled her *cavalla*.

Luckily, Zoltan had been looking out of the window from behind a curtain when a passing dog walker had stopped outside the bungalow. Zoltan had suspected Drita's screams of rage and the release of her pent-up vengeance would travel.

They'd talked about it afterwards and Drita had said it was time to leave. Zoltan didn't care either way, so he'd agreed. She'd been confirmed right when the police cars had driven past the hedge behind which he'd now parked the van. At that moment, he'd known it was almost over.

Zoltan gave a thought to Emil. It had been unsettling seeing him on the boat across the Channel. It had been obvious to Zoltan they were part of the same plan, but they hadn't acknowledged each other. Even so, Zoltan had sensed an immediate kinship. There were few people on the planet who understood him. Emil had been one.

It had been enjoyable meeting him in Norwich and catching

up on the past. They had both laughed at having to swim the last bit of the journey. But now he was gone. To think, Emil had survived the randomness of warfare. All those stray bullets and unpredictable artillery shells had missed him. The arbitrary violence in filthy jails had also passed Emil by, only for him to be shot in the street, like a dog. Perhaps Emil was lucky. His battles were over. Whereas Zoltan still opened his eyes to new days, to live with the knowledge of what he'd done in the old days.

What he felt wasn't sadness or guilt, but more a sense of knowing his actions were abhorrent. If there was an afterlife, Zoltan's journey was downwards.

Still, he quite liked jail. The routine, the comradeship, the odd treats, and the meals. He looked forward to them all. But it was the jogging around the yard and pounding weights in the gym that stilled his mind.

Zoltan had no illusion he was going to escape from this situation. No doubt he'd eventually get sent back to Montenegro if he was still alive. After all, he was serving three life sentences. It wasn't as if they could give him more time if he was already in jail until he died.

Dragan had arranged his escape. Zoltan's only worry was about being placed under super-max conditions when he returned. The guards would know his history, so Zoltan would likely receive special treatment. He shrugged. Pain he could handle. If they took his gym time away, though, he might struggle.

The main reason prison suited him fine was because one of his daughters visited him once a month and gave him family updates. She brought him a home-made cake, which the guards usually let him keep if he gave them a slice. So, Zoltan had a life. If he left Montenegro for good, she wouldn't know where to find him. He smiled. The money she would receive from Emil's son after this was over would buy her a small flat. She could build from there.

As far as Zoltan was concerned, the killings had been worth it, whatever happened to him.

When they'd dragged their captives to the bungalow, Zoltan had secured their ties, then Emil had questioned them. At first, Zoltan had watched impassively, but the smells and the sounds had brought it all back. If Emil had asked for his help, Zoltan would have become the man he used to be. Zoltan did not want that, and the world certainly didn't.

All that was decent about Zoltan had died while he was killing under the banner of war. Afterwards, like Emil, he'd detached himself from his family and loved ones, knowing that, even if he was capable of returning their affection, his anger knew no bounds. When justice had finally caught up with Zoltan, he had been okay with it. Even he accepted it was better that he lived behind bars.

Zoltan drove out of the field and headed towards Mill Road where he parked up outside the sawmill and opposite the path into Bacton Wood. They'd already dug the hole. They'd made one in the other wood, too, in case the plan changed. Zoltan smiled as he recalled Emil's thorough planning. He'd been a clever guy. He should have been a general.

Zoltan slid open the van's side panel, grabbed the upright, stomped into the wood, and found the spot. The piece of wood fitted well in position with only a little play. He jogged back to the van and buckled up his tool belt.

Lorenzo was inside, already tied to the crosspiece. It was a crude design, but it would work. Zoltan opened the rear doors to the vehicle and pulled him out. Bubbles of blood formed at Lorenzo's mouth, reassuring Zoltan that, even though he looked dead, he was still alive.

The plan had been for Zoltan and Emil to carry Lorenzo, but the man weighed nothing compared to the weights Zoltan had moved in jail. He easily picked Lorenzo up and carried him back down the path with the length of wood under one arm.

With a grunt, Zoltan rested the crosspiece on the notch carved into the upright. He'd forgotten the rope to secure the pieces. He pictured it on the driver's seat. Never mind. Lorenzo was beyond struggling.

He raised Lorenzo's head by lifting his chin, then let it drop. Lorenzo wheezed as each breath went in and out. His feet just touched the muddy ground, but they wouldn't for long.

'Water,' he gasped, or at least that was what it sounded closest to.

Zoltan heard a whop-whop-whop noise. He put the first nail between his lips, lifted one of Lorenzo's ankles up, then took the hammer from his belt. He made a tap-tap-tap sound of his own. The helicopter screamed overhead as Lorenzo shrieked below.

Zoltan threw his tool belt in the bushes but kept hold of the hammer. It was time to run.

75

Ashley raced through the country roads as fast as she dared. It was quiet, and she didn't have far to go, but farmers got up early and there was only one winner in a collision with a John Deere tractor.

Whoever they were pursuing was likely heading back to the area where Hamish had clambered from his grave what seemed a long time ago. She turned into Mill Road, which was the closest entrance to Hamish's burial spot. Other units were already there. The officers had left their vehicles and were looking at a grey van. It was the one they wanted.

Ashley leapt from her car and raced over. The side panel was open.

'It was empty,' said an officer. 'Looks bad for the victim.'

Ashley stared at the thick red smear on the floor of the vehicle, where something large and bloody had been dragged out. She suspected Drita and her boyfriend had carried Lorenzo between them, but the man sounded capable of the task himself.

With so many officers there already, they could flush their quarry out, but the problem was that they were chasing killers. She called Control again and got them to redirect the other approaching units to the main entrance. She instructed that extreme caution be shown and for all personnel to stay in their vehicles until told otherwise.

Ashley gathered the officers present around her. She explained what she knew and what she suspected. The ARV guys were the ones with the experience of dealing with this level of danger.

'How do you want to play it?' she asked them.

'You have two officers with Tasers. We'll take them in and fan out in your target area. The most important thing is finding Lorenzo. Once we've done that, you can enter, and we'll adjust. I imagine his kidnappers have fled that scene. If they're running, the helicopter should pick them up.'

Ashley nodded, then stared after them as they jogged down the leafy lane.

A Vauxhall Insignia arrived as she was updating Control. Hector got out and ran over.

'You took your time,' she said.

'I nipped into OCC and booked out a car instead of bringing my own.'

'I'm pleased to see you haven't picked up any of my less desirable habits. Well done. I think we're about to find Lorenzo.'

'I heard.'

Hector listened as she brought him up to speed.

'Right,' was his only comment.

'Actually, why are you here? You weren't on call.'

'This is my last case. I wanted to be here at the end, so I asked HQ to ring me if there were any developments.'

Ashley smiled.

'You sure got a doozy for your final one.'

Hector's eyes narrowed.

'It's certainly something I won't forget.'

'Maybe the killers will be having a picnic when our guys turn up, and it'll be nice and easy.'

Hector shook his head at Ashley.

'I see what you're doing and it's not necessary.'

'What?'

'Making jokes. Distracting me. I don't need it.'

'Perhaps *I* do.'

'You know, on the drive here, I tried to recall the fresh-faced youth who joined your team just six months ago. But he seems to be missing.'

'You've changed. That's what happens.'

'Has that person vanished permanently?'

'I'm afraid so. Once you've looked behind the veil, you can't unsee it. The things you've experienced are yours forever.'

'I suppose the choice becomes whether to look there again, or hope it gradually fades into the distant past. I...'

Hector struggled for the words, which was possibly a first. Ashley gave his arm a squeeze.

'Or you stay and do something about it, so others never know.'

As the morning light came, clouds moved in overhead. The sky felt heavy, as though it were struggling under an unmanageable burden of thunder and rain.

'I can guess what we're going to find,' he said.

'What?'

'I think we're looking for a crucifixion.'

76

Ashley blew out a breath.

'What makes you say that? Why not buried or burnt?'

'From the beginning, this was all about Lorenzo. He will receive the worst punishment. Crucifixion was the most extreme Roman death sentence. It was reserved for those they wanted to hurt and humiliate.'

'The ultimate death.'

'Quite. Roman law used it as a method of execution, but also to dishonour the convicted. Jews were crucified to take away their status. Think of Jesus.'

'I get it.'

'Do you remember Gerald told you there was a hole in which one of the PolSA team nearly broke their leg at Harrison's Wood?'

'Yes.'

'It's just occurred to me. It could have been made to place a stipe in.'

'Eh?'

'An upright for the cross. Perhaps one was dug here as well.'

'You've made me picture Lorenzo being forced to carry the top bit like in pictures of the crucifixion of Jesus.'

'The crosspiece. I shouldn't think they had time for that.'

'Is he likely to be alive?'

'The crucified sometimes died from the scourging beforehand, or they were stabbed to hasten their deaths.'

Ashley shook her head. Now she was lost for words.

'It hasn't been long, though,' said Hector. 'We should be able to save him. He will be in agony and incredibly dehydrated from bleeding and diaphoresis.'

'What the hell is that?'

'A simple explanation is excessive sweating through fear and stress. The blood loss will be from the torture. The horrific nature of the punishment induces terrible shock on the body.'

'Sounds like the Inspectors exam.'

Hector looked down at her. He held her gaze for a few seconds, then grinned.

'Don't change,' he said.

'I'll try not to,' she replied.

One of the Taser team trotted up the lane towards them.

'We've found him and secured the scene. I've called for an ambulance, but we need a first-aid kit right now.'

'So, he's breathing?' asked Ashley.

The officer, a man she knew had over twenty years' experience, gritted his teeth, then spoke softly.

'Just. We'll also need a toolkit.'

77

Ashley and Hector jogged after the officer, and he directed them to the spot. Lorenzo was positioned next to the path just as it met the wood. He'd been displayed for all to see. His treatment had been worse than Tommaso's.

'We weren't sure how to move him,' said the officer who'd escorted them down. 'He's bleeding profusely, and we didn't want to open any wounds up, but his breathing is laboured.'

Ashley stepped over and glanced at the base of the cross. They'd assumed the hole had been dug to cause distraction, like the litter strewn at the entrance to Harrison's Wood and tyres being let down. It was further proof of the meticulous preparation Emil's team had put into their operation.

Again, she wondered what type of person could do this to another human being, but then she remembered Ivan's call about the man who'd escaped from jail in Montenegro. A criminal who committed atrocities in the notoriously brutal Bosnian War.

'Between us, we should be able to lift the whole thing out and rest him on his back until the ambulance arrives. We can dress the cuts on his body and his hands and ankles to stop any external bleeding.'

Hector called for the other officers back at Mill Road to come and help. Ashley stood in front of Lorenzo and looked up at his face. He tried to raise his head, but his chin dropped again.

'Lorenzo. If you can hear me, you're safe now. We're going to lift you out of the hole and rest you on the ground, so you are able to breathe more easily. The ambulance will be here in a few minutes.'

The officers gathered around and began to extract him. Ashley briefly looked away when the top of the cross separated from the upright and Lorenzo gasped, but the post slid out and they laid him down. Ashley's phone rang. It was Control.

'Hotel Nine Nine is over your location. Thermal imaging has located a fast-moving figure at the edge of the wood, on the other side from you heading southbound. Mobile units are closing in.'

'Male or female.'

'Unclear at this point.'

'Is DCI Kettle managing from OCC?'

'That's correct. He wants your ARV and anyone with a Taser to get on the net and follow directions. Radio will be on talk-through.'

Ashley cut the call. As she sent off the requested people, ambulance sirens came into earshot. She was itching to jump in her car and tear off, but Kettle had enough resources to take the suspects down. More vehicles might confuse things. Besides, Control had mentioned only a single figure. Where was the other?

She hadn't noticed Hector leaving, but he reappeared waving a radio at her.

'Did you bring coffee and doughnuts as well?' she asked with a smile.

'No, I clearly still have much to learn.'

Ashley had kept four officers with them, in case the murderers backtracked. Their angel above would hopefully fore-warn them of that, so they grouped together and listened to the radio.

The units chasing would be double-crewed. One driving, one talking to Control. Their quarry would be referred to as the subject. With the radio on talk-through, all units could hear all conversations. The helicopter would contain the pilot and the air observer. Everyone would know it was a communication from them because there was an audible high-pitched whine in the background from the engine, but they would still use their call sign.

It was the air observer who next came on the net. The voice was without emotion.

'Hotel Nine Nine, subject has emerged from the trees. IC2 male, wearing a white T-shirt and blue jeans. Running down the centre of North Walsham Road in the direction of Ridlington. Subject has looked up and waved a hammer at us. For the information of ground units, be aware, the subject is armed. Delta Four Two, it looks as though you are the closest unit to the subject. Five seconds to contact.'

One of the ground units joined the conversation.

'Delta Four Two, that's noted, and we have the eyeball. The subject is in front. He is a tall, thick-set male, jogging at a good speed. He's aware of us. We're approaching Hall Road turning to Crostwight and the subject has not deviated, he is heading to Ridlington. Correction, the subject has jumped over a stone wall and is heading across a field in a northerly direction.'

Ashley sensed the energy and drive in the voices from the pursuing vehicle as it closed in on the fugitive. Kettle's voice came on.

'From Ground Commander, Delta Four Two, hold your position. Hotel Nine Nine has the subject in view. A November unit will have the eyeball in one minute.'

Ashley nodded. A November unit was a Taser team, whereas Quebec was the ARV. IC2 meant southern European. A thick-set male. It had to be Zoltan. Nobody would want to go against a confirmed killer holding a hammer with just a Taser if they could help it, so the safest thing would be for the ARV crew to make the arrest. Either by talking him down, or shooting him down.

More communication came from the helicopter.

'Hotel Nine Nine with further information for all units. Subject is fit. Speed is maintained. He's crossed Heath Road and appears to be skirting Ridlington.'

'From November Six Nine, the subject has just run across Heath Road in front of me and is back in the fields.'

Ashley felt her body tense as the conclusion approached. She took out her phone and brought up a map of the area. She knew Kettle would have a similar one up at OCC. Where was Zoltan going? There were thousands of hiding places, but a helicopter overhead with thermal imaging was tracking him now. He was extremely unlikely to escape. It seemed he was heading towards the coast at Happisburgh. Was he planning a last stand somewhere like the lighthouse?

The helicopter's co-pilot's monotone voice was the next one they heard.

'Hotel Nine Nine has the eyeball. The subject continues in a field towards the B1159 in the direction of Happisburgh Common.'

Ashley tried to picture Zoltan pounding down the middle of narrow country roads, then dragging himself through ploughed fields, the energy leaching from his muscles. Short of running him over or shooting him, the easiest way for him to be stopped on their terms was when he was dog-tired.

Next unit heard was the ARV with the Quebec call sign.

'Quebec One One. We're close to the B1159. Where exactly is the subject, Nine Nine?'

The firearms officer sounded as calm as the helicopter co-pilot. Ashley supposed a cool nature was a necessary requisite when you were required to point a gun.

'Yes, Quebec One One, we see you. The subject will be with you in less than a minute.'

Ashley detected the slightest tension in the air observer's voice as they closed in. Less than a minute later, the ARV replied.

'Quebec One One is in position. The subject will be in our sights when he reaches the road.'

'That's confirmed,' Hotel Nine Nine responded. 'The subject will emerge at your location in five, four, three, two, one.'

Ashley heard the clatter of the helicopter blades as it made an abrupt turn. She counted along under her breath. There was a moment of quiet, then the radio burst into life.

'Stop! Armed Police! Drop your weapon.'

After a slight pause, an officer cursed.

'Quebec One One. Subject has hurled the hammer into a bush but is running again. No shot taken. Subject is unarmed. Repeat. Subject now appears unarmed.'

She pictured Kettle's troubled face as he considered his options for a man who was still innocent until proven guilty.

'Quebec One One. We could pursue and block in.'

'Ground Commander. That's a negative, One One,' said Kettle. 'Nine Nine, where is the subject heading?'

'Hotel Nine Nine. Subject is advancing straight for November Six Nine.'

'November Six Nine. Subject directly ahead. Metres away. He's stopped. No, he's sprinting again. Eastbound, back in the fields. Subject is fatigued.'

The radio conversations continued as the teams gradually

hemmed Zoltan in. Finally, they appeared to have him stumbling towards two officers waiting with Tasers at a crossroads not far from Whimpwell Green.

'Hotel Nine Nine for November Nine Seven. Target will be in front of you in ten seconds.'

November Nine Seven was another Taser unit. Now Zoltan was unarmed, they were a good option. The helicopter counted them in.

'From Ground Commander,' interrupted Kettle. 'No warning. Take him down.'

Ashley half-expected a scream, but there was a crackle from the radio, then relaxed voices.

'November Nine Seven reporting. Subject has stopped and is kneeling. Arms in the air.'

Ashley could hear someone shouting 'lie down' in the background.

'Subject is lying on the tarmac. Hands linked at the back of his neck.'

There were a few seconds of silence, then the information they all wanted.

'Subject is cuffed.'

Ashley sat back on a tree stump. The air carried a crisp and earthy fragrance, tinged with the scent of decay. It hinted at the cycle of life and renewal. The leaves danced and twirled around her, caught in a ballet, as if celebrating the end of their innocent lives.

Ashley glanced at the faces of the officers around her. There were relieved smiles and nods of satisfaction, but no cheers. Not with the sound of nails being pulled out of wood behind them.

78

Ashley was about to check on Lorenzo when she had a terrible thought.

'Shit,' she said.

'What?' asked Hector.

'Zoltan never meant to get away.'

Hector pursed his lips. 'It sounded like he was having a bloody good go.'

'No. Zoltan was the distraction. It's Drita who's escaping.'

Hector took a moment, then a smile crept on his face.

'Clever.'

'Me or them?'

'Both. It makes sense, but how?'

'It's not too hard to get another vehicle.'

Hector clicked his fingers.

'I bet I know what they're using. The owner of the bungalow died. Their car was probably still in the garage, and I'd put money on Drita being in it now.'

Ashley looked at her watch.

'She could have had three or four hours on us and be halfway across the country.'

'Yes, but if she's driving, road cameras would have picked her up. I'll contact OCC.'

Ashley recognised Sal's voice when Hector's call was swiftly answered. Sal put them on hold. Less than a minute later, he came on the line. She couldn't make out what he said. Hector cut the call.

'Owner of the cottage had a red Fiat 500,' said Hector. 'Currently uninsured and no MOT. Emma's checking ANPR.'

They waited for Sal to ring them back, by which time Lorenzo was on a stretcher. One of the ambulance crew gave Ashley a gruesome update as two of her colleagues wheeled him away. She finished off her summary by saying the injuries didn't appear immediately life-threatening. Her expression as she spoke hinted that, for Lorenzo, that might not be the best thing. Not because of what he might have done, but because of the life-altering injuries he'd sustained.

Hector's phone rang and he put Sal on speaker.

'Okay, guys. Good news and bad. The Fiat was picked up on the A11, M11, M25, and A3.'

'Where does that lead?' asked Ashley.

'Portsmouth. It's about four hours away. She could already be there. Kettle's onto Hampshire Police now. I'll call you when I have more.'

Hector puffed out his cheeks.

'That's the first mistake they've made,' he said.

'Maybe they thought they had time.'

'Perhaps, but they didn't need to leave the original plates on the car.'

'Their plans may have changed when Emil got killed.'

Hector rubbed the sides of his forehead. 'Yes. Perhaps they

presumed we'd track them but guessed we would focus on Zoltan's cross-country performance.'

'Which means the vehicle will get dumped in Portsmouth,' said Ashley.

'Yes, and what's Portsmouth famous for?'

'Its port?'

'Exactly. It's one of the busiest recreational sailing areas in the UK. I doubt we'll find Drita now unless we're lucky. She could be on any of thousands of boats.'

'Brilliant.'

Ashley rang Kettle and had a brief discussion with him.

'Did Jasmina go back home?' she asked him.

'She's still here. She point-blank refused to go until we'd found Lorenzo, so they crashed in the room they were in. The local authority have arranged a room at a refuge, but it appears the danger's over.'

'Yes, Lorenzo won't be up to any mischief for a while. He was flayed on every inch of his body, which looks like it blinded him. His tongue has been damaged. I suppose the doctors will be able to tell us how. His fingers were pulverised. Ribs, knees, ankles, all smashed.'

'Sounds as if he'll live the rest of his life in agony.'

Ashley remembered Drita's forced prostitution for three years. She considered the number of other women who would have suffered going through his organisation's hands, and she put Lorenzo to the back of her mind.

'Is Emma about?' she asked.

'Yes.'

'Tell her I'm on my way in. She and I can break the news to Jasmina. I assume Jasmina will return to Overstrand as she planned. I'll ring Rocco when I return.'

'He's still here as well. Sitting in a different room.'

'Okay. I'll let him know as well. Has Scott arrived?'

'No, I'll check he's on his way.'

Ashley and Hector trudged to Hector's car. She gave Bacton Wood one last glance, knowing, if she could help it, she would never return.

79

FOUR DAYS LATER

Jasmina heard the doorbell and went to let Rocco in. He kissed her on both cheeks. Then he cupped her chin and held her face away from his.

'Bella,' he said.

Jasmina smiled and managed to hide her surprise at Rocco's wan and drawn face. Her nose twitched at the alcohol on his breath. It was understandable. Max was still AWOL, and his other sons were dead or dying after Lorenzo had suffered a heart attack shortly after arriving at the N & N.

'Striking,' he said half-heartedly at her hair, which she'd put into a scraped-back ponytail. 'Are you going for a new look?'

'Something like that. How is Lorenzo?'

'It's horrific. His organs are failing. I had to get out of there for a while.'

'It must be very hard for you.'

'Where are those rascals?' he asked. 'At least I still have them.'

Rocco had told her on the phone they were his reason for continuing. They were all he had left. She recalled he hadn't mentioned her.

'They're at the nursery. Maybe we could take them for a walk on the beach, but I wanted to talk to you about something delicate.'

'I'd enjoy that, and we can chat about anything.'

They talked about the children while Jasmina heated up the sausages and bacon she'd cooked before he arrived. She placed a huge plate of food on the table in front of Rocco, who leaned away with faux shock.

'It's too much.' He laughed.

Jasmina put a Marigold glove on and took the five-inch vegetable knife from the block and stood next to Rocco as he stared down at his feast. She could see through what probably used to be a fitted shirt that Rocco sported the same tattoo as Tommaso and Lorenzo. In fact, Rocco's appeared larger and more detailed.

With a practised move, she hooked her arm around his throat and pressed the blade into the small dip behind his collarbone. He shrieked as it sank in a centimetre.

'Quiet,' she snapped. 'I talk. You listen. I have a story to tell, then I want the truth from you. Or this goes down into your chest. Do you understand?'

Rocco winced, then nodded.

'Your children trafficked me and my sister, and countless others, to this country. Jelena was made to work as a whore, and so was I, but under different circumstances. Her death in a dark wood after many years of suffering was due to your two oldest sons. My family declared *krvna osveta*. Do you know what that is?'

Rocco shook his head, which caused another yelp of pain.

'Death to all those responsible,' she whispered.

'They are all dead.'

'Ah, not all, Rocco. What about you?'

Rocco's voice rose and his eyes blinked rapidly.

'I knew nothing about it. That was Lorenzo's business.'

'Did you not suspect I was kept like this? Forced to exist like this? Threatened with my sister's murder even though she was already gone, or by the slaughter of my children?'

'I love my grandkids. I would never allow them to be harmed.'

'My dad visited me last week in the garden and delivered a phone so we could keep in contact. He insisted you were part of my misery. He told me his plans for who he said was the boss, but I said no, you were innocent. It was Lorenzo and Tommaso. He promised he would find out for sure. Max had known nothing. My father let him go because he revealed the location of this place. Tommaso died horrifically, trying to keep his mouth shut. He only betrayed you after many long hours, but Lorenzo, he gave you up straight away.'

Rocco was almost shouting as the knife bit deeper into his flesh.

'No. He would have lied to save his life.'

'It was your business he took over. Those were your contacts in eastern Europe. You created who Lorenzo was, a monster, but that's not surprising, seeing as you are one, too. Now. Tell me the truth.'

She watched Rocco grimace as his mind raced, but he was in a desperately weakened state, not having slept or eaten properly for weeks. Terror broke down his defences. His voice dropped to a mumble.

'It's true, but I stopped a long time ago. I realised it was wrong.'

Jasmina laughed.

'Do you think that makes it okay?'

She pushed down on the knife, causing it to sink in another centimetre. Rocco's hands came up and grabbed her arm, but there was little strength in them. His response was a whisper.

'I'm so sorry.'

Sorry wasn't enough. Rocco was responsible for hundreds, if not thousands, of exploited people. Only one punishment was enough.

She tensed her body to ram the blade in as she'd promised her father she would. Jasmina bared her teeth, but she couldn't do it. Her kids loved Rocco. Raffaele looked like his grandfather. She realised if she killed Rocco, she would be no better than him.

She crouched and shouted in his ear.

'They wanted to burn you alive for all of your crimes. You deserve to die.'

'Do it. What are you waiting for?'

'I can't, you fool. If I do, where does it end?'

Rocco's grip tightened on her arm. The knife tip began to rise. Jasmina had lost her advantage.

'Perhaps,' he whispered, 'I should kill you.'

'Perfect. What next? Would you murder my mother or my brother? Then who? Perhaps little Rocco and Raffaele?'

'I would never hurt them.'

'Do you want the best for them?'

'Always.'

'Who do they need most in their life?'

Rocco tensed but didn't reply.

'Their mum,' she snarled. 'Or would you like to raise them in the family business?'

Rocco made a strange sound. A cross between a wail and a sob. Jasmina continued.

'Perhaps, one day, I shall tell them what became of their aunt. Explain how the great Viallis made their money. You raised a man who raped me for years. He broke me like a horse, again and again. Those children are the product of his vile crimes, and you knew. What kind of grandfather are you?'

Jasmina leaned to the side to observe his expression. Rocco's whole life seemed to pass across his eyes. His face filled with the most terrible pain, as the final wall of everything he'd ever worked for came tumbling down. Then his features softened. He peered over at the photograph on the windowsill of him, which was taken at a restaurant when he was celebrating his recent birthday. Rocco glowed with pride as Raffaele hugged him on his lap, while Rocchino tried to blow out his candles.

'I love them,' he said. 'They are provided for in my will.'

Tears poured down Jasmina's cheeks.

'Forgive me,' bellowed Rocco. Then he yanked down on Jasmina's arm, pulling the blade deeper inside his chest.

Jasmina recalled the lost years. Her stolen innocence. Remembered the pain and hopelessness. With a mighty cry, she placed her hand on his and drove the steel home, so it pierced his rotten heart.

80

Ashley puffed her cheeks out at her desk, having finally finished the paperwork for the murders in Bacton Wood and Happisburgh. Their conclusions fitted together neatly now they had a decent idea of what had happened. The cottage in Overstrand was in Vittoria's name, not Lorenzo's, which was why they hadn't discovered it. Drita appeared to be the one who had drugged Hamish the night it all started. Council CCTV had picked up her car near the club that evening.

Ashley had a meeting with Kettle shortly about Rocco. Kettle had spoken to the suspended Ally, who had agreed to give evidence against Rocco. Ally had handed over to Kettle the mobile he'd used, which contained all the messages, in the hope of them going leniently on him, but his career was over.

They suspected Rocco of being involved, or at least being aware of what Lorenzo was up to, but they had nothing to link the trafficking to Rocco.

PolSA had searched the nightclub, but there were no incriminating finds. Lorenzo's property had a safe, but all they'd found in it was Jasmina's passport, now expired, and four large bundles of cash, which they had confiscated.

Jasmina needed to apply for a new passport for her and the children before she could go home. That meant she couldn't vanish abroad just yet, but she seemed happy to stay for a while with Lorenzo no longer posing a threat. In fact, the doctors expected him to survive for only a few more days.

Jasmina was the other subject Ashley wanted to raise with Kettle. Once she returned to Montenegro, Ashley doubted she would speak to them again. Ashley had niggling doubts about Jasmina's honesty. Ashley thought her calm reaction to the deaths was too cool. As if she'd known the attacks on the Viallis were coming, even though she denied it. There would be no way of knowing, short of a confession.

When her phone rang, she answered and heard Jasmina's voice.

'Hi, Ashley. There's something you should know about Rocco. Could you visit my house later today?'

'What is it?'

'Please. I want to talk in person. You're the only one I trust. Will you come?'

'I can pop in on my way home at five, if that's okay?'

'That works for me.'

81

Jasmina sat at the kitchen table and wrote a letter for Ashley to find. After checking the clock, she grabbed the backpack that contained her children's toys and clothes and a change of outfit for her. She closed the front door, but didn't lock it, then strode from the cottage to the nursery to collect her children. They were too young to understand the concept of going on a big holiday, but they had picked up on her energy.

Jasmina thanked the staff and took the boys outside. She put Raffaele in his buggy and Rocco held on to the side, then she hurried up the road to the church, where she hoped the taxi was waiting. She almost cried when she saw the Toyota with Gosport Premium Cars on the door.

The driver spotted her coming and waved. He got out and took the backpack off her.

'I knew it was you,' he said. 'The kids, you see, after the request for child seats.'

'Ah, right,' said Jasmina, who was distracted by the reflection of herself in the vehicle's window. A blonde bob did not suit her at all. 'How long until we arrive?'

'Five hours, less probably, but depends on the traffic. Is that okay?'

'Yes, perfect.' She smiled, but a snapshot of Rocco's sad face as he died slipped into her head. He hadn't been gone long and it was already not the first time his memory had haunted her. She pushed the image away. There would be time to heal.

'We don't get many calls from up here. Are you thinking of moving to Gosport?'

'Perhaps. Is it a pleasant place to live?'

'I adore the area. There are twenty-four miles of coastline, so you're never far from the sea. You'll love the town if you enjoy sailing. I prefer it to Portsmouth, but I'm not certain the youngsters do.'

She handed him five CDs. One was singalong songs, and the others were short stories for children.

'Do you mind if we have them on later?'

'You've paid up front, darling. Anything but rap music.'

'Maybe if you turn the radio off, the kids will sleep.'

'Sure thing.'

Jasmina nodded at the silence in the car as he turned in the road and cruised out of Overstrand. She didn't want him listening to any bulletins.

After a quick glance at her watch, she forced herself to relax. With God's speed, she would meet Drita at the marina around five p.m.

Shortly after that, they would sail to France.

82

Barry was planning to leave the office at the same time as Ashley, so she asked him to follow her to Overstrand, just in case. Ashley was beginning to unwind now the case was drawing to its conclusion. Everyone from port security to local police and the Royal Navy had been notified to keep an eye out for Drita in Portsmouth, but she had vanished.

Zoltan had admitted to the murders of Tommaso, Paolo and Gianluca, and the attack on Lorenzo, but had told them he was acting alone. He'd forgotten Morgan and Zelda had met him at Drita's house. When Zoltan had been asked why they had found her DNA at the bungalow, he'd said she'd brought him food, but didn't know anything. Interestingly, none of her prints or DNA were on the scourging weapon or the saw in the garage, so if she was responsible, she must have worn gloves. Zoltan had confessed to making the cross.

Ashley arrived first at Jasmina's and got out of her Vauxhall. She was about to knock when she noticed Rocco's car parked at the kerb. Barry pulled in behind it. They stood next to Rocco's Tesla together.

'It was kind of her to let him keep seeing the grandchildren,' said Barry. 'Many women wouldn't.'

A sinking sensation came over Ashley. She placed her hand on the bonnet. It was stone cold. Barry knocked at the cottage, but nobody answered.

'Put gloves on,' she said.

Barry picked up on the tension in her voice, did as she asked, then rapped again. He tried the door handle.

'Ready?' he asked when it opened.

'Yes.'

Barry stepped inside. He stopped at the kitchen door, which was open. His nose wrinkled. She followed him in, feeling déjà vu from the smells at the torture bungalow. Rocco was slumped at the table with the black handle of a knife sticking out of him. His white shirt was nearly all red.

Barry checked around him for blood, but there wasn't much. He stood next to Rocco. 'I don't reckon it's a suicide.'

'You think?'

'I take it Jasmina didn't tell you she'd killed Rocco?'

'Very amusing. She said there was something I should know.'

'I suppose she might not be responsible.'

'True. Drita may have come back. We aren't certain there are no more people helping Emil and Zoltan.'

Barry tutted.

'It means whoever did this believed Rocco to have been involved, at least indirectly. This attack on the Romans wasn't revenge. It was a purge. They meant to murder them all, but they wanted Lorenzo and probably Rocco to suffer before they died. Both of them would have felt completely helpless and afraid. You know, the sensation of being trapped, but not being able to do anything about it. They became observers to their own fate.'

'That's rather poetic from you, Barry, but surprisingly on the money. I wonder if we've been played for fools.'

'In what way?'

'Jasmina told us Rocco wasn't involved. Perhaps she heard he was. Like the melons we are, we let her come back home, thinking it was over. That gave her a chance to finish the job her father started.'

'Icy,' said Barry. 'Although no less than the Viallis deserved.'

Ashley had been looking around the room. Something had changed.

'Some photos have disappeared, and the pictures on the fridge, too, which means she's gone for good.'

'When did she ring you?'

'About five hours ago.'

'Oh, dear.'

Ashley walked to the wall where there was a slight shadow showing a frame had been there. Rocco's picture was still on the windowsill. An envelope had been propped against it. Ashley's name was on it. She beckoned Barry over.

The envelope was closed, but not sealed, so she slid out a single sheet of folded A4 paper. She read it out.

'Thank you for coming, Ashley. I knew you would because you are a caring person. This is what happened. A victim of Lorenzo's evil was here today. She threatened to kill Rocco. In the end, Rocco did the right thing, and pulled the blade into his own body. It was an admission of his guilt. His involvement. I'm guessing this explanation might make you suspicious of me, but it is the truth.

'I have left and taken my boys. You will not find us.

'I did not recognise the woman responsible. She was a stranger.'

Ashley looked over at Rocco. Suspicious was an understatement.

'Do you reckon it was Drita?' asked Barry.

Ashley shook her head.

'My money's on Jasmina. Think about it. How often do we arrest people who've committed violent attacks who say afterwards they didn't recognise themselves, or it was as if someone took over their body?'

'Clever,' said Barry. 'She covers her arse, gives us a suspect, but doesn't mention Drita by name, and then provides a reasonable explanation of why she left. I bet Rocco's are the only fingerprints on the knife.'

Ashley had to admit Jasmina was a remarkable lady. Her endurance of the situation she'd found herself in was phenomenal. Ashley didn't want to charge her with murder. Jasmina and her sister, and her family back in Montenegro, had suffered greatly, as had her children. Ashley remembered a comment Max had made when he'd told them about Jasmina.

'When I spoke to Max, he described Jasmina as a tiger in a cage.'

'So?'

'Isn't the phrase more commonly used, a bird in a cage, to signify a beautiful woman in an oppressive situation? Caged tiger makes me imagine a dangerous animal, waiting to pounce.'

'Perhaps Max sensed her anger.'

'Maybe. You'd better go and check upstairs. I'll ring it in.'

Ashley gave Rocco a prod to see if rigor mortis had set in. It hadn't. She happened to glance in the washing-up tub. A Marigold glove floated on the surface. The liquid was murky and brown, tinged with red. It seemed the assailant had stopped to wash their hands afterwards, and the glove they wore. Ashley again thought of Jasmina's boys. They would be safe with a mother like that, but what would they learn from her?

83

Ashley checked her watch. Hector's leaving do started in thirty minutes and she was waiting for Emma to appear. Emma had asked to stay over so she could, in her words, get lashed up. Ashley heard a car pull up outside and went to open her front door.

For once, Ashley had really deliberated over what she was going to wear that night. A few days before, she'd ordered a lovely flirty dress with matching heels from the Very catalogue and had it sent express delivery. It wasn't slutty, at least she didn't think so, but it showed off a touch of one of her runner's thighs and made her appear more curvaceous up top. Ashley would give it a go.

She'd been hoping it would be a double celebration—Hector staying with the police, and Ashley getting the inspector role—but Kettle had been called to London and hadn't made his announcement. She suspected his visit concerned Ally. The case would have implications for the nation's security on many levels.

It was a reminder that if someone wanted to arrive in the UK, and then commit crimes including murder, they could, if they were well funded and organised. It was a chilling fact. Ashley supposed that, even though the details were different, it wasn't too far away from the antics the Russian poisoners had pulled over the years.

When nobody came to her door, Ashley pulled it open. Cherry was parked outside with her forehead resting on the steering wheel. Her shoulders shuddered. Ashley strode outside and opened the car door. Cherry almost fell out. Ashley held her close and finished up standing in the street hugging the woman who she guessed must have just lost her mother.

'Mum!'

Ashley glanced behind her and saw Oliver looking out of his bedroom window. He was wiping his eyes.

Ashley had helped Cherry into her lounge by the time Oliver came downstairs. He rushed into his mum's arms.

'I'm sorry, Cherry,' said Ashley. 'She was wonderful. I'll miss her.'

Cherry looked over Oliver's shoulder at her and tried to smile, but her face collapsed. Ashley wasn't sure what to do.

'Do you want a cup of tea?' she finally asked.

'No, it's fine. Am I being too rude in saying can you leave me and Oliver to be alone for a while?'

'Of course not,' said Ashley, retreating to the front door. 'Shall I come in the morning, around nine, have a chat then?'

This time, Cherry did manage a smile.

'I'd like that.'

Ashley returned home and rested her back against the front door after closing it. Life had a way of feeling permanent, a race without an end, then all of a sudden the finish line was in sight. It made Ashley think of missed opportunities. It made her think of Scott.

A pounding shuddered the door behind her. She could feel it through the wood. Ashley opened it to a beaming Emma, who plonked her handbag on the sofa and gave her a crushing hug.

'Hi, Ash.'

'If you'd knocked any harder, I wouldn't have needed to open it.'

'Sorry, just excited. I've not been out in a while.'

'I thought your husband upped his game.'

'To be fair, he has. He does work hard, so I'm trying to meet him halfway. Typical man, though. Pretty useless. I got him to take the kids to McDonald's, then shopping at Smyths Toys with their birthday vouchers. He looked like he'd run the gauntlet when he returned and fell fast asleep in an armchair.'

Ashley laughed.

'You look fab,' said Emma.

'I know! Although why are you so surprised?'

Emma giggled.

'It's great to see you looking after yourself. Even Sal noticed your snug suit trousers.'

'Praise indeed.'

Emma grabbed her handbag. 'Come on. The night is young, and I haven't got to go home.'

Ashley placed a hand on Emma's arm.

'Emma, are you glad you took him back?'

'Yes, I suppose. It all changes once you have children. I can't find them another father. Kevin's what they've got, so I need to work with him. If I'm honest, it is easier with him around now. The mistake I made was not kicking him out earlier.'

'If he doesn't step up, you can soon boot him out again.'

'Too right. I'll move Bhavini in and start a commune.'

Ashley chuckled, slipped her shoes off and put them in a carrier bag, then stuck her trainers on. There was no way she could walk there in those heels!

As she locked the door, her phone rang. The call was from

Montenegro. She'd been chasing Ivan to no avail, so she had to take it. She mouthed Ivan to Emma, who gave her a thumbs up.

'Hi, Ivan. Thanks for ringing.'

'Sorry, I've been extremely busy here, and I had nothing new for you.'

'And you do now?'

'I heard a rumour the missing daughter, Jasmina, has returned. It's like a fairy tale.'

'That's not the term I'd use.'

'No, but many people here have lived hard lives. To have hope in this country has often meant disappointment. Jasmina was assumed dead, so her return is a miracle.'

'Do you know where she is? I want to talk to her.'

'I saw your investigation on television. All those murders over there even made the news over here. I expect Jasmina will disappear for now. Perhaps to the mountains.'

'She has to give us answers about what happened here. What are the chances of you fetching her?'

Ivan chuckled.

'It's dangerous up there. They are poor, but proud folk. Even the police disappear if they ask the wrong questions. We'd need to go in mob-handed, but for that we require strong proof. Like CCTV.'

Ashley shook her head. He knew she didn't have it. Attempting to extradite Jasmina probably didn't serve the public interest either, after all she'd been through. They didn't have enough evidence for that, regardless.

'Anyway,' he said, 'it's over. Honour has been restored.'

'A lot of people died.'

'True, but it seems to me justice has been done.'

Ashley nodded. She had nothing more to add.

She cut the call thinking Ivan was probably right.

84

Ashley wanted to be the first person at The Grove, seeing as she'd arranged it, so they were five minutes early, but Kettle's car was already parked in a space. The garden appeared to glow as dusk settled over it. There was a gravel path between trees to the tented area, which was lit up by lights that swung in the gentle breeze.

'Very romantic,' said Emma, linking arms.

'Try to keep your hands off my bottom.'

'I can't help it.'

They saw a sign saying 'Tipi' and the smell of freshly cooked pizza drifted over to them as they approached the big tent. Ashley could see a few tables inside with couples chatting, and a large family laughed together at another. Kettle was waiting outside. He got straight to the point.

'Sorry I didn't get a chance to talk to you today, Ashley. Would you give us a minute, Emma?'

'Sure. I'll get a cheap round in before everyone else turns up.'

After she'd gone, Kettle held out his hand.

'Congratulations,' he said.

Ashley shook it, but her heart hadn't filled with joy.

'Thank you.'

'I know the prospect can be daunting,' he said. 'Working as an inspector is a substantial change from being a sergeant. You've started the shift from one of them to one of us.'

Ashley grinned. 'Now you say that, I'm not completely sure I want it.'

Kettle smiled. 'That's probably why you were successful.'

'Thanks for your advice. When do I start?'

'January. New year, fresh beginning. We'll get you on a couple of courses first. I think you'll love having the opportunity to see the bigger picture. The sky's the limit for you, Ashley. Reach for it.'

'Does that bigger picture include knowing what's going to happen to Ally?'

Kettle smiled, then looked away.

'Maybe.'

Ashley heard others crunching through the gravel towards them. The person who came into view first was Scott, and this time her heart did leap, although it didn't flutter for long.

He was holding hands with Michelle.

85

The couple strolled towards them. Scott looked dapper in chinos and a nice shirt. Michelle was poised elegantly in a slimming black dress and gold sandals.

'Hi, Ash,' said Scott.

'Of course, you must know each other,' said Michelle. 'I met Scott at OCC in the canteen. We happened to sit together. He wondered what I was doing tonight, so I asked Hector if he minded me bringing him along. Here we are.'

The pair shared a look that made Ashley want to hurl, or perhaps thrash them with her new shoes, which she was still clutching in a Morrisons carrier bag.

'How lovely,' she said.

'I'll buy us a drink,' said Scott. 'I'll get a couple of bottles. Red and white.'

'I'll give you a hand,' said Kettle.

Michelle came over all giddy when the men had left and Ashley couldn't help being pleased for her.

'Oh, Ashley. He's been so charming. Does he have a strange secret that nobody dares tell me about?'

'Yep. He picks his nose and eats it.'

'Yuck, although, with my recent track record, that's probably not a deal breaker.'

'Just kidding. He's a great guy. I wish I'd noticed earlier.'

Michelle gave her a hug.

'Come on, let's celebrate. I haven't been steaming since Hector told us he was celibate.'

With perfect timing, Hector had arrived and was in earshot.

'I heard that, so you need to buy me a large whisky.'

'Deal,' said Michelle. 'I'll see you both inside.'

Hector waited until she was gone before he spoke.

'Did I just spot Scott and Michelle holding hands?'

'Yep.'

'She rang and asked to bring him. I didn't think you'd mind.'

'I don't.'

'Feeling happy for them?'

'Overjoyed.'

'I can see that. Sorry, I didn't realise you felt like that about him.'

'Nor did I.'

'Weren't you hearing about the promotion today?'

'Yes. I got it.'

Hector pulled her into a hug. Her second in as many minutes. As she breathed in the scent of his familiar aftershave, she realised Hector's presence had become reassuring.

'The Lord giveth, and the Lord taketh away,' he said.

'I think someone's going to have to giveth me quite a few beers to get me through tonight.'

'Excellent. Every party needs a maudlin drunk. Did you bring me a leaving present?'

'I did. Took plenty of effort, but it's just arrived.'

Hector turned around as Gabriella walked up the path. Ashley sensed electricity in the air. Gabriella looked as though she'd stepped off the front page of a fashion magazine.

Ashley scuttled inside to put her new shoes on.

86

When everyone had arrived and was seated in the tipi, Hector tapped his glass with a spoon and stood. He had Levi's on with a thick belt, which accentuated his slim frame. His Ralph Lauren shirt had the top two buttons undone. His hair was cut a bit shorter, perhaps a little smarter. He smiled, looking the picture of health, as he stared around the tables that had been pushed together to accommodate the twelve of them.

'I feel I should say a few words,' he said.

'Spit it out,' said Sal. 'Are you in or out?'

'After careful consideration, I have taken the job in London.'

'Boo!' hollered Emma.

'But not the one with my uni friend. It's a new department the Met are setting up, to look at social media channels and all other digital formats, with an oversight nationwide, to assist in increasing conviction rates across all sentencing areas.'

Barry theatrically banged his head on the table and began to snore.

'So, I'm staying with the police,' said Hector. 'It's only for an initial twelve months. I'll be made sergeant, and I can see how it goes. I'll always think of MIT fondly. You've been like a family.'

'Addams family?' asked Gerald, who'd been the last to arrive.

Bhavini listed the team's attributes.

'Arguing, moaning, judging, gossiping, stealing food, bitching and borrowing money, but sticking together in adversity.'

Hector nodded.

'Exactly. Like a family. I also want to give a special mention to your new inspector, who has been wonderful to me since I arrived.'

They all gazed at Ashley and raised their glasses.

'Congratulations,' they chorused, but nobody looked surprised.

'So,' continued Hector, raising his drink again. 'This is au revoir, not adieu.'

'What does that mean?' asked Barry.

'It means you should have tried harder at school,' said Joan.

'To Ashley and Hector,' shouted Kettle.

There was a big cheer, then they got down to the important task of choosing their pizzas. Ashley cast an eye over at Scott and Michelle, who were sharing a moment as they chuckled at the menu. Ashley took a huge gulp of wine and looked away. She was sitting between Bhavini and Hector. Suspecting she might not receive much conversation from Hector, who had Gabriella on his other side, she turned to Bhavini.

'Pregnancy really suits you. You'll be a fantastic mother.'

'You've been a fantastic friend. We'll do this together.'

'I can't wait.'

'I was worried this baby would rip our family apart, instead it's sewing us together. Himansu even received his comeuppance.'

'Hit by lightning?'

'Hit by a divorce petition. His wife chucked him out, and he's back at his parents'.'

'Excellent. Any plans to involve him?'

'Emma talked to me about it. She said even the idiots eventually grow up, so we'll see. Although it was Himansu who spread the gossip from our day out. I told him everything when we were seeing each other, not realising what a shit he was.'

'Sounds as if he's getting his just deserts.'

'Regret pie. I hope he chokes on it.'

Gabriella rose from her seat a little later and glided outside on three-inch heels. When she was out of sight, a flushed Hector turned around to Ashley.

'Oh, brilliant,' said Ashley. 'Now you want to talk to me.'

'Do you know what the most important thing you've taught me is?'

'That I'm always right?'

'Not even close. When I joined you guys, I thought detective work was going to be a series of light-bulb moments, where the genius investigator, me, obviously, clicked his fingers and shrieked "eureka". But it's not, is it?'

'Nope.'

'In some ways, we didn't solve this case. We merely chased it to its conclusion.'

'Sometimes it works out like that. We still don't know for sure exactly what happened, but we can guess. No investigation is perfect.'

Gabriella had only nipped to fetch a cardigan from her car. Hector watched as she walked back up the path.

'How did you convince her to come?'

'I said you were an honest guy who was leaving, and it would be a chance to get to know you in a casual environment. She didn't have to marry you tonight.'

'Shame.' Hector reached over and kissed Ashley on the forehead. 'Thank you.'

'Do I need to keep Gingerpuss in my basement until you realise how fab Norfolk is?'

'Ashley!'

'Okay, okay. Should I lock *Gabriella* in there until you return?'

'That's better. Although you haven't got a basement.'

'Oh dear. I'll have to tie her to my headboard.'

Ashley comically licked her lips.

'Despicable to the end.' Hector smiled, but his face was a mix of happiness and sorrow. 'I'll miss you.'

'I bet you'd come back for her.'

Hector put his arm around Ashley's shoulders.

'I'd come back for you all.'

87

THREE WEEKS LATER

Ashley pulled into the parking spaces at the side of Coast Road next to Walcott beach. There were no worries about finding a space. When she got out, a keen wind gusted down the promenade, blowing sand along the walkway in drifts. It was not a day for ice creams.

Ashley crossed the street and strolled into the Kingfisher Café. At first she didn't think he'd shown up, but then she spotted an individual in the far corner with a baseball cap pulled down low. He had a cup of steaming coffee in front of him, so he'd already been there a little while.

Ashley sat opposite him.

'Great to see you,' she said.

The peak of the cap rose up, revealing a more relaxed face than she'd been expecting. He smiled.

'Great to see you,' he replied. 'How did you guess?'

'About you being a mole? It pretty much came out of the blue when Barry told me.'

'No, I meant, how did you realise I was undercover and not feeding intel to criminals?'

'Oh,' said Ashley with a grin. 'A few things. The toll it took on you. Some of Kettle's comments. The bits and bobs that hung around in my head and didn't make sense. The lack of progress over the last year. But mostly because I was convinced you wouldn't do it. I know we all think we can't be wrong. So, I checked the divorce records, just to be sure.'

DS Ally Williamson gave her half a smile.

'Ah, I see. And when I didn't appear, the case was closed, so to speak. Have you kept your suspicions a secret?'

'Of course, although it seems a sad way to end your career.'

'Kettle said the truth has a habit of slipping out years down the line, but I don't mind too much.'

'How did it come about?'

'Oddly, I was approached at a poker game I'd heard about. I've always played and like to think I'm a pretty shrewd player. I started talking to a woman, and she joked about buying information when she asked what I did for a living. My wife had been diagnosed with cancer at the time. Poker was a great distraction because the treatment was failing. She hated me watching her die, so I was regularly thrown out of the house.'

'I'm sorry.'

'Yes, life wasn't easy. I carried on playing, and this woman asked me again. I looked at her face, and she was serious. Funnily enough, I mentioned the details to Kettle, and he passed it up the chain. We suspected there might be a link to the drug problems we were having, so I took a few backhanders and gave them a couple of juicy titbits. Then someone else approached me on behalf of Rocco. The Romans and Vampires were making fools out of us, so we tried to do the same with them.'

'Despite knowing your career would be over when you were rumbled?'

'I asked my missus about it just before the end, and she said yes. She was desperate for something good to come out of her premature death. It felt like we'd been cheated out of our retirement plans anyway. She was a police officer when I started, so she knew the score. That's how we met. I've already served twenty-nine years, Ashley. My time was nearly over, anyway. The deal was if I got caught, I'd be pensioned off early. Truthfully, I enjoyed the challenge. I could think about something other than what I'd lost. There was guilt, of course, letting the team down, but I discovered a touch of the buzz from when I was young. You remember the thrill?'

'I do. And there was no other rat than you?'

Ally held his hands up. 'Just me.'

'But how much did it help us?'

'To be honest, not massively. Lorenzo ran such a tight ship. We still don't know the depth of Rocco's involvement, but with Lorenzo's life support being turned off, they're all dead, so it's over.'

'And what's next for you? Golf and slippers?'

'Certainly, for the short term. Perhaps I'll become a PI. They want me to stay in touch due to an angle I can't talk about.'

'Something to do with Typhon?'

Ally chuckled. 'You'll make a good DI. Whoever or whatever that serpent thing is in Europe needs stopping.'

'Thank you. So now you've gone from the day to day. How does that feel?'

'Kind of numb. Days are long. I miss my wife, and I miss you lot, but I've got a few ideas. Might take a cruise. I also fancy a trip to Oz.'

'I'm pretty sure even they don't have mullets nowadays.'

'I've heard they made a comeback.'

They both smiled at each other. They'd worked together for many years.

'That was clever work from you guys, sussing me out,' he said. 'Can't believe Barry was the person who rumbled me.'

'Every dog and all that.'

'You've got a brilliant team there. Any idea who's taking on mine?'

'Yours is being disbanded. One of your team wants back in uniform, another is retiring, one handed his notice in, and I'm getting Morgan and Zelda to replace me and Bee. We'll need new sergeants.'

'Perfect. My guys will do well with you.'

Ashley's drink arrived.

'It's a shame we didn't find out more about Typhon,' she said.

'Yeah, that is annoying. Thousands of people are dying or disappearing across Europe. There are rising reports of abductions of beautiful young men and women in Europe, where they have simply vanished, with no requests for ransoms. The odd body has shown up, so what I did was worth a try, even if it didn't help our investigation.'

'The risk reward trade-off.'

'Exactly.'

'Maybe it was just Rocco putting on a convincing Slavic accent.'

Ally laughed. Ashley took a sip of her coffee and grinned back at him.

'Perhaps Typhon will be a story for another day.'

AUTHOR'S NOTE

Thank you very much for reading my Norfolk trilogy. It was a bit of a mind-bending roller coaster, dealing with all these twists. I'm surprised I didn't have a permanent nosebleed while writing them. So, I hope my efforts translated into something very readable, with loads of surprises. At the least, I hope that nobody can say the books were predictable.

For those who've followed this after my DI Barton series came to a natural end, there's another surprise. I've written another Killer book. Obviously, I wanted to call it Barton Returns, in the manner of Batman! I could get carried away and give him a cape, but my publisher wasn't keen on either idea. If you head over to Amazon, you should be able to read the blurb now. If you get chance to leave a review for this, that would be appreciated.

Your feedback has been great for the Norfolk murders. It appears you'd like more. I had an idea for a story with a bit of prison in it, but wasn't sure what to write. So I'm going to look into something with scenes at HMP Peterborough, and perhaps a little cameo for John Barton. The Typhon organisation needs stopping after all! Depending on when you read this, if I've had the go-ahead, there might be another Ashley Knight book for you to pre-order at Amazon now, too.

As always, feel free to get in touch, and thank you for all your support.

All the best, Ross.

ABOUT THE AUTHOR

Ross Greenwood is the bestselling author of over ten crime thrillers. Before becoming a full-time writer he was most recently a prison officer and so worked everyday with murderers, rapists and thieves for four years. He lives in Peterborough.

Sign up to Ross Greenwood's mailing list for news, competitions and updates on future books.

Follow Ross on social media:

- instagram.com/rossg555
- x.com/greenwoodross
- facebook.com/RossGreenwoodAuthor
- bookbub.com/authors/ross-greenwood

ALSO BY ROSS GREENWOOD

The DI Barton Series

The Snow Killer

The Soul Killer

The Ice Killer

The Cold Killer

The Fire Killer

The Santa Killer

DS Knight Series

Death on Cromer Beach

Dear at Paradise Park

Death in Bacton Wood

Standalones

Prisoner

Jail Break

Survivor

Lifer

Chancer

Hunter

Printed in Great Britain
by Amazon

44810830R00235